MEDICAL
Pulse-racing passion

Nurse's Secret Royal Fling
JC Harroway

Unbottoning The Bachelor Doc
Deanne Anders

T0359691

MILLS & BOON

NURSE'S SECRET ROYAL FLING
© 2024 by JC Harroway
Philippine Copyright 2024
Australian Copyright 2024
New Zealand Copyright 2024

First Published 2024
First Australian Paperback Edition 2024
ISBN 978 1 038 91039 4

UNBOTTONING THE BACHELOR DOC
© 2024 by Denise Chavers
Philippine Copyright 2024
Australian Copyright 2024
New Zealand Copyright 2024

First Published 2024
First Australian Paperback Edition 2024
ISBN 978 1 038 91039 4

MIX
Paper | Supporting
responsible forestry
FSC® C001695

Published by
Harlequin Mills & Boon
An imprint of Harlequin Enterprises (Australia) Pty Limited
(ABN 47 001 180 918), a subsidiary of HarperCollins
Publishers Australia Pty Limited
(ABN 36 009 913 517)
Level 19, 201 Elizabeth Street
SYDNEY NSW 2000 AUSTRALIA

Cover art used by arrangement with Harlequin Books S.A.. All rights reserved.

Printed and bound in Australia by McPherson's Printing Group

Nurse's Secret Royal Fling

JC Harroway

MILLS & BOON

Lifelong romance addict **JC Harroway** took a break from her career as a junior doctor to raise a family and found her calling as a Harlequin author instead. She now lives in New Zealand and finds that writing feeds her very real obsession with happy endings and the endorphin rush they create. You can follow her at jcharroway.com and on Facebook, Twitter and Instagram.

Visit the Author Profile page
at millsandboon.com.au for more titles.

Dear Reader,

In writing *Nurse's Secret Royal Fling*, I was totally swept along in the magic and sparkle of my hero's royal world and the mountainous principality of Varborg. Giving Prince Andreas Cronstedt such a grounded and cynical heroine in nurse Clara Lund led to lots of juicy tension, which was offset by their red-hot romance! I hope you enjoy reading about the medical emergencies that bring them together as well as the passionate love story that unfolds.

Love,

JC x

DEDICATION

To the wonderful and talented editors who helped
create this story. To Jo Grant, who believed that
Andreas and Clara's story deserved to be told,
and to Charlotte Ellis, who encouraged me
to take my characters on an emotion-packed journey
to their HEA.

CHAPTER ONE

CLARA LUND NEEDED this prestigious job. However *delicate* the situation awaiting her behind the intimidatingly vast timber door in the guest wing of Varborg's winter palace, she could handle it.

Straightening her crisply ironed nurse's uniform, she pressed the intercom button beside the door. Talk about being thrown in at the deep end on her first shift: no welcome tour of the palace; no explanation of her night-nurse duties; no pointers on royal protocol for when she finally did meet her patient, Prince Henrik, Varborg's ruler. When the intercom remained silent, Clara pressed the button again, for longer this time.

'Yes, yes. Please enter,' a disembodied male voice, deep and cultured, barked brusquely.

Rude... But at least he'd said 'please'.

The automatic locking system disarmed with a click. Clara pushed her way inside the suite and closed the door, focussed on her salary rather than the occupant's apparent sense of entitlement. It seemed, by working for Varborg's royal family, she'd have to get used to demanding VIPs. But this second salary would increase Clara's contribution to paying off the mortgage on her family's home and hopefully ease the perpetual worry lines around her mother's eyes.

Bypassing the ridiculously opulent fresh flower arrangement on the reception table, Clara set off in search of the grumpy-sounding guest. The suite boasted wall-to-wall luxury disguised beneath understated Scandinavian elegance. Were her feet not so deeply embedded in the concrete of reality, she might have spared a moment to be impressed.

Except each room was empty.

'Hello…?' she called out as she stepped into the deserted bedroom.

A splash of water sounded from the *en suite* bathroom.

'In here,' the owner of the rich baritone said from behind the half-open door.

'Are you okay, sir?' she asked, mostly keeping the exasperation from her voice. The guest sounded younger than she'd first assumed—and mildly irritated, as if she'd kept him waiting. 'I was led to believe that there was some sort of emergency.'

If his 'delicate situation' had been that urgent, someone would have called an ambulance.

The stranger sighed. 'The situation *is* urgent to me.'

'I did buzz. *Twice*,' she pointed out, his manner ruffling her usually unflappable feathers. He sounded perfectly healthy.

'I'm aware,' he said. 'Look, I'm sort of…stuck.'

Clara rolled her eyes. She wasn't a maid. An experienced nurse with her training—which included a Master's degree in Advanced Clinical Practice— was surely above reaching for the soap for some entitled visiting dignitary or foreign ambassador? Except patients, like customers, were always right.

Think about the money... Think about the money...

'I have no desire to waste your time,' he continued in that commanding voice she found both objectionable and inconveniently appealing. 'Could you please enter so we can get this...*situation* over with?'

'Okay—are you decent?' While she'd seen it all before, she didn't want to barge in and embarrass the owner of that attractive voice.

'I'm naked, if that's what you mean,' he replied, his voice now tinged with amused challenge. 'But, rest assured, I have no immediate plans to flash you.'

Clara stifled a snigger. A sense of humour helped when patients were forced to concede their dignity and ask for assistance.

'That's good,' she quipped, pressing her lips together to contain her smile. 'We don't want a sexual harassment incident on my first night, do we?'

When her only reply was a dry chuckle that filled her belly with inexplicable flutters of excitement, Clara pushed the door fully open and poked her head inside.

Any trace of humour drained from her like water down a gold-plated plughole. There was nothing laughable about the modern-day Viking reclining regally in the generous bath, which looked as if it could happily accommodate two adults with ample room for fun and games.

Clara's mouth instantly turned dry, her pulse speeding as he arched one golden brow, his bold blue-grey stare defiant and full of questions.

'Um…hello,' she croaked, stepping from behind the door.

To her utter alarm, her face warmed. Every spirited retort deserted her, while the shocking heat of instant attraction set her entire body aflame, as if she'd rolled naked in a bed of nettles.

'You're a nurse,' he said with surprise, a frown slashing his outrageously handsome face as he looked her up and down.

Her body heated in every place his eyes landed. How could he do that? And was it her imagination, or was he vaguely familiar? She rarely watched TV, was too busy for social media and had no time for VIP-spotting.

'Well observed,' she said dryly, looking away. Not because he was naked, concealed only from the waist down by what she suspected was a dwindling foam of bubbles, but because, trapped or not, he dominated the luxurious marble bathroom like some sort of powerfully virile mountain-man.

She exhaled slowly, grateful for that modesty layer of suds. His voice alone was sexy in a bossy kind of way, but the entire package seemed to have triggered a rush of hormones—no mean feat considering that Clara deliberately avoided noticing members of the opposite sex. Relationships weren't worth her while. Even sex, the one time she'd done it, had been underwhelming, leaving her vulnerable and humiliated.

But she'd have to be anaesthetised not to notice *this* man.

'The east wing steward sent me,' she said, casually scanning the room for signs of blood or trauma, while she willed her body to revert to normal. 'But I'll happily leave again if you were expecting someone else. A plumber, perhaps…?'

He laughed, another dry chuckle that rumbled up from that deliciously broad chest. She couldn't remember the last time someone had found her funny or made her laugh in return. Absurdly, Clara searched for other amusing things to say.

Except this was work. She was a professional. She wasn't here to spar with him, no matter how carefree and giggly he made her feel.

'*Are* you hurt?' she asked sharply, pointedly glancing at the watch pinned to her pocket before scrutinising his well-defined chest, which was covered in manly hair with the barest hint of reddish gold. His shoulders were wide, his upper body ripped and bronzed. While she desperately tried not to envision herself as the second occupant of that giant bath, Clara's gaze skimmed the ladder of his abs until she reached the modesty layer of suds, frustrated to have her view cruelly interrupted.

'Don't mind me,' he drawled, snapping her to her senses. 'Have a good, long look.' He relaxed his arms on the edge of the bath as if in invitation.

'As you pointed out,' she blustered, mortified to be caught ogling the sexy, naked VIP, 'I'm a medical professional—I was assessing you for injuries.'

'Is that right?' He raised his eyebrows, a knowing smile tugging at one corner of his sensual mouth, which was surrounded by a close-cropped beard of dark facial hair flecked with similar golden tones to his body hair.

'Indeed.' Clara tilted her chin, hot shame in her veins that she'd temporarily forgotten she was there to help him; that it was her *job*, one she couldn't afford to mess up. 'And I'm pleased to find that you seem fine.'

If 'fine' denoted the kind of wildly rugged male beauty that brought to mind log cabins in the snowy mountains, fur pelts on the floor, a crackling fire…

Where the hell had that ridiculous and unwarranted fantasy come from? His raw, edgy sex appeal was as irrelevant as his VIP status. She wasn't about to undo the past eight years of struggle and heartache for something as frivolous as sexual chemistry.

From the age of sixteen, when her father had left his wife and two daughters and done a runner, Clara, the eldest, had worked part-time to contribute to the family income. At nineteen, while Clara had also been studying for her nursing degree, her mother, Alma, had developed breast cancer and hadn't been able to work for months on end while undergoing treatment. Clara's income had kept the roof over their heads and the bills paid with no help from her absent father. The emotional toll of caring for Alma, while also taking on financial responsibility for her family, had cured teenaged Clara of the foolish romantic aspirations of most of her peers.

Especially after Alma discovered her father, Lars, had re-mortgaged the house to fund one of his get-rich-quick schemes and had then ended up in prison for fraud. Now, at twenty-four, with her parents' unequal marriage as a warning, Clara's only goal was lifelong financial and emotional independence. She'd never be *any* man's puppet, wild mountain-men and Vikings included.

'I need to get back to work,' she said in her haughtiest voice, willing her eyes to steer clear of his ripped physique. 'So unless you're bleeding to death...'

She paused expectantly, faking indifference to the inconvenient attraction that, for a moment, had caught her off-guard.

'No blood. Sorry to disappoint you.' His lips twitched with playful amusement other women might have found charming.

No doubt he was used to the effect he had on poor unsuspecting women. Only, Clara had seen how love could make one partner, usually the woman, vulnerable. Her mother had excused and forgiven Lars time and time again in the name of love.

Ignoring the heat and speculation in his stare, she smiled sweetly. 'What a shame.'

'Next time, I'll try to provide you with a little

more drama,' he said, his silvery blue eyes sparkling flirtatiously.

'Let's hope there'll be no next time,' she shot back, unable to resist. Was this the flirty fun she'd missed out on as a teenager because of Lars's irresponsible approach to raising his daughters?

At that he only stared, amused and revoltingly confident in his nudity.

'So, what can I do for you?' She folded her arms across her chest, keeping her eyes on his face and not a millimetre lower. Now that he seemed to have awoken a previously dormant aspect of her womanhood, all she could think about was escape. *He* was the naked one, but she felt horribly exposed, imagining wildly romantic scenarios when, before meeting him, she'd have sworn that there wasn't a fanciful bone in her body.

'While that's normally the kind of offer I'd love to hear from a beautiful woman,' he said, his stare playfully daring, 'We've already vetoed sexual harassment, although you might need to stop looking at me as if you've been denied the last cookie in the jar.'

His comment drew another uncontrollable blush from Clara. A trickle of fear chilled her blood as if by ignoring the demands of her femininity up to now something vital might be missing from her life and somehow he could tell.

'You said you were stuck. And I'm not interested in cookies,' she lied, dragging her eyes away from his chest.

How had they got there again? Was he some sort of sickeningly handsome sorcerer, bewitching her with his hot bod, his sparkly eyes and the sheer force of his unapologetic masculinity?

'In that case,' he said, seeming to drop the cocky attitude, 'I won't keep you from your other duties any longer.'

'How generous,' she snapped, the testosterone fog around him the only excuse for her uncharacteristic attitude. 'I'd hate to have to attend to a *real* emergency and leave you...indisposed. I'm sure that bath is getting cold.'

She just couldn't seem to bite her tongue around him.

He laughed, something like respect flickering in his eyes. Validation shot excitement along Clara's nerves, lighting her up inside like the million stars in the night sky. She fisted her hands on her hips, furious at her rebellious body's response to him. If circumstances had been different, if they'd been equals, if she hadn't needed this lucrative job, she would have turned tail and left him to shiver in his cooling bathwater.

Instead, she clamped her lips together. Her family was one defaulted mortgage repayment away from losing their home.

As if finally done toying with her, the infuriating man sat up. The water swirled around his lean hips in tantalisingly hypnotic currents.

'Before you leave,' he said, the amused lilt lingering in his voice telling her he'd caught her watching those currents for a glimpse of what lay beneath. 'I wonder if you would save me an undignified crawl across the tiles and be so kind as to pass me my leg?'

CHAPTER TWO

CROWN PRINCE ANDREAS CRONSTEDT, heir to the Varborg throne, was rarely surprised by the many people he met. But the enchanting beauty who'd marched into his bathroom with her no-nonsense attitude didn't bat an eyelid at his rather unusual request.

'Of course,' she said, casting big, blue eyes around the bathroom. 'Your leg; where might I find that?'

Satisfaction spread through the ancient Viking blood in Andreas's veins like lava. She was spectacular. And obviously had no idea that he descended from a long, ancient line of Scandinavian princes.

'Try behind you, in the bedroom. Under the curtains, perhaps?' Andreas indicated the doorway, through which this fascinating and forthright woman had come. 'I'm quite impressed with myself for making such an improbable shot.'

'What is it doing all the way over there, when you're stuck in your *cold* bath?' she asked, casting him an unsympathetic look he found thrilling.

Rather than having the desired effect, her taunting reprimand, and the way she looked at him with both interest and astonishment at his stupidity, flooded his groin with heat. Too bad she was a palace employee, one of the round-the-clock nurses employed to keep Prince Henrik in excellent health, and therefore strictly off-limits.

'I'm afraid I hurled it away, unthinkingly, in a rare fit of frustration,' he said, gleefully admitting to this intriguing stranger that his current predicament was totally self-inflicted.

'So you only have yourself to blame,' she pointed out, one hand on her hip.

Had anyone ever before found him ridiculous? Had a woman ever stirred his curiosity so…intensely? Right then he couldn't recall a single time.

'I'm afraid so.' He smiled, noticing how her lips twitched, as if she was trying not to laugh.

'Interesting…' she said and turned away.

As Prince Henrik's second, less important son, Andreas had been allowed to pursue a career of his choosing. As a doctor, he met a lot of nurses, but none as unique, strikingly beautiful or unapologetically herself as this one. Where on Earth had the palace found such a refreshingly candid character?

Through the open door, he watched her stoop in search of his leg. As she looked behind the heavy curtains, Andreas willed his eager anatomy into submission. But he was only a man, not superhuman. He couldn't have stopped his stare sliding to the curve of her hips and derrière as she bent over if his life had depended upon it. Perhaps he should turn on the cold tap, shock his libido into behaving, but where was the fun in that?

And tonight, after having been rudely summoned home, his locum position in Stockholm cut short by his father's personal secretary with only the briefest of explanations—Prince Henrik was fatigued following a short illness and needed time to recover—Andreas deserved a little flirtatious interlude with a woman for whom he was just an ordinary man.

Excitement buzzed through his nervous system at the heady freedom this encounter offered. Most people recognised Varborg's physically challenged prince, a man who was not meant to rule and could never replace his late older brother, the popular Oscar. But, with *this* woman, he had the opportunity for complete anonymity; to be no one but himself for a moment.

He'd never met anyone like her, least of all in his royal life, in which women were cookie-cutter sophisticates who fitted into two categories: those who fawned and flattered him and those too intimidated by his title to utter a single word. Even the women he bedded were careful to avoid any verbal display beyond voicing their delight between the sheets, should it somehow lose them his royal favour.

On discovering he was an amputee, some went overboard on the sympathy, infantilised him. He might have lost a leg, but the rest of him worked just fine, as proved by the very functional stirring in his groin that this delightful stranger had provoked the minute she peered into the room with her cutting remarks and her prim and proper hairdo.

'Found it,' she said, returning to the bathroom, flushed and slightly breathless in a way that made him think of kissing. 'Luckily for you.'

He was lucky that she'd been the one sent to his aid. If he'd known that *she* awaited him, he might not have been so reluctant to return to the oppressive confines of the palace, all be it to the guest wing he'd insisted upon. He wasn't ready to sleep in the suite that had once belonged to Oscar. Nor did he intend to be solely at the crown's beck and call just because he'd returned to help out Prince Henrik with royal engagements. He'd taken a locum position at the local private medical clinic, his work the one thing in his life that filled him with uncomplicated pride.

'Thank you,' he said, savouring her striking face, her hair the colour of burnt caramel and the playful glint in her blue eyes. 'What's your name?'

He swept his gaze from her exquisite features down the length of her body, tracing her blistering figure underneath the nurse's uniform, in the way she'd blatantly appraised him earlier. 'I should have asked before, given the circumstances.'

'Circumstances,' she scoffed, holding out the prosthesis. 'Is that what we're calling a fit of leg-hurling impatience? I thought it was a self-inflicted situation.'

He grinned, waiting patiently for her answer, while her stare once more dipped to his torso in obvious admiration. She couldn't seem to stop checking him out.

When he made no move to take the leg, she huffed. 'My name is Clara. Clara Lund.'

A small smile tugged at his mouth—captivating, candid Clara. 'Pleased to meet you, Clara.'

Her name caressed his tongue the way he imagined her kiss would taste: breathy, bold, undaunted: like the woman herself. A woman who clearly didn't care one jot that he was someone important enough to stay at one of the Cronstedt palaces.

She frowned and shuddered a little, as if his speaking her name gave her a thrill of pleasure that was inconvenient. He understood her dilemma. Regardless of the sparks between them, he couldn't bed this woman whom the universe had delivered as if to soothe his grieving soul. Because being back home resurfaced complex emotions.

'Thank you for finding it.' He took the prosthesis, noting with satisfaction the way her eyes were averted from the layer of thinning suds that, just about, still concealed his lower half. 'You should know that not many people surprise me, Clara.'

'Well, I'm glad I could save you that undignified crawl across the tiles.'

Andreas's smile widened. The more they talked, the better he felt about being here, a place of bittersweet memories. She'd helped him forget that, one day, be it in five years or fifteen, he would have to abandon the medical career he loved and succeed his father. It wouldn't matter that, as the spare who'd been left to his own devices, he was unqualified for the role. Nor would it matter that the nation, who still referred to Andreas as 'the party prince' he'd been in his twenties, had adored Oscar, just like Prince Henrik—just like Andreas himself, in fact. He would have no choice but to turn his back on the life he'd built for himself and step into his brother's shoes.

'I'll be going, then, if that's everything…?' She glanced at the door, as if she was dying to escape.

He should let her go, but not yet.

'Yes, time to get out, I think.' Andreas propped his prosthesis against the side of the bath and pulled the plug. He braced his hands on the bath's edge as if to lever his body from the water, unable to resist one final flirtation, if only to see the censure once more sparking in her pretty eyes.

Right on cue, she flushed. 'Right… I'll…um… leave you to it.'

She cast one last look down his chest to the waterline and scurried from the room.

'I'd appreciate it if you could wait,' he called after her, a rumble of amusement trapped in his throat. 'I'd like to thank you properly—face to face, as it were. When I'm no longer naked.'

He heard a nervous squawk from the bedroom, neither a refusal nor acceptance, but some instinct told him that she'd wait.

Andreas used his upper-body strength to haul himself from the bath. He reached for a towel, impatient now to know everything there was to know about the palace's newest nurse, perhaps the only woman on the planet who'd failed to recognise him; a woman with whom he would be free simply to be an ordinary man—not Andreas, the second-choice heir.

He attached his below-knee prosthesis to his left leg and wrapped a fresh towel around his waist, swallowing down the sour taste of failure that being back here had caused to resurface. Judgement seemed to seep from the ancient palace walls. He wasn't meant to have been the one. It should have been Oscar in line to the throne.

If only Andreas had been able to save him. The defeat and guilt brought jarring flashes of his worst memory—a crumpled vehicle wreck, the smell of hot metal and petrol, the urgency to save his unconscious brother and his attempts at CPR. And then nothing but blackness until he'd woken up in hospital.

Why hadn't he died in that accident instead of Oscar? With the ruler who'd trained for the role from birth, the future of Varborg would have been secure. Whereas Andreas knew more about the human body than being a statesman.

He found Clara in the suite's living room, her back to the fire while she looked out at the shadowy, mountainous view beyond the windows. He clung to the distracting sight of her wonderful ordinariness. It made him want to be an ordinary man, not a last-resort prince. To shrug off the sense of being second best and feel invincible, the way he had when she'd moved her eyes over his nakedness. To be himself, the man she'd seen when she'd challenged him so unflinchingly.

'Beautiful, isn't it?' he said, entranced by the angles of her profile as he flicked on the lamps.

Clara turned to face him and gaped. Her throat moved on a pained-looking swallow that fanned his ego. 'You're still naked.' Her gobsmacked stare travelled down his bare torso, which was dotted with the droplets of water he'd missed in his haste to prolong their thrilling interaction.

'Not quite.' He shrugged, unabashed. 'Would you like a drink?' He poured himself a nightcap.

'No, thank you. I'm *supposed* to be working.' She fidgeted with her hair, pushing some unruly strands of honeyed gold behind her ear, while she tried valiantly to keep her eyes averted from his bare chest and the towel slung low on his hips.

Oh, yes, she felt this primal attraction as strongly as him, and the intense chemistry neither of them could dismiss, no matter how inconvenient or ill-judged.

'Well, I need to warm up after that tepid bath.' He joined her before the fire.

Something about her made him feel less alone, as if the ferocity of their attraction proved they were humans first, all other expectations second.

'You could always put some clothes on,' she snapped.

'I could.' Grateful to have their playful banter back, he made no move to oblige her. 'But then I'd miss the way you're looking at me.'

'I'm not looking at you. I'm wondering how soon I can return to my proper job.'

'Point taken. But, before you leave, tell me, do you work here full-time?' he asked, already looking forward to their next meeting.

'*Part*-time,' she stressed. 'I have another full-time job at a local hospital.'

'You work *two* jobs?' he asked, astonished by her impressive dedication.

'Some people must if they want a roof over their heads.' She cast him another of those challenging looks and then glanced around the immaculately elegant room, a barely concealed sneer on her lips.

Of course; the palace was completely over the top compared to how most normal people lived.

'Forgive me.' Andreas frowned, appalled by the arrogant assumptions he'd made about this intriguing woman's life. 'I've detained you long enough.'

But now he wanted to know everything about Clara Lund. To understand what had shaped her, what drove her, what dreams she held. Meeting her tonight had been a welcome-home gift he could never have anticipated. Knowing she worked in a place where he should feel at ease to be himself but instead felt like an imposter gave him the strength to face all that this place represented: memories, good and bad; expectations of duty and obligation at odds with his dreams; the disappointment in people's eyes, his father's included.

He placed his barely touched Scotch on the table and held out his hand, wishing he didn't have to let her go. 'It was a pleasure to meet you, Clara. Thank you for your help.'

She took his hand, her grip firm and her fingers warm, her touch calling to that part of him that was, first and foremost, a man.

'Perhaps you'll be more careful where you throw your prosthesis in future,' she said, those big, intelligent eyes teasing.

What did she see when she looked at him? Suddenly, he wanted to know.

'You haven't asked—about how I lost my leg.' He kept hold of her hand, hoping she couldn't feel the rapid acceleration of his pulse. 'Most people can't help their curiosity.'

But he'd already established this woman wasn't most people.

If she *did* ask, he'd have to confess his true identity, explain the accident and voice his worst failing to this extraordinary, ordinary woman. Would she view him differently if she knew how he'd failed his brother, his family, his nation? Would she too find him somehow lacking?

Could he stand to find out?

Her stare clung to his. 'If you wanted me to know, a complete stranger, you'd have told me.'

Andreas's breath caught in his chest, her answer more perfect than he could ever have imagined.

'And why does it matter?' she asked, her pupils dilating in the dim lighting. 'Our scars don't define us, do they?'

Her astonishing reply sliced through him like a blade. She couldn't possibly know he struggled with imposter syndrome, not because he'd lost a limb, but because he'd been raised from birth to know that he wasn't quite as important as his older brother, a brother who had then died on Andreas's watch.

'No, I suppose they don't,' he said, as fresh heat boiled inside him.

What scars had shaped beguiling, hard-working and independent Clara?

For Andreas, his injury represented what might have been, what *should* have been, if Oscar had survived the accident instead. His scars were a daily reminder of the brother he'd failed to save. And more—with Oscar dead, and his father growing older, Andreas would one day need to forgo his career and his freedom.

But she was right: there *was* more to him than his scars, his past mistakes and the future role he would one day inherit. In that moment, he was desperate to be nothing more than an ordinary man.

'May I?' he asked, slowly lifting his hand to an escaped lock of hair on her cheek.

She nodded, her eyes dipping to his mouth for a revealing second as her breathing accelerated.

This close, he could see a tiny hole in her nose from a piercing. It made him smile and strengthened his resolve to stand up to the palace's demands for his time, to cling to the medical career he loved, until he was finally forced to stop. He tucked the silky strand behind her ear, his fingers lingering over that soft golden hair.

Oh, Clara, Clara, Clara... Why is it so hard to let you walk away?

As if she'd read his mind, she gripped his wrist, holding his hand in place.

His pulse spiked. He should tell her to leave. Except her warm, feminine scent lured him as she swayed closer and wet her lips with the tip of her tongue, her hungry stare latched to his, as if she saw deep inside his soul.

'You should go,' he said in one last ditch attempt to do the right thing, to resist the madness engulfing him like a rogue wave sucking him under.

'I should.' She nodded, swallowed and inched closer.

Damn it, just one taste.

Crushing her to his bare chest, he covered her mouth with his, pressing her pliant body close, from breasts to hips. Need roared through his blood, powerful and inescapable, setting off a chain reaction of desire so intense, he lost his mind. Her lips were soft, her whimper a moan of desperation that echoed so deeply inside him he struggled to recall if he'd ever wanted a woman more.

She parted her lips and touched her tongue to his, twisting his hair in her greedy hands. He tasted sweet triumph. He wasn't alone. She felt this uncontrollable chemistry too.

Her body writhed against his as their kiss deepened. His towel loosened and slid from his hips to the floor. But he was too far gone to care, too intent on the thrilling duel of tongue against tongue, too aroused by the intense flare of mutual passion as they kissed.

With a sudden gasp, she broke free. She pushed at him, so he stepped back, releasing her at once.

Her hand flew to cover her mouth, but not before Andreas saw the evidence of her kiss-swollen lips. 'I'm sorry. I shouldn't have done that.' She looked down at his nakedness—he was hard—and stepped back towards the exit. 'You're a guest here.'

'No, I'm…here on business.' He speared his fingers through his hair, lingering arousal and fresh guilt shredding his composure. '*I'm* the one who's sorry. It was my fault.'

'Please don't have me fired,' she whispered, backing further away as if he was some sort of lecherous creep. 'I need this job.'

Fired? Guilt rattled his bones. 'There's no question that you'll lose your job.'

He'd taken advantage of the situation, kept his identity secret and indulged himself with a beautiful woman in his father's employment. Yes, she'd kissed him back, her passion as desperate as his, but he should have controlled himself. He knew better and held himself to higher standards than other men.

'Wait,' he said, reaching for his towel as she turned and headed for the exit.

He strode after her, tucking his towel around his waist. For a wild and irresponsible moment, he'd relished the freedom to be the anonymous man Clara saw, flirted with and found attractive. He would make this right and tell her his name, hope she didn't curtsey or something equally hideous, and perhaps they could laugh about the situation.

Except, by the time he reached the corridor, she'd disappeared. Andreas cursed under his breath. He closed the suite door and retraced his footsteps. The room seemed to have shrunk, the walls pressing in on him with the heavy weight of regret. He touched his lips, the lingering taste of Clara soured by the bitter taste of what might have been if he were any other man.

CHAPTER THREE

IF CLARA HAD hoped for a quiet moment the following day to analyse why she'd acted so completely out of character, flirting with and then kissing a gloriously naked stranger, she was to be sorely disappointed. No sooner had she met her newest patient at Nordic Care, a private hospital an hour's drive from the palace, than the poor elderly man collapsed and went into cardiac arrest right before her eyes.

Shocked into action, Clara hit the alarm on the wall above the patient's bed and instantly began chest compressions. The crash team arrived within seconds—two other nurses and a female registrar. The doctor began manually bagging the patient, inflating his lungs with air, while Clara gave the team a brief synopsis of the patient's medical problems.

'This is Mr Engman, a seventy-three-year-old diabetic admitted overnight with dizzy spells.'

Clara snatched a breath, the exertion of performing CPR talking all her energy. 'We'd been monitoring him for cardiac arrhythmias. I'd just taken over his care when he collapsed and lost consciousness.'

She didn't want to tell the doctor her job, but the heart monitor seemed to show ventricular fibrillation, an abnormal rhythm where the heart's ventricles quivered in an irregular and uncoordinated manner. Other staff arrived, bodies jostling in the cramped space around the bed. Emergencies like this prompted a kind of controlled, co-ordinated chaos that ensured there were enough hands on board to do everything they could to revive their patient.

Clara focussed on timing the cardiac compressions, willing Mr Engman to respond. But her stomach tightened with fear, given his frail condition and multiple comorbidities.

'Looks like ventricular fibrillation,' a male voice said from behind Clara, confirming her diagnosis.

She was too focussed on the CPR to wonder where she'd heard the vaguely familiar voice before.

'Check for a pulse, please,' the commanding voice ordered.

There was a pause while they checked if Mr Engman's heart had spontaneously restarted. Clara caught her breath, looking up at the man running the arrest protocol.

She froze, her jaw dropping.

It was *him*—from last night—the naked VIP. The man with the body of a Greek god and haunted eyes. And he was looking at her without a trace of surprise, as if he'd expected their paths to cross.

Last night, after they'd kissed as if competing for the Olympic gold medal in kissing, Clara had met others from the team of palace nursing staff who cared for Prince Henrik, praying she'd never need to see her sexy but confusing stranger again.

Except there he was—a sexy mountain-man in scrubs.

Clara snatched her gaze away from his, fury and humiliation turning her stomach. While she'd been high from the kiss and begging for her job, he'd secretively held on to some pretty pertinent information. So this was the *business* he'd vaguely referred to. He was a *doctor.* Why hadn't he just come out and said that last night? She'd assumed he was a diplomat or a visiting ambassador, and he'd said nothing to the contrary. He'd commented on her uniform but had failed to declare that they worked in the same field. She'd even told him she had a second job at a nearby hospital, just before he'd lured her with his vulnerable stare and his talk of scars into that disastrous kiss which might have cost her a lucrative and prestigious job at the palace.

'No pulse,' Naked VIP said. 'Are you okay to continue compressions, Nurse Lund?'

Mortified that she'd lusted after and kissed someone so apparently shifty, Clara nodded and restarted the chest compressions. This was why she couldn't trust men. The last time she'd been intimate with a guy, he'd slept with her and then avoided her. Ever since, she'd resolutely refused to give anyone the power to hurt and humiliate her. Until last night…

She should have known better. After all, she'd learned to rely only on herself after her father, the one man who should have offered unconditional emotional and financial support, had repeatedly let her down. Growing up, she'd never known from one day to the next if Lars would come through the door at the end of the day, if the bills she knew worried her hard-working mother would be paid or if her father's latest dodgy deal would topple, plunging the entire family into a deeper pit of debt and despair.

One of Clara's nurse colleagues stuck gel pads to Mr Engman's chest and Naked VIP—she really needed to discover his name—positioned the defibrillator paddles in place.

'Stand clear. Defibrillating—two hundred joules,' he said, delivering the shock to the man's failing heart in line with the Advanced Cardiac Life Support protocol.

Clara couldn't bear to look at him. He looked far too gorgeous in the hospital's navy-blue scrubs, and being lured by his irrelevant good looks was how she'd found herself in this embarrassing situation in the first place.

'Nothing,' her stranger said, watching the erratic trace on the cardiac monitor.

'It's been three minutes,' Clara told him, resuming the chest compressions, glad to have an excuse to look away from his annoyingly riveting lips.

He nodded, taking a vial of adrenaline from the trolley and administering it intravenously in an attempt to normalise the heart's rhythm.

Why had she kissed him? She'd allowed him to get under her skin, weakened by desire stronger than anything she'd ever known. Flirting with him had felt carefree, whereas growing up with her unreliable father and having to care for her mother had given Clara an over-inflated sense of responsibility. They'd talked about scars and he'd seemed momentarily lost, a feeling she'd understood well as a bewildered teenager.

Until that unexpected interlude in the palace's guest suite, she hadn't realised that Lars Lund's selfish actions meant that she'd missed out on a wild and misspent youth. But with *him*, a sexy, naked stranger, she'd felt young and vibrantly alive.

She'd have to stop thinking of him naked. It was foolish to think about him in any state given that he was just another man she couldn't trust.

'Pause please,' the man in question said. All eyes settled on the heart monitor, every member of staff awaiting Naked VIP's next instruction with bated breath.

'He's still in VF,' he said. 'Stand clear—defibrillating again.'

With the second shock delivered, Mr Engman's heart stuttered back into sinus rhythm, the patient breathing again of his own accord. There was a collective sigh of relief. Clara sagged, her head woozy from the physical exertion and the adrenaline rush.

'Okay, we'll be moving Mr Engman around to ICU,' her midnight mystery man said. 'Nurse Lund, can you please call Mr Engman's next of kin?'

'Of course.' Clara nodded and placed a high-flow oxygen mask on their still groggy patient. This necessitated stepping closer to *Dr* Naked VIP.

Big mistake. He smelled delicious, reminding her

of how it had felt to be held in those strong arms last night: safe, protected, desired.

The wild desperation of that kiss—his big body engulfing hers, each of their lips chasing the other's, demanding and sensual—had surely ruined her for all future kisses. For a second, before she'd pushed him away, Clara hadn't been able to come up with a single reason she shouldn't sleep with him right there and then.

Swallowing hard, Clara fought off visions of him naked and proud, a spectacular specimen of manhood. The magnificence of his manhood was of no consequence whatsoever. And, more importantly, Clara wasn't interested in kissing, naked or otherwise. His deception made her realise just how out of her depth she was when it came to relationships.

She reattached an electrode that had come loose during CPR to Mr Engman's chest. The mystery doctor drew some blood from the patient's arm, thrusting the vials at the registrar.

'Check his cardiac enzymes and do an ECG, please. We need to exclude a myocardial infarction or cardiomyopathy.'

'I can do the ECG, if you want,' Clara said to the harassed-looking registrar, who gave a grateful nod and hurried away to order the blood work, leaving Clara alone with the patient and *him*.

An awkward silence descended.

Clara felt his observation like sun on her face as she tucked in the blanket on Mr Engman's bed. The patient was obliviously out of it, but this wasn't the time or the place for a personal conversation.

She looked up, their stares locking. 'Any other tests you'd like, *doctor*?'

She emphasised his title, showing him, and more importantly herself, that whatever had happened during last night's moment of insanity wouldn't be happening again. She couldn't trust one glorious hair on his devious head.

An image of Alma Lund, weary, sick and scared, flashed behind her eyes. Her mother had been through so much, and had always worked hard to provide a stable and comfortable home for Clara and her younger sister Freja, latterly with no help from her husband.

Clara wanted to slap herself; she knew better than to risk anything for a man, especially the income that kept them in their family home.

'No thank you, Nurse Lund.' Curiosity flickered over his expression, his blue eyes impressed and carrying the same hint of vulnerability that, last night, had made her lose her mind.

Well, in the cold light of day, her head was back in charge. She didn't need his admiration. She didn't need to know his name. She didn't need him at all, not even for phenomenal naked kissing. What she needed were her two jobs, her peace of mind and her self-reliance.

'We need to talk,' he said, pausing at the gap in the curtains around Mr Engman's bed.

'Didn't we have that opportunity last night?' she

shot back, feeling decidedly uncharitable, given that she'd allowed herself to be duped by a charming smile, some witty repartee and a hot body.

'Last night, I was…distracted,' he admitted, pressing his lips together grimly as he continued to stare.

And just like that Clara's body returned to the scene of the crime—her pulse going crazy, her blood so hot she must surely have given off steam and the taste of him fresh on her lips.

A wave of fear and foolishness whipped through her chest. Even now—with every reason in the world not to; when last night's rash and unprecedented impulse to kiss a fellow lost soul might have cost her the job at the palace; when he held all of the power—she craved another kiss.

'Well, today I have my head screwed on correctly,' she said, willing it to be true.

It was only when he'd finally exited the ward moments later that Clara could finally breathe easy. Whatever he had to say, whatever his real name and his reasons for being secretive, he was just another man showing her the only person she could truly rely on was herself.

CHAPTER FOUR

LATER THAT MORNING, Andreas waited outside the acute medical ward for Clara Lund to emerge. She pushed through the doors and headed for the lifts, an assault to every one of his heightened senses. Today's uniform was navy, the fitted cut reminding Andreas how it had felt to have that insanely gorgeous body pressed against him last night while their tongues had duelled for dominance of their kiss.

He approached, his heart knocking at his ribs at the sight of her hair pulled back into a tight bun, leaving her slender neck exposed. Heaven help him; even now, when he had a whole heap of explaining to do, he wanted to remove the clips and tunnel his hands in all of that silkiness as he kissed her again and again until her eyes glazed with arousal once more.

'Clara,' he said, intercepting her outside the lift. 'Is now a good time to talk?'

If she remained ignorant of his identity after their reunion over this morning's crash call, it was time he filled in the blanks.

She glanced up, her expression carefully neutral. 'I'm on my lunch break, doctor.'

Her voice was deservedly dismissive; he missed

her playfulness. 'I appreciate that,' he said, regretting that he hadn't warned her about them working at the same hospital the moment he'd discovered the fact from palace security last night after she'd left. 'But what I have to say won't take long. I'll accompany you to the canteen. It will give me a chance to explain a few things.'

'Like how you're a doctor, not a diplomat?' Suspicion narrowed her eyes. 'I've already figured that out all by myself, thanks. The scrubs and white coat kind of give it away.'

She jabbed at the already lit up call button, as if desperate to escape.

Andreas winced with remorse but he was so glad to see her feisty side. Her anger was better than her indifference.

'It's…complicated,' he said, wishing he'd explained himself last night, in private.

Technically a prince *was* a diplomat, a representative of the nation he served.

'I'm kind of both, for the time being,' he added, frustrated by the thought that, given its way, Prince Henrik's office would have him abandon his career now and commit fully to royal duties. If he capitulated to the palace's demands, he would have to give up treating patients, give up his freedom to flirt with fascinating women like Clara and give up everything he'd known his entire adult life.

A dull throb of resentment tightened his chest. He loved his job and had worked hard for his career. He was good at being a doctor. Being back in

Varborg meant readjusting to the demands of his two personas: Andreas the man, free to do what he liked, and Andreas the prince.

'Great,' she scoffed, shaking her head with disbelief. 'That's cleared everything up.'

Andreas smiled to himself, his spirits already roused by a moment of her company. He had no idea if she was still upset by the kiss or because he'd concealed his profession, and he really had no time for complications of the fiery, blue-eyed variety. Except, the part of him that was just a man demanded that, for this particular woman, he *make* time.

'I know I should have mentioned that I'm a doctor last night,' he said as the lift arrived and the doors opened. 'I've just started a locum geriatrician position here.'

'Yes, you should.' She stepped inside. 'But, now that you've explained, I'll wish you a good day, doctor.'

Ducking inside the lift before the doors closed, Andreas continued, 'Listen, Clara, now that we're alone, I want to apologise again for last night.'

'Oh?' Completely unfazed, she glanced down her pert little nose at him, impressive given their height difference. It made him think of the Swedish term of endearment *sötnos*, the literal translation of which was 'sweet nose'.

'Don't worry.' She huffed, stabbing once more at the second-floor button as if her impatience alone could make the lift ascend faster. '*I* regret it too.'

She was so desperate to get away from him now.

Andreas inched closer and rested his gaze on that kissable mouth, now pinched with irritation. 'Oh, I don't regret the kissing for one second, *sötnos*.'

Alone with her in this confined space, there was no avoiding her bewitching scent or the erotic memories blasting him from all angles.

'I'm not your sweetie,' she snapped, flinging the endearment back in his face as if it were poison.

But her pupils dilated, her pulse flickered in her neck and her eyes dipped to his mouth every few seconds as if she too could remember every steamy detail of the night before.

'You might regret it now,' he taunted, 'But last night you enjoyed kissing me. I was there. I felt your body against mine, your fingers tugging at my hair…heard your sexy little whimpers.'

They had unfinished business.

'Maybe I did,' she admitted, planting her hands on her hips and leaning closer. 'But so did *you*.'

Andreas held up his hands in surrender. 'You'll get no argument from me. I wanted to kiss you the minute you laughed at me for hurling my leg.'

She huffed again, frustrated. 'But I didn't enjoy it enough to lose my job over or do it again.'

She was breathless now, her eyes ablaze with challenge and something else—something wild, reckless and needy that helped him to see the last lie for what it was.

But enough games; she might want nothing more to do with him when he told her his other secret.

Being a public figure came with complications that some people couldn't tolerate.

'And *that's* why I'm apologising,' he said, turning serious as guilt at his abuse of power sent chills down his spine. 'That you felt your job was at risk is unforgivable. I would never allow you to face repercussions when the kiss was fully my responsibility.'

Now he had her attention. She blinked, as if she was momentarily confused, then her stare hardened.

'Well, I hope you don't expect me to be grateful.' Her lip curled in distaste. 'Just because I've seen the goods...' her stare dipped to his groin '...doesn't mean I'm interested in making a purchase.'

When their eyes met again, he unleashed a victorious grin. If only she'd resisted checking him out last night when his towel had slipped, he might believe her now.

'I'd rather be homeless,' she continued, her colour high, her voice breathy. 'So, if you think I somehow owe you for your discretion, you can think again.'

Adrenaline rushed his system, urgent and fiery, compelling him to act. 'Exactly what kind of man do you think I am?' he asked, his voice deceptively calm despite the accusations she was hurling his way.

She obviously didn't trust him, but did she truly think him capable of blackmailing her into sex?

'I don't know you.' She raised her chin in defiance. 'So far, you've proved yourself utterly untrustworthy. You had a perfect opportunity to tell me you were a doctor last night, but you didn't. Even now when you've *come to explain*—' she made finger quotes '—you're being vague. Maybe you enjoyed misleading me. Maybe you're used to getting your own way and manipulating people. Maybe you expected a whole lot more than a kiss.'

At her goading, all his good intentions to make amends and come clean evaporated. If only she knew what he'd wanted in the moment when their tongues had been duelling, her luscious body restless against his, craving more. And, for all her denial, their undeniable magnetism was generating enough sparks to set the lift alight.

But maybe he'd been wrong about her; maybe he couldn't be the real Andreas with her after all.

'You're right—you *don't* know me,' he said, catching the sound of her sharply inhaled breath as his stare raked her features, from the icy chips in her irises to the plump fullness of those lovely lips. 'So let me enlighten you. I don't need to bribe or manipulate women into my bed. They come eagerly and leave satisfied.'

His heartbeat raced, thick arousal boiling in his belly.

'Oh, I bet they do.' She snorted in disgust. 'Well, *I* have no intention of being one of those women.'

But she was panting hard and had stepped up close, raising her face to his so one mutual move would send them back into each other's arms.

'Are you sure about that, *sötnos*?' he asked lazily. 'Because you're looking at me like I'm the last cookie in the jar again.'

But he needed to master their chemistry, and fast. With her two jobs, she'd be everywhere he looked. Just as she knew nothing about him, he knew little about her beyond her education and employment history. Nothing about the things that counted: her integrity, her moral compass, her loyalty.

His public position necessitated discretion in the people he invited into his life, even casually. And, while it was perfectly acceptable for hospital staff to fraternise, he still hadn't explained the small detail of his royal life. Would she treat him differently when she knew that he was Varborg's heir that should never have been?

Just then, while they faced each other, eyes locked in challenge, the lift arrived on the staff-only floor.

The doors slid open, breaking the sexually charged impasse.

Andreas stepped back, breathing through the wild thudding of his heart. How had the conversation veered in a completely tangential direction from the one he'd planned? What was it about this woman that left him struggling to walk away? And what had caused her distrust and general cynicism towards men, when it was obvious to anyone with eyes how hot they were for each other?

Waiting outside the lift slightly out of breath, as if he'd taken the stairs at full pelt, was Andreas's bodyguard, Nils.

'Your Highness, there's been a security breach

in the emergency department.' Nils flicked a brief look at Clara who, as a staff member both at Nordic Care and at the palace, would be well known to the security team that monitored Andreas's every move. 'You need to come with me now, sir.'

Defeat rumbled in Andreas's chest. He winced as he took in Clara's stunned confusion.

'Who's this?' she asked, her jaw dropping. 'And what did he just call you?'

She'd made it perfectly clear today that she had little trust for him, and now he'd missed the opportunity to have her hear the news from him direct.

'Give me a moment,' Andreas instructed Nils, who dutifully stepped aside out of earshot.

Andreas turned to Clara, his control of the situation now tugged like a rug from under his feet. If she'd wanted nothing more to do with him when she'd thought he was just a man who'd failed to declare his profession, his royal baggage, the ultimate complication, would likely be the final straw. It shouldn't matter. He'd come back to Varborg for family reasons, not for fun. Except that addictive lure of being just himself with this woman was hard to fight.

Taking Clara's elbow, he led her into an alcove beside the lifts. 'This is why I wanted to speak with you. I intended to explain my…heritage, my role at the palace…but then we got side-tracked again.'

He dropped his hand, instantly missing the feel of her silky skin beneath his fingertips, more off-kilter than ever with her this close physically, while emotionally he could literally see her slipping further away.

As if she'd finally pieced the jigsaw together, her hand covered her mouth, horrified. 'This isn't a joke. You're really a prince…?'

'I'm afraid so.'

What he wouldn't give to be just a doctor in that moment, to have her look at him the way she had last night, right before that kiss. He could escape for ever in eyes like hers. But escape wasn't an option.

'I thought you were familiar… But you're a doctor,' she said, clearly trying to make sense of the scattered pieces of information, the panicked tone of her voice telling him all he needed to know about her current regrets. 'You were staying in the guest wing.'

Andreas sighed, resigned. 'I refused to occupy the suite prepared for me in the family wing.' He swallowed, forcing himself to continue. 'It once belonged to my brother.'

Andreas had a hard enough time with his grief, and unfavourably comparing himself to Oscar, without occupying his rooms.

'And I've grown used to sparse but comfortable doctor's digs at hospitals,' he finished, braced for her transformation as reality sunk in.

Last night, when she'd blasted into his predictable, privileged life like a tornado—and again this morning, while they'd worked together to treat their patient—he'd foolishly clung to the hope of something real and unguarded with this exceptional woman he couldn't seem to forget.

But, now that she knew the truth, he would no longer be just Andreas the man and doctor, in her eyes. He would be something else—something two-dimensional, a caricature.

'You let me believe you were a nobody...' She scowled and shook her head, as if dazed. 'I kissed a prince...?'

She might as well have said she'd kissed a frog for all the contempt with which she spoke his title.

'Oh, don't worry.' Desire heated his blood as he stepped closer and watched her eyes widen, her breath catch and arousal flush her skin. 'Prince or not, I remember every second of our kiss and, what's more, so do you.'

'I do...' She blinked up at him, clearly stunned into an honest admission. 'But I'm sorry—it won't happen again.'

Hot, sharp jealousy sliced through him. 'So you were willing to flirt with me and kiss me when you assumed me to be a guest of the royal family but, now you know I'm Prince Henrik's son, you want nothing more to do with me—is that it?'

Futility stiffened his muscles. Part of him, the same part that refused to give up his career until he had no choice, refused to accept that the fantasy of this woman was over. He wanted to remind her of the inferno they'd generated when they'd been in each other's arms, him naked and her wild for him.

'I…' Her mortified stare darted to Nils. 'Can't we just forget it happened?' she snapped.

Andreas raised his brows dubiously. 'We could try and forget, if that's what you want.'

Ever since Oscar's death, what Andreas wanted, be it his medical career or the woman who now seemed horrified by his true identity, hadn't been his choice to make. And, when it came to this woman and the kind of chemistry they shared, forgetting the way she'd looked at him with heat and desire would be an uphill challenge.

But he would have to find a way to work alongside her until it was time for him to hang up his stethoscope for good.

Sensing Nils' urgency, he tilted his head with regret, his duty to his family tugging him away.

'Either way, we'll need to talk about the kissing some other time,' he said. 'I must go.'

Taking one last look at her, he took out his frustration on the stairs as he headed for the armoured vehicle awaiting him outside.

CHAPTER FIVE

TWO DAYS LATER, Clara returned to the palace for her next night shift, her stomach twisted into knots of dread and humiliation. Half of her was desperate to avoid seeing Andreas again—*Prince* Andreas—the other half had no idea what she wanted, beyond wishing she could turn back time and never have met him in the first place. How dared he flirt with her twice, but keep such an important identity a secret?

Following the footman to Prince Henrik's private rooms, her face heated with the memory of how she'd snogged, ogled and then insulted the heir to the throne. She stifled a snort of disbelief. Her actions had been bad enough when she'd assumed Andreas was a hunky diplomat and then a doctor.

Now, she was so confused, because Andreas was right—she *did* recall every thrilling second of that kiss and she had no hope of forgetting. She might not trust him, but her body didn't seem to care that, for a woman like Clara, an ordinary nobody with financial woes and a notorious convicted conman for a father, he was the most ridiculously out-of-reach man in the universe.

She had such little experience with relationships, thanks to Lars and those lost teenage years and thanks to the guy who'd taken her virginity and then acted as if they were strangers. Her attraction to Andreas of all men was…laughable.

The only sensible course of action was to keep her distance. No more lusting after him, no more bickering and no more reliving his look of defeat when he'd accused her of wanting nothing more to do with him.

Resolved, Clara waited while the footman tapped quietly on the door. She dragged in a shaky breath, preparing herself to finally meet her patient, Andreas's father. After signing her confidentiality agreement on the first night, she'd been given the prince's medical records.

The prognosis wasn't good. After a short battle with prostate cancer, Prince Henrik had recently been diagnosed with stage four disease and was currently undergoing a course of radiotherapy for painful bone metastases.

Clara's heart ached for the older man, and for Andreas. Having nursed her mother through breast cancer treatment a few years ago, she knew exactly what the family was going through—although Andreas had shown no obvious signs that he was even aware that his father's disease was terminal, beyond stating that he was both a doctor and a diplomat *for the time being*.

Had that cryptic reference been because he knew he would soon need to forgo his medical career and succeed his father? Compassion clenched her heart. She understood how it felt to be tugged in all direc-

tions. She'd just started her nursing degree when
Alma Lund had been diagnosed. Clara had considered dropping out to care for her mother full time,
but fortunately her mother wouldn't hear of it. At
least Clara had been able to continue with her career, her independence invaluable, whereas Andreas
would likely have no choice but to give up medicine.
He couldn't rule Varborg *and* work at the hospital.

The door opened. Prince Henrik's private butler
appeared and quietly ushered Clara inside.

'His majesty is uncomfortable tonight and can-
not sleep,' the man she'd been informed was named
Møller said, his face etched in concern. 'I believe
his pain management requires addressing.'

Clara nodded, trying to shove her patient's son
from her mind. But she couldn't seem to block out
the vulnerability she'd seen in his eyes when he'd
accused her of treating him differently because he'd
grown up here, surrounded by wealth and privilege.

Why had that look of defeat in Andreas's eyes
called to her on such a profound level? Was it just
that, for all their differences, she could empathise
with him both about his father's illness and the loss
of his career? Or was the idea he might be torn between his two roles deeply unsettling? She shook
her head, disgusted with herself. How did all roads
lead back to Andreas?

She followed Møller's stiff gait through a series
of ante rooms, her nerves growing with every step.
But the prince was a patient like any other; all Clara
needed to do was her job.

They arrived outside another door and the butler knocked, waiting to be admitted into what Clara soon saw was the prince's private sitting room.

The man sat in an arm chair before a sleek contemporary fireplace built into a marble surround. Clara approached and curtseyed, as she'd been taught, waiting for Prince Henrik to address her first.

'Your name is Clara?' he asked, his face pale, his eyes red with fatigue.

'Yes, Your Highness.'

She'd seen him a handful of times in the media. His head was on Varborg's stamps and coins. But in person it was the likeness to his virile, handsome son that made Clara's heart gallop with longing to see Andreas again.

Huh! Her resolve clearly meant nothing...

But how could she ignore the prince she'd kissed—the man to whom, for all her denials, she was obviously still drawn—when his life was about to change irrevocably because his father was terminally ill?

'Can I help you, sir?' Clara stepped closer, urged by the butler, who then discreetly left the room.

'I'm in pain,' the prince said. 'My bones ache and this blasted thing isn't working.'

He indicated the syringe driver strapped to his arm, which had been prescribed to administer analgesia while he was undergoing treatment.

'Can I examine your arm, sir?' Empathy for the

older man, a man from whom Andreas had inherited his grey-blue eyes, tugged at her heartstrings.

Varborg's ruler was beloved by the nation. For fifty years he'd ruled with diligence and dignity, despite his share of adversity—losing his wife when his sons had been teenagers and, more recently, his oldest son, Oscar. If only she'd done her homework on her patient's past sooner, she might have recognised Andreas.

Prince Henrik nodded and slipped his arm free of his blue velvet dressing gown. Focussed on her work, and not the tragic losses of Varborg's royal family, Clara peeled away the dressing from the needle site, finding an angry red patch of skin where the cannula had extravasated.

'I'm afraid it's slipped out.' She disposed of the cannula in the nearby sharps bin. 'I'll need to re-site the needle, if that's okay.'

'Of course, dear. I'm pretty much a pin cushion at this stage,' he said with a sad smile that gave his stare the same aching vulnerability she'd witnessed in Andreas. Did these two proud men know how similar they were?

Trying not to think about his deceptive son, Clara pulled on gloves and grabbed a fresh subcutaneous cannula, some antiseptic wipes and a new adhesive dressing.

'I hear you've met my son,' the prince said, watching her with shrewd eyes that spoke of sharp intelligence and an ability to read people easily.

'I have. We work together at Nordic Care.' Clara willed herself not to blush.

While she held this prestigious position she couldn't expect to have any secrets. She only hoped that the prince was unaware of her late-night antics with his naked son.

In the days since she'd discovered Andreas's true identity, she'd scoured the Internet for any information she could find on Europe's most eligible and unusual prince. There'd been tales of his military career, his work as a doctor and photographs of his playboy antics—an immaculately dressed Andreas attending various glitzy functions accompanied by a string of beautiful society women. The latter had caused such searing jealousy, she'd had to slam closed her laptop in disgust.

'Ah, yes, the day job...' Prince Henrik sighed and closed his eyes as Clara cleaned a patch of skin on his arm with the antiseptic wipes. 'Tell me, is he a good doctor?'

'Yes,' she said simply, recalling the way they'd worked together to revive Mr Engman. 'He's very well respected. A favourite with the patients, I'm told.' Many of whom had volunteered to Clara what a compassionate and caring man they found the heir to the throne; how natural and grounded he appeared to his patients, treating them with empathy and respect.

But why was the prince asking *her*, the palace's newest member of staff? Surely he and Andreas spoke about his work?

'Just a small scratch now, sir,' she said, burning up with questions about their relationship she would never dare to ask. At Prince Henrik's silent nod, Clara inserted the subcutaneous needle just beneath the skin, securing it with the dressing. Then she reattached the syringe driver and adjusted the dose of pain killers.

She shouldn't care what kind of relationship Andreas had with his dying father *or* whom he dated. He was handsome, intelligent and a *prince*: of course he was a catch for any woman willing to forgo her independence and put *his* life first.

Intense chemistry or not, that woman wasn't Clara.

For all her father's faults, Alma had loved Lars Lund. Young Clara had loved him too, craving his attention. But, where her mother had forgiven him countless times for his erratic employment history and excused his unreliability, teenaged Clara had grown more and more wary with each disappointment. She'd seen the fallout and had witnessed Alma struggling to put on a brave face when Lars had lost yet another job, or pretend all was well when the electricity had been cut off. Clara had been the one taking care of Freja after school while Alma had worked longer hours. She'd understood that her parents' marriage was unequal; that loving the wrong man, having his children, had left Alma vulnerable.

Even after her father had left for good to pursue his dubious, get-rich-quick schemes, the final one sending him to prison, he'd burdened the family with deeper debt. It wasn't until after his death that Clara's mother had discovered he'd re-mortgaged the house.

'We don't get on terribly well, my son and I,' Prince Henrik said, taking her by surprise.

He opened his shrewd eyes and Clara froze, uncertain how to reply. But her curiosity for Andreas went wild. The more she learned about the man behind the headlines, the harder it was to ignore him the way she wanted to.

'He resents me, you see,' the older man said, as if to himself, his stare far away. 'I've reminded him of his birth right and his responsibilities to the crown.'

Without comment, Clara silently disposed of her gloves.

She had no idea how Andreas felt about anything, his relationship with his father and his crown prince duties included. They were virtual strangers.

She understood complex relationships, having experienced years of rejection and disappointment with her own untrustworthy father. But, whereas Lars had passed away while serving his sentence for fraud before Clara had had a chance to face him with some home truths, at least *this* father and son still had time to air their grievances and reconcile their differences.

But not much time.

'Are you feeling more comfortable now, sir?' Clara stooped at the prince's side, adjusting the blanket across his knees. His eyes had fallen closed once more, the tension around his mouth easing as the pain medication began to work.

'I gave him too much freedom when he was younger, you see…' he continued. 'I allowed the boy to choose a career for himself, when perhaps I should have had greater expectations of him as a prince.'

Clara's skin prickled with discomfort, as if she were eavesdropping. Patients voiced all sorts of things in their most vulnerable moments. Part of her wanted to leave the prince to his privacy but, if he wanted to talk as her patient, she would listen.

'I promised his mother before she died that I would allow the boys to have as normal a life as possible…' He was slurring now, obviously on the cusp of sleep. 'It wasn't always possible for Oscar, but with Andreas… I tried my best, but I missed their mother, so very much…'

Compassion squeezed Clara's heart. She blinked away the sting in her eyes, recalling the stark terror she'd experienced on more than one occasion when she imagined losing her mother. Prince Henrik was a man like any other. He was still grieving for his wife and wondering if he'd been a good enough father to his sons. Like many families, Varborg's first family had their issues, for all their power and privilege.

In desperation, Clara cast around for sight of the butler lurking in a doorway. Perhaps together they could encourage the prince back to bed. Spying a call button next to the prince's arm chair, Clara gave it the briefest of pushes, hoping it wouldn't sound in the room and wake the dozing man.

Within seconds, the butler appeared. Clara explained the issue with the syringe driver, keeping the man's privileged confessions to herself. But, as she made her way back to the staff sitting-room, her feet dragged, her heart heavy.

The more she learned about Andreas, the murkier the picture that emerged. Did he resent his father for calling him back to Varborg? Did he know the prince was terminally ill? That would surely devastate him; and how would he feel, having to give up his career as a doctor?

But the hardest question of all to answer was why she cared so much when she'd vowed to keep him at arm's length.

CHAPTER SIX

THE EMBOSSED AND gilded envelope had arrived the following day—an invitation to Prince Henrik's private Jubilee Banquet, an intimate celebration of his fifty years on the throne.

When the gown box had been delivered shortly afterwards, she'd assumed that the formal wear was part of the clothing allowance that came with her salary. She hadn't been able to resist peeling back the layers of gossamer tissue paper and trying on the most extravagant garment she'd ever handled... just once.

And now, three days later, she was wearing the gown for real—a black, lace beaded sheath that clung to her body and flared at her feet, her heart beating into her throat with awe as she was ushered inside an opulent banquet hall in the formal and ceremonial wing of the palace.

Clara swallowed, any ridiculous fantasy that she and Andreas might have anything in common, or that he needed *her* concern, crushed into the plush carpet so thick she could have been walking on a cloud.

This part of the winter residence was often open to the public, but tonight it glittered in celebration. The cold marble of the columns and ornate cornices was warmed by the six enormous chandeliers that hung from the ceiling, as well as a million twinkling lights strung like a net of stars across the night sky. To one side, row after row of banquet tables were precisely laid with glittering crystal glassware, ornate gilded centrepieces and cascading fresh flower arrangements. A chamber orchestra occupied a raised dais, where guests danced to ballroom versions of popular Scandinavian folk songs.

Utterly overwhelmed, Clara slipped discreetly around the edge of the room, hoping to blend into the gold-edged midnight-blue drapes that lined the walls, stretching from the floor to the vaulted ceiling.

She scanned the room, casually searching out her nursing colleagues among the Varborg elite. Her pulse fluttered frantically, her body hopeful, her mind full of dread.

Was *he* there—Prince Andreas?

She hadn't seen him since the day she'd discovered his identity. That had left plenty of time to promise that, next time they met, she would keep things strictly professional and properly deferential.

She'd just spied her nursing colleagues on the other side of the dance floor when her stare landed on the hottest man in any room.

Andreas.

She froze. Her mouth dried. She couldn't look away as euphoria spiked her blood. How had she ever once mistaken him for an ordinary man? He'd been utterly spectacular naked, seriously sexy in his hospital scrubs but, dressed in his formal attire, he looked every inch an untouchable heartthrob prince.

Desire, thick, hot and confusing, pounded through her veins.

An impressive row of medals adorned the lapel of his dark tailcoat, the breast pocket bearing the Cronstedt royal coat of arms. His crisp white dress-shirt and waistcoat contrasted with the midnight-blue sash worn across his broad chest, the colour complementing his mesmerising eyes. Nearly every other man there was clean-shaven but, unlike them, he wore his beard, neatly trimmed short, and his golden hair swept back from his aristocratic face, just an inch too long so the ends curled above his collar.

A true, unapologetic Viking.

Horribly turned on, Clara sank deeper into the shadows. Why did her treacherous body hate her so much, when her head had already made all the decisions? She gripped the folds of velvet, wishing she could disappear into the curtains so she wouldn't have to witness him sharing that dazzling smile of his with the stunning and elegant society women who, unlike Clara, were a part of his world.

Moving on from one conversation, Andreas addressed the mountain of a man at his side—Nils, the bodyguard from the hospital—before conversing with a regal blonde wearing a tiara made of diamonds that Clara would bet a year's salary were real.

Clara's skin prickled with humiliation. Here, in

Andreas's world, she was so utterly and obviously out of her depth, an imposter in a hired gown.

Nils spoke into a discreet microphone attached to the earpiece he was wearing, his stare landing on Clara across the vast room, as if he'd just been informed of her precise location.

Clara froze. Would she be told to leave in front of all these important people? In front of *him*? Perhaps it wasn't too late to duck out before Andreas saw her. She should never have come. She couldn't face him. He would surely see through her disguise to the scared little girl inside who'd been abandoned by one parent and forced to grow up fast to help care for the other. What would Crown Prince Andreas Cronstedt need with a woman like that when he could kiss any woman he chose?

The bodyguard whispered to Andreas. With a charming smile, Andreas concluded his conversation with a portly man in his sixties, turned and stared straight at Clara.

A soft gasp left her dry throat.

He'd asked Nils about *her*; the room was obviously awash with his spies.

From so far away, she couldn't read his expression. Was he annoyed to see her there after their childish squabble in the lift? What on earth did it matter who regretted the kiss, who'd enjoyed it, who recalled every detail when it was unlikely ever to happen again?

Desperately clinging to the indifference she'd spent days perfecting, Clara raised her chin and gripped her clutch, which contained her embossed invitation, like a shield.

Without taking his eyes off hers for one second, Andreas marched her way.

Her palms began to sweat.

His long strides sliced through the parting crowd.

Her ears buzzed with tinnitus.

Still he descended, full of purpose and so achingly beautiful, looking at him stung Clara's eyes.

People had started to notice his determined trajectory. Clara grew hot under their curious stares. Whispers began to spread from person to person like a highly contagious virus. Clara's pulse throbbed frantically in her fingertips and toes. Her head grew light from lack of oxygen. She gulped down a few breaths, trying to look away from his intense eye contact, but she couldn't make her body obey her commands. Was this what a stroke felt like? She could only stand and wait for him to arrive, her only armour her determination to stay immune to his overwhelming magnetism.

'You made it,' he said with a small, restrained smile.

He seemed taller and broader in his exquisitely tailored attire, every inch the regal, self-assured leader he was born to be.

Ignoring his devastating hotness, Clara lowered her gaze. 'Your Royal Highness.'

Her voice croaked as she bent her knees in the deep curtsey she'd been practising in her heels and gown all afternoon.

All around them, people were staring, likely thinking who exactly could have inspired Prince Andreas's inexhaustible pursuit across a room full of important people who, like him, belonged there.

When she looked up, Andreas's mouth wore a tight smile and his eyes were grey and stormy with what looked like fury.

'Please *never* do that again,' he said, his voice low for her ears only.

Clara blinked up at him, a barrage of questions and comments dying on her tongue. How did he expect her to act? She hadn't been trained on the proper etiquette for addressing a prince you'd kissed, seen naked and then tried to ignore. But there was no time to wonder what social *faux pas* she'd made.

He held out his hand. 'Ms Lund, would you do me the honour of a dance?'

Clara quailed inside, dread freezing her diamanté-clad feet to the lush carpet. She had no idea how to dance to this kind of music. She'd make a fool of herself and, worse, a fool of him in a room full of his snobby, aristocratic peers.

She opened her mouth, praying that it wouldn't be considered an act of high treason to politely refuse a crown prince a dance, when Andreas spoke again.

'Before you decline…' he angled his head closer '…shall I remind you that we agreed to talk about a certain, very pressing matter?'

He was so calm, so composed, they might have been discussing the weather. But surely they couldn't settle their unfinished business, *the kissing*, in front of all these people?

Clara's entire body burned hot, her skin hyper-sensitised under his observation. She could barely stand upright just thinking about the heat, fizz and excitement of that kiss. Just looking at him all dressed up made that reckless, carefree part of her that felt alive every time she talked to him ache to do it again.

'Your Royal Highness,' she said, placing her hand in his, 'I merely hoped to spare you the public spectacle of me treading on your toes. I have no idea how to dance like this.'

'I'll lead you,' he said, self-assured, smiling at several of the gawking crowd. 'Just keep your eyes on mine.'

The onlookers parted for them as, unconcerned, Andreas led her to the dance floor. He executed a short bow, gripped her hand and placed his other hand between her shoulder blades. 'Allow me to worry what your feet are doing.'

'That's easy for you to say,' Clara muttered, her body melting under his touch. 'But I much prefer to rely on my own two feet.'

Before she could make further complaints, he swept her along into the dancing crowd. Clara gasped, the thrill of once more being this close to him rendering her speechless. The warmth of his body seeped into her palm where it rested on his shoulder. The spicy scent of his cologne, delicious notes of pine forest and wood smoke, sent her head swimming back to fantasy land. The all-consuming focus of his eye contact made her forget that she was being watched by hundreds of onlookers as he effortlessly spun her in time to the music, his strong arms and skilled dance moves preventing her from taking a wrong step.

She laughed, the thrilling abandon of dancing with so expert a partner suppressing her reservations and insecurities. She might as well have been flying. Andreas grinned at her delight, spinning her a little faster so the hem of her dress fanned out, holding her a little closer so she was forced to surrender her body and dignity to him entirely, the way she'd surrendered to that kiss.

Alive once more, all she could do was smile. But this wasn't reality. Reality was her bank balance; the shameful online headlines bearing her family name; the sting of humiliation she'd experienced outside the hospital lift, when she'd realised with a sinking stomach that, no matter what her body craved, him and her could never be.

As the tempo of the music slowed, she felt Andreas's body stiffen a little, as if he was aware of the change in her mood.

'I want to apologise for rushing off that day at the hospital. I'm afraid that, no matter how much I value my work, I must put my family first.'

Clara gave a small sharp shake of her head, stunned by the regret in his voice, the implication that Prince Henrik was right—their relationship was strained. 'There's no need to apologise, Your Royal

Highness. I'm embarrassed that I didn't know you straight away when you're so…famous.'

His fingers flexed against her bare back, or she might have imagined it, because he looked perfectly polite, no hint of the heat from that first night.

But what did she expect—that she, ordinary Clara Lund, was special? Maybe he wanted to explain that, given his wild and notorious past, he kissed everyone he met that way…

'You accused me of manipulation.' His jaw clenched. 'But the truth is, when you didn't recognise me, I found the anonymity liberating. You fascinated me, with your hair primly pinned back but with your bold and spunky attitude on display.'

Clara exhaled a sound of disbelief as shameful prickles of heat danced over her skin. 'I'm outspoken. The way I spoke to you must be an act of treason. Not to mention the…kissing.' She hissed the last word. 'Two hundred years ago I'd have probably been imprisoned or sent to the guillotine.'

He smiled, a glimmer of playfulness in his eyes that unfurled something deep inside her—that longing to be the young woman she was in years. Clara wished they were at work, where at least she could pretend they were equals, but here, among the glitz and glamour, the titles and ceremony, it was obvious that they had nothing in common.

'You weren't outspoken, you were honest. That hardly ever happens to me. I've never met a woman like you.' He sobered. 'In truth, I was struggling to be back here that night. Just for a few moments, I wanted to just be myself with you. Selfish, I know.'

Why was he struggling to be home? Was it the prince's diagnosis and his regrets over his career? And couldn't he be himself with everyone? Hadn't she felt the same? For a few moments in his company, she'd felt more vibrantly alive than she'd ever felt before.

'And I guarantee that, these days...' his lips twitched with amusement '...kissing a prince carries no such penalty.'

In spite of the confusing mix of desire and unease swirling inside her, Clara laughed. If only they were alone, they could have a candid conversation and get to know each other better. Discover if they had other things in common.

Ridiculous! He was a prince. They weren't on a date. He probably had official duties tonight, given that Prince Henrik was, as yet, nowhere to be seen. And she was out of her depth. Feeling foolish at how easily she'd been seduced to feel emotionally close to a man who was from another world, Clara changed the subject.

'You look very...regal. Did you earn all those medals?'

'Yes,' he stated simply, obviously reluctant to talk about his military service. 'You look beautiful in that dress,' he said instead. 'I knew it would suit you.'

Clara stiffened, her confusion growing. '*You* picked out this dress?'

He gave a half-shrug, as if the gesture was no big deal.

'Why?' Something spiky and hard settled in her stomach. She was so naïve.

'I thought you'd like it.' A frown tugged down his beautiful mouth. 'Consider it a gift—an apology for making you feel that your job here was compromised by my actions.'

Clara's throat burned with humiliation. Of course he wouldn't understand the symbolism of what for him was a seemingly innocent gesture.

Seeing red, Clara hardened her stare. 'Well, then, I insist on paying you back.'

As if the dress was tainted, her skin began to chafe and itch underneath.

He maintained his bland smile but a muscle ticked in his jaw. 'That's not necessary.'

'It's necessary to *me*.' A flush crept up her neck. 'I don't like to be beholden to anyone. I pay my own way in the world.'

Chills rattled her bones. She shouldn't have come tonight. She didn't belong here, not like this: pretending to fit in, wearing a borrowed dress, playing Cinderella in his arms when any second now the clock would strike midnight and he'd see how implausible their flirtation was.

'Why so independent, *sötnos*?' He gripped her waist a little tighter, as if he could literally repair the damage he would never understand by holding onto her. 'I simply assumed you might find the gift welcome. After all, you work so hard.'

Shaking her head with disbelief, Clara forced her feet to remember that they were under her own control, not his. 'That's an easy thing for you to ask when you grew up here. But seeing as you appreciate my candour, Your Royal Highness, know this: I've been contributing to my family's income since I was sixteen and my father upped and left us with nothing but his debts, never to return.'

Stricken, Andreas appeared instantly contrite, but it was little comfort.

'I'm sorry,' he said, a flicker of panic in his stare. 'Please accept my apologies for the dress. It won't happen again.'

Appalled by the burn of irrational tears behind her eyes, Clara tried to remove her hand from his.

She *never* cried.

'I should have known,' she said, shaking her head when he refused to relinquish his grip, the panic in his eyes now full-blown.

She wouldn't make a scene, but nor would she play his puppet, regardless of their audience.

'For a minute there,' she continued, 'I'd almost convinced myself that we were, in some ways, equals. That we had something important in common. But the cold hard reality is that I was fooling myself.'

His stare turned steely, the muscles of his clenched jaw standing out beneath his facial hair. 'We *are* equals. Two human beings drawn to each other.'

Clara scoffed at his naïvety.

'Are we?' She fought to keep her voice as calm and quiet as she could, given the humiliation pounding in her head. 'In that case, what's it to be? Repayment for the dress? Or do you prefer I return the garment? I can take it off right now, in fact.'

Indignant, she skidded her feet to a halt and reached for the side zip under her arm.

Andreas's eyes blazed with an inferno of heat.

'Don't you dare,' he growled, taking her arm.

With a benign smile on his face, he guided her from the dance floor and through an inconspicuous door tucked into the corner, manned by two liveried footmen.

Awash with shame for her outburst—and spitting mad that, for all her independence and distrust, she'd been naïve enough to fall under his spell out there on the dance floor—Clara accepted her fate. She'd done it now; he would kick her out and wash his hands of her.

And it would be for the best. She was so laughably out of her depth in his world. Their stark differences had only been highlighted by the extravagance of the stupidly beautiful dress that now felt like a prison straitjacket.

But, for one heady moment out there in his arms, as he'd twirled her round and round, nothing else had seemed to matter—not his title, or her family debts, or even the misguided attraction she just couldn't seem to fight. He'd been just a man, and she a woman.

Except when the dancing had stopped, and her

feet were firmly back on the ground, reality had struck. They came from impossibly different worlds: his full of glitter and magic, and hers the real world.

CHAPTER SEVEN

LENGTHENING HIS STRIDE, Andreas ducked into the nearby Blue Room, his blood on fire. From the minute he'd spied Clara from across the ballroom, the sophisticated black lace gown he'd chosen hugging the curves of her sensational body like a glove, he'd been deafened by a roar of desire. As he'd crossed the endless-seeming distance between them, urgency had pounded through his head. He'd wanted to blindfold every other man present. Better still, he should have called off the banquet, sent everyone home and selfishly had her to himself.

Except she didn't want him…

The door closed behind them—no doubt Nils's doing, so he could stand sentry.

Clara tugged her hand from his. Reeling from the loss of her touch and the tightness gripping his insides like a fist, he scrubbed a hand through his hair.

'What are you trying to do to me?' His breathing turned harsh as he fought for the control that had seemed second nature to him until he'd met this woman. 'Threatening to take off that dress?'

As if of its own accord, his frantic stare traced her lush curves, the cascading lace no barrier to his vivid and debauched imagination about what delights lay underneath.

'You should have asked someone else to dance,' she snapped, ignoring the reference to their chemistry. 'I told you I couldn't do it.'

'You did it just fine, until you stopped trusting me. And I wanted to dance with you, *sötnos*.'

He paced closer, catching the sparks of hurt in her eyes. 'This isn't about dancing or dresses,' he said, shame thickening his voice. 'I hurt you.'

She pressed her lovely lips together and hid her eyes from him by looking down.

'I'm sorry,' he said. 'I hate that I let you down over something that looks so beautiful. If I'd known how…insulting you would find the gesture, I never would have done it.'

Guilt punched him in the gut, its force no match for the arousal coiled in his belly because she was close, so close, her scent bewitching.

'All I seem to do is apologise.' He scrubbed a hand down his face. He'd crossed the line and been selfish and entitled. He should never have asked her to dance, because the minute he'd taken her in his arms he'd no longer been able to pretend that he had their chemistry under control. When she'd talked about removing the dress, vulnerable but defiant before him, he'd almost fallen to his knees.

But he needed to grapple back control. He didn't want to hurt her more than he had already. He didn't want to let her down the way she'd obviously been let down before by her father.

'It doesn't matter.' She looked down and Andreas wanted to punch something—preferably himself.

'It matters to *me*.' He paced away in frustration, spinning to face her once more. 'I got carried away. I thought we made a connection. But then you seemed disgusted by my title. I told myself I would leave you alone, but then I learned you'd been invited tonight. I saw that dress and imagined you in it and then you came, wearing it, looking stunning, the only person in the room I genuinely wanted to see.'

She frowned, confused.

'Why me?' she asked, as fearless as ever. 'When you had that entire room to choose from, every other woman more on your level than I will ever be, no matter how fancy you dress me up?'

She was right: they were from different backgrounds. She had her own demons—financial strains and trust issues he knew nothing about. By asking her to dance, by dragging her into the goldfish bowl of his life, he'd surely exposed her to the rife speculation that would follow—the last thing she deserved. He'd have to spend the remainder of the evening running damage limitation—playing the playboy prince of old, dancing with every single woman in the room in order to head off the gossips and society bloodhounds who always seemed to bay for his blood. Andreas the stand-in—never more so than tonight, when his father, the man they'd all assembled to celebrate, was indisposed with a bad headache.

His first public appearance for his father and he'd messed up. But, as long as he lived, he would never regret it fully. For a brief time, when she'd trusted him on the dance floor, he'd felt invincible with her in his arms.

'Because I'm selfish, okay?' Andreas winced, hating that he'd made her feel so small. 'The fact that you're different, that you don't seem to care about all of this—' he waved his arm to encompass the ornate room in which they stood, the vast banquet hall beyond, the very palace itself '—is what I like about you. I wanted you, grounding me the way you did that first night when you reminded me that—away from perceptions and duty to my family, away from the shoes of my dead brother that I must one day fill—sometimes I can just be myself: the real Andreas.'

Clara hesitated, her stare softening. 'And who is the real Andreas? The compassionate doctor taking the frail hand of an elderly patient? Or is he the party prince in those pictures on the Internet, invited to all the best gatherings, usually with some glamorous woman on his arm?'

'I admit, I've been both in my time.' Fascinated by her thrilling jealousy, he stepped closer and watched her breathing speed up, caught the enticing waft of her perfume that almost made his eyes roll closed in ecstasy. 'Are you jealous, *sötnos*?'

His blood surged at her sense of possession. She might feel that they came from different worlds, but she couldn't conceal how she felt physically. She wanted him in return—man, doctor and prince.

'Not at all,' she bluffed, clearing her throat in a

nervous gesture. 'I'm just disorientated, wondering what I'm doing here, how I should address you—or if I should even acknowledge you at all, given that we're from such starkly different worlds and clearly have *nothing* in common.'

'You can call me Andreas,' he said, ignoring the parts of her argument he deemed irrelevant as he focussed on her parted lips, slicked by some berry-coloured gloss he wanted more than anything to taste.

Oh, how he wanted to hear his name on her lips—preferably cried out in passion. But, now that she knew his true identity, would she give him her honest desire, as she had that first night? Or would she demure like a timid mouse simply because he'd been born into an historic family, something over which he'd had no control?

Clara licked her lips, as if aware of his observation and the direction of his thoughts. 'That hardly seems reverential enough, given the circumstances.'

Stepping closer, he drew her stare back to his, finding it full of her signature defiance. Triumph electrified his nerve endings at the resolute tilt of her chin. Clara was no mouse.

'That is exactly why I insist on it. When I'm with you, I'm just me. *You* are the one person I can rely on to treat me with brutal honesty. Don't turn on me now, *sötnos*, when I need an ally within these walls more than ever.'

He caught her soft gasp of astonishment and

watched as her pupils dilated and compassion re-placed all that fire in her eyes.

'Why do you need an ally in your family home?' she asked in a confused whisper, voicing the one question designed to strip him bare of his layers of armour. '*You* belong here.'

Andreas swallowed and tugged at the hem of his waistcoat, a reminder that he at least looked the part he'd been born to play. Except he'd spent most of his adult life free to live another role, to forge his own path, to just be a man who belonged in Clara's world.

'I do,' he agreed, desperate to talk about anything other than his royal life with this woman he wanted so badly, he could taste it. 'But I wasn't born the heir, wasn't raised for the position. So you see there are many out there, perhaps my father included, who believe I'm not fit to follow him to the throne. That it should have been my elder brother Oscar standing here today, charming the crowds and dancing with the most beautiful woman in the room.'

As the ugly truth spilled free, he glanced away from her frowning face, jealousy a hot slash through his chest at the idea of Clara dancing with the brother he'd loved. Should he also spill at her feet his guilt and regrets over Oscar's death? His secret fear that those with no confidence in him were right because, as a doctor and brother, he'd failed Oscar so completely?

No; he wanted her too much to risk it.

'That's not true,' she whispered, horrified.

'Isn't it?' he asked. 'I'm the spare, don't forget. My father certainly made that clear while I was growing up.'

'Is that why you refused your brother's rooms—why you're still in the guest wing? Perhaps you should talk to your father about this. Perhaps you're wrong about his reasons and how he feels.'

She reached for his arm, bringing him back from a dark place with her touch. But it was too much; it caught him off-guard, the desire that was never far away since that first night a roar in his head.

'While I appreciate your directness, *sötnos*, and your suggestions, do we know each other well enough for such advice? Because I might be prompted to ask why you work two jobs when one is all anyone could expect, or why you insist on paying your father's debts.'

She flushed but held her ground. 'Helping out my family financially is *my* choice.'

'As is choosing to forge my own path rather than stepping into my dead brother's shoes. But we don't always get what we want, do we? Sometimes, we must be something others need us to be.'

Clara's eyes widened, as if his words resonated deeply.

'Still think we have little in common?' he asked while they faced each other at an impasse, equals with, he suspected, more similarities than they had differences. Except, unlike him, she was free to choose how to live her life. He'd long ago come to terms with his…mostly.

Sighing with defeat, Andreas again rubbed a hand down his face.

'I asked you to dance so I could clear the air,' he said, his hands itching to touch her once more. 'Except, yet again, I underestimated the impact of our chemistry.'

Her jaw dropped, the arousal shining in her eyes urging him to lay his cards on the table.

'Even here when I must be on show, play this role that feels…borrowed, it's inescapable.' That simmer of heat in his blood he felt around her boiled over. 'That day at Nordic Care, you said we should forget our attraction. Do you still feel the same?'

'I'm certainly trying to forget it.' Colour flushed her chest and neck. 'But… I… I don't know.'

'Whereas I feel the opposite,' he admitted, a sting of disappointment in his throat. '*You* are all I can think about, even when my priority should be temporarily standing in for my father.'

Her eyes shot to his.

'I've shocked you with my own directness,' he continued, determined now to lay his feelings out. 'Would you prefer that I lie to you? That I conceal how much I want you? Deceive and manipulate you into my bed instead, as you once accused me?'

She shook her head with conviction, her stare bold on his. 'No. But—'

'Be honest with me, *sötnos*,' he urged. 'The way you've always been. Because, whatever our other differences, our bodies don't seem to care. In this—' he pointed between them, illustrating the sexual tension coiling between them like smoke '—we are absolute equals.'

She dragged in a ragged breath, as if resolved. 'I want you too.'

The sweet-sounding words left her in a rush.

'But I can't lose my job and it feels…dangerous.' Her breath came faster, her breasts rising and falling.

'I guarantee your job will be safe.' He stepped closer, taking her hand and placing it over the medals she'd admired on his chest to show his sincerity. 'You have my word—as a prince, as a Knight of Varborg and a string of other titles.'

She regarded him silently and thoughtfully for long seconds, her lip snagged under teeth. Then she rolled back her shoulders. 'No one can know.'

Andreas nodded solemnly, his pulse pounding with excitement at this negotiation of terms. 'I never again want to hurt you as I did tonight—I hate letting people down. So, tell me what you need for this to work.'

She tilted her face up so her breath brushed his lips. 'I'm not interested in relationships, so it can only be a physical thing,' she said, adding another condition of her own.

'Agreed.' Curiosity shoved a list of questions to the forefront of his mind as he inched closer, his body restless with desire. 'At present, I have more than enough to consider without…romantic complications.'

At some point in the future, he would need to

address his marital state, settle down, find a wife, produce an heir and put the needs of the principality first. But for now he could focus on pleasure and freedom—focus on Clara.

'A fling, then,' he said. Satisfaction bloomed in his chest.

'A brief fling,' she countered, her eyes swimming with need as she stared up at him.

He nodded, already forming a plan to safeguard her privacy. He didn't want his public prominence to scare her off before they'd even begun.

'I have one final condition,' he said, tugging her hand so their bodies were almost touching. 'And this one is non-negotiable, I'm afraid.'

'Oh?' A playful glint shone in her eyes. 'How very bossy of you.'

Andreas smiled. As he had that first night, he reached for a strand of her hair and eased it behind her ear, allowing his fingertips slowly to trace the curve of her cheek and down to the tip of her earlobe, where a tiny pearl earring dangled.

She shuddered and need rumbled in his chest on a stifled groan.

He stared into her eyes and rested his hand on her waist, the very air in the room seeming to crackle and hiss with electricity.

'No more curtseys. No more "Your Royal Highness",' he stated, his gaze falling to the soft excited pant of her breath over those gloss-slicked lips he wanted so badly to taste.

'It's only proper,' she said, one corner of her

mouth tugged in a knowing and defiant smile. 'After all, I *am* one of your subjects.'

His fingers curled into the fabric of her dress, an animalistic growl sounding in his head. 'Not when I'm inside you, making you come.'

Galvanised by her low moan, he hauled her close, crushing her to his chest. Their lips found the others in a rush of desperation and mutual, almost palpable, relief as they kissed. Her curves moulded to his chest and hips in all the right places, the heat of her fanning the inferno in his veins, the scent of her a dizzying cloud that made time recede. Andreas cupped the back of her head, directing her mouth, their tongues meeting and surging wildly, so nothing else seemed to matter. There was just this moment: just a man and woman; just passion and need.

Her fingers twisted in his hair, tugging, greedy to have him where she wanted him. Andreas paced forward, pressing her against the back of a sofa, his mind and body consumed by her, as he'd been since that first meeting in the guest suite when she'd effortlessly blown him away. He fisted the fabric of her dress over her hip, hoisting the dress up high enough to slide his hand around one silky bare thigh.

'Andreas,' she moaned, just as he'd hoped, dropping her head back to expose her neck to his ravaging mouth.

The sound of his name on her lips was more rewarding than anything he'd imagined. Cupping one cheek of her backside, he lifted her, depositing her bottom on the edge of the furniture so he could slot himself between her parted thighs.

He grew hard between her legs as he ran his lips over her jaw, up to her earlobe and down the silky column of her neck, sucking in her scent, filling his senses with her taste, licking and nibbling her satin-like skin. He couldn't get enough. It was as if her skin was laced with some sort of potent aphrodisiac. He'd walk away smelling of her, the scent of her torturing him for the rest of the night.

Her hands were inside his waistcoat, her touch through his shirt hot like a brand. He kissed her again, his tongue in her mouth as she dipped her hands lower to cup his buttocks, drawing his hips to hers, massaging his arousal between their bodies so Andreas almost lost his mind. This was insane. He needed to stop. But his fingers swiped the lacy edge of her underwear over her backside and sanity fled.

'Andreas…please…' she whispered, her eyes closed and her head back so her throat was exposed to him, already pink from the scrape of his facial hair and ferocity of his desire.

Her beauty was a painful throb beneath his ribs. The marks he'd left on her skin called to the primitive part of his brain, the part acting on instinct alone. If she kept calling his name in that breathy voice, he feared what he'd do next. Indulging in one last kiss, he ripped his mouth from hers, his breathing wild and painful.

'Look at me, *sötnos*,' he demanded, sliding his

fingers under the lace of her underwear to stroke the molten heat between her legs. 'Open your eyes.'

She obeyed, blinking up at him, her lips parted on a series of soft gasps as he stroked her over and over.

With his other hand, he reached for her wrist and pressed her palm over his erection, steely hard behind his fly.

'Tell me we're equals now, when I'm so hard for you it hurts and you're wet for me. Tell me. I need to hear you say it. I need to know you believe it. I don't want a puppet in my bed. I want you.'

She gripped his arm, her stare slumberous with arousal but alive with the sparks of fire that were pure Clara.

'We're equals,' she said on a ragged breath, dragging his mouth back to hers as her hips bucked against his hand.

'That's right, we are,' he murmured against her lips, against the wild kisses she snatched from him in between moans. Andreas kissed her back, the taste of triumph sweet and satisfying as he stroked her faster, sliding a finger inside her core.

'Except,' he said, rearing back to gaze into her eyes, 'I've never wanted anyone as much as I want you.'

His words seemed to tip her over the edge into bliss. She climaxed, shuddering in his arms as he kissed her through the spasms with slow thrusts of his tongue. When she was spent, she leaned her weight against him, her face buried against his neck while she caught her breath.

Andreas's heart thundered in his chest, his arm holding her tight. He slid his hand from between her legs and brushed down the hem of her dress, literally blocking out the sight of temptation. One glimpse of her naked thigh, a flash of black lace, and he might not make it back to the banquet where he was to give an after-dinner tribute to his father.

Just then, there was an insistent rap of knuckles on the door. Nils had been instructed to give him as much time as possible.

'Just a moment,' Andreas called, frustration a tight knot under his ribs.

Clara deserved more than a quick clandestine fumble. She deserved seduction and satin sheets, romance and adoration. Especially after the way he'd inadvertently hurt her over the dress. But his time with her was up. His absence at the banquet must have been noticed, and his official duties called.

'I have to get back,' he said, his hands reluctant to leave Clara's waist. He tilted up her chin and pressed a soft kiss to her lovely lips. 'I have people to schmooze, an after-dinner speech to give. Hopefully my father will be recovered from his headache and join us for the rest of the night.'

How had he completely blanked out the visiting dignitaries awaiting an audience with him as a stand-in for his father? With Clara in his arms, he'd forget his own name…

She nodded, stood and looked up at him. 'Of course. You should go.'

She was flushed from her orgasm, more beau-

tiful than ever. She cast her eyes over him and
then straightened the row of medals on his lapel,
which had gone awry during their passionate tryst.
'There—perfect.'

He reached for her hand, raised it to his lips and
pressed a lingering kiss over her knuckles. 'It was
a pleasure negotiating with you, Ms Lund. I look
forward to our next meeting, more than you could
ever imagine.'

She smiled, her eyelids heavy, and his breath
caught. How he wished he could whisk her away
somewhere private, just the two of them.

But Clara's cold, hard reality was calling to them
both. Taking once last glance at her breath-taking
image, committing how she looked to memory, he
tugged his jacket into place, ran a hand through his
hair and left the room, pulling on his persona as he
re-joined the evening's festivities.

She was right: they *were* from different worlds.
Hers was less privileged, but she had greater freedom. But as long as he was careful with her feelings—as long as he never again let her down, as
long as he protected her from speculation, from
the royal-watchers and press critics who judged his
every move—they could meet on common ground
as equals.

CHAPTER EIGHT

THREE NIGHTS AFTER the banquet, Andreas was enjoying a highly erotic dream featuring his favourite nurse when he was roughly awoken by the intercom buzzer.

'Andreas, it's Clara. I need to speak to you.' The urgency of her voice shot panic through his system.

He jolted into a sitting position. 'Come in.'

He disarmed the door lock and reached for his prosthesis. His pulse bounded with surges of familiar adrenaline. He was used to being woken in the middle of the night by a pager, but never here, at home.

'What's wrong?' he asked as she appeared in his bedroom seconds later. He moved his eyes over her from head to toe. 'Are you hurt?' Why else would she come to him in the middle of the night, her voice carrying a desperate edge that made his teeth grind?

She shook her head. 'I'm concerned for Prince Henrik. I need a second opinion. It's snowing a blizzard outside, and the prince's personal physician is stuck in a snow drift.' She wrung her hands, wearing a deep frown of worry. 'I've left the prince with the other nurse on duty tonight because I wanted to be the one to wake you.'

Andreas stood and shrugged on his robe, too dis-

tracted by concern for his father to enjoy the way
Clara flicked her stare over his nakedness before
he tied the belt.

'You did the right thing in coming to me, *sötnos*.' He gripped her upper arms, deeply touched
that she'd sought out his help. 'I'll come right away.'

He scrubbed a hand over his face to clear the
last fog of sleep and reached for the medical bag
he kept on hand at all times. What could be wrong
with his father?

He recalled the last conversation he'd had with
the prince. His father had been a little tired, but
otherwise seemed in good health. They'd talked
mainly of business: the upcoming visit of the Swedish prime minister; the plans for the annual staff
Christmas party; the list of new charities seeking
royal patronage. But Andreas trusted Clara's clinical
judgement and she wouldn't have woken him lightly.

'Tell me what your concerns are,' he said as they
left the suite.

'Prince Henrik became acutely breathless a short
while ago,' Clara said. 'His temperature is normal,
pulse and blood pressure elevated. No history of
chest pain, but obviously I'm worried about pneu-
monia or a pulmonary embolus, although I've listened to his chest and can't hear any evidence of
consolidation.'

Concealing his own concern, Andreas placed
his hand on her shoulder, squeezing for both their
comfort.

'What are his oxygen saturations?' he asked as

they rushed from the guest wing towards his father's suite, fear now a metallic taste in his mouth.

'Ninety-seven,' she answered.

Andreas breathed a small sigh of relief.

'Someone has taken a motor sled to fetch the doctor,' Clara said, keeping pace with his longer strides. 'But it could take an hour. I know it's not strictly ethical for you to treat your father,' she continued as they entered the family wing of the palace, 'But I figured it was okay in such urgent and unusual circumstances.'

Andreas sent her a grateful smile, wishing he could drag her into his arms, but his father needed help. 'Thank you for taking such good care of the prince.'

There would be time later to tell her how he valued her inspiring dedication. How humbled he was that she'd come to him for advice. How privileged he felt because Clara was so fiercely independent, she demanded nothing from him.

Outside the prince's suite, Clara rested her hand on his arm. 'Andreas, are you sure you are okay to see Prince Henrik like this? He's quite distressed.'

For a second, she looked as if she might say more, but then she blinked and the moment passed.

'I appreciate your consideration of my feelings. Thank you.'

Of course she saw and understood him. Of course a nurse of her calibre would grasp the complex emotions pounding through him. Seeing a parent incapacitated was upsetting for anyone, even more so when that man was also your ruler, someone Andreas had always seen as a larger-than-life figure.

What she couldn't know was how the fear for his father chilling him to the bone was amplified by what had happened to Oscar. The last time Andreas had tried to medically help a family member, he'd failed, with devastating consequences for him, his family and the nation. He'd tried everything he could to treat and then revive his brother, but his efforts hadn't been enough.

But he couldn't think about his failings now. He needed to stay calm and objective. He rapped on the door once out of observance of royal protocol, urgency driving him to enter the suite of rooms without waiting to be admitted.

The prince's butler greeted them, the older man's face stricken and pale. 'The doctor is still thirty minutes away, Your Royal Highness. Should I call for the helicopter, sir?'

'Of course not, Møller. There's a blizzard raging outside,' Andreas said, fighting the sickening trepidation twisting his gut. 'I will assess the prince so we know what we're dealing with.'

The butler stood aside and Andreas and Clara entered his father's bedroom, a room he hadn't been in since he'd been a young boy.

No matter how hard he'd tried to prepare, given his training and Clara's words of warning, shock lashed at Andreas like the icy rain pelting the windows outside. His father was seated on the edge of the bed, another nurse at his side. He wore an oxygen mask, but his hands were braced on his thighs and his breathing was fast and laboured.

Fear and compassion tugged at Andreas's heart as he approached. 'Pappa, I need to listen to your chest.'

If he focussed on his training, treated the man before him like any other patient, he could keep the waves of panic at bay. Only this wasn't *any* patient. This was his father, his ruler, a proud and unemotional man much beloved by their nation, and something was wrong.

He reached for his father's radial pulse, noting it was elevated but regular.

'Do you have any chest pain?' His mind trawled the same differential diagnoses for acute shortness of breath that Clara had considered.

Prince Henrik shook his head, his eyes wild with distress, sweat beading on his forehead.

'Dizzy,' he gasped, gripping Andreas's hand with vice-like force.

Clara handed Andreas a stethoscope. He listened to the breath sounds, searching Clara's concerned expression for clues, because something was off. He felt as if he was the last person to know some sort of well-kept secret, his sense of isolation flaring anew. Yes, he belonged here, as Clara had pointed out, but he'd spent so long away pursuing his career that there was no one at the palace he could confide in.

Only Clara.

He focussed on the whoosh of air transmitted through the stethoscope, swallowing down his rising sense of apprehension. His father's office had given little away when it came to the 'brief illness' rendering the normally fit and active prince indisposed. But was there something more medically sinister going on than Andreas had been led to believe?

He should have pushed for more information on the prince's health when he'd returned. He didn't blame Clara, or any of the medical staff who were loyal to the prince, respectful of his privacy and duty-bound to keep his medical information confidential. But had Andreas, a doctor, failed to see something that had been right under his nose? And, if there was something serious going on, why hadn't his father confided in him?

That familiar feeling of inadequacy settled like a stone in his stomach. Would he ever be good enough in his father's eyes or would he always be the less important son? They hadn't been close for years, but they were the only family each other had left. Except now it seemed that Prince Henrik couldn't even trust his doctor son with potentially important information.

Something in Clara's stare, something she could no longer hide from him because of their growing emotional closeness, told Andreas that, unlike him, she knew the full story.

Guilt lashed him. Since his return to Varborg, he'd been self-absorbed with his struggles to reconcile the demands of his two roles, doctor and heir, because being Prince Andreas had forced him to confront his greatest failure—losing Oscar. But instinct told him this was more than a 'brief illness'. As his son and as his heir, Andreas had a right to know if his father's health was in danger.

'You're right,' he said to Clara, removing the earpieces of the stethoscope. 'Breath sounds are completely normal.'

He beckoned her a short distance away so they could talk. 'There's no sign of infection or acute heart failure. No obvious pneumothorax or pleural effusion. But without a chest X-ray or a scan to exclude anything more subtle but sinister our diagnostic abilities are limited.'

Clara frowned, glancing at Prince Henrik. 'So what do we do?' she whispered, looking up at him with absolute faith.

At least *she* believed in him, even if no one else did.

Remembering that he was good at his job, Andreas dragged in a shuddering breath, grateful for Clara's presence.

'I think the most likely diagnosis of exclusion is a panic attack,' he said, hoping for his father's sake that he was right, because they could easily treat that here and now. 'It's worth a shot; if we can slow down his breathing, then we'll know.'

She nodded, her expression staying impressively neutral. Andreas wasn't the prince's doctor. It wasn't Clara's place to inform him of his father's medical history. But none of that helped with his feelings of inadequacy.

Andreas sat on the bed at his father's side and

took the older man's warm and capable hand.
'Pappa, you're breathing too fast. We need to slow
that down. Purse your lips like you're going to blow
out a candle…that's it. Now breathe nice and slowly.
In, two, three and out, two, three, four, five.'

While Andreas repeated the instructions in as
calm a voice as he could muster, given the sickening, doubt-fuelled lurch of his stomach, Clara
stooped in front of the prince and pursed her lips,
demonstrating the slower breathing technique in
time to Andreas's voice.

It took a few minutes of synchronised breathing,
but eventually his father calmed, his grip on Andreas's hand reassuringly strong and unwavering,
reminding Andreas of the proud statesman who'd
ruled Varborg steadfastly for fifty years.

Hot with shame, he wondered how they'd ended
up so estranged. The chasm between them had been
so wide for so long, they knew little about each other's personal lives, fears and dreams.

'Give the prince some privacy, please.' Andreas
instructed the butler and other nurse to vacate the
room. 'Would you like Clara to stay so we can make
you comfortable, Pappa?'

Taking some slow, shuddering breaths, his father
nodded, slowly recovering his strength and composure.

Clara plumped the pillows and together they re-
positioned Prince Henrik back into bed.

'I think you had a panic attack, Pappa,' Andreas
said, the doctor in him needing to understand why

just as much as the son. 'Your physician is on his
way, and I'm sure he'll organise some tests, in case
we're missing something.'

'Thank you, son,' Prince Henrik said, shakily.
'That was…alarming. I'm grateful that you were
here. I'm not sure what came over me.'

Andreas startled, glancing away from the man
he'd looked up to his whole life. He couldn't recall
a single time when Prince Henrik had relied on him
emotionally. Not after Andreas's mother had died,
when Prince Henrik had become focussed on Oscar
as the heir, nor after the accident that had stolen the
life of his eldest son. They'd grieved differently,
separately, never seeing eye to eye.

'No need to thank me, Pappa. I'm always here for
you. I'll stay until your doctor arrives.' He needed
to understand what might have caused his father's
acute distress tonight.

Clara placed a fresh glass of water next to the
bed. 'Can I get you anything else, sir?'

'No, thank you, dear,' his father said with a fond
smile that spoke not only of his immediate recovery,
but also their close relationship. Of course Prince
Henrik respected Clara. She was an exceptional
nurse: gifted and smart, humble and empathetic.
And, maybe most importantly, loyal.

Clara glanced at Andreas. 'I'll leave you two
alone. Call if you need me.'

Her stare brimmed with empathy that filled Andreas with fresh dread. Before she could leave the
room, he caught up with her, resting his hand on

her arm. 'Thank you for coming to me for help,' he said, wishing he could crush her in his arms and escape into their passion. 'The prince is lucky to have you on his staff.'

'He's lucky to have *you* as a son,' she replied, her compassionate stare leaving him exposed and raw, feelings he would prefer to conceal from the woman he was trying to seduce. 'Why don't you sit with him a while, perhaps talk?'

With his throat tight with confusion and fear, Andreas nodded and re-joined his father. The alarming realisations of tonight proved that there were conversations long overdue. Seeing his father incapacitated had brought home the reality of Andreas's situation. Even if there was no sinister explanation for his father's current state of health, no one lived for ever. Like Andreas, the prince was human, as vulnerable to illness, weakness and scars, both physical and emotional, as the next man.

Prince Henrik would one day die, as was the natural order of the world, and Andreas would take his place on Varborg's throne. His days of freedom to pursue the career he loved, a career that gave him a deep sense of pride, achievement and validation, were numbered. His personal freedoms too, such as his fling with Clara. Like it or not, prepared or not, Andreas would one day need to make these sacrifices and commit fully to the role he would inherit.

It might even be sooner than he'd imagined.

CHAPTER NINE

CLARA OPENED HER EYES the next morning, disorientated after only a couple of hours' sleep. She glanced around her bedroom in the staff quarters at the palace, her first thought of Andreas.

Last night, it had been obvious that her suspicions were correct: he *was* unaware of Prince Henrik's diagnosis and terminal prognosis. She'd witnessed the moment he'd figured out something serious was going on. She'd had to look away from the pain and confusion dulling his stare, her loyalties so horribly torn between father and son.

Only now, off-duty at the palace, could she be there for Andreas. She reached for her phone and sent him a text, asking after both men. On her way to the shower, she opened the curtains. The snow drift outside the window reached halfway up the pane. There was no way her little car would make it to the main roads. It looked as if she was snowed in. She made the call to Nordic Care, informing them she wouldn't make her late shift.

Under the spray of hot water, Clara tried to process everything that had happened since the Jubilee Banquet. After they'd agreed to have a secret fling that night in the Blue Room, she'd vowed to hold herself emotionally distant, and she'd tried her best.

But the blizzard had brought about exceptional and unforeseen circumstances. Her professional reliance on him was only natural—Andreas was a geriatrician. But now, faced with the evidence that Clara knew more about the prince's medical condition than his own son, a doctor, the thrilling affair they'd negotiated seemed almost trivial.

Don't turn on me now...when I need an ally...

His heartfelt plea from the night of the banquet twisted her stomach. He had so much weight on his shoulders: the imminent loss of his father; the enforced end of his medical career; the transition to the most important role of his life, as ruler. How would he deal with all of that? How could she help him adjust?

Her phone was stubbornly silent as she dressed in her everyday clothes—jeans and a beautiful jumper hand-knitted by Alma. She'd just applied moisturiser, mascara and lip gloss and fitted her nose stud when there was a tap at the door. Expecting another of the nurses, or the staffing manager with an update on the conditions on the roads, she pulled open the door.

Andreas stood on the threshold, his eyes haunted and fatigued. He'd come to *her* of all people. Did he have no one else he trusted to talk to?

Clara's heart cracked open for him. 'I'm so sorry.'

'You know his prognosis, of course,' he said, shock etched into his haggard expression.

Even grieving, he was unbearably beautiful, dressed in a forest-green sweater and dark jeans, his hair carelessly pushed back from his face. She wanted to hold him, her protective urges on high alert. Instead, she glanced along the deserted corridor and then, when she saw that they were alone, reached for his hand.

'I'm sorry. He's my patient,' she whispered.

Andreas of all people would understand that she had a professional duty of confidentiality, but she hated that he seemed to have been the last to know.

'I'm not blaming you,' he said, flatly, 'But he's *my* father. *Someone* should have told me. *He* should have told me.'

She nodded, stunned speechless by his understandable pain and confusion.

'He trusts me to rule Varborg because he has no choice,' he continued, his voice gruff with bitterness. 'But he doesn't trust me, his heir, his son, a *doctor*, with his confidences, even when I'm the person this impacts the most.'

Of course he would hate to stop practising medicine. Sick to her stomach with wretchedness, Clara inched closer and took his other hand. 'It's a shock.'

'I should have seen the signs,' he said, briefly closing his eyes.

She wanted to be there for Andreas, but she was trapped in an impossible position of torn loyalties, already too close to this family to be totally objective.

'You can't blame yourself. And maybe *because* you're his son,' she continued cautiously, *'Because* he loves you, he's tried to spare you the distressing news.'

Andreas frowned, unconvinced.

His relationship with his father was none of her business. They weren't friends. They weren't even properly lovers. But she understood exactly what he was going through. Clara's mother had tried to spare her daughters from worry in the beginning, before she'd faced surgery and had no longer been able to hide the symptoms.

A door slammed somewhere overhead. Clara forced herself to step back. Someone might see them or overhear their conversation. They'd agreed to be discreet about their relationship.

'How *is* the prince this morning?' she asked, to cover up her caution.

'He's feeling much better, enough to refuse me the minute details of his medical records.' His voice was bitter, his expression disbelieving. 'It's as if he doesn't understand me at all. I'm a doctor; maybe I could…help.'

Clara winced in empathy. She understood his feelings of futility, but beyond supporting his father there was nothing else he could do. And she couldn't blame Prince Henrik for not wanting to rake over it all again.

'Is there anything I can do for you?' she asked. Maybe sharing her own experiences would make him feel less alone.

He looked away, clearly struggling with complex emotions. When he looked back, his stare was imploring. 'I'm…overwhelmed by it all. Powerless. I can't think straight. I need to get away from here, clear my head. Will you come?'

Clara swallowed her immediate 'yes'. She'd promised to guard her feelings, but how could she deny him a single thing when she understood his current vulnerability? Someone he loved, his *parent*, had cancer. Whereas Clara's mother had been given the all-clear, Prince Henrik had been told to put his affairs in order. And for Andreas the news carried another layer of devastation. His birth right meant he would soon have to choose: his career or the crown.

Except, he had no real choice.

'I'll go anywhere with you,' Clara said, deciding she would double her efforts to protect herself while also being there for Andreas. 'But have you seen the snow?'

'Trust me,' he said, his stare both pleading and hopeful.

'I do.' she said.

'Grab your boots,' he instructed, some of the tension leaving his body.

Clara hurried into her room to snatch them up, along with her phone.

He led her to a part of the palace she'd never visited before. There, in a large boot room, he shrugged on a fur-lined parka emblazoned with the palace crest from a selection of sizes hanging along the wall, and then passed one to Clara, along with some mittens and a hat.

Despite the sadness in the air, excitement fizzed in her veins. Would they be digging snow? Cross-country skiing? It didn't matter. He'd come to her in his hour of need. She'd do anything to help him process the news he'd received last night, including escape with him.

Outside, the snow in the courtyard had been shovelled away and there at the top of the driveway sat a gleaming, royal-blue snow-mobile bearing the royal crest and the words House of Cronstedt.

'Can you drive that?' Clara asked, hesitating for a second as she pulled on the hat. She didn't want the heir to the throne to be injured on her watch.

Andreas smiled broadly for the first time, his eyes bright with confidence and excitement. 'Of course I can. You can't get anywhere in winter up here without one.' He took her gloved hand, leading her towards the machine. 'Oscar and I used to have races.'

'Of course you did.' She laughed, picturing the scene. 'That sounds terrifying.'

'Jump on,' he said with a sexy wink that snatched her breath away.

She hadn't imagined exactly how they would implement their secret affair, but she'd guessed it would involve late-night texts and clandestine meetings in discreet hotels. This, on the other hand— spending time with the *real* Andreas, getting to know him better, understanding his passions and doubts—was way more dangerous to Clara.

She sat at the back. Andreas swung his leg over the seat in front and started the ignition.

'Hold tight,' he called over the hum of the engine.

Clara scooted forward to encircle his waist with her arms and his hips with her thighs so she felt the thud of his heart under her cheek. The engine revved beneath her, setting them in motion, and Clara squealed, gripping him tighter.

Then they were off, skimming the undisturbed snow which glittered in the sun like a sheet of diamonds, and headed for the native forest at the perimeter of the landscaped palace grounds. Andreas drove the snow-mobile with impressive skill, weaving them with ease over the bumpy landscape and between the tall pine trees.

The wind whipped at Clara's cheeks and hair. Her smile was so wide, her teeth were cold. This reminded her of the night of the Jubilee Banquet, when she'd danced in his arms and felt as if she were flying. The wild sense of freedom was back—the heady abandon she'd experienced far too infrequently, thanks to Lars Lund's irresponsible approach to caring for his family and raising his daughters. How many more experiences had she passed up during her teens and early twenties, time she would never get back?

She gripped Andreas's waist tighter and rested her face against his shoulder, protected from the bitter wind by the imposing breadth of his chest. Other women might get carried away by the absurd romance of this situation but Clara was weighed down by reality, even as she sped along with the sun on her back and Andreas's solid warmth seeping into her front.

Ever since they'd danced together, when she'd come alive in his arms both on the dance floor and later in the Blue Room, she'd told herself that their fling didn't make him hers. He'd said they were equals that night, when he'd forced her to admit how badly she wanted him, but deep down world-weary Clara knew better. In all the areas that mattered—their upbringings, their expectations, their priorities—they were worlds apart.

And, even if she wanted him, he belonged to Varborg first and foremost and to his future princess second. That woman would be content to walk at his side, stand in his shadow, give Varborg and him an heir and never question the inherent power imbalance of their relationship. That didn't stop Clara wanting the only thing she could allow herself—a temporary interlude in his bed, freshly stamped with an expiry date.

Finally, they emerged from the trees into a clearing. Andreas slowed the snow-mobile, bringing it to a halt and killed the engine. Clara raised her face from his shoulder and gasped with awe at the sight of a picture-perfect log cabin nestled among the fir trees with a backdrop of Varborg's northern mountain range.

'Oh… It's so beautiful,' Clara said, mesmerised. 'Who lives here?'

Like the surrounding forest, the cabin was dressed

in a thick layer of snow, glittering in the sunshine like a scene from a winter wonderland.

'No one.' Andreas held out his hand, helping her from the back of the snow-mobile with a more care-free smile on his face. 'It's a hunting lodge built by one of my Cronstedt ancestors.'

Already he seemed less tense, as if he felt more at home here than among the grandeur and cere-mony of the palace.

'Oscar and I came here all the time as boys,' he continued, confirming her suspicion. 'It was the only place we could be free to play—build bon-fires and tree houses and camp out in the summer. There's a lake over that ridge where we'd go ice-fishing in winter.'

She could envision the young prince he must have been so clearly in her mind's eye—scamper-ing around after his big brother, away from the strict protocol and public gaze of his royal life. No won-der he chose to hide out here when he needed space.

The barest flicker of pain crossed his eyes as he tugged her close. 'Now I'm the only person who spends time here.'

She blinked up at him, her heart beating wildly at the power of the cabin's solitude and the positive change already evident in Andreas.

'It's idyllic,' she said with wonder in her voice, touched that he'd brought her to this special place—a place clearly dear to him, a place linked to his fondest childhood memories of his brother.

Clara's eyes burned, close to tears for his losses.

But she *never* cried—not even when Alma Lund had haltingly confessed her cancer diagnosis to her daughters. Nor when, weeks later, nineteen-year-old Clara had swallowed her pride and called her father, begging him to come home and support his wife, the mother of his daughters, during her treatment. Of course, Lars hadn't even done it for Clara and Freja. He'd made excuses and let them down once more. She should have known better than to rely on him.

'Can we go inside?' she asked, glancing at the charming cabin, the windows of which glowed with warm, orange light, hoping to escape the humiliating rejection of that final conversation with her father.

'Of course. I asked the housekeeper to start the fires and stock the fridge.' He took her hand and led her up the steps of the covered veranda, which housed outdoor seating carved from old tree trunks and covered with reindeer pelts.

'Are you hungry?' he asked when they were inside, taking her coat and hanging it next to his on wooden pegs beside the door.

Clara stilled, overwhelmed by the sumptuous interior. The fire was roaring, warming the entire living space which boasted high-vaulted ceilings crossed with wooden beams, massive picture windows framing the views and luxurious furniture. Breakfast was laid out, the dining table romantically set for two.

She shivered, in spite of the warmth and the cosy

décor. Thinking about her father reminded her how out of her depth she was when it came to relationships. She wasn't a sophisticated seductress. After her one intimate relationship with a man who'd never called her again—proof that she'd been wasting her time with men—it had been easier to avoid disappointment than to give anyone else the power to hurt her again. And she'd been preoccupied, too busy with studying, working and helping out with her mother to devote the time to the kind of relationship *she* wanted—one on equal terms.

But Andreas wasn't just any man. She trusted him.

As if he could read the turmoil in her mind, Andreas stared down at her, his eyes dark with emotions, his expression turning serious.

'I've never brought anyone here before.' He brushed some hair from her cheek, the way he had the first night they'd kissed.

It made her feel precious. His words felt like a promise, an acknowledgement that he trusted her with his private life; that, despite his playboy past, Clara was different...for now. It sounded naïve, except she *was* different. She wasn't planning to fall in love with him, so her heart was safe. She wanted nothing from him, beyond them being equals, and perhaps more of that reckless, carefree feeling he brought out in her.

'In that case, thank you for bringing me here.' With her heart galloping, she stood on tip toes and pressed her cold lips to his warm ones, sucking in the crisp scent of snow and pine forest that seemed to cling to his skin.

She pulled back and he cupped her cheek in his palm, his earnest stare searching hers. 'No, thank *you*—for trusting me, for blindly following me, for escaping with me.'

Clara released a soft, shuddering sigh, his touch filling her body with enough heat to melt the snow outside. A part of her—a deep-seated part, home to her deepest fears—understood his need to flee reality. How many times had she experienced the same shameful urge in the middle of a long, dark night of worrying about her mother? She'd been too young to shoulder such responsibility alone, but with her father's refusal to come home there had been no one else to care for Alma.

'I wanted to tell you at the palace,' she whispered, that lost and scared part of her exposed, 'That I understand what you're going through today. My mother was diagnosed with breast cancer when I was nineteen.'

His lips flattened, his brows pinched together. 'I'm so sorry, *sötnos.*'

Clara shook her head, rushing on. 'She's fine now, but at the time there was only me and my fifteen-year-old sister to care for her. I helped out at home, drove her to her chemotherapy appointments, sat awake on her worst nights, willing her to get better.'

Clara's voice broke. Speaking about her beloved mother's illness brought those painful memories back, along with resentment at Lars for heaping too much on his daughter's shoulders. But Alma Lund had been one of the lucky ones.

'It's not the same as your situation,' she said, 'But you're not alone, Andreas. Your confusion and hurt and anger are all normal reactions.'

He cupped her face with both hands. 'Thank you for confiding that in me. That you understand, that I can talk to you, helps more than you'll ever know. Your inner strength is truly inspiring, Clara.'

'So is yours.' She couldn't seem to catch her breath, as if the air in her lungs were frozen. 'You've been through so much.'

How was she expected to keep her distance when he trusted her, had opened up to *her*, of all the people he must have in his life? But maybe he had few people with whom he felt truly understood and seen for himself. Maybe he had few people who expected nothing from him. Maybe he too was weighed down by responsibility.

'Right now, strong is the last thing I feel,' he admitted, taking her hand and holding it to his chest over the wild thump of his heart while his hungry stare traced her mouth. 'It's taking every shred of restraint I possess not to kiss you and touch you and bury myself so deep inside you that I lose myself in you, just for a few moments.'

Clara dragged in a ragged breath, recognising the same urgent needs in herself. This craving for him was building out of control. It was as if their chemistry was being fanned hotter by the fact that time was running out. Reality was chasing their tails.

Soon, when Andreas was forced to give up his career, they would no longer work together at Nordic Care. Clara's nursing position at the palace would end with Prince Henrik's death. They would have no excuse to see each other. And, while she could sleep with a prince—especially when, to her, he was simply Andreas—she couldn't sleep with Varborg's ruler, an altogether more serious and intimidating man.

'Then do it,' she said boldly, her body an inferno from the fire he'd lit inside her with that first sexy smile, when he'd been resplendent in his bath like a marauding Viking. 'It's the only thing I want from you.'

For a moment he froze, frowned, as if her words were too good to be true.

'Except,' she said, before she threw herself into his arms, 'We said we'd be equals in this. And, the thing is, I'm nowhere near as experienced as you. In fact, I've only done this once, with a guy I met at college. He pursued me, took me on romantic dates, bought me flowers, made me feel special…and then, the minute I slept with him, he lost interest. I found out he'd done that to lots of girls in my year, which was…humiliating. So I just gave up on men after that. It was easier to avoid disappointment than to risk being hurt and let down. Not to mention that it wasn't even very good and…'

His fingers landed on her lips, his eyes blazing

into hers. 'I don't care about your inexperience. It doesn't matter. That guy is an idiot.'

'It matters to *me*. I vowed that the next time I was intimate with someone it would be on equal terms and with honest expectations. That *I'd* be in control.'

He nodded, taking her seriously.

'The way you made me feel the night of the banquet,' she ploughed on, 'Alive, joyous, powerful. I've never experienced that with anyone else. I want to make you feel the same way.'

This complex, hurting man standing before her was everything; the sight, scent and feel of him filled her senses, making her feel alive again. She wanted to rock his world. She wanted to help him lose himself. They could escape the sometimes cold, harsh and cruel reality of life together.

'So, will you show me what you like?' she finished.

His pupils dilated, his jaw flexing as he took a pained-looking swallow. With a growl that Clara felt resonate throughout every inch of her body, Andreas hauled her close, crushing her mouth to his.

For a few moments, she lost herself in the fiery passion of their kiss. Andreas made it easy, holding her so tight her feet barely touched the floor; kissing her with such domination she forgot to breathe and turned dizzy; pressing her so close, she wasn't sure where her body ended and his began.

'You might kill me...' He groaned against her

lips, pulling back to stare hard into her eyes. 'Just when I thought you couldn't be more perfect.'

Clara snorted, almost euphoric with desire. 'I'm very far from that. And I'm certain killing the heir to the throne *is* a punishable offence.'

'Then,' he said, cupping her face and kissing her once more, 'It's a good thing that right now, with you, I'm just Andreas.'

Then he took her hand and led her through the lodge to the master bedroom.

CHAPTER TEN

CLARA GLANCED AROUND the luxurious room, her body burning with need. Fur pelts covered the hardwood floor in front of the fire, which crackled and flickered, casting a warm glow. A massive carved timber bed covered with snowy white linen dominated the room.

She spun to face Andreas, reached up on tip toes and pressed her lips to his, blocking her mind to everything but the way he made her feel. She didn't want to think about the risks she was taking by allowing him this close, or reality awaiting them beyond this room. She just wanted the promise they'd negotiated: the two of them together, just a man and a woman as equals.

'I want you,' she said, slipping her hands under his jumper, seeking out his warm, golden skin, tracing every dip and bulge of the muscles she remembered from the bath. Impatient, she broke free of his kiss and pushed up his sweater so she could see his magnificent body once more, confirmation that, in this moment, he was real and he was hers.

'There's no rush,' he said, tugging his sweater over his head and tossing it to the chair beside the bed before dragging her into his arms, where the heat of him nearly burned her alive.

'I can't help myself.' She sighed. 'I've seen you naked, don't forget—*twice*.'

Clara moved her stare over the breadth of his bare chest, her hands skimming warm flesh as she went. He was beautiful, so masculine the woman in her trembled with longing for the empowering connection they shared.

'I thought I caught you checking me out last night.' A satisfied smiled kicked up his mouth. He raised her chin, his breath whispering over her lips. 'So it's only fair if I now feast my eyes on every inch of this body that has tortured me night and day since we met.'

His warm hands slid under her jumper, deftly freeing the clasp of her bra with one flick of his fingers. He kissed her in a long and thorough exploration that left her shifting restlessly against him to appease the molten ache between her legs.

How had this man, unlike any other, inspired such desperate need? Was it just the way he looked at her, the way he'd always looked at her, as if to him she was…exceptional and unique? Had she spent too long shutting down this side of herself, so one look at him had sent her hormones into revolt?

They reached for the hem of her sweater in unison, Andreas removing both it and her bra in one swift move so she shivered before him, not with nerves but with delicious anticipation. Goose pimples rose on her skin, but she was burning up. Chest to chest with Andreas, naked skin to naked skin, she felt as if she might incinerate to ash.

'Touch me,' she begged when he only stared at her nakedness.

His eyes blazed as he raised his hands to caress her bare breasts. 'You are breathtakingly beautiful.' His voice was gruff with desire.

Clara gasped but it wasn't enough. It was nowhere near enough for that reckless part of her that craved the life-affirming freedom of his touch.

'I wanted you that first time I saw you,' he said, his thumbs toying her nipples to taut peaks. 'With your hair all prim and proper and your uniform fuelling some pretty raunchy nurse fantasies I never knew I had.'

Clara laughed and bit down on her lower lip to try and contain the swell of pleasure weakening her legs, but languid heat radiated out from his expert touch, infecting her entire body.

'I wanted you too,' she said, dropping her head back so her throat was exposed to his kisses. 'You looked so rugged and wild; I was tempted to join you in that giant bath.'

Her hands roamed his shoulders, his back and arms, the sheer strength of him. She couldn't seem to touch him enough.

'I knew it would be like this between us,' he said, pressing her erect nipples between his fingers so darts of pleasure arced to her pelvis. 'I felt the sparks the first time you looked at me as if you wanted to roll your eyes, as if you didn't care *who* I was.'

Clara moaned at his words and the pleasure he

was wreaking with just his fingers and thumbs. She was already lost, whereas he seemed far too in control. Raising on tip toes to kiss him, she slid one hand down his body, his skin scalding her palm until she reached the impressive hard length of him pressing at the front of his jeans. He groaned into their kiss, gripping her tighter so she was crushed against the fiery heat of him, enclosed in his powerful arms.

But she felt powerful too, the knowledge that she could affect him as much as he affected her almost as drugging as his heated kisses.

He walked her back towards the bed. 'Lie back,' he ordered, as her thighs hit the edge of the bed. 'I want to see all of you.'

Leaning over her, he pressed kisses over her neck and chest, taking one nipple into his mouth and sucking until Clara's head spun with thick, paralysing desire. Why had she never prioritised this exploration of passion before? Surely she'd been denying herself something as essential as breathing? But would it be like this with anyone else? Her one fumbling foray into sex had been underwhelmingly brief and disappointing.

Perhaps this magic was down to Andreas. Because she'd yet to render him anywhere near as helpless as he was making her, she reached for the fly of his jeans.

His hips jerked and he took her hand, pinning her wrist to the bed. 'I believe there is a nudity imbalance to redress,' he said, smiling wickedly as he captured the other nipple with his lips, laving it with the flat of his tongue. 'You've seen me naked twice, after all.'

'Andreas…' Clara moaned, writhing beneath him on the bed as he continued to torture her breasts with the sensual pleasure of his mouth. She wasn't even naked and he'd driven her so close to the edge.

'Keep calling me that, *sötnos*,' he ordered, keeping his mouth on her breast.

He undid her jeans and together they shimmied them off with increasingly frantic tugs and shoves. Clara wanted him naked again, his weight on top of her, the heat of him scalding her, the feel of him inside her.

'Almost good enough,' he said, leaning back to move his eyes over her body from head to toe. 'But not quite perfect.'

Taking hold of her underwear, he peeled it off so slowly, so intently, with his stare scouring her nudity, Clara thought she might explode from longing.

'Don't mind me,' she whispered, her voice hoarse with want even as she tried to lighten the moment with humour. 'Have a good look.'

Andreas's eyes blazed in the firelight, showing her that he recalled the reference from the first night they'd met when *he'd* been the naked one and she'd ogled him shamelessly.

'Oh, I will, don't worry. You asked me to show you what I like and it's this—you. I intend to see and kiss and pleasure every inch of you until you sob my name. Until you never think to call me anything else but Andreas. Until to you I'm just the man who wants you so badly, he's struggling to draw breath right now.'

Everything in Clara clenched hard. How was she supposed to stay immune when he said things like that? When he looked down at her as if she was something rare, to be valued? When he made her feel as if this connection of theirs was as important to him as it was to her?

True to his word, he kissed a path across her ribs, to her belly button and lower. Clara gasped as he covered her sex with his mouth, sending fiery darts of pleasure through her every nerve. Reflexively, her fingers speared through his hair and she held on tight, her body tossed from pleasure to ecstasy to want in a cycle that happened again and again, until she was certain there was nowhere left to climb. Until she was indeed sobbing his name, as he wanted. Until she burned in white-hot fire.

Then he stopped. 'I want to be inside you when you come.' He reared back to remove his jeans and underwear so his erection sprang free, prouder and impossibly bigger than the last time she'd seen him aroused.

Aware that, for all her talk of equality and control she'd yet to do one thing to turn him on, Clara sat up and reached for him, encircling his hard length with her hand, then leaning forward to kiss him in return.

'Clara…' Andreas groaned, his stare fierce on

hers as his fingers slid through her hair, holding her to him.

'Don't you like it?' she asked, stroking the silky soft and steely hardness of him with her fingers, thumb and the tip of her tongue.

'I like it too much.' He hissed through his teeth as she took him inside her mouth, his stare glitteringly hard while he cupped her face and watched.

She'd barely taken two or three swipes of him with her tongue when he yanked her away and pulled open the bedside drawer for a condom.

'I was enjoying myself,' Clara said, pouting as he tore into the condom and stretched it on.

'So was I.' Following her down onto the bed, Andreas removed his prosthesis and tossed it to the floor.

'Come here,' he said, reaching for her, his strong arms rolling her on top. 'I love the smell of your hair,' he said as it fell around them like two curtains. 'Like spring meadows.'

Gripping the back of her neck, he dragged her lips down to his, groaning when she pushed her tongue into his mouth, the way she'd licked him seconds ago. He cupped her buttocks in his hands where she sat astride his hips, pressing her close so her sensitised core met his hard length and stars danced behind her eyes as she forgot to breathe.

'Andreas,' she pleaded, looking down at him while he commanded her hips to a torturous rhythm, up and down, over and over, sliding them together so they gasped in unison. Then, with a deft and speedy roll, he switched their positions so that he was now on top, his expression harsh with desire. Cupping her breast, he sucked the nipple to a hard peak.

'You make me so hard,' he said, his thumb rubbing the sensitive nipple he'd primed with his mouth as he watched her pleasured cries.

'I want to make you feel good,' she said, feeling him between her legs, nudging at her entrance so she spread her legs wider in invitation. 'I want you to lose yourself.'

He brushed her lips with his in a series of slow, sensual kisses. 'I like who I am when I'm with you. I like how you see me. How you're not afraid to challenge me. You make me feel as if I can be myself.'

'You can,' Clara whispered, watching arousal and vulnerability cross his beautiful stare, certain that this moment couldn't be any more perfect. Then he pushed inside her, inch by inch, until they were one.

Every muscle in Andreas's body pulled taut as though he might explode and cease to exist. Clara gasped her pleasure against his lips, staring up at him as if he was the answer to prayers, she hadn't even known she had.

Holding himself still because she felt too good, he kissed her with languid swipes of his tongue against hers, coaxing out her moans, his whispered name, her pleading expression.

But still he held them both suspended. A connection like theirs deserved savouring. If he could have kept her here indefinitely in his favourite place, he would have, slaking his uncontrollable hunger for her over and over until his world made crystal-clear sense. Until he'd garnered the strength to face everything he must.

'Thank you for escaping with me,' he said, entwining his fingers through hers as he slowly thrust inside her.

He wanted to pleasure her to the point of exhaustion. His selfish need for her shocked him. She gave so much of herself, met him fearlessly, even in moments when their differences outweighed their similarities. And he couldn't seem to get enough.

'I'm so glad I met you.' He reared back and stared into her intensely vulnerable eyes, wondering how, when she'd claimed to being the less experienced, he'd ended up feeling so moved, humbled and entranced by her responsiveness and her honest passion.

'Don't stop,' she pleaded, her hands in his hair, stroking his shoulders, his back, her nails a gentle scrape that made every nerve in his body sing. It was taking every scrap of self-control he possessed not to rush to the finish. But he'd exhaust himself to make this good for her, after she'd not only trusted him with her body and her pleasure but had also opened herself to him emotionally, telling him about her mother and had been there for him when he'd needed her most.

'You're amazing,' he said, refusing to think what he'd have done if she hadn't been snowed in at the palace. He'd known it from the start when she'd strode into his bathroom and jolted his world off its axis. Shifting his weight, he rocked his hips, watching her arousal streak across her beautiful face, the flames between them fanning higher.

'Andreas!' she cried, her stare clinging to his, giving him everything he could possibly need: connection; acceptance; unity. But that was Clara: fiercely loyal; inspiringly compassionate; unflinchingly brave. He moved inside her, his kisses as wild as the beat of his heart. Every part of him coalesced, mind, body and soul, to this one moment where he truly was lost in Clara.

'Andreas… Andreas,' she said his name, calling to that inner part of him that, for some reason, with her had always found peace. Maybe because she took him at face value. Because, as she'd said, she wanted nothing from him but this.

Because he didn't want to think about tomorrow, or how long they'd have to enjoy each other as lovers, he drove himself harder. 'Lose yourself with me, Clara,' he groaned against her neck, sweat breaking out and slicking their bodies even closer together.

Temperatures soared. Hearts thudded. Stares were locked and vulnerable.

Another cry was snatched from her throat. He dived to swallow it up, thrusting his tongue into her mouth as she climaxed, her nails digging into his back, her muffled sobs sweet music to his ears.

She was his—perfection.

He followed her, the powerful spasms of his orgasm endlessly racking his body as they clung to each other, panting and sweaty and equally laid bare.

'I didn't know it could be like that,' she said breathlessly a few minutes later, wonder in her voice. 'I've heard the myths, read it in romance novels, but… wow.'

'Wow indeed, *sötnos*,' Andreas said, pressing kisses to her smiling lips, her flushed cheeks, her closed eyelids while his heart fought to get back inside his chest. 'It's not always like that, but I'd say that definitely makes us equals.'

He rolled over, scooping an arm around her shoulders to hold her close while his awareness sharpened at the periphery, the intrusion of reality returning. He clung to Clara, clung to her uncomplicated company and the relentless attraction that had helped him to escape his troubles for a while.

But he couldn't escape with Clara for ever. He couldn't even stay at the lodge with her indefinitely, no matter how sorely he was tempted. He'd have to return to the palace and be there for his father, plan an exit strategy for his career.

His throat tightened with grief—for his father, the man, the ruler; the only family Andreas had left. And for himself: for that part of him that was proud of what he'd achieved; for the loss of the life he'd assumed he'd have for many years to come; for the demise of his freedom.

Clara rested her head on his chest, her hand stroking his abdomen in a way that would soon make him hard again. Andreas focussed on breathing, on the feel of her body against his, of the scent of her all over his skin. Considering today had begun with the devastating news of his father's diagnosis—and the bitter taste of failure that he'd not only missed the signs, but had also been the last person to know—that he could feel anything like the kind of pleasure and contentment that had just ripped through him was a testament to how badly he wanted this woman. Right now, she was the only thing keeping him grounded.

Except he'd also have to sacrifice even Clara.

'Do you think your Cronstedt ancestor, the one who built this place, brought his mistress here?' she asked sleepily, her lips pressing against his chest.

'Prince Erno, my great-great-grandfather? Probably. He did have a mistress, a famously beautiful one.' Had Erno Cronstedt sought solace from the demands of his position in the arms of a woman? 'Except, you're not my mistress.'

'No,' she stated simply, leaning up on her hand to peer down at him curiously, a small smile on her lips.

'I should be so lucky,' he said, stealing a kiss, because she was too far away and he already ached for her again.

Clara laughed, glancing at the fire in the hearth. 'It's dying down; I'll throw on another couple of logs.'

Before he could stop her, she slid from the bed

and crossed the room, completely naked and completely comfortable.

Andreas folded one arm behind his head, propping himself up for a better view, his mouth dry with lust and longing. How could she do that to him, turn him on and make him ravenous, within minutes of great sex? Was it some sort of power she had over him? Or was it that their connection was deeper because they worked together and because Clara also cared for his dying father? Because she saw him like no other and understood his feelings?

Every other thought in his head evaporated as she stooped and placed two more logs on the embers and then returned to the bedside, her stunning naked body cast with an orange glow from the fire.

'If this hadn't already been my favourite place in the whole world,' he said, his voice gruff with thick desire, 'It would definitely be now. I'll never be able to look at that fire again without seeing your glorious body.'

She smiled. 'I am your eternal servant, Your Royal Highness.' She gave a mock curtsey and then joined him under the sheets.

'Don't,' he said, clasping her chin, directing her mouth to his. 'We made a deal: no more curtseys.'

He kissed her, pushing his tongue against hers to try and calm the wild need uncurling in him once more. But her careless reminder had broken the spell. No matter how good it had felt to flee the palace with Clara, no matter how thoroughly he'd lost himself inside the warm haven of her body, he couldn't hide for ever from his life, his responsibilities and the difficult days ahead.

Prince Henrik needed him—the nation, too. But could he bear to lose everything in one fell swoop: his father, his career *and* Clara?

'I'm sorry,' she whispered, the playfulness draining from her eyes. 'It's too soon to joke about that, right?'

Andreas sighed, reaching for her and sliding her body under his so their rapid heartbeats aligned. 'I would normally have a sense of humour. It's just that this is the one place I've always felt I can be myself.'

He touched the glinting green gemstone in her nose, one of many facets that made Clara unique. 'And I want to be myself with you. Always.'

She nodded, regarding him thoughtfully, her stare filled with compassion when he'd rather see it burn with desire. How could she make him feel more naked than he'd ever felt in his life? He was supposed to be the one in control of this rampant attraction, he was supposed to be the one with more experience, but instead he was close to unravelling, his need for her unstoppable.

'I'm glad that you have somewhere you feel safe and free.' Her stare flicked between his eyes, as if she saw him deep to the centre of his damaged soul. 'You feel close to Oscar here too, don't you?'

He pressed a kiss to her lips. 'You have a gift for seeing people clearly, did you know that?'

He'd always appreciated her directness. But now that he'd faced the reality his father was terminal—

now that he'd escaped with Clara to this magical and unique place; now that they'd finally surrendered to their desires—his past mistakes were the last thing he wanted to discuss.

Except Clara had been there for him this morning when he'd needed someone like he'd never needed anyone before. She understood what he was going through because of her experiences with her mother. His world was on its head, the sands of time slipping through his fingers, and no amount of holding on would slow the inevitable. Discovering his father's prognosis had changed *everything*.

'I do feel close to Oscar here,' he said with a small sigh of surrender. 'We had the best times growing up.'

'You must miss him terribly,' she whispered, her fingers stroking his back hypnotically.

Andreas watched Clara's parted lips, craving a distraction from the shame, guilt and pain of re-membering. It would be so easy to kiss her again, to refocus on their passion, to seduce her into silence and get lost once more. But his recent experience with his father had taught him that he couldn't hide from his feelings for ever. They caught up with him one way or another, often when he was most vul-nerable and least expecting it.

'We were so close as boys,' he said. 'Not so much as teens, but then close again as adults before he died.'

He rolled onto his back, tucking Clara against his side so he could stare blindly at the ceiling. He didn't want to see her reaction if he had to talk about this. He wanted her to look at him with arousal, need and desperation, not pity and blame.

'Lots of siblings drift apart as teenagers,' she said, resting her cheek on his chest. 'My sister and I used to fight all the time.'

'Now, why is that so easy to imagine?' he teased, stealing another kiss for strength. 'The truth is, I hero-worshipped Oscar. He was smart and funny and always won the snow-mobile races.'

Clara smiled indulgently, her eyes bright with empathy. 'What happened to change that?'

'Nothing *he* did.' Andreas stroked his fingers up and down her back, from her nape to the top of her buttocks, her warm, silky skin comforting even as he stepped out of the shameful shadows and into the harsh light. Would she change towards him once she knew all the ugliness of his past? Could he bear that now that he'd found something real with her?

'I was fourteen and Oscar was sixteen when our mother died,' he said, because she'd always been easy to confide in. 'It seemed that, overnight, we stopped doing everything together. Oscar was suddenly too busy for races. He was always squirrelled away in Pappa's study or attending statesman classes or meeting with important dignitaries.'

'And you felt left out,' she whispered. 'That's understandable.'

Her statement jabbed at his ribs like a blow, the emotions too complex for a simple yes or no answer. He clenched his jaw, debating whether to share more. He didn't want her to see him this way—hung up on the past, a man who'd failed and let down his loved ones, at odds with his dying father.

He craved the way she'd looked at him in the bath that first day; the way she'd looked at him as he'd twirled her around the ballroom; the way she'd looked at him when she'd asked him to show her his desires.

'I didn't understand it fully at the time,' he continued, the inexplicable urge to be honest burning in his throat. 'But of course Oscar was in training to rule. I didn't blame him, after all; it was his birth right. But I was a kid, and a relatively sheltered one at that. There was a part of me that couldn't help but vie for a little of our father's attention.'

'Of course not. You were grieving for your mother. A part of you must have felt as if you'd lost your father and brother too,' Clara said simply, pressing her lips to his chest so he felt raw inside.

Was that true? It seemed obvious now.

Andreas stared hard into her eyes, as if he could draw on Clara's innate strength and intuition. 'After a while I gave up that fight. Oscar was focussed on the role he'd been born for and Prince Henrik threw himself into preparing his heir.'

'Perhaps your father was grieving too,' she said quietly.

'Perhaps. For a while, I acted out, frequented wild parties, saw the sense of freedom as a green light for anything I chose to do.'

'I've seen the pictures on the Internet.' Clara smiled sadly in understanding.

He nodded. 'Then I got wise and realised that, while I might not be as important as Oscar, I had freedom. I could choose how to fill my time and live my life. So I knuckled down, went to university, earned a medical degree and then joined the armed forces.'

'You are just as important as the next person,' she said, pushing up onto her elbows, her stare glittering with sincerity. 'Even if you'd chosen to simply be that playboy version of yourself and nothing more.'

Andreas hauled her closer and kissed her again, part of him splintering apart that she understood his motivations when he'd been blind to them, perhaps until this very second. 'And you are wise beyond your years, Nurse Lund.'

'We both had to grow up fast,' she said, her insight slicing through him like a blade.

He'd never thought of it that way, but of course losing his mother and effectively losing his brother and father to more important duties had left his teenage self lonely and confused. No wonder he'd acted out. No wonder he'd pushed himself into a medical career he could be proud of, as if he'd had something to prove to the father and older brother he loved.

And it had worked—right up to the moment when he'd been unable to save Oscar.

'And now you must soon give up all of your hard

work,' she said hesitantly. 'It must be difficult. I can't imagine ever giving up nursing.'

Something rumbled in his chest, an unsettled gnaw of uncertainty, as if her statement was another blow to the convictions that had seen him through his adult life to date. But of course Clara fiercely valued her independence, another of her attractive qualities.

'I've always known that my family must come first,' he said, dejected because, whereas Clara could continue with her career, he would be taking another path. Their worlds, the common ground they'd shared as medical colleagues, would diverge.

He continued, refusing to think about him and Clara parting ways. 'But naïvely I never truly thought about what it would mean for the career I love and take pride in until the accident that killed Oscar. I was there when he died. I tried to save him. That's how I lost my leg.'

And now, with his father's news, he had even less time left as a doctor than he'd hoped. He would have to step into Oscar's shoes, final confirmation that his brother was gone for ever…

'I'm so sorry.' She pressed her lips to his neck.

'The palace wanted me to give up medicine immediately after Oscar's funeral,' he said, recalling the rows that had driven the wedge deeper between he and his father. 'I woke up in hospital to discover my brother hadn't made it, that my leg had to be amputated; that I had to set all of that aside, put on my uniform and attend his televised state funeral. I refused to even consider giving up my career on top of everything else. And I'm glad I didn't succumb to pressure. I needed to heal and recover. I needed a reason to strap on that prosthesis every day, to do my exercises, to learn to walk again. In a way, the drive to get back to work saved me.'

Clara stroked her fingers through his hair. 'A strong motivation to recover helps. It must have been a horrendous time for you.'

'Of course, now I'm going to lose my father too. None of our past issues matter.'

He swallowed, the sense of failure intensifying. 'Not our mutual stubbornness that used to drive my mother mad, or our differences of opinion on how to rule the principality or our inability to even discuss what happened to Oscar—none of it matters.'

Defeated, he clamped his lips together, sickened by his pity party. Giving up his career, while regrettable, wasn't the end of the world. He'd adapt; he'd adapted before, to losing a limb. He could pour all his energy into his royal role. He'd do it for Oscar and try to be as good a ruler as his brother would have been.

'I'm so sorry, Andreas.' Clara wrapped her arms around his shoulders and held him tight. 'But I think you're wrong. I think that stuff with your father *does* matter. You have an opportunity not many people get, to talk about the things that have impacted your relationship before it's too late.'

Andreas stiffened. 'The men of this family don't really talk about their feelings. It's an unspoken rule to suck it up and get on with it. Even when Prince Henrik told me his diagnosis, he showed no emotion, and when I pressed for more information he as good as told me to mind my own business.'

He didn't need verbal confirmation from Prince Henrik that, as the second son, he wasn't the heir his father had hoped for. He carried enough self-doubt. If he messed up as heir, he'd not only be letting down his father and the nation, he'd also be failing the brother he hadn't been able to save in life.

'I appreciate your opinion.' He tried to keep his voice even. 'But some things are best left alone. My father is a proud man who's used to being in charge. He won't tolerate being questioned, and I've no desire to upset him during whatever time he has left. And besides, every time we do speak on an emotive subject, a part of me seems to revert to being that young boy so eager for his approval.'

He was done with that.

'We have a complex relationship, *sötnos*.' He pressed a kiss to her forehead to lessen the sting of his words, part of him regretting that he'd opened himself up quite so much.

'Don't do that.' She pulled away, drawing the sheet higher to cover her breasts. 'Don't patronise me. I know all about complex parental relationships.'

'I didn't mean to upset you,' he said, contrite. 'Will you tell me about it?'

Her frown deepened, pain in her eyes. 'By the time my father left us—I was sixteen—he'd already let me down one time too many. For three years I survived without him. Yes, I worked hard to help out Mum, but we were happier somehow, just the three of us. When my mother got sick, I was so scared. One day, I swallowed my pride and called him. I begged him to come home and help care for his wife and to support Freja, who was only fifteen. Do you know what he did? He made excuses, dismissed my concerns, said he'd try, but he had a big deal on the horizon. It was so humiliating. Before I'd even hung up the phone I knew he wouldn't come back. He didn't care about any of us. He chose his own selfish pursuits over his wife and daughters.'

'I'm sorry.' How he wished he could brush away her sadness and wished he'd been more careful with his words, or simply seduced her again rather than talking.

'I got smart—got on with my life,' she continued as if he hadn't interrupted. 'I never relied on him again, never needed him. I stopped presenting myself for his rejection.'

She turned to face him. 'But, by cutting myself off, I never had the chance to tell him how badly he'd let me down, how much he'd hurt me…and I never had the opportunity to work through forgiving him. He died two years ago. I hadn't seen him or spoken to him since that last phone call.'

He took her hand and raised it to his lips, lingering over the kiss he placed on her knuckles to show her the depth of his regret. 'If you could confront him today, what would you say?'

Clara raised her chin. 'That I no longer need him for anything. That he can't hurt or disappoint me any more. That I'm sorry he couldn't be a better man.'

Andreas's heart ached for this beautiful woman who gave so much of herself to others and somehow, intuitively, saw what they needed. His protective urges flared. He wanted to take care of her, to give her as much as she'd given him. To protect her from ever again feeling that degree of hurt and disappointment. But, of course, he *would* react that way to a wonderful woman he was not only sleeping with, but working with while she cared for his terminally ill father. Their lives were repeatedly entwined.

'I think you're wrong, too, *sötnos*,' he said. 'A while ago, you said we're from different worlds, but I think we're more similar than either of us realise.'

They'd faced similar emotional issues, dealing with them differently.

'Maybe,' she said, kissing him so he started to lose track of his thoughts. 'And maybe we should be doing other things than talking before we have to go back to reality.'

Relief washed over him as they retreated to their passion. 'I like the way you think.' In fact, he liked everything about Clara—*everything*. He rolled her underneath him, pressing his lips to hers to block out the doubts and the pain, the past and the future.

But her confessions tumbled through his mind. Bringing her here, to a place he cherished, he felt closer to her than ever. Hearing how badly she'd been hurt by her father, he vowed to take special care of her until he had to give her up.

Because he never wanted to be the one to let her down.

CHAPTER ELEVEN

A WEEK LATER, Clara was working a shift at Nordic Care, well and truly thrust back into reality. She checked the vital signs of her frail, elderly patient, Mrs Kaase, noting her most recent blood pressure on the chart. Needing a second opinion on the case, she'd summoned the registrar for advice.

Despite speaking to Andreas daily, she hadn't seen him since that magical day at the hunting lodge. They'd worked opposite shifts at the hospital, and whenever she'd worked at the palace he'd been busy with his increasing workload of royal engagements. He'd been furious over a leak to the press on the state of Prince Henrik's health, warning Clara that the palace had been forced to issue a public statement announcing his diagnosis. The story, complete with a video clip of Andreas arriving at a prominent children's charity for which he was patron, flooded the media.

Clara had watched it a hundred times just to see a glimpse of his dazzling smile. But watching his life unfold from afar, like the rest of the nation, made him seem so untouchable, they might as well have been strangers again. The absence of him served as a timely reminder: no matter how close she felt to Varborg's heir, he didn't belong to her.

Just then, the door to Mrs Kaase's room opened. Clara looked up, expecting the new registrar, Dr Nilsen.

But it was Andreas.

Their eyes met. Clara's skin tingled, as if imprinted with his every touch. If she'd known he was working today, she'd have applied mascara and the perfume he liked. Before she could fully register the heat and hunger in his stare, she realised he wasn't alone. Sister stood possessively at his side, casting Clara a disapproving look.

Clara forced her expression into something appropriate. 'I called Dr Nilsen.'

Ignoring her body's instant response to the sight of Andreas, she glanced nervously at Sister.

'Dr Cronstedt is very busy, Nurse,' Sister said, as if protecting him from predatory females. 'There's a film crew arriving soon to interview him.'

'Yes, thank you, Sister,' Andreas interjected. 'I have plenty of time to review Nurse Lund's patient.' He held Clara's stare, as if conveying a secret message with his eyes. 'I'm not supposed to be working today, but I was missing my favourite nurses here at Nordic Care.'

He winked at Sister, who flushed with delight. When he looked back at Clara, his expression innocent, his sinful lips twitched.

She swallowed, lightheaded with lust. She recalled the feel of those lips against every inch of her skin, especially between her legs. Disgusted by her weakness for him, she looked away. One day in

his bed, and she was ready to forget her professionalism and hurl herself at him at work. But her need
for him was a choice, not a necessity. She could kick
the habit any time.

'So, what's bothering you, Clara?' He glanced
at sleeping Mrs Kaase and stepped closer, reaching for her chart.

Desperation to touch him curled tightly inside
Clara like an over-wound spring. Okay, maybe for
now she was hooked, but just because he'd taught
her that sex could be phenomenal when it was
with the right person didn't mean she should act
all starry-eyed. Even if they'd been alone, they had
work to do.

'I'm concerned about Mrs Kaase's increasing
breathlessness,' Clara said, conscious that Andreas
most likely had a hundred other things to do rather
than investigate her clinical hunch.

'Is that all?' Sister asked. 'Maybe you should have
run this past me before calling the doctor.'

'I'm here now, Sister.' Andreas said, staring at
Clara encouragingly. 'Go on.'

His observation lit her up as if she were made of
electric currents, every one of them connected to
the pleasure centres in her brain. But on closer inspection there was a tightness around his mouth,
fatigue in his eyes. He seemed…distracted. He had
so much going on. *She* was the least of his priorities, and that was fine with her.

Except this was about their patient. 'She's seven

days' post-right ventricular myocardial infarction,' she continued, undaunted.

'So you're thinking right heart failure?' he asked, his confidence in her clinical acumen obvious from the impressed approval shining in his eyes. Most doctors wouldn't have asked for her opinion.

'Yes…' she said, hating the hesitation in her voice.

She shouldn't doubt herself or her powers of observation and critical thinking just because they'd slept together. Was it just the presence of the sour-faced sister, who assumed Andreas the heir was too busy to care about his patients, when Clara knew better because she knew *him*? Or was it the things they'd shared about their respective fathers? He'd pretty quickly shut down her suggestion that he speak to Prince Henrik, letting her know when she'd crossed the line, and she'd had to pull him up on his thoughtless assumption that he was the only one with a complex father-child relationship.

But Clara didn't need his approval to do her job.

'She has worsening peripheral oedema and weight gain,' she continued, pressing home her argument. 'She's also complaining of non-specific abdominal pain.'

'I agree. It sounds like right-sided failure,' he said. 'Let's examine Mrs Kaase.'

He gently placed a hand on the patient's shoulder to wake her. 'Mrs Kaase, I need to have a listen to your heart and lungs, okay?'

The patient nodded sleepily, and Clara helped her into a sitting position. With his auscultation complete, Andreas looped his stethoscope around his neck and palpated the patient's abdomen, encouraging Clara to do the same, particularly focussing on the right-upper quadrant, where she felt an unmistakeable liver edge that indicated hepatomegaly.

'The jugular venous pressure is elevated,' he said to Clara, indicating the distended vein in the woman's neck. 'I'll site a central line to monitor the central venous pressure and order an echo.'

He addressed the patient. 'Nurse Lund and I are a little concerned that your heart isn't pumping very effectively.'

The elderly lady reached for his hand. Andreas wrapped his large, capable hands around Mrs Kaase's frail one and something in Clara's chest jolted. The medical profession would lose a great doctor when Varborg's heir became ruler. But the hospital's loss would be the nation's gain. Just like the older brother he admired so much, Andreas would excel at anything.

If only he could resolve his issues with Prince Henrik. If only he'd talk to the man before it was too late. If he fully embraced the role that was his by birth, rather than seeing himself second choice, he'd not only be good, he'd be incredible.

Her stomach swooped with the realisation that soon they'd no longer be working together. It shouldn't bother her, but maybe she was getting too close. Maybe that was why she was so invested in his happiness, why his praise and collaboration affected her so deeply… But she couldn't become reliant on him.

'I'll speak to the High Dependency Unit and organise her transfer,' he said. 'Is she on diuretics?'

Clara nodded, handing him Mrs Kaase's drug chart. 'I'll set up a central line tray.'

Grateful to escape for a moment, she left Andreas to explain the minimally invasive procedure to the patient, while she collected the portable ultrasound machine and the equipment he would need to site the central venous catheter. Her hands trembled as she gathered wrapped sterile syringes and dressings. Just because professionally and intimately Andreas treated her as his equal didn't mean she should forget her hard-won autonomy. If she wasn't careful, if she confused amazing sex and professional camaraderie for other feelings, she could so easily be hurt, given her lack of experience with relationships.

Feelings made a person vulnerable. She'd seen that in her parents' marriage; had seen her mother's tendency to forgive her neglectful husband again and again in the name of love. Clara had no intention of falling into the same trap.

Assisted by Clara, Andreas skilfully sited the central line in the internal jugular vein in Mrs Kaase's neck before accompanying Clara and the patient to the HDU. After handing over their patient, they left the ward together, an awkward silence descending.

'I've missed you,' he said finally.

The stark need, heat and restraint in his eyes all but sent Clara bursting into flames. Gone was the dedicated doctor and the regal prince. In his place stood the stripped-back man—a complex and flawed man she now knew intimately. But she needed to be careful.

'Me too,' she whispered, her entire body molten-hot.

His eyes sparked with triumph, his sexy mouth tugged in a knowing smile. Despite her warnings to herself, she ached for him. She'd do almost anything to feel his lips on her skin, to hear him groan her name, to feel him fill that empty place deep in her core. But this physical dependency to him was linked to Andreas's skills as a lover. It certainly didn't mean that she was *emotionally* dependent.

'Come to me—tonight.' It was an order, pure and simple, filled with sensual assurance.

She dragged in a breath, desperate to agree, every inch of her clamouring for the pleasure behind the promise. But she hesitated. They paused outside Clara's ward. He leaned against the wall, his head cocked in challenge, awaiting her answer. They stood a perfectly professional distance apart, but the air between them was thick with pheromones. She might as well be naked and wrapped around him, so intense was his invisible force field drawing her in.

Clara glanced down the corridor, horribly torn. Her body was fully on board but her head couldn't shake off the words of caution. Maybe it was the ticking clock. Maybe it was Sister's reminder of his importance, of how he was regarded public property, how he would soon be promoted to the 'top job'. Maybe it was that pesky reality of hers.

'What if someone sees me at the palace when I'm off-duty?' No one could know.

'We'll meet somewhere after dark,' he said, his eyes sparkling with excitement, making a pulse thrum between her legs. 'We'll leave your car and I'll smuggle you into the palace in mine. I'll text you an out-of-the-way meeting place.'

Clara swallowed, adrenaline a wild rush in her veins, her stare obsessively glued to his sexy mouth. She wanted him too much, the longing also a reason for hesitation.

Being smuggled into the palace on her night off seemed way riskier than that day at the lodge, when she'd already had a legitimate work-related reason to be at the palace. What if she was caught in his suite? She wasn't one of his society sophisticates; she was a normal woman.

With Prince Henrik's diagnosis public knowledge, media speculation and interest in Andreas had sky-rocketed. If anyone got wind of their...affair... if her family shame of her father's notoriety, debts and prison sentence came out, not only would she have to relive the humiliation but Andreas would be tainted by association.

She should tell him, before he found out some other way. But not here. Not now.

'It feels...risky.' She should return to the ward and her duties. Except he was looking at her the way he'd done when she'd been naked, when he'd

moved inside her, when he'd watched her climax…
triumphantly confident.

As if tired of her caution, Andreas glanced along
the corridor and then sprang into action, taking her
hand and dragging her into a vacant treatment room.
The minute the door closed, she was in his arms,
their lips crashing together, their tongues thrusting,
their hands restlessly fisting each other's clothes.

His powerful body pinned her to the back of the
door, the heat of him a stifling inferno. She rubbed
her body against his, seeking the friction that would
help quench the fire, but her uniform was too tight;
she couldn't open her legs wide enough to have him
where she wanted. She clung to him, kissing him
back with so much pent-up desire, she would surely
leave scorch marks on his white coat.

He growled, pulling back while his greedy hands
caressed her hips, her waist, her breasts. 'Please,
sötnos. I can't spend another night without you. I'm
going out of my mind. *You* are the real reason I
came in today.'

Before she could answer, he kissed her fiercely
once more, his lips then sliding down her neck, hitting all her sensitive spots, coiling the desire between her legs tighter. Clara tried to cling to the
elusive threads of her argument, but her brain was
paralysed with pleasure. It was as if that day at the
cabin had primed her body to respond to him, only
him, on reflex. She was panting, slick heat in her
pelvis, her drugged-up mind ready to agree to any
liaison he suggested.

'I can't think straight for wanting you.' He stroked her nipple through her clothes and she dropped her head back against the door, exposing her neck to his open-mouthed kisses.

This was crazy. They were at work; this room was regularly used. But she couldn't seem to stop kissing him, the thrill of his need for her, of finding him hard, making her bold and, oh, so reckless.

She cupped his erection through his scrubs. He groaned against her skin, the scrape of his facial hair sending shivers through her every nerve. But she couldn't go back to work with stubble rash from his beard. Somehow that thought gave her the strength to shove him back a pace.

'Okay. I'll meet you later,' she said. 'But the location has to be absolutely safe. If I think there's a chance we'll be seen together, I won't stop.'

He braced his hand on the door over her head, and stared down at her with hooded eyes. 'Bring your toothbrush; you'll be staying the night. I need to get my fill of you in case we are forced to spend another week like the last.'

At the thought of spending the entire night in his bed, trickles of elation zapped along her nerves, setting off a series of shudders. 'I can't wait. But now I have to go.'

Yanking his neck, she pressed one last kiss to his lips, which were curled in a self-satisfied smile. She ducked away and checked her reflection in the mirror over the sink. Debauched: there was no other way to describe the flush to her skin, the excitement in her eyes and the kiss-swollen state of her lips.

'Don't you have somewhere to be?' she asked, flicking him an accusing stare in the mirror before splashing her face with cold water.

He leaned against the door they'd just utilised, his arms crossed over his chest while he watched her smugly.

'The interview is in an hour,' he said, looking as if he might reach for her again. 'A public relations exercise dreamt up by the palace—let's show the nation a candid glimpse of the heir doing his day job while he still has it…'

At the defeat in his muttered words, Clara turned to face him. 'I'm sorry.'

'It's fine.' He shrugged, his stare vulnerable, bewildered by the sacrifices he had to make. 'But our secret rendezvous will be the only thing getting me through this afternoon.'

Clara nodded, uncertain what to say. Andreas didn't have to trust her with his feelings on giving up medicine. He'd made it clear at the cabin that her advice that he should talk to Prince Henrik was unwelcome.

'I'll let you get back to work,' he said, carelessly swiping his fingers through his hair. 'Until tonight.'

He opened the door, turning to wink at Clara before he ducked outside.

Clara rushed back to the ward, her stomach knotted with excitement for tonight which, with everything that was going on for him, could be their last.

Either way, he deserved to know her most shameful secret. He deserved to know the risks they were taking with their affair.

She would tell him tonight.

CHAPTER TWELVE

ANDREAS PULLED THE CAR into the underground garage at the palace, his excited pulse a deafening rage in his ears. He was only flesh and blood, and having Clara close enough to touch but still out of reach while he drove had tested his limits to the max.

'Are you sure no one saw me?' she asked from the passenger seat, still ducked down, out of sight.

'Positive,' he said, turning off the engine. 'The windows are tinted.'

He didn't add that he'd asked Nils to do a dry run of their route to ensure there'd be no hidden surprises. Clara was skittish enough without knowing that, since the press release confirming his father's diagnosis, media interest in Andreas had tripled. There was nothing like bad news to fuel speculation about Varborg's future ruler. He'd resolutely avoided watching the news, but he'd been told that several international newspapers were running stories on the tragedy-struck Cronstedt family, rehashing the death of Andreas's mother and Oscar as entertainment for the masses.

He understood Clara's caution. The idea of her facing the kind of public and media interest he'd experienced these past few days, left him chilled to the bone. He'd do everything in his power to safeguard her privacy. He'd vowed to protect her and he wouldn't let her down.

Andreas unclipped his seatbelt. 'Come here.'

He leaned over the centre console, cupping Clara's face to give her the proper kiss he'd had to hold inside for eight endless days. He pressed kisses to her closed eyelids, the tip of her nose, the angle of her jaw and that sensitive place on her neck.

'I missed you so much,' he mumbled against her soft lips, his heart thudding with urgency.

Why had he ever taken his previous freedom and relative privacy for granted? Soon his life would be unrecognisable—every second of his time scheduled, people constantly surrounding him, public appearances and interviews to be done, like this afternoon's. His grip on his old life was slipping, and Clara was the one thing that made his situation tolerable.

He held her tighter. 'I'm adding a new condition—we can't leave it that long again.'

His time for indulging in flings, his time for working alongside Clara, was running out. Every second with her felt precious.

'We've been busy,' she said, pulling him closer so the gear stick jabbed his ribs. 'And we need to be careful at the hospital. No more steamy gropes in the treatment room, although Sister might not let anyone else near you.'

'Right now, I can't think of anything more important than kissing you.' Andreas groaned; she was too far away, had too many clothes on, was talking too much.

But Clara's words had struck a nerve. Constitutionally, he belonged to Varborg. He was obliged to marry, produce an heir, and secure the next generation of Cronstedt princes and princesses. He'd always known it would take an exceptional woman to walk at his side through the circus that would be his life from here on out. But, since meeting Clara, his desires had solidified. He didn't want a cardboard cut-out for a wife. He wanted something real with someone who understood him beyond the public role he played. Someone to grow at his side. Someone he could respect, love and care for.

But right now he only cared about one woman. He breathed in the scent of her skin and slid his hand along her thigh, which was covered in thick black stockings that disappeared under a tight woollen skirt.

She gripped his tie, pulling his mouth back to hers.

'I like you all dressed up,' she said. 'You look extremely hot in an untouchable kind of way. Is this what you wore for the interview?'

'You can touch all you want, *sötnos*.' Andreas grinned, his hand locating an inch of bare skin at her waist. 'But, yes, I wore this for part of the filming. They also had me dress in scrubs and examine a few people at the hospital—make Varborg's heir relatable to the masses.'

Clara slid her fingers through his hair, pushing it

back from his face, staring up at him thoughtfully. 'You are relatable; you don't have to try.'

'Maybe you should be on my PR team.' Andreas gripped her hand and kissed her knuckles one by one. She saw things in him no one else saw; believed in him without agenda.

'If we don't move right now,' he said, reaching for the door handle at his back, 'You'll be riding me in this seat with the steering wheel at your back.'

Spurred into action by Clara's nervous squawk and the desire pounding through his blood, Andreas exited the vehicle and rushed her towards the lift to the guest suite he was still using.

She kissed him again, driving him wild with delicate darts of her tongue against his. 'You won't be able to smuggle me in like this much longer,' she said as they tumbled out of the lift, tugging at each other's clothes, pausing every few steps to kiss. 'Especially when you move into your own suite.'

She shoved at his suit jacket and he tossed it on the floor. 'I'll build a secret tunnel from your house to mine,' he said, only half-joking, 'So you can come to me any time you want.'

He refused to think of them ending when every other aspect of his life was so uncertain.

He *needed* her. She laughed but a shadow crossed her eyes. There was something hesitant about her tonight, more than her fear of discovery. It was making him jittery.

'Why are we wasting time talking,' he said,

'When that's been all we could do for eight excruciating days?'

He reached for her, losing himself in her kisses, gripping her waist and guiding her into the bedroom. Clara pulled the hem of his shirt free of his trousers and slid her hands up his back, restlessly pressing her body against his. He removed her sweater and popped open her bra, his hands greedily caressing her beautiful breasts as they spilled free.

'Because I've missed you,' she said simply, honestly, perfectly.

That was his Clara…

The possessive direction of his thoughts caught him off-guard. She wasn't his. This was a fling; even if he wanted something more permanent, that wasn't what *she* wanted. He didn't want to hurt her, disappoint her or let her down, and his father's diagnosis had curtailed his freedoms. Just as Oscar had done, he must put duty first. He couldn't drag someone as unique and guileless as Clara into his world of ancient protocol and public service. She cherished her independence and her career. He wouldn't change a single thing about her.

Right here, right now, this was all they had because he couldn't fail another person he cared about.

Unease compounded his desperation for her. He quickly peeled the remaining clothes from her body, taking one indulgent second to rake his gaze over her nakedness, his hands skimming her skin as if committing the softness, every dip and swell to memory.

'You're so beautiful; you steal my breath.' He tugged her close, the heat of her burning through his clothes. 'Later, I'm taking you in my giant bath, the scene of our first meeting. But first... I need you.'

He thumbed her nipples erect, smiling when she moaned his name and dropped her head back so he could ravage her neck with kisses.

'I need you too,' she said on a sigh, taking hold of his tie once more and tugging him by the neck towards the bed. She sat down and hurriedly undid his belt and fly, looking up at him with wicked intent. He'd barely survived the last time she put her gorgeous mouth on him. And he was strung so taut, the tick-tock of the clock flooding his body with a sense of panic, that this time he might actually fracture apart.

With a look of thrilling determination, Clara encircled his erection, licked up the length of him and then took him inside her mouth. She hummed a satisfied sound of delight. He closed his eyes, a surge of arousal filling him to bursting point. How could she do this to him—render him unstable with her touch and that look that said she saw him exactly as he was? Just a man.

But there was something wild about her tonight. Had she reached her limit in the eight days they'd been forced apart by work schedules and life? Or was she too hungrily preparing for future famine when they'd be once more forced apart, maybe for good. No; he couldn't think about that.

Spurred into action, he yanked back his hips. He

tossed off his clothes and prosthesis and prowled over her naked body. He kissed her lips, her breasts, her stomach and then dived between her legs to kiss and lick her into a sobbing frenzy. He was addicted to her taste. Addicted to everything, from the stud in her nose to the sharp wit of her tongue and the sound of her moans when she climaxed.

She cried out his name now, her hands twisting in his hair. He teased her sensitive nipples to hard peaks so she was writhing, needy for him, her hands restless and grabby.

'We won't be sleeping tonight,' he said, settling his weight over her. 'I want to make up for those eight days with as many orgasms as is humanly possible.'

He slid his hand to the slick heat between her legs, watching her eyes darken with need.

'Yes…' She dug her nails into his shoulders and spread her thighs wide so their hips aligned.

On fire from within, his heartbeat banged, dangerously high.

'I can't get enough of you,' he panted, tearing his mouth away from her kisses. He cupped her thigh, his hips grinding between her parted legs as if out of his control. He'd never been this hot for a woman. The deprivation had sharpened the ache for her, only her, and one look at her passion-dazed expression told him she felt the same way.

Clara held his face and brought their lips back together in a rush of frantic and deep kisses. She cupped his buttocks, urging him closer, tilting her hips to meet him and shrouding him in her scalding heat as he pushed inside her with a groan of profound relief.

'Andreas!' she cried.

He reared up on his elbows and captured one nipple with his mouth. She crossed her ankles in the small of his back so he sank deeper inside her. Their bodies moved together in a frenzied rhythm as they tried to quench the need riding them both so hard.

How would he ever find the strength to let her go, having taken his entire adult life to find someone so remarkable? In that moment, he could have sworn that Clara was as essential as the very air he breathed.

He rolled them, holding her hips so they stayed locked together. She sat astride him and rode him, her hair a wild tumble around her flushed face. He cupped her pert breasts and stroked her nipples with his thumbs. She shattered, her stare locked to his, her cries ringing out around the room, until he jack-knifed into a sitting position and kissed them up.

With one final roar, he crushed her to his chest and spilled himself inside her, a part of his soul surely branded hers for all eternity.

Clara relaxed back against Andreas's hard chest, so languid in the warm scented bubble bath that she might have fallen asleep if she hadn't been so attuned to every subtle shift of Andreas's touch. They'd lit what seemed like a hundred candles around the bath and left the blinds open so they could look out at the view of the snow-capped mountains and inky night sky.

Her skin tingled with awareness, the throbbing pulse between her legs barely satiated, even after that incredible orgasm. How would she survive the loss of such pleasure when this fling came to an end? And end it must. Clara was an ordinary woman, too cynical for relationships. Even if she'd wanted more from Andreas, it would be an impossible fairy tale. He would rule Varborg, marry his princess and produce his own heirs, and Clara would watch from the side-lines. Although, she had no clue how she would see pictures of him in the media and not want him with this all-encompassing need...

'I'm sorry about the condom, *sötnos*,' he said, pressing his lips to the side of her neck so she shivered with delight.

'I'm sorry too. But, despite having only one previous partner, I'm still on birth control.'

They'd been so wild for each other after their eight days apart, they'd forgotten all about protection.

'I'm normally very sexually responsible,' he said, his hands sliding up and down her thighs under the water. 'You just make me...insatiable.'

'Insatiable, huh?' Clara smiled like the cat that had stolen the cream, the flutters in her chest telling her just how much she trusted Andreas.

Now that they were finally alone, she should tell him about her father's prison sentence. But she was so relaxed, his touch so hypnotic, it was hard to think about anything but him. And, once her secret was out, she'd have nowhere left to hide. That most vulnerable part of herself, the part she'd always protected from hurt by avoiding relationships, would be exposed. He'd know *everything*.

His lips skimmed the sensitive place on her neck, distracting her once more. 'Will you watch my interview when it airs? Let me know how badly it comes across?'

'Of course, but I doubt it will be bad. You're a prince and a doctor, and you're single. Half of Varborg will be in love with you before the show ends.'

Now it was his turn to chuckle, while spikes of jealousy pricked Clara's skin. But he didn't belong to her.

'Did they ask you any questions you didn't want to answer?' she asked to detract from the helpless, jittery feeling in the pit of her stomach.

'I'd already vetoed any questions relating to Oscar's death,' he said. 'But they asked if I'm currently seeking a princess to marry—only to be expected in my position. My personal life is considered public property.'

Clara flinched. Wasn't she temporarily part of his personal life? Because she'd rather have run naked out into the snow than know if Andreas was officially courting some foreign princess or lucky aristocrat closer to home, she latched onto another topic.

'Will you tell me about Oscar?' she whispered,

resting her head on his shoulder so his next kiss landed on her cheek. 'I'd love to know what he was like.'

Andreas took a deep breath, his chest expanding at her back.

'It's so hard to paint one picture,' he said on a sigh. 'He was so many things.'

'Like you, then,' Clara said, lifting his hand to press a kiss to his fingers.

'He was good at everything.' His voice lightened with admiration. 'But somehow humble too. He could ski like a champion, speak five languages and he always had a joke up his sleeve, ready to drop it into conversation if and when appropriate.'

Clara smiled, pressing a breathy kiss to his lips. 'Very useful skills for a statesman. How many languages do *you* speak?'

'Only three, I'm afraid.'

'What a dreadful under-achiever,' she teased, and he laughed. 'Hot and intelligent and kind—the palace may need to ramp up security once that interview airs.' But her teasing cost her another jealous roll of her stomach.

He chuckled. After a few seconds, he stiffened. 'Oscar's death was a great loss for the future of Varborg. He had big plans to modernise the principality. We discussed it often—how things would be different for our children.'

'What kind of plans?' Clara didn't want to imagine Andreas's fair-haired children.

He shrugged, sending out ripples of bathwater.

'Ways to challenge the old guard traditionalists, a more equal distribution of duties between royal siblings, that kind of thing.'

'Things you can still implement yourself, if you choose.' She entwined her fingers with his, cautious of making him withdraw, the way he had at the cabin when she'd pushed too hard.

'I guess. We didn't discuss it until we were adults, but we were both lonely growing up so…segregated. We needed to develop our own interests and be independent, but when it came to our royal life we could have acted as a team rather than being divided. Not that it matters now.'

Clara stilled, aware of the thud of his heart at her back and the matching rhythm in her chest. Every second of their time was precious, but Andreas's past issues with his place in the Cronstedt family were holding him back from being his wonderfully authentic self. He'd made it clear that he wouldn't be addressing those issues with his father. But, if she could get him talking, maybe it would help him to believe in his ability to rule.

'Will you tell me about the accident?' she whispered. 'I promise I'll never speak of it to another soul.'

'I know you won't, *sötnos*.' Andreas pressed his lips to her temple. 'You and I share a sense of loyalty. I trust you.'

Clara swallowed, her eyes stinging with longing. He trusted her but she was hiding something from him: her most shameful family secret. She needed to tell him, and soon.

'Oscar and I were both in the army, in different regiments,' he said, staring ahead as if staring into the past. 'We were attending the same training exercise. It was all perfectly standard until it wasn't. Oscar was in a vehicle crossing rough terrain when it hit a concealed ditch and rolled.'

Clara sat frozen, a shiver running through her, although the water was still warm.

'I heard it on the radio,' he continued. 'The medical corps were training nearby, so we rushed to help. We managed to free the driver, but Oscar was unconscious in the passenger seat, the crushed cab of the vehicle trapping him.'

His heart thudded against her back and Clara gripped his hand tighter, wishing she could undo his pain and loss.

'We cleared the shattered windscreen,' he continued, 'And I half-climbed in so I could preserve Oscar's airway while we waited for the cutting crew. I could tell it looked bad for him. He had an obvious head injury, and a scalp wound that was bleeding profusely, but all I could do in that position was stabilise his neck, pressure-dress the wound and protect his airway.'

Tears tracked down Clara's cheeks. He must have felt so scared and helpless.

'I was too emotionally attached to be objective,' Andreas said. 'But I refused to leave him, even when he went into cardiac arrest. I performed CPR, even when I was ordered to step down by my superior officer so someone else could take over. Even when someone noticed the petrol leaking, I refused to leave my brother.'

Clara turned to face him, the full horror of what must have happened hitting her like a blow.

He nodded, his face pale with grief, as if he was reliving the accident. 'The wreck burst into flames. I was thrown clear, but I broke both my legs.'

'I'm so sorry,' she whispered, pressing her lips to his in silent apology. Why had she asked him? Because she just selfishly wanted to know everything about him, for her own insatiable needs.

'They saved the right leg, but the left was fractured and badly burned, and became infected. They had to amputate three days before Oscar's funeral.'

'Andreas…' She sat astride his lap, holding onto both his hands as if she'd never let go. 'You could have died too.'

He shook his head, dismissing her concern. 'He was my brother, my senior in rank, my country's heir to the throne and I couldn't save him.'

Clara's vision blurred with sadness. She gripped his face. '*No one* could have saved him. You did everything humanly possible. It was a terrible accident.'

'A part of me knows that.' A sad smile tugged his lips; he didn't believe her. 'But the rest of me just feels guilty. I'm a *doctor*. I let him down. And why was it me to survive and not him?'

'You know why.' Clara rested her forehead against his. 'Life is random and sometimes unfair.'

She didn't need to tell Andreas that. He was an intelligent man of the world, a leader, who'd had more than his fair share of family tragedy.

'*He* should be here now,' Andreas said as if he hadn't heard, as he gripped her upper arms so they were locked together in this horrible moment of grief and heartache. 'He was meant to be the one to succeed Prince Henrik.'

Clara shook her head violently. The idea of never having met Andreas was too horrible to contemplate.

'You feel responsible because of your profession,' she said passionately. 'Because he was your big brother, a man you loved and respected; because the family you were born into has a hereditary hierarchy most families don't have. But it wasn't your fault.'

He stared up at her, pain shifting across his beautiful eyes. And something else—need. His arms came around her waist and he held her so close, burying his face against the erratic thud of her heart. It was as if their connection, this wild storm of desire that never seemed to lessen, went way beyond physical in that moment.

But it couldn't. She wouldn't let it mean more. She was strong. She would be there for him, embrace their intimacies until it was time for them to part and then she'd deal with the fallout once it was over.

Clara stroked his hair and held him to her heart as if she could fix the broken pieces of him. His life was in turmoil. He was grieving for the past and the future. He was hurting, carrying unnecessary guilt over Oscar's death and feeling that he was second best to a dead man because of his family's succession, and because he had unresolved issues with Prince Henrik. If what he'd told her the day at the cabin was true, he and Prince Henrik had never really spoken about Oscar's death. Perhaps if Andreas knew that no one else blamed him, including his father, he could start to forgive himself. It might ease his struggles with the royal role he felt he didn't deserve.

But, just like Andreas hadn't been able to save Oscar, Clara couldn't save Andreas. He needed to do that himself.

'What can I do to help you?' she asked, aching for him.

His arms tightened around her waist. 'You help me simply by being here. Things make sense when I'm with you. You understand me. You see me, the real me. You always have.'

Clara held him while he crushed her to him.

Right now, while the rest of his life was tugging him in all directions, he might feel as if he needed her, but she couldn't forget her reality. Her valued independence, her own shameful past and her determination for equality in any future relationship.

'I know you think I should talk to the prince about the past, about Oscar,' he continued. 'And maybe you're right. But, what with my crash course on ruling Varborg, stepping in to fulfil most of my father's engagements and planning a state funeral in minute detail, the prince and I already have many things on our minds.'

'I'm sorry. I didn't mean to pry.' Her voice sounded sickeningly small, the feeling she'd been dismissed once more causing a hot ache in her throat. It made memories of her final phone call to her father resurface, when he'd trivialised her concerns and refused to make her any promises.

But she didn't need promises from Andreas. This was just sex.

'And I didn't mean to offload.' He dragged her lips to his. 'Let's forgive each other.'

Clara nodded and smiled, because he'd done nothing wrong. He was just dealing with his lot in life in the best way he knew how. It wasn't Andreas's fault that she'd learned from her own regrets or that she would hate to see him miss his chance to heal some of the scars holding him back before his father died. But she needed to accept that sometimes she just couldn't fix what was broken.

'I've handed in my notice at Nordic Care,' he said, looking up at her with such grief and vulnerability, she shoved aside her selfish thoughts on what that would mean for her.

'That's good.' She pressed her lips to his. 'You have a lot going on.'

But she understood his reluctance to end his locum job. He was clinging to the one thing he could control, the one thing he could ensure he was good at—his career.

But he had so much more to give.

'You're like your brother, Andreas,' she said imploringly. 'You'll be good at anything you set your mind to, including ruling this nation of ours.'

His expression shifted from despair to bewilderment. 'You asked how you could help...and my answer is just be yourself. Don't ever change, *sötnos*.'

He brushed her lips with his on a ragged sigh, pulling back to search her stare. 'You are the only good thing I can hold onto right now.' His hands restlessly skimmed her back and her shoulders, his fingers tunnelling into her hair. 'I need you, Clara. I want you.'

Gripping the back of her neck, he dragged her mouth back to his. His kiss grew deeper, his hands roaming her body as if he was committing the shape of her to memory.

Clara surrendered, kissing him back, losing herself again. Every time she veered away from the passion and connection they found in each other's arms, she came unstuck, her mind spinning out, searching for answers and solutions that were right there in front of her.

For, however long they had left, *this* was all that mattered.

His hands gripped her hips under the water, drawing her close. He was hard between her legs. Rising up on her knees, she guided him inside her body, each of them sighing with relief as they stared into each other's eyes.

For now, he was hers—her wild mountain-man, her Viking.

As she rocked above him and he moved inside her, passion spiralling as they clung to each other, and Clara clinging to the only part of him she could have, she promised herself she would hold something back.

She would protect her heart the way she'd always done because, of all men, Andreas had the power to do the most damage.

CHAPTER THIRTEEN

THREE DAYS LATER, Clara was just about to leave the palace after her night shift when she received a text from her sister, Freja.

Have you seen this?

The message accompanied a link to a celebrity news site. The main article featured a grainy picture of Andreas and Clara kissing goodbye at her car the morning after she'd spent the night in his bed at the palace.

Her stomach dropped at the sickening headline: *How Much Longer Can the Heir Play the Field?*

Horrified, her pulse went through the roof. She could almost taste the public's rejection, hear their judgement and contempt that she wasn't good enough for Varborg's heir. But, worse, if her identity was revealed, if the connection between Lars Lund and her got out, her family's humiliating past might hurt Andreas at a time when he must feel as if his life was falling apart.

Tears pricked her eyes. Her father's disgrace shouldn't be her burden to bear, but she'd been hardwired most of her life to feel the sting of rejection. And that guilty part of her, that should have already come clean to Andreas, now had nowhere left to hide.

It was time to face him.

Willing herself to calm down, Clara texted Andreas.

We need to talk.

Against her better judgement, she scoured the picture again. The photographer had clearly been hiding some distance away, using a telephoto lens. Clara was only visible from behind, but her parked car was in the background. The registration number had been blurred out, but it would only take some nosy journalist a few seconds of sleuthing to find out her identity and the paper trail of shame that would lead to her door.

Andreas's reply was swift.

Come to the green sitting room in the family wing. Sorry, I can't get away.

With acid burning her throat, Clara hurried to the room she knew of but had never been inside, grateful for the sense of legitimacy her uniform provided.

Her rapid steps matched the panicked bounding of her heart. What if poor Prince Henrik had seen the photo? What if the palace press office was aware of the identity of Andreas's unsuitable mystery woman? Would she be fired or banned from seeing Andreas?

An ache settled under her ribs, its potency suspicious of grief. But she'd always known this day would come, that she'd have to give him up; she'd just hoped for a little more time. Knocking on the door, she waited for the call to enter and then ducked quickly inside.

He wasn't alone.

Even with a firestorm of fear in her veins, her heart lurched at the arresting sight of Andreas. His immaculately tailored navy suit caressed his lean and sculpted body to perfection. He looked up from adjusting his crisp white cuffs, which glinted with onyx cuff links, his stare burning into hers from across the room.

Taking one look at Clara's face, Andreas stiffened.

'Leave us,' he instructed the valet, who ceased his efforts brushing invisible specks of lint from Andreas's suit and hastily fled.

'What is it, *sötnos*?' A small frown tugged down his mouth as he crossed the room.

Clara rested her eyes on his, her heart actually stuttering to a stop. The flood of desire for him was almost strong enough to dispel her profound embarrassment—almost.

Last night, snuggled on the sofa with her mum and Freja, with mugs of hot chocolate, she'd watched Andreas's interview. She'd sat spellbound, her eyes glued to the screen as the skilled programmers painted a portrait of Andreas the doctor, Andreas the veteran, Andreas the heir.

Now, chilled to the bone, she was fooling herself

to think she could have any part of such a magnificent man. He was wildly dashing, every inch the eligible prince and commanding statesman he feared he might never be. But he couldn't fight his upbringing, his genetics and the historic breeding of his family line. He was a prince. He always had been, from the day he'd been born. Clara had just forgotten that, allowing herself to be swept along by lust, by her professional regard and the way he'd made her feel special. But *he* was the special one.

'You're scaring me, Clara.' He gripped her upper arms. 'Are you hurt? Is it Prince Henrik?'

Clara shook her head and blurted out her reason for disturbing him. 'There's a photo of us together online.'

She blinked to stave off tears; her revelation would be final confirmation that this was over. Had she already tarnished his reputation by association? And at a time when he had so much else going on.

A muscle clenched in his jaw, but he didn't seem surprised. 'I've been made aware.' He reached for her hands. 'I'm sorry. The announcement of Prince Henrik's state of health has, I'm afraid, caused an increased interest in my personal life.'

She frowned, her head foggy with desire, confusion and guilt. Could she blame the public? She too had watched the candid thirty-minute interview of Varborg's heir with rapt fascination bordering on obsession, her hot drink forgotten.

'No, *I'm* sorry.' She tugged her hands from his,

feeling shabby and creased in her uniform, more aware than ever before of their massive differences.

With his face cloaked in his signature close-cropped beard, he was more handsome rogue than prince of the realm, but of course that was a massive part of his Viking appeal.

He frowned. 'Why are *you* apologising? It's me they were after, not you.' He ran a hand through his tamed hair. '*I* should be the one apologising for not protecting you better, for exposing you to the seedier side of life in the public gaze. I know you wanted to keep us a secret. For now, they don't seem to know who you are.'

His hands gripped her elbows and he pressed a desperate kiss to her lips. Clara's body reacted, as always, to his kiss.

'You don't understand,' she said, extricating herself from his touch. She wanted nothing more than to curl up in his arms and hide from her past, from the ugliness and risk she'd exposed him to. But shame was a painful gripe in her belly.

'I understand all too well.' His voice rose, fury sparking in his grey stare. 'It's an invasion of my privacy and yours. *I* expect it, but they have no right to target you. I won't let that happen. I swear to you, Clara. I'll protect you.'

'I need to tell you something.' Clara shook her head, trying to stay on track, but shock and desire threatened to derail her thoughts. She could no longer deny that her need for this man was now a full-blown addiction. She'd realised that last night, watching him on the screen.

'Sötnos...' He stepped closer and wrapped her in his arms so she was engulfed by his warmth and the scent of his cologne. 'Please don't distress yourself over this. Let me deal with it. I have people. I'll ensure that you remain anonymous.'

He tilted her chin, brushing his thumb over her bottom lip, his stare dipping there. 'It's just a fishing expedition—social commentary from strangers who don't know me but think I should be married by now, or some such rubbish.'

Clara recoiled from his touch, turning her head away. The idea of Andreas with another woman hit her like a slap to the face. But of course there would be other women after her, until finally his princess: a sophisticated beauty with the appropriate pedigree, well-schooled in dealing with press intrusion, her closet devoid of tawdry family skeletons. The kind of woman who would look at home on the arm of the immaculate and urbane prince before her.

Hating her own weakness, her self-doubt-fuelled envy, Clara snapped, 'I don't need you to rescue me or protect me; I can take care of myself.'

Andreas frowned, his gaze flicking to the clock on the wall. 'So it's okay for you to want to help me, but not for me to help you?'

Clara dragged in a calming breath. He clearly had places to be, important people to see. Her sad family drama would be swiftly passed to some lackey in the palace press office.

'I won't keep you,' Clara said, rolling back her shoulders, 'But I need you to listen. I told you about my father running out on us, but the bit I left out was that he was something of a swindler. Not only did he get into all kinds of debt while my parents were together, he also re-mortgaged our family home behind my mother's back. But the worst thing he did was defraud a bunch of people in some sort of pyramid scheme. He went to prison, Andreas. He died in prison. That's why I never had the chance to confront him, because I refused to visit.'

'Clara—'

'I know I should have told you before.' She blinked, refusing to cry for the father who'd let her down so badly. 'But I'm not exactly proud of the fact. I thought, if we were careful, it never needed to come out.'

'It doesn't matter,' he stated flatly, moving towards her and then stopping, presumably in response to her expression.

'Of course it matters,' she snapped, her fears spilling free. 'We promised we'd be careful, but now look what's happened. I'm…news. I never wanted any of this. I just wanted *you*.'

'I'm right here.' He gripped her cold hand and rested it over his chest where his heart thudded against her palm, vibrant and steady.

Clara looked away from his impeccable appearance; he felt more out of reach than ever. 'And you may as well be on the moon, don't you see?' she cried. 'We've always been too different and now the whole world will see that. You'll be embarrassed. Prince Henrik will be embarrassed. Neither of you need a scandal right now.'

She tugged her hand free and backed away from him. She couldn't think when he touched her—that was how they'd ended up in this mess.

'I'll probably lose my job,' she continued, 'And my mother has been through enough without having the whole sordid story regurgitated.'

Tension built in the silence as she finally faced him.

'Are you ending this?' A fierce scowl slashed his handsome face. 'Because I know what I need, and I told you, it's you.'

Confused, Clara shook her head. For a brief moment, him, their connection had been the one easy thing she'd wanted. But it was no longer easy.

'I'm not sure we ever really got started,' she said sadly. She didn't want to leave him, not yet. 'But this photograph certainly complicates things.'

'I told you, I'll take care of it,' he said.

'How? You're royalty,' she argued, deaf to his promises. In Clara's experience, believing in those only made you more vulnerable. 'If people find out you're fraternising with the penniless daughter of a convicted criminal, it could damage your reputation!'

'Don't do this.' He gripped her face, staring at her with panic in his eyes. 'Don't let strangers come between us.'

Tilting her mouth up, he delivered a crushing kiss

as if he could make her believe in him, that he'd deal with the issue.

Her lips parted on a shocked gasp. His tongue surged into her mouth, coaxing. Because she'd always been helpless to their desire for each other, Clara's brain shut down, her body clinging to the pleasure of his kiss to block out all the ugliness in which she felt coated.

This beautiful man, who could have any woman, wanted *her*. The power of it surged through her. *This*, them together, made sense and blocked out reality.

His fingers tangled in her hair, spilling it loose from its bun. His body heat scorched her. His hard chest brushed her sensitive nipples, his thigh pressing between her legs as he backed her up against a table. There was an ominous rattle of something heavy, perhaps a lamp, but Clara was too inflamed to care. She clung to him, drowning, so far out of her depth with this man that her only certainty was that she should walk away. But it was as if her heart knew best and wanted him, no matter what.

'Andreas,' she moaned, spearing her fingers through his hair as he trailed kisses down her neck and slid one hand up her thigh, under her uniform and into her underwear. 'You have to go,' she gasped, palming his erection through his trousers, aware that she was holding him up for whatever important princely engagement he was immaculately dressed.

'I don't care.' He shoved down her underwear and

unbuckled his belt. 'I only care about you. About this. About us.'

Frantic now with desire, Clara tackled his fly, freeing him from the confines of his suit.

'You can't leave me, not yet.' With a grunt, he hauled her around the waist and deposited her backside on the edge of the table. He kissed her again, his fingers working her nipple through her uniform and bra.

'I won't,' she cried as they broke free of their kisses to fumble together.

Clara hiked up her skirt and spread her thighs. Andreas shoved down his trousers, just enough to free him from his underwear.

'Soon. I'll let you go soon,' he said, staring into her eyes as he pushed inside her. A low growl rumbled in the back of his throat. His hands clutched at her waist, hips and breasts with thrilling heated possession.

'I want you, Clara…' He groaned against her neck, thrusting inside her. 'You asked me what I needed and the answer is *this*. *You*.'

He pulled back, stark need in his eyes.

'I want you too.' Clara sighed and shuddered, gripping his hips with her thighs and clinging to him as they rode this storm of need together.

'Tell me you're still mine, *sötnos*,' he muttered between kisses, his hands holding her hips so tightly, she wondered if he'd leave marks. 'Tell me we're still in this together—different but equals. Tell me.'

His thrusts grew more frantic, his kisses deep

and demanding, his eye contact so intense, Clara could only hold on and give him her all in return.

'I'm yours,' Clara said, stifling her cries against his lips as pleasure shook her from head to toe, heightened by the glitter of triumph and possession in his stare.

Andreas gave a rough cry and crushed her in his arms as they climaxed together, the furious need finally abating. For long seconds they stayed locked together, hearts thudding, breaths panting.

He moved first, slipping from her body. He stepped back, helping her slide from the table. He buttoned up and Clara shakily scooped her underwear from the floor, stepping inside the garment while her mind raced and her body tried to recover.

What was she doing? She was out of control for this man: risking her emotions; making him promises she might not have the strength to keep; giving him everything when she'd vowed to hold something back as a shield around her inexperienced heart.

He touched her hand and she looked up. Apart from slightly dishevelled hair and a bit of colour on his cheekbones, he was still perfect, still achingly beautiful, still a prince. Sadness, maybe even pity, touched his eyes. 'I've always known about your father, Clara.'

Horrified, she frowned, searching his stare for the truth as ice shifted through her veins.

Andreas's beautiful mouth flattened into a grim

line. 'No one works for my family without a police check and a background check.'

He'd known…all this time? For all his talk of equality…

'You consented to be vetted when you landed the job,' he explained. 'Palace security investigate everyone who works here: their past, their family and their employment history. It's all thoroughly scrutinised.' His lip curled with the barest hint of distaste. 'The price you pay for any association with me, I'm afraid. I wish it wasn't necessary, just like I wish I could spare you the paparazzi.'

He shrugged with sad inevitability.

Clara shrivelled inside, as if what they'd just done had left her dirty. She looked away from him, their differences neon-bright, and the trust she'd foolishly imagined shattered on the floor like shards of glass.

'Why didn't you say anything?' Humiliation burned her eyes as she forced herself to look at him.

All this time she'd thought that on some level they were equals, just Clara and Andreas enjoying their chemistry, but in reality he'd always held all of the power in the relationship.

'It didn't matter to me,' he said flatly. '*You* did nothing wrong. It's like you said the first time we met—our scars don't define us.'

The lump in her throat expanded. How could she have been so naïve?

Andreas raised her chin. 'If you care for me at all, please don't let them come between us. We know who we are, what we value, and we know each other. You know me, Clara. If I say it doesn't matter to me, it doesn't matter.'

Numb, Clara nodded. She *did* know this man. She knew her feelings for him were reckless. She knew he'd seen the deeply vulnerable part of her that she'd always kept guarded. She knew that, if she wasn't careful with her heart, she could fall for him and he could destroy her.

I'll let you go soon...

She winced, hating the words she'd been too pleasure-drunk to analyse when he'd spoken them earlier. She didn't want to be *this* Clara: uncertain, emotionally exposed, scared. She wanted to be her old self, the woman who could take care of herself, needed no one and had her life all figured out.

'I need to go,' she said, clearing her throat. 'I have to drive home and change and head to Nordic Care. I'm doing a late shift.'

He cupped her face. 'I'll take care of the press. Trust me.'

She nodded numbly, kissing him and then moving to the door. She *did* trust him, but it changed nothing. She'd let Andreas too close. She'd wanted him and he'd wanted her and their fling had seemed harmless. But danger was everywhere, overwhelming.

At the door, she turned to look at him one last time. His back was to her. He checked his watch, tugging on his cuffs, and pressed a buzzer on the desk, presumably summoning the valet once more.

He was unspeakably beautiful. The demands on

him were staggering. She'd wanted to ease his burdens, not add to them. She'd wanted to be there for him, not rely on him. She'd wanted to enjoy their affair and then walk away unscathed.

But it was like he'd once said: 'you don't always get what you want'.

CHAPTER FOURTEEN

ANDREAS'S FINAL SHIFT at Nordic Care arrived two days later, much sooner than planned. With a heavy, grieving heart, he strode onto Clara's ward, his eyes scanning for sight of her. Even now, when tension seemed to colour their every interaction, he selfishly craved her like a drug.

Curtains were drawn around the bed of one of his patients. From the urgent comings and goings, Andreas surmised some sort of emergency was taking place. Curious, he entered the bay. Clara, the ward sister and the new registrar, Dr Nilsen, attended to an elderly man, who was breathless.

'Hello, Mr Hagen.' He addressed the patient he'd admitted a week earlier with uncontrolled diabetes and infected venous ulceration of the lower leg, and looked to Clara for guidance as to the nature of the emergency.

Their eyes met. Pressure built in his chest. He'd missed her so much. Her obvious concern for their patient triggered his protective urges. How he ached to comfort her, to spirit them both away—maybe to the hunting lodge so they could be alone, and work out everything that felt tense between them since she'd panicked about her father, and go to bed until the pieces of his world slotted back into place.

But there was no time for any of that.

'What's the situation?' he asked, scanning the monitors. The patient was clearly in respiratory distress, his respiratory rate elevated and his blood oxygen saturations ninety-four percent.

Clara frowned, as if he had no right to be there. 'Acute shortness of breath. Dr Nilsen was on the ward.' She looked away.

'Good, but I know this patient well.' Stifling an irrational flinch of rejection, Andreas took the man's pulse, which was fast but regular, noting the fine beads of sweat on his brow. That Clara had bypassed him and gone straight to another doctor irked. It shouldn't matter, but it was another sign of her dwindling trust. Not that he could blame her; after today, he wouldn't even work at Nordic Care.

'I think it's acute left ventricular failure,' the registrar said while Clara silently passed Andreas an ECG tracing.

'Any chest pain?' Andreas asked, reaching for his stethoscope to listen to Mr Hagen's lungs.

'No,' Clara answered, while the registrar set about siting an intravenous cannula in the man's antecubital fossa.

Andreas listened to the patient's chest, hearing the unmistakeable crackle of pulmonary oedema, or fluid in the lower lobes of the lungs.

'Let's get some intravenous diuretic and morphine, please, Nurse Lund,' he said, taking control of the situation while trying not to draw parallels with his first day there a few short weeks ago.

So much had happened since they'd met, kissed and faced their first emergency together. He felt as if he'd known Clara a lifetime. But how did *she* feel? Did she still relate to the real him, or was she too overwhelmed by the inconveniences of his public life to keep sight of what they'd shared?

Clara left the bay to fetch the medication, returning with two vials and a syringe, which she handed to the registrar, who quickly drew up the drugs and injected them through the IV cannula.

She couldn't even look at him. It was as if she'd already made up her mind and deemed him too much trouble. Andreas concealed his sigh. He might want to protect her, but he couldn't make any guarantees. He didn't want to let her down or fail her in any way.

'Have you listened to Mr Hagen's chest?' he asked, handing over his stethoscope.

The patient's distress eased as the drugs worked. 'Nurse Lund is going to have a listen, Mr Hagen.'

They'd always collaborated on cases and trusted each other's clinical skills and diligence, regardless of the traditional role demarcations of doctor and nurse. They were a team. He wasn't about to act differently now that his personal circumstances dictated that his other job, the one he would inherit, demanded more of his time.

'We need a chest X-ray, bloods and an echo.' He addressed the team. 'He also needs a catheter to monitor urine output. I'll speak to cardiology, make an urgent referral. We need to exclude a silent myocardial infarction.'

There was a flurry of activity, a dividing up of the tasks. Andreas explained the diagnosis and the tests he's ordered to Mr Hagen, and then sat at a computer station to write in the patient's notes.

He kept one eye on Clara while she went about her duties but she wouldn't meet his eye. He'd just finished speaking to his cardiology colleagues when he spied her heading for the ward exit with her bag slung over her shoulder.

He caught up with her just as she left the ward. 'Clara, can we talk?'

She cast a wary glance around the foyer before pushing through the door to the stairwell, a place of relative privacy.

'Why didn't you call me about Mr Hagen?' he asked when the door closed, unable to keep the hurt or accusation from his voice. He stood as close as he dared, desperate to reach for her. But she was rigid and remote.

'I assumed you were busy,' she said, her expression hurt. 'I understand that today is your last day at Nordic Care.' She shrugged, resigned. 'Hospital rumour mill.'

Andreas winced, reaching for her bare arm, the feel of her skin a jolt of desire to his system. 'I'm sorry. I meant to tell you. I've been stuck in A and E most of the morning. The seasonal flu rush has started.'

'It's fine.' She shook her head, her cheeks flushed, as if she was embarrassed by her hurt feelings.

Despair gripped his throat. He stepped closer, dropping his voice. 'You know how I've struggled with giving up work. I've tried to delay the inevitable as long as possible.'

She nodded. 'I understand. You don't have to explain.'

'Yes, I *do*,' he muttered, willing her to look at him properly.

She was slipping through his fingers.

'Everything came to a head this morning,' he said, desperate to downplay the matter so she didn't get too spooked and end this right now. 'More leaks to the press about Father's radiotherapy, speculation about how long he has left. The palace communication team are scrambling to control the flow of information, but tensions are high.'

Sometimes he felt as if his entire world was crumbling. He swallowed, relieved to see the compassion in her stare. 'It's finally forced me to face facts.' He took her hand, needing to touch her. 'I can no longer spread myself so thinly.'

'Of course you can't.' Clara tilted her head in understanding and concern. 'And the demands on you are only going to increase.'

Andreas clenched his jaw in frustration. He wished they were anywhere but there, where they could barely look at each other for fear of discovery, let alone have a meaningful conversation.

'Can you come over tonight?' he asked with

a desperate edge to his voice that he hoped she wouldn't hear. 'We can talk, in private.'

'I finish at six…' She hesitated, glancing down at her feet. 'But perhaps we should…cool it off for a while.'

'This again…?' With his pulse pounding in panic, he rested his hand on her waist, as if he could physically stop her withdrawing. But lately every time they were together felt as if it might be the last time.

'Look, all this media fuss will die down,' he said, willing her to trust him enough to overlook the gossip. 'I know you're nervous about exposure, but I'm dealing with it. I won't let you down.'

Her trust had been badly damaged in the past, so it was no wonder she struggled to completely trust a man like him: a man with baggage. A man whose life was public property.

But couldn't she see that he'd move mountains to protect her?

She sighed, her eyes on their clasped together hands. 'There have been…whisperings on the ward. I think people recognised me from that photo.' She looked up, her fear and uncertainty etched into her face. 'I still need to work here after you've gone, Andreas.'

Nausea rolled through his gut. She was right— after today, he wouldn't be at work to collaborate with her or to be there for her. He didn't want to leave Nordic Care and leave Clara to the wolves. He wanted to look after her. That was what people did when they cared about someone. That was what

Clara herself did all the time: with her patients, her family, even with Andreas.

Except, just like the rest of his life, her trust in him, the connection they'd shared, seemed to be crumbling before his eyes. Without even trying, he was failing her.

'I'm sorry,' he said simply, because he couldn't make her any promises. He had to leave his career. 'I know it's a lot to take on. Of course you must protect yourself.'

With Prince Henrik's diagnosis, with a change of ruler imminent, the media heat on Andreas was only likely to increase. No matter how much he wanted to protect Clara, he was sickeningly aware that, unless she was part of his life, what he could do to keep her family and her safe and safeguard their privacy was limited.

Maybe that was the solution… But she didn't *want* his help.

Fear laced his blood. He'd dated women in the past who'd ended the relationship because they wanted no part of life in the public eye. He'd hoped Clara was different—that she understood him, saw the role, the stage, the act, for what it was: something he did, not something he was. Desperation for her raced through his blood. He didn't want to lose her over this.

'You know all that stuff,' he said, his voice close to begging, 'The media, the photos, the PR moves— that's not the real me. It's just a role I put on, the same way we put on our roles as doctor and nurse when we put on our white coat and uniform.'

'I know.' She inclined her head, regarding him with sad eyes. 'And I've always understood that you have other priorities beyond me.' Her hand rested on his arm. 'I walked willingly into this affair. This isn't a bid for my share of your attention.'

'And just because I'm leaving here sooner than I planned,' he argued, 'Doesn't mean that I'm walking away from *us*. We can still see each other.'

His teeth ground together with frustration. He was already failing at his career and his royal role. And, by selfishly craving Clara, he'd exposed her to speculation, letting her down too.

His stomach dropped. Maybe he should do the right thing and let her go…

He would hate to drag her name into the press and then have her snubbed or criticised for not fitting some arbitrary mould. In his eyes, she was perfect just as she was.

'I'm just trying to be realistic,' she said. 'We agreed it was temporary.'

'Damn realistic,' he snapped, dragging her into his arms and kissing her, his misery finally spilling over. 'Give me a little longer, *sötnos*.'

He was full-blown begging now, his heart pounding against hers as she looked up at him with uncertainty.

A door below them opened, footsteps echoing on the stairs.

Clara stepped out of his embrace, a guilty look on her face. 'I'll try.'

Casting him one last inscrutable look, she descended the stairs and disappeared. Andreas curled his fingers into fists. He'd always known it would take a special woman to tolerate his life. Since they'd begun their affair, he'd experienced brief flashes of inspiration when he'd wondered if Clara might be that very woman.

But now… Was he failing her? Did he risk hurting her by asking her to stay? A man in his position, with the eyes of the world watching and the weight of a nation on his shoulders—not to mention the self-imposed burden of honouring both his father and his brother as the future of Varborg's monarchy—couldn't afford to be wrong about anything, including Clara.

He couldn't bear to make a mistake. If he wasn't careful, he'd let Clara down. He'd let himself down. And he'd let Oscar down.

None of that was an option.

CHAPTER FIFTEEN

LATER THAT EVENING, shaken from the power of her orgasm, Clara clung to Andreas, certain that she'd never let him go. His groan died against her neck where he'd pressed so many passionate kisses she felt sure he'd leave a mark on her skin.

Not that she cared. The reckless part that was wild for him welcomed a sign of his possession. A reminder that, for a brief time, this connection she'd never felt with anyone else had been real.

He pulled back, slipping from her body, looking down to where she was sprawled on the sofa. This time, they hadn't even made it to the bedroom. Even when they were about to discuss the end of their fling, they couldn't keep their hands off each other.

But Clara was a realist. Their time together was coming to an end. Despite the ache in her heart, and the confusion slashed across Andreas's beautiful face, she smiled up at him sadly.

'It's not over, Clara,' he said defiantly, his breaths gusting. 'Not by a long shot.'

He tucked himself back into his jeans and zipped up.

Close to tears, her blood still thick with endorphins, Clara scooped up her underwear from the floor and wordlessly replaced the garment. She needed to be fully clothed for this talk.

'Maybe not.' She stood and moved away, desperate to escape him and the scent of sex, the cloud of pheromones urging her to keep her mouth shut and get lost in his arms once more. 'But we knew it wasn't going to last for ever. We *agreed*.'

'I understand you're scared for your family's reputation,' he said, his tone that of a coaxing parent for a frightened child, 'But I could protect you, all of you.'

'How?' she asked, incredulous. 'Because, of course I'm scared. My family have been through enough and so have yours. I work here. I still have to face Prince Henrik, and I don't want Mum to have to relive the shame of my father's conviction. But it feels as if it's only a matter of time before it's all dredged up in public.'

'There are vacant properties on the estate.' He reached for her, gripping her upper arms. 'You could all move in until interest in my personal life dies down. The press couldn't get to you there.'

Clara frowned, horrified, her heart cracking that he understood her so little. 'Listen to what you're suggesting. Us moving into a palace property would be confirmation that you and I are involved in some sort of seedy tryst. And my mother and I would still need to leave to go to work and my sister to college.'

'Clara…' He cupped her face and stared into her eyes. 'I have more money than I'll ever know what to do with. I can support you and your family, in-definitely.'

Clara yanked herself free. 'Are you suggesting that I give up my job too? And what—be a kept woman, waiting in some hidden away cottage for your clandestine visits when you have a break in your important schedule or when the royal itch requires scratching?'

'Stop.' His voice was low but authoritative, his scowl the only sign of his fury. 'It wouldn't be like that. I'm not suggesting for ever. I'm just trying to help, because I care about you.'

'I care about you too.' Clara paced out of his reach, suddenly too hot *and* too cold. 'But I told you from the start—I need my independence.'

She levelled him with a defiant stare. 'I watched Mum take second place to my father, quietly toiling away to put food on the table while he chased dream after dream, scheme after scheme, only to put us more and more in debt. I never understood how she could forgive him, time and again. How nothing he did seemed to destroy her love.'

'I'm not your father.' He scrubbed a hand through his already dishevelled hair. 'I'm not trying to steal your independence. I just don't want this to end over one grainy photo online. I thought you understood me, my life, my dreams, the part of me the public don't get to see. I showed you all of me.'

'I *do* understand you.' She rushed back to him because she just couldn't stay away. 'I don't want this to end either.' Hot tears pricked the back of her eyes. The situation was impossible and always had been—a hopeless fantasy.

But, for Clara, it wasn't just fear of exposure. There were other more terrifying feelings making her irrational and confused. She'd opened up to Andreas and become vulnerable in a way she'd never been with another person. She'd told him her most shameful family secrets. She'd worked with him, laid in his arms and held him through his struggles and grief.

Despite all her tough self-talk and caution, all her warnings about holding something back, she'd somehow fallen in love with him. And she was scared, so scared.

As if he knew the tender contents of her heart, he reached for her, roughly tugging her into his arms, pressing his mouth to hers with fierce and desperate possession. Clara embraced the kiss, her tongue surging to meet his, squeezing her eyes tightly shut as if she could block out the rest of the world and just be with him like this: just the two of them, no intrusions, no expectations, no fear.

When they were intimate, everything seemed to make sense. But the minute it was over she couldn't help but see how strongly she was kidding herself. She wasn't the woman for him, not long term. Having him would mean losing her independence. She wouldn't become like her mother, loving a man on whom she couldn't depend. Abandoning the hardworking provider Clara had become out of necessity would not only make her reliant, it would shatter any hope of Andreas and her being equals. She might love him, but if she let go of that hope she would struggle to love and respect herself.

And the longer she stayed, the greater the risk that she'd break when this ended. Wasn't it better to go now, on *her* terms?

They broke apart, panting.

Clara shook her head. 'I can't do it,' she whispered. 'I can't be this needy, frightened version of myself. I can't rely on you, or anyone, don't you see that?' Not when he could never love her in return. It would be too great a sacrifice.

Pain shifted through his eyes. 'Can't or won't? All I'm hearing are excuses. You can still be yourself and want me as I am. I'm not trying to change you, or contain you, or clip your wings. You said you wanted us to be equals, but maybe it's *me* you find wanting.'

Clara shook her head, hot licks of shame flooding her face. He was right: they were similar, both broken, damaged and scarred. Her fear was compounding his because he was scared to embrace the role he'd been born for: scared to fail his nation, his dying father and maybe even his beloved Oscar.

Just then, the room's intercom connected.

'Your Highness, there's been an accident in the Banquet Hall. Someone fell from a ladder while decorating for the Christmas party. Can you come?'

Without hesitation, Andreas marched to the intercom, pressed the connection button and spoke. 'I'll be there. Call an ambulance.'

He rushed to the bedroom and returned seconds later with his medical bag.

'I'll come with you,' Clara said. No matter what their personal issues, they were still a team.

He paused at the door, as if about to point out that her presence at the palace when she was off duty would expose their secret affair, but he said nothing.

Clara shoved aside her fears. She loved him and she couldn't have him. What was a little workplace humiliation compared to that?

The Banquet Hall had been transformed by two enormous Christmas trees, and twinkling festive garlands hung from every column and doorway. The casualty, a woman in her fifties, was surrounded by a small group of concerned staff members.

Clara and Andreas kneeled at her side.

'She's unconscious,' Clara said, feeling for breath.

'There's a pulse,' Andreas replied.

'She's barely breathing,' Clara added, seeing an obvious compound fracture of her lower leg.

Andreas produced a bag and mask from his medical case, which he placed over the woman's mouth and nose, and began rhythmically inflating her lungs with air.

'Can you stabilise her neck?' He glanced at Clara. 'She might have a spinal fracture.'

Clara held the woman's head steady while Andreas continued to inflate her lungs. Their eyes met, their concerns shared. Any movement could destabilise a fractured vertebra. But, until the paramedics arrived with a neck splint, all they had was each other.

'Has an ambulance been called?' Andreas asked the nearby staff in a choked voice.

Several of them nodded.

'Can someone get a clean towel from housekeeping?' he instructed, his face pale and slashed with worry. 'And cover that leg wound, please.'

Clara's throat tightened. Andreas seemed frantic.

'Do you know her name?' Clara whispered, her bruised and battered heart going out to him.

'Kari. She's worked here over twenty years. She's always in charge of the staff Christmas party. I... I've met her grandchildren.'

He clearly felt responsible for this woman.

Clara stared at his anguished face, trying to communicate her support without words. Personally, things between them were horribly uncertain, the emotional divide widening with their mismatched expectations and the things holding them back, but she was still there for him.

'Can we have some privacy, please?' Andreas spoke with authority to the onlookers. 'Jens and Magda, you stay. The rest of you, thank you for your help, but we'll take it from here.'

When they were alone, the two remaining staff members having moved a short distance away, Andreas swallowed, his expression pained. 'Thank you for being here. I appreciate your support.'

'It was an accident,' Clara whispered, knowing that he would torture himself if something serious happened to this member of his staff, a woman he'd known most of his life. She knew him so well, this Viking of hers. And the last thing Clara wanted was to add to his burdens. Maybe she could hold on a little longer—lock up her heart and give their relationship some more time until he'd come to terms with the changes in his life.

But, oh, the risk was massive...

Kari stirred, regaining consciousness. She groaned in pain, trying to swipe away the mask covering her face.

'Kari, hold still,' Andreas said. 'You've had a fall, bumped your head.'

While Clara tried to keep the casualty immobilised, someone returned with a clean towel and Andreas set aside the Ambu bag to cover the lower leg fracture, which had punctured the skin and would be prone to infection if left exposed.

The paramedics arrived with oxygen, a hard collar and back board. While Clara fitted a nasal oxygen catheter in place, Andreas explained what had happened to the paramedics. The ambulance crew fitted the neck brace and back board, and administered some painkillers. Andreas and Clara helped out by splinting Kari's fractured leg so she could be transported to hospital.

'I'm going with her in the ambulance,' Andreas said distractedly as the paramedics lifted Kari onto a stretcher.

Clara nodded, their break-up set aside for now. 'Will you call me later? Let me know how she is?'

He nodded and met her stare, the things they'd left unsaid hovering between them. His accusation from earlier reverberated in her head.

Maybe it's me you find wanting...

Clara swallowed, desperate to hold him. There was nothing lacking in him; the deficiency lay with *her*. She'd never been in love before and she was terrified to love him openly, freely, honestly because of how vulnerable she'd be.

But they weren't alone and he had enough to deal with.

As the paramedics wheeled Kari away, Clara watched Andreas leave, every part of her aching with love for him. She made her way back to the guest wing, her resolve strengthening. She would give him a little more time, perhaps until Christmas, but then she *would* walk away. She would bury her feelings, because loving him changed nothing. If she became the person making all of the sacrifices, her love would never survive. Better to be alone and heartbroken than be on the wrong side of an unequal relationship.

After all, being self-sufficient was second nature.

CHAPTER SIXTEEN

A WEEK LATER, after a night shift at the palace, Clara returned home, her plan to indulge in some well-earned self-care—a long soak in the bath, painting her fingernails and styling her hair in an elegant up-do.

Tonight was the staff Christmas party and she wanted to look her best for Andreas. They'd only managed to see each other twice since Kari's accident. Both times, he'd sneaked Clara into the palace and they'd made love as if it was the last time, and had carefully avoided any talk of breaking up. The cracks in Clara's heart had deepened each time, but Christmas was only two weeks away.

In the bathroom, Clara removed the contents of a brown paper bag from the pharmacy, a flutter of nervous anticipation in her stomach: gold nail polish, volumising hairspray…and a pregnancy test. She could no longer ignore the fact that her period was three days late when she was unfailingly regular; her breasts were sore and she was more tired than usual. She took the test and filled the bath, pouring in some scented bubble bath to take her mind off the little white plastic stick.

What would she do if it turned positive? More importantly, how would Andreas react?

She stripped off her clothes, her gaze drawn to the test, which already boasted two pink lines: positive. Her hand fell protectively to her abdomen, her heart thumping wildly. Those two pink lines changed *everything*. She was pregnant with Andreas's baby.

After her bath, she dressed in the green vintage dress she'd borrowed from Alma, fitting matching glass earrings with trembling hands. She stared at her reflection, half in awe of the woman staring back, half panic-stricken. The dress complemented her skin tone, so she appeared radiant, and there was a new strength to the set of her posture, as if she was already inhabiting her new role as a mother.

She was adamant—the baby's happiness would be paramount.

Her phone pinged with an incoming text from Andreas.

Can't wait to see you tonight.

Clara blinked back tears, refusing to ruin her mascara. Now she had bigger issues than when to walk away from the man she loved but could never have. Now she'd have to tell him about the pregnancy—tonight.

She sat on the bed and typed a reply.

Me too.

Then she deleted it and threw down her phone. That wasn't entirely true. Part of her was dreading their conversation. What would Andreas expect of her now? Would he want shared custody of their child or would he be forced constitutionally to disown the baby? After all, they weren't married.

Nauseated, Clara slipped her feet into her heels and fastened the buckles, her mind racing with the many implications. She'd have to pull back on the hours she worked as her pregnancy progressed. She'd need to take maternity leave, and then what? There was an excellent state-run crèche near Nordic Care that her colleagues talked about but would Andreas approve? Would he demand a private facility beyond Clara's budget?

And what about their child's privacy? Would simply being related to Andreas make the baby a target? How would Clara keep their child safe and keep her independence? What if, as a prince, Andreas's custodial rights to their child surpassed her own? What if he wanted to raise their child as a prince or princess without Clara? What if he made all the decisions and she was powerless?

Standing, she smoothed her palms over the silky fabric of the dress. She wouldn't allow any harm befall her child. Her mother had raised two daughters as good as alone, and Clara could do the same. She would protect this baby with her life and provide for its every need, with Andreas's input or without it.

'I'm glad you're feeling better,' Andreas said to Kari at the Christmas party. 'Thank you for the festive transformation. The hall looks magical.'

The room glittered with a thousand lights and was bedecked with two enormous Christmas trees. That Kari was there after all her hard work, albeit on crutches, her broken leg in plaster, raised his dampened spirits.

Why hadn't Clara replied to his text?

They hadn't raised the subject of ending their fling since the night of Kari's accident. The past week had passed in a busy blur. Clara had taken extra shifts at the hospital to cover staff illness and Andreas had been occupied with a state visit to Finland and with preparations for this evening's festivities. He'd even supervised the renovation of his new suite of rooms. He was determined to stamp his own mark on ruling the principality, and the first step was feeling comfortable enough to make the role his own.

His stomach twisted in recognition of how he'd decorated with Clara in mind. Foolish, given his inability to see beyond the life-changing events of the next few months. But, if he could just hold onto her and protect her a little longer until the intense media interest died down, then he could think straight.

Andreas moved on to welcome another group, glancing at Prince Henrik, who was doing the same thing on the other side of the hall. His father had insisted on being present, and for now showed good energy levels, but Andreas was determined to keep an eye on him.

The Cronstedt family couldn't exist without the hundreds of people filling the ballroom, their tireless work behind the scenes as vital as the prince's ribbon-cutting ceremonies, diplomatic speeches and weekly audiences with Varborg's Prime Minister.

Speaking of vital…was Clara there?

Discreetly, he scanned the room before asking after the palace administration manager's small children. His jaw ached from smiling, his reserves of small talk running low. He needed to see Clara, to know that he could convince her to stay his for a little while longer.

He'd just moved on from a conversation with the housekeeping team when he spied Clara talking to her fellow nurses and the prince's personal physician. Even though the other doctor was in his fifties and happily married, a white-hot shaft of jealousy pierced Andreas's chest as he watched her smile up at the man.

She looked radiant and seemed so carefree, so Clara.

When was the last time she'd smiled at him that carefree way? Was his desperation for her hurting her, crushing her sense of independence? Would he fail her if he didn't let her go soon? But every time he tried to imagine being without her he rushed the other way, clinging tighter.

With everything going on in his life, they seemed to have lurched from one crisis to another, the only highlights the blissful moments of intimacy they managed to snatch.

Something jolted in his chest as he watched her. Were those moments of intimacy enough? Clara deserved more. She deserved peace of mind, security and privacy. She deserved a man who was focussed only on her, a man who'd protect her and never fail her. These were all things Andreas longed to give her but, because of his position, couldn't guarantee.

At his side, Nils spoke. 'Your Highness...'

Andreas came to. He'd been staring, mesmerised by her, as he'd been from the start. Deviating from the planned route around the room, Andreas walked her way.

'I wanted to thank you all personally,' he said to the entire group, 'For taking such good care of Prince Henrik. As you can see—' he tilted his head in his father's direction '—he's feeling much restored tonight, and that's down to all of you.'

Clara hadn't yet met his eye, and he couldn't be seen to favour one staff member over any other, not when gossip had already spread since the night she'd attended Kari's accident by his side.

If it were down to him, he'd whisk her away to his new bedroom and make love to her all night until he convinced her that she wanted him, the real Andreas, more than she wanted her career, her independence and her anonymity.

At last, he allowed his gaze briefly to settle on Clara. It hurt to look at her beauty and not touch her. But, on closer inspection, she appeared pale. Was she unwell, or had she reached her decision and would soon tell him it was over?

Sensing Nils's discomfort, because Andreas was on a tight schedule to talk to at least half of the staff, he prepared to walk away, panic surging through him. Then, at the last second, she looked up, looked right at him and the party around him seemed to stutter to a stop.

He stared hard, pouring all his feelings for this woman into his eye contact so she would see how much he cared, how much he wanted her, how he wished he could be just a man she was free to care for in return, without risk.

She looked away.

Crestfallen, Andreas was spurred into action. He plastered on his smile and moved on to greet the next group, but not before he instructed Nils, 'Bring her to me at the end of the festivities—the Blue Room.'

All he had to do was make it through the party. It was going to be a very long night.

For the rest of the evening, Clara watched Andreas from afar, a sense of déjà vu chilling her to the bone. The first time they'd danced in that very hall, she'd known that he was a natural born leader. He'd been torn between the role he'd trained for and the role that was his birth right, because he lived with deep unresolved guilt over his brother's death.

But his royal status shone as people vied for his attention. He was a prince. He had it all—charisma, kindness and empathy. How could she avoid falling head over heels in love with a man like him?

Swallowing the lump in her throat, Clara paced to the window of the Blue Room, the place where she'd been instructed by Nils to meet Andreas. This was the room where they'd negotiated their fling. How fitting that this would also be the scene of the conversation to come.

Clara stared out at the illuminated balcony and beyond to the vast, snow-capped mountain range that separated Varborg from the rest of Scandinavia. It was a stunning night. Crisp, cloudless skies were an inky blank canvas for the multitude of stars.

Clara's vision blurred, fear a metallic taste in her mouth. How would he take her news? How would she tell him that she was carrying his baby and still hold on to her heart? How would she find the strength to walk away? Because she must, and sooner than she'd promised. Now that there was the baby's happiness and safety to consider, she needed to be stronger than ever.

Just then, the sky above the mountain tops began to dance with the magical wonder of the Aurora Borealis, or northern lights, the green light streaking the blackness. Clara watched, mesmerised. There was magic here, in Andreas's world. But the clock was about to strike midnight and she couldn't stay.

A sound in the room behind Clara drew her attention. She spun to find Andreas observing her, his face dark with repressed need.

'You look breath-taking tonight,' he said.

Clara swallowed, her pulse a painful thud in her throat.

'More so than nature's display outside, even.' His stare latched to hers, but he didn't step closer or try to touch her. 'Green suits you, *sötnos*. You should wear it more often.'

'Thank you. This dress belonged to my mother.' She glanced down at the simple silky sheath. 'I'm recycling.'

She looked up and swept her gaze over him from head to toe, the ache in her chest sharpening at his refined splendour. 'You look very regal, every inch the prince you were born to be.'

A small frown pinched his eyebrows together. 'And yet here, with you, I'm just Andreas.'

Clara nodded, her heart cracking open a little wider. Just because she'd fallen in love with him didn't mean that she could have him as her own. He needed a woman content to exist in his shadow and, while Clara might tolerate that in public for appearances' sake, it would destroy her to know that they weren't equals in their private lives—to know that she loved him desperately, but that he didn't love her.

But how could they ever be true equals? He was a prince, a ruler, and she was a penniless nobody in a borrowed dress.

'I need to tell you something,' she said, cautiously stepping closer, because even when she was ready to walk away she wanted him with terrifying desperation.

'Okay.' His frown deepened.

Clara raised her chin, resolute. 'I'm pregnant.'

His body seemed to sag with relief, excitement

in his eyes. He almost stumbled as he lurched for her, gripping her arms.

'Are you sure?' His pulse ticked furiously in his neck.

Clara nodded. 'My period was three days late so I did a test this afternoon. It was positive, but obviously it's very early days.'

She shrugged, her own joy at the news diminished, because in the deepest part of her soul she'd dared to imagine that, if she ever had a child, it would be with a man who loved her and who she could love freely in return.

But this wasn't a fairy tale. This was reality. Ahead lay confusion and doubt for the future and fear that her parental rights would be restrained because of her baby's paternity.

With his face wreathed in delight, Andreas hauled her into his arms. Clara rested her head against his crisp white shirt, against the soothing thud of his heart. She closed her eyes, dragging in the scent of him, fighting tears.

'That's wonderful news.' He pulled back, his stare swooping to her flat stomach. 'Are you feeling okay?'

She nodded numbly. 'I'm fine, Andreas. A little tired, perhaps.'

'Do you want to sit while we talk?' he asked, clearly still dazed.

Clara shook her head. 'I wanted you to know straight away, but we don't have to sort everything out right now.' She needed more time to think things through.

Doubt flashed in his sparking eyes for a split second before he rallied. 'What's there to sort out? You're carrying a Cronstedt prince or princess. I'm going to be a father.'

His awestruck grin made her vision blur. She hated being the one to burst his bubble. 'I'm glad that you're happy.' She winced and ducked her head. 'But the prince-princess thing doesn't count. We're not married. I'm just an ordinary woman.'

Andreas laughed, clutching her back to his chest. 'A hundred years ago that might have mattered, but today my heir is my heir. Besides,' he said, 'We'll *get* married.'

Clara swallowed, dread sliding through her veins. 'Just like that—you decide and I have no say or rights? Don't you think you should ask me what *I* want?'

She might as well be a brood mare.

All her greatest fears rolled in like storm clouds in the sky. *He* was the important one in this relationship. *He* had all the power. Was she meekly to agree to his sterile marriage proposal, give up her career and simply exist as a royal appendage, too lovesick to question the arrangement?

'I'm sorry.' He gripped her shoulders, peering at her with confusion. 'What *do* you want? I assumed that you'd be overjoyed by this news, but you must also be in shock.'

'I *am* happy,' Clara said, a massive part of her,

the part that loved him and ached for a ridiculous fantasy, feeling anything but. 'But…there's so much to think about. I want us to raise this child together, but we shouldn't rush this conversation. Let's take a few days to come to terms with the news and then we can discuss a way forward.'

Once her shock wore off, maybe she'd have the strength to tell him how she felt about him.

Andreas's expression darkened. 'There is only *one* way forward, Clara. I'm a Cronstedt. My child, *our* child, will one day rule Varborg. I'm sorry, but there's no getting around that.'

'I understand.' Clara shook her head, which was fuzzy with confusion, her heart sore with grief. 'But that's a separate issue. I don't want some sort of pragmatic royal marriage.'

She might have felt differently about the institution if he'd loved her, if he'd proposed in some romantic way rather than with ruthless practicality. But she'd never once envisioned being trapped in a loveless marriage, a relationship in name only, for show when the cameras were rolling or to give their child a sense of legitimacy.

'Then we'll live together,' he stated, adamant. 'Raise our child together. It's unconventional for my family, but I'll make it all right. After all, I plan on modernisation. What's more modern than co-habitation and co-parenting?'

'You're not hearing me, Andreas,' she said, her stomach twisted into knots with grief. 'I can't live like this, the way you do.'

Not if she couldn't have all of him, including his heart. The civilised, unconventional relationship he proposed would be doomed from the start. She'd be the one making all the sacrifices, without even gaining the reward of his love in return. She'd be just like her mother: loving a man who couldn't possibly care as deeply for her; forced to sacrifice her career, her independence, to put his needs first; vulnerable, her options limited because they'd made a child together, a child she would always prioritise above herself.

'I can't lose everything that I am,' she continued, trying to keep her voice even. 'My job, my independence, my autonomy.'

'You can still have those things and be with me, Clara. I'll take care of you and our child. Protect you both. Support you always. I won't let either of you down.' He frowned, disbelief entering his eyes. 'Unless it's *me* you don't want…'

His voice was flat, but there was a question in the last word, a question that split Clara's heart in two. She held her hand over her mouth to hold in a sob. She wanted him so badly she was crushed by the weight of her desire. But this was no longer about what *she* wanted. It was time to be realistic. To set aside this fantasy and focus on making a secure life for their child, who would never have to grow up too quickly, the way they'd both had to.

'You once said that we don't always get what we want,' she whispered, wishing she believed in dreams, wishing she could escape into his magical world, wishing he could love her as deeply as she loved him. 'That sometimes we must be something others need us to be.'

He frowned, staring as if carved from stone.

She faltered. But she needed to be strong for all of them—herself, Andreas and the baby.

'You need to be Prince Andreas Cronstedt,' she said, sweeping her eyes over his immaculate suit, and his tie bearing the royal crest. 'You need to rule Varborg, because that's who you were born to be.'

'How two-dimensional I sound—a cardboard cut-out.' Disappointment dimmed his stare. He clenched his jaw and stood a little taller. 'And what do *you* need?'

Desperately trying to hold in her tears, to stand her ground and not reach for him, Clara exhaled a shuddering breath. 'I need to be a mother.'

He nodded once. 'And us?'

'I'm sorry,' Clara said, tears finally spilling over her eyelids to land on her cheeks. 'I'm so sorry. I can't.'

Clara fled, finally giving herself over to the body-racking sobs once she was safely ensconced in the back of a taxi and speeding into the night.

CHAPTER SEVENTEEN

THREE DAYS LATER, Andreas ducked his head as he alighted from the House of Cronstedt jet, the bitterly cold wind stinging his face. He descended the plane's metal staircase and slid into the back seat of his car beside Nils.

He'd been forced to keep his engagement, a visit to Oslo, but now that he was home, now that he'd given her as much space as he could tolerate, he wanted only one thing: Clara.

But she didn't want him.

He scowled at his reflection in the car's window. It was dark out, after eleven p.m., and his mood was as black as the landscape. Clara's dismissal and lack of faith in him the night of the Christmas party had stung worse than any pain he'd ever known. Nothing had felt right since he'd allowed her to run away, as if all the colour had leached out of the world.

He balled his hands into fists, failure choking him. His baby was smaller than a pea, but he'd already broken his word and let his child and Clara down. He'd been so wary of failing her as he'd failed Oscar that he'd said the wrong things and pushed her further away, given up too easily. Just as he hadn't fought hard enough for Oscar, he hadn't fought hard enough for Clara; hadn't told her that he loved her and begged her to stay.

And the price of those mistakes crushed him. He missed the sound of her laughter, the scent of her skin and the tiny gem twinkling in her nose, like her own personal star. He missed her passion, her massive heart and the way she made him twice the man he was alone.

The car pulled up at the palace and Andreas stalked inside. He would go for a swim, do length after length after length until he collapsed with exhaustion. Maybe then he'd know what to do, how to change her mind and fix this.

'Your Highness,' Møller said, appearing from the shadows. 'Prince Henrik requests an audience, sir.'

'Is the prince unwell, Møller?'

'No, sir.'

'Very well.'

Andreas found his father in his library, behind the great slab of a desk that had once seemed vast and intimidating to Andreas the boy. But now he saw it for what it was—just a functional piece of furniture.

'You wanted to see me, Pappa.'

Prince Henrik stood and joined Andreas near the fire, a sheaf of documents in his hand.

'Take a seat, son.'

Andreas folded himself onto an arm chair opposite his father.

'Everything is finalised.' The prince tapped the folder that contained the state funeral plans for

Prince Henrik: Operation Aurora. 'A copy for your final approval.'

Andreas nodded, taking the folder and then staring into the flames. He respected his father's wishes for the funeral. That didn't make his dying any easier to bear.

'You are an inspiration, Pappa,' he said, his voice strangled with emotion. 'I'll try to do you proud. You have my word on that.'

Especially when, despite being a doctor, he could do so little for his father now. But, when he thought of the future, Clara was always at his side. What if, without her, he would never be whole?

'I did things my way, just as you will do things yours,' the prince said, walking to his drinks cabinet and pouring two tumblers of Torv, Varborg's finest whisky. 'Varborg will be lucky to have you as its ruler.'

Startled by his father's declaration, Andreas took the offered glass. He'd always seen his father as a proud, emotionally distant but otherwise honourable man. Could Clara have been right? Had Andreas's guilt and grief over Oscar blinded him to the truth? Should he have confronted his demons and spoken to his father sooner?

The prince took a seat. 'My decisions weren't always the right ones. We are all human, after all. After your mother died, I worried that I gave you too much freedom. I missed her so terribly, and she'd made me promise I would try to give both our boys as normal an upbringing as possible. It wasn't always feasible with Oscar,' his father said, sipping his drink. 'I had to prepare him for the reality of his situation, but with you… I tried my best. And look what you've achieved.'

Prince Henrik glanced his way. 'I am incredibly proud of you, Doctor Cronstedt.'

Andreas held his breath. 'Even when it should have been Oscar sitting here with you today, discussing the succession?'

Prince Henrik frowned. 'Life doesn't work like that. There are no guarantees. We play with the hand we've been dealt.'

Andreas looked down at his hand wrapped around the crystal tumbler, his knuckles white. He was going to be a father—time to be the man his child would need. 'I want you to know that I fought with everything I had to save Oscar. I just wish I could have done more.'

The panic flared in his chest, as if he was back inside that crushed vehicle.

'Of course you did. You're a doctor,' the prince said. 'You've saved countless lives.'

Andreas faced his father. 'Except I couldn't save the most important person to me, to our family, to Varborg.'

The older man stared, a rare display of emotion shifting over his expression. 'I could have lost you both that day. I've read the official inquiry into the accident. I know what you did to try and save your brother. You were incredibly brave and fearless and determined. *No one* could have done more.'

Andreas swallowed, his throat too tight to take a sip of whisky. 'I blamed myself for a long time.'

'I'm sure, but no one else blames you,' his father said. 'You are a credit to me and to Varborg. I should have told you that before today. Time to lay Oscar to rest, perhaps, and live *your* life.'

'How…?' Andreas's voice broke.

Prince Henrik tilted his head, compassion in his eyes. 'The mark of a life well-lived is that you have far fewer regrets than blessings. I was blessed with a meaningful role, marrying the love of my life and with my two sons. What more can a man ask?'

Andreas stared ahead, wondering if it could be as simple as minimising regret. Could he honour his brother, his family, his nation, by chasing what he needed to be happy?

'Pappa,' Andreas said eventually, 'I have something to tell you. Another blessing for the tally— you're going to be a grandfather.'

Prince Henrik smiled, nodding his head sagely. 'Indeed, another blessing. Congratulations.'

Andreas's heart skipped a beat, the expectant flutter of excitement, a certainty that if he could win back Clara anything was possible. 'Don't you want to know who the mother is?' he asked, wishing he would one day be able to count as many blessings as his father.

Prince Henrik shrugged. 'Does it matter? If you've found love, that's all I care about. Because this job—and it's best to think of it that way if you can—will be so much easier if you have someone you love at your side.'

Andreas knocked back the whisky in a single swallow, pulled out his phone and checked his schedule for the next day. He had a visit to the local army barracks that he couldn't reschedule, but then he would find Clara and tell her that he loved her.

Because he *had* found love with a woman who was his equal in every way that mattered. He didn't want to spend another day without her, so he'd have to persuade her that their fears—his that he'd let her down and hers that she couldn't be independent—weren't good enough reasons for them to be apart.

Clara opened the door of her family's home, kicked off her shoes and barely made it to the sofa before she collapsed in a wretched heap of exhaustion. She should head up to the shower, peel off her creased Nordic Care uniform and hide under the spray until she'd cried out, but she couldn't seem to move.

Was it possible to feel so broken, but still have her heart beat? Was it because it beat for him, Andreas? Did it know better than her head what was right for her?

Reaching for a beautiful, hand-made crocheted throw her mother had made while recovering from her cancer treatment, Clara pulled it over herself and curled into a foetal ball. Would she ever feel warm again?

Alma appeared from the kitchen with two mugs

of hot chocolate. 'You look frozen. They say there's more snow due tonight.'

She placed the mugs on a side table, sat on the sofa and reached for Clara's foot, tugging it into her lap so she could massage Clara's aching instep.

'My first job was waitressing,' Alma said, telling the story Clara had heard before. 'I would come home from work in tears, my feet were so sore.'

'You're so strong, Mama,' Clara whispered, trying not to cry. 'What's your secret?'

Alma made a dismissive sound. 'I'm a woman. We're born strong. Look at you, for instance.'

Clara smiled, but her eyes burned with unshed tears. If only she'd been strong enough to resist Andreas. But no, she would never wish away meeting him. Falling in love had given her the most precious of gifts: her baby. *Their* baby.

'But strength comes from being yourself and being happy,' Alma continued. 'I've always taught you and Freja to unapologetically love yourselves.'

Clara sighed. 'Being happy is…complicated. And what happens if you love someone else, if their happiness feels more important than your own?'

She'd seen Alma's love for Lars, how one-sided it had been. How soul-destroying it must have felt to be so let down by him.

Alma released Clara's foot and took a good look at her daughter, understanding dawning. 'Then the key is finding someone who loves you like that in return.'

'Exactly.' Clara offered up her other foot for a rub,

bombarded by the image of Andreas's expression when she'd rejected him. 'Complicated.'

'Is this about your father?' Alma asked, working her magic on Clara's foot. 'You know he wasn't always the man he became in the end. We were crazy about each other, loved each other passionately for many years. We made two beautiful and kind daughters before we lost our way as a couple.'

Clara stilled, her heart pounding rapidly. It was hard to imagine her parents young and madly in love. 'So you don't regret loving him, despite the way it turned out in the end?'

Alma frowned. 'I know Lars let you down when he left. I wish he'd been there for you and Freja. What *I* regret is that you took on too much responsibility when I got sick,' Alma continued, peering at Clara a little too closely for comfort. 'You were barely an adult. Lars and I should have protected you better. But I'm fine now. You don't need to worry about me. You have to live your own life.'

Clara smiled sadly certain that, by leaving Andreas the night of the Christmas party when she'd been too overwhelmed to think straight, she'd walked away from her only chance to feel happy.

'I made my choices, as did Lars,' Alma Lund continued, as if sensing the depth of Clara's despair. 'I've lived with them, made more choices. That's all any of us can do. We can't hold ourselves back from love in case it fades or turns sour or dies. And you shouldn't let my choices, your father's choices, stop you from making your own. That's not the independent woman I know.'

Tears seeped from the corners of Clara's eyes and tracked into her hair at her temples. She was so sick of crying, so tired of feeling empty. She wanted to live, to feel young and vibrantly alive, the way she did with Andreas.

'I *am* in love, Mama,' she whispered. 'And I'm having his baby.'

Alma gasped, tears of joy glittering in her eyes. 'And does he love you?'

Clara shrugged, her heart a rock. 'I don't know. I couldn't tell him how I feel and he's…kind of preoccupied with important stuff.'

Alma snorted. 'Nothing is more important than love, Clara. You will soon know that when my grandbaby is born.'

Clara smiled indulgently, thinking about Andreas. Ruling Varborg *was* pretty important.

'You must tell him how you feel,' Alma said. 'You are so much stronger than me. There's nothing you can't do, including being honest with this man. If he's worthy of your love, then tell him, see where love takes you. It will be an adventure you'll never regret, even if it isn't perfect or doesn't last for ever.'

'You're right.' Clara sniffed, her tears drying up. 'I *should* tell him. He likes my outspoken streak.'

'See? I like this man already.' Alma smiled. 'Let's have him over for dinner.'

Clara laughed. She couldn't wait to see the look

on Alma's face when Prince Andreas walked through the door.

Except he was just Andreas, and if she ever met him Alma Lund would see that. But only if Clara stopped feeling sorry for herself and told him that she loved him—the *real* him.

'A grandbaby.' Alma clapped her hands excitedly and reached for her knitting bag. 'I can't believe it.'

'Are you staying up?' Clara said, shrugging off the throw and heading for the shower. 'I might head to bed. I'm exhausted.'

'You get some rest. I'll be up in a while. I just want to make a start on baby clothes.'

Clara smiled fondly as she plodded upstairs. She didn't have the heart to tell her mother that her grandbaby was going to be a prince or princess. It wouldn't make a blind bit of difference to the home knits.

As she lay in bed, she made the baby a promise. Andreas deserved to know that she loved him, that he was her first and only choice; that, for her and for their baby, he was the best man possible.

CHAPTER EIGHTEEN

THE METAL BARRIER was icy-cold. Clara clung tightly, refusing to relinquish her spot at the front of the waiting crowd. Varborg's dashing heir to the throne was a popular man. If one more onlooker screamed his name in Clara's ear, she was going to lose it.

None of these people knew the real him. They only saw the two-dimensional version, the sexy Viking who lived in a palace, whereas Clara knew his passions and his dreams. She knew the feel of his skin and the shape of his smile. She knew the rhythm of his heart and the deepest regrets of his soul.

She loved him, pure and simple, and she needed him to know.

But maybe she'd left it too late…

The doors at the front of the army barracks opened and the waiting crown roared, even before Andreas appeared. Clara held her hands over her ears, scared that the noise would somehow hurt their baby, but her eyes were glued to Andreas as he emerged.

Her legs trembled with desire. He was wearing his dress uniform, the navy-blue coat trimmed with white epaulettes making his broad shoulders appear wider, the row of medals on his chest testament to the calibre of man he was. He smiled a movie-star smile, waving at the crowd before shaking the hands of the officials lined up between the exit and his car idling a short distance away.

The people sharing Clara's section of barrier screamed his name and waved Varborg's flag, clamouring for a closer glimpse of him, perhaps a wave, a direct smile.

Clara knew exactly what they wanted because she clamoured too. Those things were just as precious to her, perhaps more so, because she loved Andreas the man, and the fans out there in the cold only admired and respected Andreas the prince.

Leaning over the barrier, she willed him to look her way. One look in his eyes and she'd know if he'd already moved on and made practical arrangements for their baby, but forgotten Clara. The woman beside her screamed his name in earnest. For a moment, it looked as if he might head straight to his car after passing along the military line-up, but then he spied a little girl holding a small posy of flowers and he approached the crowd-control barrier, stooping to share a few words with the lucky child.

Clara held her breath, tears prickling the backs of her eyes. He was going to make such a wonderful father and she hadn't given him a chance to be ecstatic about her news. She'd ruined it with her fear that he could never love her back. But loving someone didn't make a person weak, it made them strong. Love was the most powerful force in the universe. It made humans do extraordinary things, such as Andreas fighting to save the brother he loved. She didn't have to fear her love for him, she just had to embrace it and let it work its magic.

'Prince Andreas!' Clara's neighbour cried as he worked his way along the row, shaking hands, answering questions, smiling for his admirers.

Clara froze, her stare tracing every inch of him. He had shadows under his eyes, as if he hadn't slept. She wanted to hold him so badly, she hooked her feet up on the edge of the barrier and leaned closer as he approached.

Andreas reached for the hand of the woman at Clara's side, his stare flitting over the crowd behind as he tried to acknowledge as many onlookers as possible. The woman began to gush, telling him how much she admired him, how handsome he looked in his uniform, how sorry she was to hear that his father was terminal...

The noise around Clara dimmed to silence. He was close enough to touch now. If she just reached out...

He turned his head, saw her and froze. 'Clara...'

Clara blinked, her eyes hot with tears. She stared, seeing in his beautiful eyes that she still had a chance to tell him how she felt. That it wasn't too late.

Snapped from his shock at seeing her, Andreas removed his hand from Clara's persistent neighbour's grasp. He gave Nils some instructions, his eyes never leaving Clara's.

Her heart soared with excitement. She would go

to him, tell him that she loved the real him, and all his other versions, and ask him to give her another chance. Tell him that with her he would always be safe to be himself. Just then, Clara felt a weight slumping against her shoulder, sliding down, shoving her sideways.

She dragged her eyes from Andreas and watched with horror as the frantic fan next to her slid to the floor in a faint. Clara spread her arms wide, trying to push back the crowd, to stop them from trampling the poor woman to death. But it was like trying to hold back the tide with her bare hands. Trying not to panic for her own safety and that of the baby, Clara stooped at her neighbour's side and held her head to protect it from hitting the ground.

There was a rush of movement, the barrier parting, soldiers shouting, the crowd around her clearing. Andreas appeared, kneeling opposite her, his expression one of frenzied concern.

'Are you okay?' he asked, his arms spread wide to protect Clara and the fan from any stray onlookers.

Clara nodded, desperate to touch him, to kiss him and beg him to hear her out. 'She's fainted.'

Clara removed her scarf and propped it between the woman's head and the cold, hard ground. Andreas felt for a pulse and instructed one of the nearby soldiers to lift the woman's legs to return the blood back to her head. Within seconds, Nils had organised a circle of soldiers, a human barrier to stand guard around her, the casualty and Andreas.

The woman stirred, coming to. 'Prince Andreas...'

she said, sounding delirious that her rescuer was the man she'd come there to see.

'You're okay,' he said. 'You just fainted. We're going to get you some help. Just relax.'

The woman tried to sit up, sliding a hand through her hair to ensure she looked her best. Clara smiled up at him; she could relate.

'You're here,' he said to Clara, as if dazed.

Clara nodded. 'We need to finish that conversation.'

As paramedics arrived and began tending to the woman, Andreas took Clara's hand, his grip determined. 'Come with me, *sötnos.*'

He stood, helping Clara to her feet, and Nils urged them towards the car.

Hope surged in Clara's chest as she climbed into the black car with the tinted windows, her head light, as if she too might pass out.

Andreas dragged Clara into the back of the car, his adrenaline so high, his head spun.

'Tell me you're okay,' he pleaded, his hands on her shoulders, holding her distant so he could scour every inch of her for evidence of trauma.

'I'm fine.' She smiled. 'A little jealous at the effect you have on women, but apart from that, I'm good.'

Andreas crushed her in his arms, his sense of humour abandoned. He pressed his lips to her temple and breathed in the scent of her hair. 'I've never been more scared than when I saw you go down in the middle of that crowd. I almost ripped apart that barrier with my bare hands to get to you.'

He pulled back, his stare flitting over her face to make sure she was real. 'And the baby's okay?' He glanced down at her stomach, as if he had X-ray vision.

Clara rested her hand there. 'I think so.'

'Clara…' His voice broke, his face crumpling with anguish. 'I love you.'

She'd come to him. That had to mean something. Perhaps she was ready to give him another chance. He slid his hands from her shoulders to cup her face. 'I love you, and I need you, and I want you.'

Speechless, she blinked, her eyes shining with tears.

'I've tried to give you some time. But I can't take it any more. I need you to understand how deeply I've fallen in love with you and how I'll do anything, *anything*, to have you in my life.'

She gripped his wrists, and for a panicked second he thought she would tug his hands away, but she didn't. The move reminded him of their first meeting, their first kiss.

But he had to say everything he needed to say.

'I know the idea of my life is hard for you, but I'll abdicate if I have to. You don't have to give up your career. I wouldn't change a single wonderful thing about you. Or we can work together,' he rushed on. 'I want to build a dedicated rehabilitation hospital for wounded veterans. You can help me. We can build something to be proud of together—equals.'

'Andreas…' she whispered, tears spilling over her eyelids.

'We can raise our baby together,' he said, brushing the tears away with his thumbs and pressing kisses to her damp cheeks. 'We don't have to marry if it's not what you want, but I'll spend every day of my life being there for you, as you deserve. You and our child will always be my first priority. You'll always be able to rely on me.'

'Andreas, I love you too,' she said.

Andreas did a double-take, staring at her mouth in case he'd misheard.

She smiled and his heart soared with hope. 'I love you. I came today to see you, to tell you. I should have told you the night of the Christmas party.'

Still a little confused, he shook his head. 'You do?'

'Of course. I love you.' She laughed with joy. 'The real you and all your other amazing versions—doctor, ruler, prince. I've known for ages, but I just got scared. I've never been in love before. I couldn't handle how vulnerable it made me feel. But it also makes me strong. Loving you means I can face anything life might throw at us.'

She cupped his face, her fingers curling into his hair. 'I'm sorry about the things I said. How I made you feel inadequate. But my fear was about *me*, about *my* hang-ups, not about you. You're everything I want. You're not my father, you're *you*. That will always be enough for me. I choose *you*. Even if there was no baby, no throne, no palace—'

'Palaces,' he interrupted, his heart as light as a feather. But she needed to know what she was entering into.

'Palaces,' she continued, completely unfazed, 'I would still choose you. Because I know *you*. You're a man of passion and integrity. Varborg is lucky to have you. *I* would be lucky to have you.'

Andreas dragged her close and kissed her. Joy spread through his body as their lips met, melded together then parted.

'Clara,' he said, pulling back to stare into her beautiful eyes, eyes that shone with love for him. 'I want you to know that you can trust me. I won't hurt you. I'll love you and respect you and cherish you every day. Even if our relationship fails for some reason—and I'll devote my life to ensuring that it doesn't—I'll still love you, still respect you, still take care of you.'

She laughed, pressed her lips to his, pushed him back against the seat and sat astride his lap. 'No, *I'll* take care of *you*.'

Andreas grinned up at her, his hands gripping her hips. 'We can settle the details later, *sötnos*. All that matters to me is that you're mine.'

She nodded, her stare bright with resolve, with her signature passion, with love. This time when they kissed Andreas held onto her for all he was worth. He would never stifle or try to change this incredible woman. He would worship her, subtly care for her behind her back and love her.

'Where are we going?' she asked, pulling back from their kiss to glance out of the window.

Andreas unbuttoned her coat and slid his hands inside her jumper. He needed the feel of her soft skin under his palms, telling him she was real, she was *his*.

'Bed, I hope,' he said, tugging her mouth back to his. 'Or, if you prefer, my giant bath tub, or wherever you fancy… As long as I'm inside you, I don't care.'

She pressed kisses down the side of his neck while her fingers tackled the metal buttons of his uniform coat. 'In that case, I have a request—a negotiation, even.'

He grinned, loving the way this conversation was going. 'I'm all yours, *sötnos*.'

Andreas lay back against the seat and spread his thighs under her backside, shunting their hips closer so the heat between her legs burned through his trousers where he was hard for her.

'Can we go to the cabin?' She loosened his tie, using it to pull his mouth closer. 'I thought we could try out those fur pelts before the fire in true Viking style.'

Andreas closed his eyes as her lips caressed his earlobe, overcome with the passion and love for his sweet nose, his *sötnos*, his equal in every way.

His hand reached for the intercom to speak to the driver behind the tinted-glass partition. 'The hunting lodge, please, Tor. And call the housekeeper.' His speech was slurred with desire as Clara rocked her hips against his. 'Have him light the fires. Tell him I'm bringing my princess.'

'Yes, Your Royal Highness,' Tor said.

Clara took off his tie, her expression approving and serious with concentration as she exposed his chest and pressed her lips to his skin.

He pressed the button again. 'And, Tor?' he mumbled, dragging his lips free of Clara's wild kisses while he popped the clasp of her bra with his other hand. 'Put your foot down.'

EPILOGUE

Five months later…

CLARA LAZILY CURLED her toes into the padded seat of the sun lounger as desire, thick and drugging, pooled in her belly. From under the wide brim of her sun hat, she watched with almost fanatical concentration as Andreas swam lengths of the pool at Varborg's summer palace near the capital.

Her husband's lean and powerful body barely caused a ripple on the azure blue surface as his muscular arms sliced through the water, his back flexing and clenching with every stroke.

What was it about him and water? Clara's palms itched to get hold of him; to trace every muscle; to feel his skin and the springy golden hair of his magnificent chest; to sink her nails into those broad shoulders of his, while she cried out his name with the passion that was never far away when they were together.

Or when they were apart, come to think of it. Desperate to have him finish his swim and pay her some much-needed attention, Clara forced herself to look away from Europe's hottest, but no longer most eligible, prince. Just because she loved the security of being held in those strong arms didn't mean it was seemly to drool.

After all, she was a princess. They'd married in a small private ceremony on Christmas Eve, with only Prince Henrik, Alma and Freja as guests.

Now what had she been doing before she'd become so thoroughly distracted…?

Clara glanced at the paperwork on her lap, closing the folder and setting it aside. Building work was well under way on their veterans' rehabilitation centre, which was due to open in three months' time. With any luck, Clara would make the opening ceremony, having safely delivered their baby. But there were other projects in the pipeline: a grief counselling centre; a charity hospital in honour of Oscar; a state-of-the-art hospice facility in memory of Prince Henrik, who'd sadly lost his battle with cancer just after Christmas. Clara and Andreas had found endless ways to use their medical training to help others. That they could continue to work alongside each other was the icing on the cake.

Clara heard a splash. Andreas finished his swim and hauled his golden, tanned, athletic body from the pool using his considerable upper-body strength, all those gorgeous muscles she now knew by heart rippling.

Pretending to be asleep under her sunglasses, Clara watched him shuck off his swimming trunks, attach his prosthesis and wrap a towel around his hips, concealing his magnificent manhood from her greedy gaze.

Her core clenched as he carelessly slicked back his hair from his handsome face. She lay frozen so she could enjoy the hungry look on his face as he glanced her way. Mesmerised by his wild, Viking beauty, she watched him skirt the pool and walk her way. The water droplets on his chest glistened in the sunlight.

The molten heat between Clara's legs built to an inferno as he paced closer.

'I know you're awake, *sötnos*. I felt you watching me.'

He paused beside her lounger and looked down at her with predatory intent, his stare raking every part of her bikini-clad body, pausing at her breasts— which were almost spilling free of the tiny bikini top—the mound of her pregnant belly and lower, to where a triangle of fabric was all that concealed how much she wanted him.

But of course he knew. They were constantly wild for each other. Clara scraped her teeth over her bottom lip, her eyes tracing one particular droplet of water that slid down his bronzed chest and the ladder of his abs into the gold-tinged trail of hair that began below his navel.

'Can I help it if I like you all wet?' She sighed with longing.

Before he could answer, she swung her legs over the side of the lounger and stood before him, her fingertip tracing another droplet intent on a similar path.

Quick as lightning, his fingers encircled her wrist, guiding her hand lower to press against his hardness under the towel.

'Careful, *sötnos*.' His eyes blazed with arousal. 'I don't want to tire you out and we've already made love twice today.'

Clara scooped her arms around his waist and pressed her still needy body against his, her baby bump getting in the way.

'You know what they say…' She raised her face to his and melted into his strong arms as he kissed her, the passionate surges of his tongue against hers spreading flames along her every nerve. 'Third time lucky.' She pulled back, aware that his towel had slipped, and he stood naked, proud and beautiful in the sunlight.

He cupped her face, his stare full of desire, promise and love. 'I'm the lucky one,' he said, tilting up her chin to press another kiss to her lips. 'But whatever my princess wants, she shall have.'

His hands skimmed her breasts, her waist and her hips until he filled them with the cheeks of her backside, pressing her close.

Clara sighed, her heart full to bursting with love for the only man who could make her fairy-tale ending come true. 'I want *you*, Andreas. Always.'

* * * * *

Unbottoning The Bachelor Doc

Deanne Anders

MILLS & BOON

Deanne Anders was reading romance while her friends were still reading Nancy Drew, and she knew she'd hit the jackpot when she found a shelf of Harlequin Modern in her local library. Years later she discovered the fun of writing her own. Deanne lives in Florida with her husband and their spoiled Pomeranian. During the day she works as a nursing supervisor. With her love of everything medical and romance, writing for Harlequin Medical Romance is a dream come true.

Visit the Author Profile page
at millsandboon.com.au.

Dear Reader,

Welcome to Nashville's Legacy Women's Clinic, where the doctors and midwives always work together to make every patient feel like a VIP, including some of country music's biggest stars.

I love the city of Nashville, Tennessee. It has an energy that is like no other. Home of the Grand Ole Opry and local downtown bars where you can hear young musicians perform day and night, it's no wonder that it has become known as Music City. So when I decided to base my next three books on a trio of midwives, I knew I had to include the country music scene in their stories.

So put your best country duds on and have a great time as Sky and Jared find their lives suddenly filled with country music stars, glamorous parties and, most importantly, the magic of that first kiss.

And as Sky would say, "Don't forget to have fun along the way."

Deanne Anders

DEDICATION

This book is dedicated to Beth Diamond, one of the most dedicated and caring L&D nurses that I ever had the privilege of working with. Small in stature she might have been, but she was mighty in her love for God, her family and her friends.

CHAPTER ONE

SKYLAR BENTON HURRIED to the last seat available around the large conference table. It was the first Thursday of the month and she wasn't surprised to find the room crowded. Everyone who worked at Legacy Women's Clinic, from the medical assistants to the four physicians employed at the practice, wanted to be present for their monthly meeting. Lori, one of the other midwives, believed that it was the dedication of the staff that was responsible for their attendance. While Sky wouldn't argue that they had one of the most dedicated OB-GYN offices in Nashville, she was pretty sure that it was the dozens of hot, delicious doughnuts that their office manager, Tanya, brought in for the meeting that was the true draw.

"You look rough. Didn't you get any sleep last night?" Lori asked from beside her.

"Thanks a lot. I'll be sure to remind you how awful you look next time you have to pull an all-nighter." Not that it would be true. Her friend couldn't look bad if she tried to.

"It's just all part of the glamorous life of a midwife," Lori said, bumping her shoulder against Sky's.

Sky didn't feel very glamorous, sitting there in rumpled scrubs that she'd worn for the last twenty-four hours. It was great having a thriving midwifery practice, but it wasn't the same as an obstetrician's. A midwife worked with their patient for hours before the birth, sometimes acting not only as the provider of care but also in some ways as a doula who provided more hands-on support through the labor process. That was how she'd spent all of last night with three of her patients that were in labor.

And she still had one more delivery to do before she could go home and crash. Unfortunately, it was her patient's first baby and things weren't progressing as quickly as either one of them would like.

The smell of freshly baked doughnuts drifted down the length of the table as one of the boxes came closer. Her hand reached for the soft, glazed pastry before her brain could scold her on the lack of nutrients in her vice of choice. Closing her eyes, she embraced the rush of sugar as the doughnut all but melted in her mouth. Holding back a moan as she licked the sticky sweetness off her lips, she opened her eyes and froze. Across the table, dark brown eyes met hers and held. How had she not noticed him when she sat down? Refusing to be the first one to look away, Sky took another bite and chewed slowly while she tried to figure out what was going on. Dr. Jared Warner usually made a point of avoiding her, just as she did her best to get his attention. It had turned into a game of sorts between the two of them. One she had begun to actually enjoy.

Unable to help herself, she licked her lips again. Jared's eyes darted down as she made a point of dragging her tongue all the way around her mouth. His eyes met hers once more before he looked away.

"Chicken," Sky said, too soft for the man to hear her.

"What?" Lori asked.

"Nothing," Sky said, suddenly remembering where she was. Glancing around the room she was relieved to see that no one had been watching as she'd done her best to rock her stone-cold coworker.

Of course, she normally was more aware of her surroundings and made sure not to get caught teasing him, and she'd never gone this far with her teasing. He was just so much of a stick-in-the-mud, never wanting to step out of his well-beaten, boring path. He was always work, then more work. He didn't joke. He didn't tease. He never wanted to play. He was missing all the fun there was to have in life. Why that irritated her so much, she didn't know. Maybe it was because she saw herself, the person she'd been before she'd came to Nashville, in him. Or maybe it was because of the first time she'd seen him smile in a delivery. Picturing him with that big grin on his face, holding that screaming baby, still warmed her heart. It had been so natural. And so unexpected from a man who had always hid his emotions from not only her but everyone around them. After that, watching him return to that stony, totally boring exterior, she'd decided to make it her job to crack him open and see what was really inside. And so had begun her game of "shock the doc."

There were times when she just couldn't keep herself from ruffling his feathers with some silent nonsensical gestures. What was the harm? She'd even caught him smiling a few times when she'd flashed him a silly face. So what if she made herself look foolish. He had a really nice smile and it was a pity that he didn't let people see it more. Still, he was her boss's son, and she didn't want to ever disappoint the senior Dr. Warner with behavior he might not approve of, so it wasn't something she would normally do in a crowded room of her coworkers.

As Sky tried to concentrate on finishing her doughnut, making sure to keep her eyes to herself now, the door to the conference room opened and the elder Dr. Warner rushed in. With his silver hair combed back and his kind baby blue eyes, he looked like someone's favorite grandpa. "Good morning, everyone. I hope you are all doing well on this beautiful spring morning."

He took his seat at the front of the table and Tanya handed him a tablet. "Thank you, Tanya, I know each of you has a busy day today, so let's get started. First off, I'd like to welcome two new colleagues. I hope you've all met our new resident midwife, Brianna Rogers. She's a recent graduate of Vanderbilt and came to us highly recommended."

"Go Commodores," yelled one of the med techs from the other side of the table.

Everyone laughed at the man's shout-out for Nashville's largest university, which the majority of the staff had attended. Sky waved down the table at the young woman that had joined the practice a few days earlier. While Lori would be Brianna's primary preceptor, there would be times when Sky would be helping, and secretly Sky was hoping Brianna would stay after her residency was done. Their practice was growing, and it would be nice to have a third midwife on staff.

"Also, I want you to welcome Dr. Knox Collins, who will be filling in for Dr. Hennison, who, I'm sure you all know, just welcomed another baby boy."

As Dr. Warner began going through the monthly budget, Sky nudged Lori's arm and shot a sideways glance at the dangerously hot man sitting to Dr. Warner's left. How was it possible that she had missed seeing him? It had been all the office had talked about since they'd discovered that Nashville's own bad-boy doctor was going to be their new ad locum doc. With both his parents legendary country music stars, Knox had been covered by all the local media growing up. Sky just hoped that once it got out that he had returned home the media would not be hounding the office.

"And lastly, I'd like to share with you a special opportunity that has just become available to the practice." Dr. Warner handed the tablet back to the office manager and looked around the table, stopping when his eyes met Sky's. "It seems one of our midwives has been highly recommended to one of Nashville's rising stars. As most of Nashville is aware, Mindy and Trey Carter have recently relocated here from Chattanooga and are expecting their first child in just three months."

"They're the ones with the reality show, right?" asked the medical assistant sitting next to Sky.

"I've seen that show," Tanya said. "Cute couple and very talented."

Sky knew of the couple too. They'd made big news when their debut album had hit record sale numbers. With their reality show beginning to air, there probably wasn't a single person in Music City that hadn't heard of the young couple.

"I've met them personally and they are a lovely couple that are very excited about the birth of their first child. Both Mindy and her husband plan to be very involved. Of course, as always, everyone will be expected to keep our patients' information private. Also, as an added bonus, the couple has requested that their midwife and doctor be involved to a certain point with their new show."

Everyone around the table started talking at once, some excited about the prospect and some of the staff shocked by the request. Their practice had cared for high-profile patients before, including famous musicians, but this was different. This was big and exciting.

"Yes, yes… I know this is an unusual request, but it comes with a very large donation to Legacy House," the senior Dr. Warner said, silencing everyone in the room. Legacy House was the home for pregnant women in need that Dr. Warner had established not long after he'd opened the Legacy Clinic after seeing that some of his younger patients didn't have the support at home that they needed during their pregnancy and postdelivery. While the home depended mainly on donations, everyone in their office played a part in supporting it with their time and talents, doing everything from tutoring to home repairs. Still, Sky knew the home provided care for a lot of women and it wasn't unusual for their budget to run short some months. Sky had always suspected that Dr. Warner personally covered those months. She also suspected it was one of the reasons the doctor was still practicing instead of retiring, or at least cutting back on his hours, as other doctors his age often did.

"So, as you can see, this is an opportunity that we are lucky to be able to accept. *If* we accept. As always, we all need to remember to keep our patients' information private." Dr. Warner stood, signaling that their meeting was over. "Thank y'all for coming today. Jared and Sky, can the two of you give me a few more minutes, please?"

Jared looked from his father to Sky. He wasn't sure what his father was up to, but from the meeting he had an idea. A really bad idea that included the midwife sitting across from him. The same midwife who only a few minutes earlier had made him squirm in his seat. The same one who seemed to love to annoy him. The same one who enjoyed playing silly games instead of taking life seriously.

"Isn't this exciting?" his dad asked as he walked over and took a seat next to Jared, his eyes dancing with a joy for life Jared had never understood, considering all the man had been through, with the loss of a child and then later his wife.

Exciting? It was more like a nightmare. "Maybe you should tell us exactly what the plan is. I take it that the three of us are going to have something to do with this new VIP patient and her husband?"

"I'm so glad that you are ready to jump in here to help, Jared. I knew I could count on you and Sky," his father said. With anyone else, Jared would have thought he was being sarcastic. But not his father. No, Dr. Jack Warner didn't do sarcasm. He always chose to see the best in others. It was part of his charm and sometimes it made Jared wish he was truly his father's son. Maybe then he'd be able to relate to his father's optimistic nature.

But after spending two years of his life in and out of foster homes, Jared's eyes had been permanently opened to what really went on in the world. There were no rose-colored glasses in his life.

"Excuse me, Dr. Warner," Sky said, "I'm sorry to interrupt, but I need to get back over to the hospital. I have a primigravida that has been laboring for several hours."

"How many hours? Has her water broken?" Jared asked. The risk of infection increased significantly during prolonged rupture of membranes.

"Her water broke spontaneously at four centimeters, only four hours ago. She's afebrile and the baby's heart tones are fine. Anything else,

Doctor?" The fire in Sky's eyes warned him that she was ready to ignite, something Jared didn't appreciate. Even though Sky worked independently, if something went wrong and her patient required a cesarean section, it would become his responsibility. His questions had been appropriate.

"Just keep me updated. I took over call at seven and I will start making rounds as soon as we are done here."

"Okay, then," Jared's father said, plainly trying to act as peacekeeper, "let's get on with it. I met with Mindy and Trey yesterday, along with their manager, and they are all very nice people. I think working with them will be a pleasure." His dad looked across the table. "Sky, it seems that you took care of one of Mindy's band members, Jenny Mack, during her pregnancy and delivery a few years ago and she has, almost literally according to Mindy, sung your praises to her boss."

"I remember her. She had to schedule her appointments around rehearsal and gig dates. I don't think she was with the Carters then."

It always amazed Jared how Sky could remember her patients so clearly. He tried to remember his patients' names, but between his obstetrics practice and the gyn surgeries he performed, he found it impossible unless something really stood out about the patient. It wasn't how he had planned his career, but it was what it was. He was doing his best to build a practice and hopefully take over for his father someday. He had to see as many patients as possible, which sometimes limited their interaction more than he would like.

"Well, she seems to remember you too, and Mindy is very excited about meeting you. She is determined to have a midwifery delivery. Her husband, on the other hand, has some concerns. That's where you come in, Jared. In order to give this young couple the delivery they both want, I'm going to need the two of you to work closely together."

"What exactly do you need me to do?" Jared asked. He definitely wasn't one to discourage an expectant father from having a doctor oversee the birth of his child.

"I need the two of you to work as a team. This couple has a lot of pressure on them right now. They're new to the superstar level of country music and from what I can tell, the reality show is causing some…shall we say *stress* on the two of them. It's not good for either one of them, especially Mindy and the baby. Her last pregnancy ended in a miscarriage at nineteen weeks." Turning to him, his father looked him in the eye. "I know I can trust the two of you to do what is best for this couple and work together as the professional colleagues that you are."

Jared glanced at his dad and then over to Sky, who had gone unusually quiet. There were dark rings under her eyes and strands of blond hair hung loose around her face where it had come out of the band she kept it tied up in. He hadn't noticed that this morning. It had been all he could do to keep himself on his side of the table when all he'd wanted to do was lick that sticky sugar off those luscious lips of hers.

"What about the reality show? Do they really expect us to be part of that?" she asked, and Jared wasn't surprised to see a flicker of excitement in her tired eyes. She was the outgoing, flashy type of person they usually had on those kinds of shows. Not that he had any intention on being on the show himself. He didn't care for all that "reality" drama. He'd had enough drama as a child. Just the thought sent shivers through him.

"From what I can gather, you would only be there on the sidelines as you interact with them as providers for the pregnancy," his father said. "And don't forget what this will mean for

Legacy House. Things are tough financially for a lot of people right now. Some of our regular donors have had to cut back on their giving. This donation would cover the rest of this year's budget. And then there's the possibility that they will tell others about the work Legacy House does. The two of you might even have an opportunity to tell others about it."

Sky's phone vibrated with a message, and she got up from the table as she read it. "I need to get back to the hospital."

She reached for the last doughnut left on the table before standing and heading to the door, then she stopped and looked back at his father. "Is it really that bad, Jack?"

The reassuring smile that was as much a part of his father as breathing faltered. "It's not just the lack of regular donations that's straining our budget. A lot of people are struggling right now, which means more young girls are coming to us for help. We are close to having to turn them away for the first time in twenty years."

Sky's eyes locked on Jared, then narrowed. Her chin went up and he felt like one of those unfortunate ants caught under a magnifying glass about to be zapped. "Whatever they need us to do, we're in, aren't we, Jared?"

Jared's mouth dropped open to argue, but then he shut it. How could he get out of this without looking like a jerk? It wasn't that he didn't want to help Legacy House. He'd been helping out at the home since he was a teenager. But working with this free-spirited midwife who acted like life was just another game would be a disaster. Look at how she'd resented him asking basic questions about her patients. How could they coordinate their care of their patient if she reacted that way every time he asked a question?

And then there was her unprofessional teasing of him. Those big warm smiles and sassy winks rattled him. How much worse would it be if he had to work even closer with her?

Without waiting for his agreement, she spun around and headed for the door, the doughnut still in her hand.

"Well, I'm glad that's settled," his dad said, taking off his glasses and laying them down on the table.

"Why me?" Jared asked. "You know I'm not good at all that schmoozing with people. Wouldn't it make more sense for you to do this? Wouldn't the husband feel better having someone with your experience?"

"You're fine with people when you want to

be. You just hold yourself back. You need to relax more. You're thirty-six years old. It's time you get out in the world and experience life instead of spending all your time working."

"You're one to talk. You've been going strong for almost forty years now. If anyone needs to slow down, it's you."

"When I was your age, I was married and building a home for me and Katie. The years we had together were the best years of my life. And when you came into our life you made us the family we always wanted to be. I want that for you, what I had with your mom, because no matter what you think right now, there will come a time when you'll need someone. Someone that understands you and will be by you no matter what happens."

His father suddenly looked ten years older than he had when he'd been rallying the troops at their monthly meeting. Was it the memory that he'd once had a family that didn't include Jared? Was it the memory of the little girl he'd lost? Jared knew he'd never taken the little girl's place in his parents' hearts. Not that he had wanted to. The Warners had been good to him and had treated him like their own. He had no resentment of their daughter, though at times he knew he'd disappointed them by not being able to be the outgoing, happy child they'd deserved. Maybe if in his younger years he'd been surrounded by the secure love they'd always given him, things would have been different. Maybe he would have been different. But that wasn't his reality. The life he'd lived being raised by a sickly grandmother and then later in foster homes had made him who he was. He couldn't change his past.

But it wasn't the time for them to get into an old argument that he knew he wasn't going to win. Jared lived his life just like he liked it: drama free. He worked hard and in his off time enjoyed the peace and quiet of the home he'd built for himself. He didn't need anyone else in his life. And he certainly didn't want to ever rely on another person for his happiness. Everyone he'd relied on as a child had left him or sent him away. By the time he'd been adopted by Jack and Katie, he'd learned his lesson. Not that he didn't care for them. They had been the best thing that had ever happened to him.

"But back to the Carters. You're overthinking this, Jared. I have full confidence in both your and Sky's professionalism. I know the two of you will make a great team."

He could see he wasn't going to get out of this. His dad had made up his mind. As Nana

Marie used to tell him when he had to do something he didn't want to do, *Boy, put on your big boy pants and get it done.*

And so it was time for him to accept the inevitable and make the best of the situation. His only hope of getting out of this would be for Sky to refuse to work with him, and he couldn't count on that. Still, it wouldn't hurt to talk to her. Unlike his father, she would see that the two of them working together could only lead to disaster. He just had to find a way to get her to agree with him.

CHAPTER TWO

"You're doing great," Sky said as she wiped Liza's forehead with a cool rag.

"No, I'm not. I'm so tired. And I gave in and got an epidural after I swore I wouldn't need one. My sister is never going to let me live it down," Liza said.

"Well, I'm not telling her," Sky said, then looked pointedly at the young man at her patient's side. Waiting for him to take the hint was almost painful. Liza's husband almost looked as bad as she did. "No one will ever know, will they, Eric?"

"Oh, no, no...of course not," Eric said.

Liza looked over at him, disbelieving. "You're going to keep a secret? You are the worst blabbermouth in the whole family."

Eric shrugged his shoulders and looked up at Sky from the chair at his wife's bedside with a look of guilt that belonged more on a five-year-old child's face than that of a grown man. Sky looked away before Liza could see her grin.

"The most important thing is that you're fully dilated now. We could start pushing, or we could turn you over on your side and let you rest for half an hour." Sky was hoping that Liza would choose to rest a while. The baby hadn't progressed down as much as she'd like before they started pushing. Sky was tired and she knew Liza was even more tired at this point. The two of them could both use a power nap while the contractions did their own magic of bringing the baby down lower.

"Is that okay to do? Won't the baby's head end up funny shaped?" Eric asked.

"It's perfectly fine. Your baby's head has to mold as it comes down the birthing canal. That's why baby's heads sometimes look funny when they're born, but they don't stay that way." Sky found the things that new dads worried about amusing.

"And Baby Stella's heart tones are perfect. It will give the baby some time to move down now that Liza is relaxed, and a little rest will help when she's ready to push." Sky was a strong advocate of letting the patient's body tell them when it was time to push unless there was concern for getting the baby out quickly.

"I'd like to rest a bit, if it's okay," Liza said.

Tammy, the labor and delivery nurse, came into the room and they discussed their plan to give Liza a break. After positioning Liza on her left side to rest, Sky lowered the lights in the room and stepped outside.

"Dr. Warner was looking for you," Tammy said, then clarified, "the young one."

So much for a power nap. Sky reached down deep and tried to find the patience she would need to deal with Jared in the moods they both were in. She was tired, and he was aggravated about being forced to work with her. If she hadn't been so tired, she would have looked forward to their interaction. She'd enjoyed placing him in a situation where he couldn't refuse the opportunity his father had given them. Seeing the uptight doc squirm was always entertaining. He was so cute when he was flustered. And those rare times when she made him smile, those she treasured.

But that wouldn't be the reason Jared had followed her straight over to the unit. He'd said he was on call, and he always rounded on the patients he was covering whether they were his patients or one of the midwives' patients. But while Dr. Hennison and the senior Dr. Warner usually just checked in with her or Lori, trusting them to share if there were any concerns or complications with their patient, Jared took it a couple steps further. He made it a habit to check the midwife patient's medical records and ask questions of the nurses taking care of them, as if Sky was withholding some information from him.

She had never understood why Lori wasn't bothered by this as much as Sky was. The relationship between the doctors and midwives in their practice was a collaboration and she believed sometimes Jared came close to crossing the line. Of course, as there was an understanding that if there were complications in the labor process the practice's doctors would assume care for any necessary procedures, such as surgery, it could be said that Jared's level of interest was reasonable. But still, all of his questioning made her feel as if he didn't believe midwives were equal partners in the practice. There was even a rumor that he had tried to talk his father out of hiring midwives into the practice, and it made her more than a little bit defensive when she had to deal with him, just like she had been earlier that morning when he'd questioned her in front of his father.

"Tammy told me that your patient was complete. Why isn't she pushing?" Jared asked the moment she took a seat in the nurses' station.

Sky looked at Tammy, who cast an apologetic smile her way. There was something about Jared, even though he could be as prickly as a porcupine, that made the staff trust him. Maybe it was the way he always had their backs when the staff was negotiating with the hospital administration. Or maybe it was the fact that Jared never left the staff to handle a difficult patient on their own. Or maybe it was simply that he didn't talk down to them, instead he respected them for the job they did.

If only Sky could get him to respect the midwives the same way. If only he could see that they had a place in the delivery room just as much as he did. There was a story there, and someday she would find out what it was.

"Liza just got an epidural and has chosen to rest a few minutes before we begin pushing." Sky wouldn't let him make her second-guess herself. She had done this hundreds of times. "As you can see on the monitor, the baby's heart tones have good variability along with accelerations."

"See, this is why we can't work together. You resent every question I ask," Jared said, turning toward her, his voice too intense for her lack of sleep.

Sky looked at him and blinked. Was this about her patient or was this about them teaming up to care for Mindy Carter? "I guess you couldn't talk your dad into taking over the Carters' case?"

His eyes refused to acknowledge that she'd seen right through him. His lips straightened into a flat line, but not before she saw him grimace. She'd seen it many times when she'd tried to get a rise out of him. It was as if the man was trying to convince her that he was above having human emotions. But she knew better. She'd seen the way his eyes had watched her lips that morning in their meeting. Was it possible that Jared was as curious about her as she was about him? Was there even the possibility that he was more than curious? Was the way he watched her this morning a sign that he might be interested in her in other ways?

Or maybe not. Maybe it was just her that felt that electric buzz that seemed to arc between the two of them. The only time she ever got any type of response from Jared himself was when they were playing one of their silent games, which just mostly seemed to annoy him. This morning could have been nothing more serious than the man was hungry.

"I simply voiced my belief that it would be better for my father to be the one that represented the practice with such a high-profile case. Don't you agree?"

The truth was she did agree with Jared. Even though she enjoyed her game of irritating him, the two of them had never worked well together. She resented his overpowering need to meddle, and he didn't trust her. It would probably be a nightmare, but she still understood why the senior Dr. Warner wanted his son to be the one to take the lead in this collaboration. It was a known fact that Jared was being mentored by his father to take over the practice someday. It was better to find out now if Jared could take the pressure that was sure to go along with the job.

"I respect your father enough to believe he knows what he is doing," she replied, though she did wonder if she was the right midwife for this job even though she had been highly recommended. The Carters had become unbelievably famous and certainly more well-to-do, as her grandmother would have called them. Sky had been raised in a simple two-bedroom house along with her six siblings and her grandmother in Tennessee's rural mountains. She'd had little to no training on how to behave with people like the Carters.

"Look, Jared, your father has made his decision, and for the sake of the practice and for Legacy House, we have to go through with this no matter how much you don't like me." There. Now the real problem was on the table for the two of them to address. The only way to deal with this was head-on. If the two of them couldn't be friends, the least they could do was learn to work together. Otherwise it was going to be a miserable three months.

"I didn't say I didn't like you. This has nothing to do with how I feel about you." Jared's brows crinkled with confusion. "I don't even know you that well."

"And we've worked together for over three years. Doesn't that seem a little strange to you?" The wrinkles in his forehead got deeper as he stared at her. Was he really this disconnected from all the staff? Or was it just her?

"I know you are a good midwife," Jared said, which coming from him was a huge compliment. Maybe there was hope for them after all.

"And I know you are a very thorough doctor." She'd had her patients' records combed through by him so many times that there was no doubt of that. "So let's start there and maybe by the time this is over we will both have learned more about each other."

His forehead relaxed, but his eyes narrowed as if he suspected that he was being tricked somehow. Maybe it hadn't been such a good idea teasing him so much in the conference room this morning. But it had been fun, and she figured fun was something Jared could use more of in his life. And what could be more fun, or more disastrous, than being on a reality show together with a couple of country music stars?

"How about we go to the first meeting with Mindy and Trey and their manager and see how it goes? It might be that once they meet us they decide we're not a good fit for them. Will you at least agree to that?" Sky looked over to the monitor displaying the laboring patient's fetal heart tones. Liza's tracing was beginning to show signs of head compression, a sure sign that the baby was progressing down into the birth canal.

"I've got to get back to my patient," she said as she stood to leave. "Let me know what you decide. Instead of looking at this as a form of punishment, maybe we should look at this as a great way to do something different and unique. Who knows, you might find that you like being in the spotlight. It might even be fun."

Without waiting for him to give her an answer, she walked out and headed to her patient's room. Somewhere in her pep talk she'd found herself getting excited about working with the music stars despite having to work with Jared. At least she told herself that it was the hobnobbing with the rich and famous that excited—and scared—her. She didn't want to admit that she hoped she might finally tear open that cold box Dr. Jared Warner hid inside of.

And who knew? Maybe she'd find the man wasn't made out of ice. Maybe she'd find the man was just waiting for a chance to come out and play.

CHAPTER THREE

JARED HAD KNOWN this was a mistake the moment Sky had gotten into his truck. They were both headed to the same place, so it had only made sense for the two of them to share the ride. But once the car door had shut, he'd been at a loss for what to say to the one person he'd done his best to avoid since she'd come to work at the practice.

There had always been an awkwardness between the two of them. It was something he didn't want to examine, because it might lead to a more uncomfortable problem. Awkwardness he could handle, but sometimes this felt more…personal. As if something unsaid between them,which made it very important that he avoid her as much as possible. Of course, that wasn't how Sky approached him at all. She was always pulling one of her silent pranks, flirting with him like she'd done at the last staff meeting or winking at him across a nurses' sta-

tion when no one was looking, all of which he
knew she did just to make him uncomfortable.
It was those times when he wondered exactly
what her intention was. It was like she was just
having fun with him, while he was squirming
with adult responses that he had no right to be
feeling for a coworker. Not that she was acting
that way this morning. No, there was none of
her usual cheekiness. None of her teasing or
her laughter. This morning she was so subdued
that he worried she might be sick.

Not that he was complaining. The last thing
he needed was to walk into a room with their
new patient and have Sky pull one of her stunts,
throwing him off his game.

The morning traffic had been heavy as the
Nashville workforce started their day. They had
been on the road for almost thirty minutes by
the time they left Nashville and headed out of
town on I-24 toward Clarksville to the ranch
where the Carters had recently relocated. He'd
spent his time concentrating on getting them
safely through the snarl of traffic, but now that
they had left the city, the silence surrounding
them was deafening. He needed to say something, but he didn't know what. He wasn't a
casual conversationalist. He spoke when he
needed to. He greeted the office and hospi-

tal staff every day. Sometimes he even joined in on the Monday morning college football debate. He even knew which staff members to avoid if Vanderbilt had lost their Saturday game.

But this one-on-one stuff? He wasn't good at it. And, like so many other things in his life, he had learned to avoid it.

"Have you ever met anyone famous?" Sky asked. Even though her question came from out of the blue, he was glad that one of them had finally broken the silence.

"I operated on the mayor's wife a few years ago," he said, though he'd be more likely to recognize the tumor he had removed from her than to recognize the woman, even if her picture was plastered on a roadside billboard.

"Hmm," Sky said. He glanced over to see her staring down at her hands. Her top lip was poked out and she was chewing on her bottom one. Seeing this vulnerable side of Sky bothered him. He was used to feeling out of place. Being shuffled from foster home to foster home after his grandmother's death, he'd never felt that there was a place for him. Even now, after being adopted by the kindest couple in the state of Tennessee, he still didn't know where he belonged. It was like something was off with him but he couldn't put his finger on what it was, nor could he figure out how to correct it.

"Nervous about meeting the Carters?" he asked, though that didn't make sense. She was always so confident.

And why was he suddenly so worried about Sky and her feelings? He didn't do feelings. Feelings just complicated things. It was just another sign that this plan of his father's for them to work together was doomed.

"I just don't want to embarrass the practice," Sky said, before turning toward the window.

"I'm sure they put their cowboy boots on the same way everyone else does," he said as he followed his car's GPS instructions and took the next exit.

"Maybe," she said, still sounding nothing like the midwife he was used to dealing with.

"What's wrong? I thought you were excited about this," Jared said, though he told himself he needed to stop with the questioning. He had already passed the point of casual conversation.

"I am, kind of. I just don't know what to expect. What if they're not the nice couple everybody says they are? What if they're really stuck-up? What if they don't like me?"

"Why would you think that?" Was it possible that the flamboyantly outgoing Sky was having some type of confidence crisis? "Your patients always love you. That's why we're here today."

"I'm being silly. Of course they'll like me," she said before letting out an exaggerated sigh. Jared wasn't sure if she was trying to convince him or herself.

Then she sat up straighter and seemed to relax as she continued to stare out at where the cityscape had turned to open fields. "Oh, isn't this pretty? It's hard to believe we're only a few miles from the city."

Jared took his own deep breath, relieved that she'd moved on from all her misgivings. He had enough of his own to worry about.

"This must be it," she said, straining her neck to see the sign stating they had arrived at The Midnight Ranch. A plain dirt road ran between two fenced-in fields, then disappeared around a curve of trees. "Look, they have horses."

Three horses, one black and two a rusty brown, stopped their grazing and watched the car as it passed. Sky turned around in her seat to admire them, her body almost vibrating with excitement. This was more like the Sky he was used to dealing with.

"I've always thought that horses live a great life. Just look at the three of them. Wouldn't it be nice to have the freedom they have?" Sky asked.

"I guess they have a good life. Most are fed and cared for. Of course, they're really not that free. It's not like they are let loose to roam. They have to stay behind a fence." Jared had never given a horse's life much thought, but Sky was probably right—if their owners cared for them, they had a pretty safe life.

"I hadn't thought about that. I wonder if they resent looking over the railing at the pasture next door and not being able to get to it," Sky said, turning back around in her seat.

Jared hadn't meant to take away her enjoyment of seeing the horses. "We all have to live with boundaries."

"But most of the time, at least when we are adults, we set our own boundaries," Sky said, her voice dropping to almost a whisper. "I think that's worse than having others do that to us."

The pain in Sky's voice surprised him. If anyone lived life without boundaries, it was her.

A few yards farther down the winding drive they came to a wrought iron gate.

"Smile for the camera," Jared said as he

rolled down the truck's window to punch in the code the Carters' manager had emailed to him.

Before he could stop her, Sky undid her seat belt and crawled over the truck console, her body brushing against his as she leaned out of his window. She was almost sitting in his lap and his body reacted immediately, his arms coming around her waist to keep her from falling out onto the road. The smile she gave the camera was one of her one-thousand-watt smiles. It was the same smile she would send him across the nurses' station that he knew she gave him to make him uncomfortable. It was a smile so beautiful that it took his breath away. His body hardened under her, and his arms tightened around her on instinct. "Don't you think you should at least wait for the reality show before you start performing?"

"I was just having a bit of fun? Maybe you should try it before you start criticizing me. You might find you like it," she said as she moved back into her seat, his arms falling away from her and his body suddenly cold without the warmth of hers.

He'd regretted the words the moment he'd said them. She was right. She was just being her normal self. It wasn't her fault that he'd responded to her the way he had. He straightened in his seat, refusing to let himself dwell on that unwanted need he'd felt to close his arms around her. It didn't make sense. It was almost laughable.

And laugh was what she'd do if she knew just what having his hands on her had done to him. Halfway around the next curve, he was glad to see the house come into view. He needed to get out of the truck and put some distance between the two of them.

It was two stories with an outside balcony running the length of the top floor. With large cedar posts and a front porch that ran the length of the house, Jared could tell that the architect had tried to create the look of a simple country home, but the size of the house made that almost impossible. Just the grandeur of the tall, double-glass front doors spoke of luxury that was way out of Jared's price range.

"Wow," Sky said, her voice low as if someone might be listening. "If my grandmamma could just see this."

Jared didn't know anything about Sky's grandmother, but he knew his own grandmother would never believe that he had been invited to a house this grand. Still, he'd give anything to have been driving Nana Marie up to this big house. Just to be able to show her that he'd done it. He'd made something of his life. Not that this represented his life... His life was more simple, quiet and safe. But most of all, *his*. He'd never have to worry about someone taking his home away from him. And that was the most important thing to him.

But still, his nana would have enjoyed this. All of this. She'd followed all the country music stars when she'd been alive, yet she'd never met one, even though a lot of them lived just minutes away from her. She was too busy working and raising him. Then she'd been too sick to leave the house, but somehow she'd still taken care of him. He'd once told her that when he was grown and rich he'd buy her the nicest house in Nashville. His five-year-old brain hadn't even known someplace like this existed.

As his truck came to a stop behind a black SUV parked in the circular drive, a woman whose gray hair was piled as high as the heels she was wearing rushed down the front porch stairs toward them. With bright red lipstick that matched her suit, she marched toward them with an intensity that made Jared want to put the truck in Reverse and speed back down the road toward town.

"Who do you think that is?" Sky asked,

showing no signs of being intimidated by the woman.

"A fire-breathing dragon?" Jared questioned as he unbuckled his seat belt and opened the door.

Sky looked over at him and laughed as she undid her own buckle. Her eyes danced with the humor she was known for. "Don't worry. If she starts spitting fire I'll protect you."

He was pleased to see that she was back to her normal ridiculousness after recovering from her earlier dip in confidence—which didn't make sense, as he'd always found this flirty, flippant side of her irritating.

Before the two of them could make it around to the front of the truck, the woman in red bore down on them, waving a stack of papers in their faces. "I need your signatures on these nondisclosure forms before I can allow you inside."

"Marjorie, can you at least let them come inside before you start hounding them with all that privacy nonsense?" a young woman called after her.

Jared looked up to the front door, where a young woman, no more than twenty-five or -six, stood with her arms resting on her rounded abdomen. Dressed as she was in jeans and a T-shirt, with her long, blond hair flowing over her shoulders, he could have passed her on the street and never known she was one of country music's fastest rising stars.

"It's not nonsense, Mindy. You have to stop thinking like an amateur singer. The information these two will have could be worth a lot. We can't have them going around spilling information about you and Trey to the public."

"I think the physician-patient relationship covers that," Jared said as he headed up the stairs to meet their new patient, ignoring the irritating woman and her papers who had just insulted both him and Sky with her demands.

"I'm sorry," Mindy Carter said as she held out a slender hand to him and then to Sky, who had followed him up the stairs.

"Marjorie means well. It's just that all this," the young woman said, holding out her arms, "came at us really fast and we haven't been able to catch our breath in the last few months. She takes her responsibility as our agent very seriously."

"It's very serious business," the woman said when she caught up with them, her breath labored as she climbed the last step. "You can't trust everybody here like you could at home.

And the reality show is just making the media more gossip hungry."

"Aunt Marj, it's okay. The Legacy Clinic has a great reputation," a man Jared recognized as Trey Carter said as he stepped outside to join them.

"That's right, Miss Marjorie, and the two of us are thrilled to have this opportunity to take care of your family." Sky stepped toward the woman and offered her hand, her smile showing none of the dread that Jared felt.

"Look at us keeping the two of you standing out here. Please come in and I'll get you both something to drink," Mindy said. "We appreciate you coming here to talk to us. I know most doctors don't make house calls anymore."

"How about I get us all some iced tea and you sit down and rest?" Trey suggested, holding the door open for them to enter.

Jared stepped into the foyer, following Sky, and was surprised to see that it opened straight into a sitting area surrounding a massive stone fireplace. Across the room there was a table that could fit twenty easily, but still the room seemed comfortable enough with no sign of the glitz and glamour he had been expecting.

"You are not allowed to mention anything about Mindy and Trey's home to anyone until after the latest reality taping is aired tomorrow night," Marjorie said as she followed them into the sitting area and took a seat, not waiting for them to sit before raising those insulting forms at them again. "These aren't just to cover Mindy and Trey. The producer of *Carters' Way* is insisting on them too."

"Oh, we understand perfectly your concerns," Sky said, her voice dripping with a sweetness he hadn't known she possessed. "We'll be happy to take them with us and have the practice's legal team review them. But I think we can all agree that the most important thing we discuss today is Mindy and her baby. Don't you think?"

And as if Sky had performed a miracle, or an exorcism, the woman's eyes softened and she smiled for the first time. "Of course, nothing is as important as Mindy and the baby."

The doorbell rang and the woman immediately sprang into action, flying off her seat and heading to the door. "That should be the party planner."

"I know she's a bit much," Trey said as he set a tray with the tea glasses down on the short table beside one of the couches, "but she's just being protective. Once she gets to know you, she'll calm down. And if she likes you, she'll be just as protective toward you. She's really just a super animated teddy bear. Her bites are rare and her love is genuine."

Jared stared at the man, taken aback by words that could have described the grandmother he had just been thinking of earlier. "I understand. You're lucky to have her."

"So, Mindy, how have you been feeling?" Jared asked, changing the subject when Sky turned toward him, uncomfortable with the way she was studying him.

"I'm good," Mindy said, rubbing her hands over her abdomen.

"We received your records from your doctor and they show your due date as August 1, which would make you almost twenty-eight weeks. Does that sound right?" Sky asked.

"I'll be twenty-eight weeks this Thursday," Mindy said, moving to sit closer to Trey as he took the seat next to her.

For the next half hour they discussed everything from Mindy's medical history to her birth plan. When they came to her history of a miscarriage the year before, Jared saw Trey wrap his arm around his wife. It appeared that Trey's aunt wasn't the only one in the family that was protective. It was very evident that the relationship the couple shared wasn't just something they pretended for the cameras. They seemed to have the kind of bond that Jared never understood. In theory, yes, he understood the human need for companionship. But to trust someone with that much of yourself? To risk losing someone again? No, that was definitely not something he was capable of doing.

So why did looking at the two of them make him feel empty in a way he'd never felt before?

"They're a cute couple," Sky said, as he started the truck to head back to town. "I don't think we'll have any trouble working with them."

"I guess," he said.

"Didn't you like them?" she asked. She'd turned toward him. It always made him feel uncomfortable, being the focus of all her attention.

He'd watched her with Mindy while she'd done most of the questioning, which had really been an informal health review. She was naturally good with people. He wasn't sure if she interacted with other people like she normally did with him, though somehow he doubted it. It seemed he caught most of her unwanted attention whenever they were in a room together. She just couldn't help but try to get a rise out of him, as if there was some perverse part of her that liked to make him uncomfortable, though he didn't understand why.

But she hadn't been that way today. Today she'd acted professional, something he very much appreciated.

"It's not important that we like them. It's just important that we give Mindy and the baby the best of care, which is something I'm sure we will do."

"Thank you," Sky said, giving him one of those big smiles that always sent a spark of unwanted pleasure through him.

"What are you thanking me for?" He forced his eyes back to the road that led off the ranch, but not before he saw the lovely way her eyes mirrored her smile.

"For trusting me. For having faith in me. In us. I know you have a problem working with midwives."

His hands tightened on the steering wheel. He didn't want to relive the reason he had trust issues with midwives. Did Sky somehow know his history? Did she know that it had been a midwife that had delivered him? That while he'd taken his first breath his mother had been bleeding to death? He didn't want to expose that secret part of his life. It was his own private pain to endure. "I don't have a problem working with midwives. I just want to be available and prepared if I'm needed."

"Whatever," she said, shrugging her shoulders as if it didn't matter that he didn't want to discuss it with her. "What did you think about the request to interview us on the reality show? I think it would be a great chance to give Legacy House a plug if we can work it into the conversation. It could bring in donations from all across the country."

He was glad she'd changed the subject, though it was another one he didn't want to think about. He had to agree that it would be good to get more revenue coming into the home to lift some of the pressure from his father. And with everything his dad had done for him, it was a small thing to have to answer a few questions for the show.

"I don't understand why they call it a reality show. In what world is the Carters' life a reality? If they want a real reality show they need to have a show about an exhausted mom and dad who go to work every day for minimum wage so they can come home and sit around the table with their kids and worry about how they are going to pay the bills." At least, that was the reality that he'd seen when he was a kid in foster care. He hadn't been dreaming of a big house with huge fireplaces and horses running around in pastures. He'd just wanted to know there was someone out there who'd make sure he got his next meal.

"I guess people wouldn't find that entertaining enough. Though if they'd had a hidden camera at my grandma's house when me and my siblings had been growing up," Sky said, her voice filled with laughter, "we could have entertained the whole country with our antics at the dinner table. My grandma could have won an award just for all the ways she could cook the deer sausage my uncle Ben brought us. Not that we complained. We were just happy to get a meal."

"What about your parents? They wouldn't have wanted to be on your reality show?" he asked.

Sky's laughter died and Jared knew he'd asked the wrong question. But then, as suddenly as her laughter had stopped, it started again. "My parents couldn't take the reality of raising seven kids. If it hadn't been for my mom's mother we would have been homeless."

Jared sat up a little straighter. Was it really possible that he and Sky had come from such similar situations? Yet here she was laughing about her childhood while his memories before the Warners had adopted him were anything but humorous.

"How do you do that?" he asked, before he could stop himself.

"Do what?"

"You talk about your parents leaving you when you were a child, and it sounds like things weren't easy at your grandmother's house, but you just laugh it all off. How can you do that?" Maybe the question was a little personal, but he couldn't help himself. He had never understood Sky's happy-go-lucky lifestyle. For some reason, now that he'd learned more about her, it was suddenly very important that he did.

Sky didn't answer him for more than a few moments, and he wasn't sure that she was going to. He looked over to see her chewing on her bottom lip again, deep in thought. Then she took a deep breath and began. "I can't deny that at one time I was bitter about my childhood. I acted out as most teenagers do, I think, but now that I look back on it, I was mostly just angry. Living in a small town where everyone knew that we had been dumped by our parents wasn't easy on me or my siblings. Not that times had been easy before my parents left us.

"No one wants to feel that they were unwanted. But my grandmother was a special woman. When our parents left us, I was angry and scared. We didn't know her well. Our mom had only taken us to see her mom a couple times that I could remember. But from the moment we got there she acted like having us dumped on her was the best thing that had ever happened in her life."

Jared could definitely relate to that feeling. "So you just got over it?"

"I wouldn't say I got over it as much as I decided that I wasn't going to let their actions determine how I spent the rest of my life. Not that it was something that happened overnight. Life isn't that easy. Right when you feel like everything is going your way, there's always something, or someone, who decides you don't deserve to be happy."

Jared looked over to see Sky staring out the window. "Why do I feel like you are leaving something out?"

Sky turned and gave him a smile that was filled with more sadness than happiness. He'd never known that a smile could be so sad, and he didn't like seeing it on her face at all.

"I'm sorry. I didn't mean to make you uncomfortable."

His words sounded ridiculous even to himself. All his questions had been uncomfortable. He was asking her to share things with him that he didn't have the right to know. What had he been thinking? Was he so self-absorbed in trying to figure her out that he'd not considered her feelings? He certainly hadn't wanted to drag out all his own painful history for her to sort through.

"It's okay. And it isn't something I left out. It's someone." Sky sat up straighter beside him. He saw her chin had gone up and her eyes were staring straight ahead. She looked like someone preparing for a head-on battle. "I was engaged, or at least promised to be engaged, to my high school boyfriend. After graduation, he wanted to go off to college but all I could afford was community college. I thought everything was going great. I had gotten into the local nursing school and he was in pre-med. We had made plans for the future. Then, suddenly, he changed. The calls and messages just stopped. His first visit home, he brought a girl with him."

Jared glanced over at her. Her eyes had gone from hurt to hard and her lips were sealed so tight that he wasn't sure she'd ever smile again. "When I cornered him and asked him what was going on, he seemed shocked to think I had really expected him to abide by all the promises we had made to each other. Apparently, I wasn't good enough for the new life he'd planned. He didn't need a backwoods wife. He needed someone he could be proud of."

Jared's hands tightened again on the steering wheel. He'd had enough humiliating remarks aimed at him as a child to recognize the pain she felt. And he knew it didn't go away. You carried those scars with you for the rest of your life—though looking at Sky you would never know that she had been hurt that way. "You know that he was wrong, right? Any man would be proud of you."

"Maybe. But I know something even better now. I know it doesn't matter what a man thinks of me. What matters is that I'm proud of myself."

Jared's hands relaxed. He liked her observation better than his own.

"So yeah, that's my sad story. I've had some knocks in life, but haven't we all? I just choose to not let them hold me down. Life is short. I choose to enjoy it as much as possible and I think the key to that is having a positive attitude. And if some days I don't feel like smiling, I smile anyhow. There's a reason they say fake it till you make it. Besides, even though most people would think my life was hard, I wasn't alone. You're never alone when you have as many siblings as I do."

He spent the rest of the ride home listening to Sky tell stories of her and her family's escapades in the Tennessee mountains. She'd been more open and honest with him than he'd ever been with anyone. He'd never even confided about his life before the adoption to his own mother, the most caring woman he'd ever met. How was it that Sky could reveal such a painful thing about her past so easily?

Once they arrived back at the office, Jared was glad to get to work. Their house call to celebrity music stars had the office backed up with patients, so he grabbed a chart off his first examination room door and went to work.

It wasn't until later that night when he'd finally finished rounds and made it home that he let himself think about what Sky had told him about her family. For some reason he'd always assumed that Sky, with her over-the-top, happy-go-lucky nature, had come from one of those picture-perfect worlds. Somehow, finding that she'd survived the life she'd described that morning, while laughing through it all, gave him a new respect for her, though he wasn't sure about her statement about faking it. That didn't seem healthy to him. How long were you expected to fake it? Wasn't it better to deal with your feelings?

Not that he'd dealt with his own in a very healthy way. He didn't need a counselor to tell him that he let his past hold him back—his father had been telling him that for years. Yet now, hearing Sky's story, he found himself wanting to move past all those barriers he'd sealed himself behind.

But what then? What would happen if he let go of all the pain and loss he'd experienced as a child? What could his life be like if he chose to live like Sky? Jared had faced a lot in his life, but he knew that the possibility of letting go of the past and moving forward was the scariest thing he had ever considered doing.

CHAPTER FOUR

SKY STARED WITH more interest than was appropriate as one jean-clad leg followed the other
one down the ladder from the Legacy House
attic. She didn't need to see the brown head of
hair that eventually followed the hard muscled
body as he climbed farther down the stairs to
know that they belonged to Jared. She'd seen
his truck outside when she'd arrived. She'd
known he was here. But knowing that Jared
was here and then being treated to this version of Jared was not the same. This version of
Jared looked nothing like he did in his white
lab jacket, which was always neatly pressed
and buttoned all the way up to its stiff collar.
This Jared was much more interesting.

As he wiped his dust-covered hands against
the sides of his jeans, she had the outrageous
urge to reach out and brush those streaks of dirt
off him. When he turned toward her, she clasped

her hands behind her back just in case they decided to go rogue and get her into trouble.

"Good morning, Jared," she said, making sure her voice was filled with as much of her normal morning cheer as possible even while her heart rate was climbing up into the danger zone. She stared up into those deep brown eyes that were always so serious and couldn't help but wonder if she would ever know the real Jared. Even today, with his clothes covered in dirt, there was a tense line etched between his eyes as he studied her. After all she'd shared with him earlier in the week, she'd thought he'd be more relaxed around her.

"What are you doing here?" he asked.

"I brought some donated maternity clothes that I received from one of my patients. What about you? Looking for ghosts in the attic?"

He lifted an eyebrow. Yeah, it was a stupid question. Jared wasn't someone who would spend his time ghost hunting. It was more something that Sky herself might do. Well, maybe not ghost hunting, but she would enjoy going through any old trunks that might be stored in the attic.

"There's a problem with one of the electrical outlets in the living room. It looks like a squirrel or a rat might have gotten in and chewed on some wires. I'm going to get an electrician out here today to deal with it."

Okay, maybe searching through the attic wasn't a good idea.

A girl carrying a laundry basket came through the hallway and Sky moved to the side to let her get around them.

"Hey, Jasmine. How are you feeling?" Jared asked, the lines between his eyebrows coming together into a small knot now as he concentrated on the girl. Sky looked closer at the young woman who couldn't be more than eighteen. There were dark shadows below her brown eyes and her face had that puffy, swollen look that no midwife wanted to see. Her stomach was rounded and by its size she appeared to be in her third trimester.

The girl gave Sky a look that wasn't very trusting. "I'm Sky. I'm a midwife that works with Dr. Warner."

"I'm fine," Jasmine said, her voice flat. With her experience dealing with teenage patients, Sky knew that the word *fine* was used to give only the most limited amount of information. There was something off with Jasmine though. Her eyes weren't just tired, they were empty, something that Sky didn't normally see in healthy young girls who were expecting.

"Are you taking the blood pressure medicine I prescribed?" Jared asked.

"Yeah, Ms. Mason gives it to me every morning and checks my blood pressure twice a day just like you asked. But it makes me feel tired," Jasmine said, shuffling her feet and hitching the basket onto her hip.

"I'll talk to Maggie and see if she can bring you in to see me tomorrow. I might need to adjust your medications," Jared said, once again aware of how lucky they were to have someone as devoted to her job as house manager as Maggie Mason. "And we'll get another scan on the baby."

Jasmine's lips turned up in a half smile at the mention of the baby before she walked past them. She got to the end of the hall, then turned back toward them. "Thanks, Dr. Warner."

Sky waited till Jasmine had turned the corner and disappeared. "What's going on with her?"

Jared folded the ladder back up into the attic opening. "Physically, her blood pressure has been climbing for the last month. Mentally, I'm not sure. I can't get her to talk to me about it. I've asked her if she wants to talk to a counselor or if she would like another doctor, but she says no. It was one of the reasons I came by today. I want to check if Maggie has any idea what's going on with Jasmine."

The door to the attic slammed as Jared pushed it shut with more force than was necessary. This was the closest she had ever seen Jared to losing his temper. He really was worried about the girl.

"How about I talk to her?" Sky asked.

Jared looked down at her, his body close to hers in the small hallway. For a moment she forgot what they'd been talking about. Those rogue hands of hers wanted to reach out and walk down all those hard muscles clearly outlined by his shirt. It was a normal reaction by a woman attracted to a man, this need to touch that she was experiencing. With another man she might have expressed her interest.

But this was Jared. The only games she was allowed to play with him had to be silent and mostly platonic since they'd always been in the workplace. And most of the time he didn't even seem to enjoy those.

So why was she standing there ogling the man? It had to be this new relationship outside of the clinic that was causing all this confusion inside her. Yes, she'd admit, at least to herself, that she was attracted to Jared.

And though she had always told herself that

she just liked to tease him, there was a part of her that wanted him to notice her. To look at her, the woman, not the midwife. She'd been thinking about him ever since they'd visited the Carters. She'd told him almost all of her life story, something that had probably surprised her more than him. She didn't share her past with many people. She'd been judged for being abandoned and coming from almost nothing for most of her life, so now she refused to have people look at her with pity or judgment.

But Jared had done neither of those things. He'd even taken up for her, letting her know that her ex, Daniel, had been wrong, and expressing his belief that she was someone to be proud of.

She realized that she'd been staring at him for too long when his head tilted to the side, studying her deeply. "I mean… I'd like to help her and she might talk to me since I'm not involved with her care. How old is she? She looks so young. Well, everything but her eyes looked young. Her eyes are sad. Empty."

"She's seventeen. You see it too?" Jared asked, as if surprised that she could see that the girl was hurting.

"Yeah. Something is bothering her. She's due in what, three months?"

"She's almost thirty-two weeks. The baby has some intrauterine growth restriction. Another reason I'm worried about her," Jared said.

"I'm going to help Maggie today with some of the heavy cleaning. I'll try to talk to Jasmine. It's a lot to be pregnant and seventeen. I assume that she doesn't have a lot of support from her parents if she's living here." Sky tried not to judge Jasmine's parents. She remembered when her own sister had become pregnant at seventeen. It had been Sky that had been the most upset with Jill. The last thing Sky had wanted for her sister was to be in a situation where she was responsible for a child she was unable to care for. But their grandmother, even after spending the last ten years of her life raising them, had supported Sky's sister.

"Her mother came to the first few appointments with her. They seemed close. But then Jasmine asked me about moving into Legacy House. She's never told me what happened. And I haven't asked Maggie if she knew. I didn't want to make Jasmine feel like she couldn't trust her."

Sky was surprised by just how intuitive Jared was being. He'd always appeared so disconnected. Not uncaring—she'd seen him worry

over his patients just like the rest of them did—
he just didn't let very many people into his life.
Or at least that was how it seemed to her. It
could be he had a legion of girlfriends he left
every morning when he headed to work.

Okay, that was ridiculous and it might have
come from a bit of jealousy that she would prefer to ignore. Besides, whether or not he had
women in his life wasn't the point. It was the
fact that he seemed to hold himself back from
being involved with the people he saw every
day. People like her.

Maybe he just didn't find regular people interesting. Maybe that was why he tended to
keep to himself. Or maybe he was actually
studying them all. Maybe that was why he'd
questioned her about her attitude toward her
life.

She shook her head and tried to concentrate
on the issues Jasmine might be having. That
was what was important now. Not Sky's own
insecurities. "I'll see what I can find out. And
if there's some way for me to help her, I will.
She might just need some reassurance that Legacy House will be here for her. If it's an issue
with her parents… Well, I might not be the person to talk to but I'll find someone to help her.

If nothing else, I can be a friend to her. Someone she can reach out to if she needs someone."

"Right now the most important thing is to keep her blood pressure under control. If the medication doesn't help I'm going to put her on bed rest."

They started down the hall to the kitchen, where Sky knew she would find Maggie and some of the other staff preparing lunch. They'd been lucky to find someone like Maggie to run the home after the original manager, Mrs. Hudson, had retired. Maggie had spent most of her nursing career working in the office with the elder Dr. Warner. The fact that Maggie was her best friend Lori's mom made it even better.

Sky's phone pinged with a message and she pulled it from her pocket. She read the message twice, making sure she understood what Mindy was asking before she let out a squeal. "You are not going to believe this," she said to Jared, her hand coming out and grabbing his arm to stop him. "Mindy and Trey want us to come to the party they are having tomorrow night. The one Marjorie said all the country music stars were coming to."

She looked at Jared and saw none of the excitement she was feeling. "You have to come. The invitation is for the two of us. Together."

Still, he just stood there and looked at her. "Please?"

His shoulders slumped and she knew she'd won. She squealed again and threw her arms around his neck. His body tensed under hers, but she didn't care.

She, Sky Benton, from so far back in the hills of Tennessee that they had to pipe in sunshine, was going to an A-list party with all the music stars of Nashville. And she wasn't going to let Jared Warner ruin it.

CHAPTER FIVE

SKY WAS SPEECHLESS. After not being able to stop herself from talking nonstop on her first trip with Jared to Mindy and Trey's home, now she didn't know what to say. Her speechlessness surprised even her. She always knew what to say—or at least knew how to fake it. But this? This was too amazing. It was a dream come true for a little girl whose grandmother had listened to the *Grand Ole Opry* on the radio on Saturday nights.

The welcoming but overly large room she'd sat in just days earlier was filled with people. Some were people she'd seen on countless music award shows and others she recognized from the Carters' reality show. Some of the men were dressed in fancy suits while others wore jeans and cowboy hats. The women were dressed both casually and formally too.

And while Jared was dressed in an appropriate, if somewhat subdued, black suit, Sky had decided to go all out. With Lori's help, she'd found the perfect dress at a downtown boutique. Navy blue with a fitted bodice and a short flared skirt, the dress had enough glitter on it to make her feel glamorous and ready to party. It was a standout dress. One she had thought would give her the confidence she needed tonight.

Except now that she was here, seeing all of these beautiful, talented people, her confidence had disappeared as her memories of the past kept telling her that she didn't belong here. She did her best to shake them off.

"So, where do we start?" she asked Jared, glad to have him at her back. She'd been alone when she'd arrived in town after leaving her small hometown hospital. She'd never been to a city as big as Nashville before. But she hadn't run home then and she wasn't about to run home now. She'd decided that life was for living, not holding yourself back because you didn't believe you deserved something. This was a once-in-a-lifetime opportunity for her. She would not look back later with regret.

Before Jared could answer, she saw Mindy headed their way and Sky took a step toward her. After the first step, it seemed the next came easier. She could do this.

"I'm so glad you could come," Mindy said. Dressed in a flowing silver dress that accentuated her rounded abdomen, she was the most beautiful woman in the room.

"We're glad to be here," Sky said, taking hold of Jared's arm as that "I definitely don't belong here" feeling returned.

"Come in," Trey said as he joined his wife, wrapping his arm around her waist before holding out a hand to Jared. "Our producer was just asking about you. I promised to introduce the two of you."

"You're beginning to act like Marjorie. They just arrived. Can't they have a few minutes before you and Joe start talking business?" Mindy asked her husband.

"It's fine," Jared said. "I have some questions about the show and the interview they want to do that I wanted to talk to you about."

Mindy let out a heavy sigh, then linked her arm in Sky's. "Let me get you a drink and show you around. Don't get me wrong, I love Joe, but you'll get to meet him later. There are a lot more interesting people here that you need to meet."

Sky let go of Jared's arm and let Mindy pull her into the middle of the room. She looked back at Jared, who was already deep in conversation with Trey. She'd thought it would be Jared feeling out of place here, not her, but she'd been wrong. Of course, Jared had been raised in Nashville. Maybe that was why he wasn't showing signs of being starstruck like she was.

Just when she thought she'd gotten control of her nervousness about being around so many talented people, she was swallowed up into a crowd of the who's who of Nashville. There were singers and famous band members. There was even a Tennessee senator. Everywhere Sky looked, she saw another person she recognized from a video she'd enjoyed or a song she'd just been singing along with on the radio. By the time Mindy pulled her into the kitchen area, Sky was in celebrity overload.

"Would you like a drink?" Mindy asked her. "The bar is open in the family room, but I've got water and Cokes here."

"A water is fine," Sky said, taking a seat at the island, relieved to get away from the noise for a moment. "I'm sorry to pull you away from your guests."

"I need the break," Mindy said, taking the seat beside hers. "It's our first party to host in Nashville and I love it, but I don't think I was truly prepared for it."

"I can't imagine what the last year has been like for you. You have your first number one album. Your move to a new city. And then all the touring with the pregnancy. How do you do it all?"

"It's been wild, but it's the kind of crazy that we both love. And Trey has done everything he can to make it easier on me. Especially since the pregnancy. After the miscarriage he was very supportive, insisting that we decrease our tours for the next couple of months. But then everything took off. We had our first number one hit and we had to run with it. It was what we both had been working for and there wasn't a guarantee we'd get another chance."

Sky couldn't help but be a little envious of the relationship Mindy and Trey shared. What would it be like to have someone looking out for you? Someone who would be there when you got home? Someone you could count on? Someone you could share a dream with? But most importantly, someone you could trust not to break your heart? Sky had trusted her heart to someone before and she wasn't sure if she would ever have the courage to do that again.

Not that she had any right to complain. She dated often enough. She just made sure the other person always knew that she was only looking to have fun.

"We'd planned to wait a while before getting pregnant again after the miscarriage," Mindy said, rubbing her abdomen, "but this little one was meant to be. They're our special rainbow baby. The best surprise we could ever have hoped for. That's why we don't want to know the sex of the baby. We feel it should be a surprise until they're here."

Sky believed that all babies were special, but there was something so bittersweet about the babies that followed the loss of another child. "I love that. And you can trust that neither Jared nor I will share that information."

"I know. Jenny told me what a great experience she had with you as her midwife, but I was still nervous about meeting you."

"Why?" Sky asked. It had been only natural for her to be nervous about meeting someone like Mindy and Trey. They were stars. But her? She was just a simple midwife from nowhere Tennessee.

Mindy sighed and leaned back in her chair. "I knew that things were going to change if we ever made it to the top of the charts. And then there was the reality show. We'd just started to have a small amount of success when we agreed to the show. We were prepared to lose some of our privacy, but I wasn't prepared for the way the people around us changed."

Sky remembered how her friends and even some of her family acted when she'd made the decision to leave her hometown and head to the big city. She'd never understood why they couldn't see that there was nothing for her there. She'd been made to feel like she was letting them down even though they knew how hard it was to watch her ex walk around with the woman whom he'd decided fit his needs for a wife better than her.

"When a friend of mine let it out that I was pregnant, the media went crazy. We were so happy about the pregnancy, but we didn't want to share it yet. We'd just got over the media attention that my miscarriage received, and I'd made it plain to everyone who we told that I didn't want to share the pregnancy. Not yet, at least. We knew it would have to come out with the reality show and everything, but we wanted to wait. I guess I just didn't feel I could trust someone after that. But when I met you and Jared, you made me feel better. You were interested in me, Mindy, not Mindy Carter of the Carters. Does that make sense?"

"It makes perfect sense, and I'm sorry someone you thought you could trust let you down that way. I hope you know now that you can trust me. My goal is always to put mother and baby first. That's why I have a frank talk with all my patients as far as their birth plan. Your health and that of the baby will come first for me and Jared. Where they come from, their background, that's not a priority." Sky stopped to take a sip of her water.

"About Jared," Mindy said, "I hope it doesn't bother you that we asked to have the two of you work together. I really want a midwife to care for me, but Trey wanted to go the traditional route."

"It doesn't bother me. Jared and I are both happy to work with the two of you," Sky said. This was pretty much what Jack had told her and Jared the day he'd first spoken to them about Mindy and Trey. While Sky knew that some midwives would have been insulted by the request, she hadn't been. She knew that she could provide the care that Mindy and her baby would need. She'd reviewed Mindy's records closely and there were no risk factors that would keep Mindy from having a midwifery delivery. But if Trey needed the reassurance of Jared being involved, that was okay too.

"About you and Jared," Mindy said, her eyes

lighting up with humor, "am I imagining that there's something there besides work going on between the two of you?"

For the second time that night, she was speechless. She took a big gulp of water, paying close attention to swallow it without choking, then set the bottle down. She liked Mindy but she didn't know her well enough to admit her secret attraction to Jared. She wouldn't even admit that to Lori. "We're colleagues. That's all."

It was the truth, yet she felt a small amount of guilt for not admitting to her unexpected interest in Jared. Mindy had been open with her about her fears and how someone had let her down. It had been more than just the normal patient-and-provider sharing of information. This had been more personal.

There was something about Mindy that put Sky at ease. And it had helped put all the absurdity of the crowd in the other rooms into perspective for her. Not too long ago, Mindy was just a normal person working to make her dream come true, just like Sky had been when she'd worked to become a midwife. How many of the people out there surrounded now by fame and fortune had started just like the two of them? Like Jared had said, they put their cowboy boots on just like she did.

"Thank you for helping me get over my nervousness tonight." Sky set her bottle down again and turned to Mindy. "I'm not usually like this. It's just…my world is so much different than this. This is…"

"Extreme?" Mindy asked, standing and taking Sky's arm again.

"Yes!" Sky said as they headed back into the crowd, this time feeling more confident. "So, let's go get crazy too."

Jared looked over the crowd, trying to find Sky. He'd had a good talk with the producer of the Carters' reality show. While Sky didn't seem to have any problem being on the show, he didn't like the idea of opening up his personal life to the public. He knew it wasn't like he or Sky were going to be featured except for the small part of being health care providers for Mindy. Still, he'd made the producer promise that there would be no unnecessary information given out about the two of them. With the handsome donation the producer had agreed to for Legacy House, Jared knew he'd made the best of the situation that he could. They'd do an interview or two and it would be over with. Now he just needed to find Sky so they could leave.

Sometime since he'd left the party to join the producer Joe and Trey in his office, a band had set up. The music was good, of course—he wouldn't expect anything less with the caliber of musicians in the room. When a man he recognized as a Hall of Fame singer joined in with his own guitar, Jared stopped to listen for a moment. His own hands itched to feel those guitar strings under his fingers. To feel the vibration of the music flow into him along with the emotions it brought him.

When the song ended and the applause started, he made his way back through the crowd to the other side of the room, where a dance floor had been set up. The band started back with a line dance favorite from the 1990s and it only took him a minute to spot Sky among the dancers. Then he recognized the man she was smiling at beside her. Nick Thomas was a local boy who'd formed one of the top bands in the city. He hadn't gained the fame that most of the people in the room had, but from the local media reviews it was only time before his band hit it big.

But it wasn't Nick that held Jared's attention. It was Sky. And it wasn't the way her short skirt twirled around her shapely legs as she danced or the way her head of blond curls bounced with her movements. It was her smile. That happy, wide-mouthed smile that made him want to join her in the dance. That made him want to pull her to him and swing her around and around with the rhythm of the music until they both were breathless.

The song ended and she said something to Nick, then turned toward him. He knew the moment she saw him as their eyes locked and her smile changed to that mischievous one she loved to tempt him with. His body tensed with an edginess he'd never felt before as she walked slowly toward him. The crowd faded away as she took his hand and began pulling him toward the dance floor. The band started to play a slow, sad song filled with the sweet strains of a fiddle.

"Dance with me," Sky said, her blue eyes sparkling with a fevered excitement that flowed over onto him.

He knew he shouldn't. This wasn't a date. They were there purely as professional colleagues. Nothing more.

But as her arms wrapped around his neck, his own arms found their way around her waist, pulling her closer. And when she laid her head against him, he let himself relax against her. What could it hurt to share one dance?

It only took a minute for his body to answer that question. It was as if a fire had been lit inside him as his body reacted to the feel of Sky against him. His muscles tightened and he went stone hard. He tried to keep his breathing as even as possible as they swayed to the music, her body rubbing against him with each movement. He glanced down and their eyes met. As she drew in a breath that appeared as labored as his, his eyes went to her lips, the same lips that had teased him for months. For a moment he considered tasting them. Would they be soft and supple? Or would they be firm and needy? He had just started to lean down when the couple next to them bumped into him, breaking whatever spell he'd been under.

What could one dance hurt? It could destroy his whole reputation if he let himself lose control on the dance floor.

With a willpower he hadn't known he possessed, he pulled himself back from the brink of doing something that would scandalize the whole room. But when the song ended and she stepped away from him, his arms felt empty. It had only been one dance. The fact that her body had molded so perfectly to his didn't mean a thing. But he'd danced with many women before Sky and he'd never felt anything like this before.

"We should go," he said, though his traitorous feet refused to move.

"Why? Do we have plans?" she asked, her voice soft and breathy. His body responded as once more she stepped toward him.

He wanted to pull her back into his arms, to kiss that mouth that had teased him for the last six months. Only he couldn't kiss her now any more than he could have kissed her all those other times. He had to restrain himself just like he'd done over and over when she had tempted him. He needed to put things back to the way they'd been before that dance. Before he'd felt how right her body felt against his.

It should be simple. One step. Just take one step and walk away. But this was Sky. Nothing about the woman was simple. They constantly butted heads at work. She'd teased and tortured him for months with her sexy smile and sassy winks.

Someone tapped him on the shoulder and broke the spell that had held him captive. Turning, he saw that it was Nick standing behind him.

"If you aren't going to dance with the lady, I'd like to," Nick said, his oh-so perfect smile making Jared's teeth clench on the words he wanted to say.

"No. We were just leaving," Jared said, managing to get the words out before taking Sky's hand and pulling her behind him.

It wasn't until they were at the door that he was reminded of where they were and why they'd come. None of this was supposed to be about him and Sky. Nor was the possessive way he'd just acted professional.

It sobered him to know how close he'd come to making a scene by telling Nick right where to shove his invitation. They were there to represent his father's practice and to help gain more donations for Legacy House. He remembered how beaten down his dad had looked when he'd shared that Legacy House could be in trouble financially. And Jared had almost blown everything, nearly embarrassed his dad in front of the very people whose help they needed. His father deserved a better son than that.

He let go of Sky's hand and took a physical step away as his brain took a figurative step back from the line his body had been prepared to cross.

"I'm sorry," he said. "I shouldn't have spoken for you. If you want to go back to Nick I understand."

* * *

Emotions bounced around inside of Sky like she was a pinball machine. Shock with a small amount of pleasure from the way Jared had reacted to Nick's interest in her. Anger at the way he'd spoken for her without giving her a chance to tell the other man she wasn't interested. And finally, the worst part, pain from the way he was now prepared to let her return to Nick after the intimate dance the two of them had just shared.

She looked across the room to see that Mindy was involved in a conversation with one of last year's CMA winners. It felt rude to leave without thanking her for the invitation.

She looked over at the ramrod-straight statue that Jared had become and her anger pushed all of the other emotions out of its way. Stomping her high heeled feet through the crowd, she left Jared behind. She didn't care if he followed her or not.

She'd made it outside the house and halfway across the drive by the time Jared caught up with her. When he walked around to her side of the truck to open her door, she was already opening it. Changing her mind, she slammed it shut and turned on him.

"I don't understand you," she said, the truth

of the statement hitting her hard. She didn't understand him because he had never let her get close enough. She'd been teasing this man for over six months now, trying to get a response out of him. Yes, she wanted to make him smile, but now she wondered if it had been more than that. The more time they spent together, the more she wondered if she'd been secretly wanting him to seek her out. To return her interest.

And for a few moments tonight, she'd thought he had been interested. Then the old Jared who she'd watched turn away from her over and over found that control he was famous for, leaving Sky now confused and hurt. Why couldn't the man just relax and enjoy the moment? Had he not felt that all-consuming need for her that she had felt for him? Had she been the only one who had experienced that magical moment on the dance floor?

"I was having so much fun." She wouldn't cry, not in front of him. She'd promised herself that she would never cry again when someone walked away from her, yet the tears felt so close now. "And then you ruined it. Why? Why couldn't you have just enjoyed the moment? Was it me? Was it something I did?"

"We didn't come here to dance," Jared said,

his eyes emotionless and his body rigid as he ignored her questions.

How could this be the same man who had held her just minutes before? How could this be the same man whose body had reacted so eagerly to hers? Did he think she hadn't noticed the way his body had hardened against hers? Hadn't he felt the way she'd melted against the heat of him?

"Well, maybe you didn't, but I did."

"We were supposed to represent the practice and try to get donations," he said, his stern jaw turning up in challenge.

"We were supposed to blend in with the crowd while representing the practice and earning some goodwill for Legacy House. That was what I was doing with Nick. He's a good friend of Mindy and Trey's. They'd told him about what the home does to help local women. He's from Nashville. He was interested in helping."

"It wasn't Legacy House he was interested in on the dance floor. That wasn't why he wanted to dance with you."

"He wasn't the person I was dancing with. I was dancing with *you*. So maybe you should explain to me why it was that you agreed to dance with me? It certainly wasn't because you wanted to *represent the practice*." She filled the last three words with as much sarcasm as was possible.

They faced each other, both of them breathless from the emotions that swirled around them. Along with the anger, she felt a certain thrill running through her because she'd been able to make Jared show at least some sort of emotion for her. He might deny how he'd responded to her on that dance floor, but she knew better. He'd felt something for her when he'd held her. He'd wanted her. And she'd wanted him.

Unfortunately, it was just as plain to her that he wasn't going to admit it. That for a few minutes she'd made him drop that facade of detachment he wore. And if it truly wasn't something he wanted, it didn't matter. He wasn't the first man that hadn't wanted her. Her ex had made that plain when after years together he'd walked away from her without a second thought.

"I'm sorry if I embarrassed you and the practice," Sky said. "That wasn't my intention."

"You didn't embarrass me."

All the emotions that she had been feeling drained out of her as suddenly as they had come. She felt empty and so very tired. She opened the door and climbed into the truck. She turned away from Jared when he climbed in beside her and started the engine.

She'd assumed she'd leave the party tonight floating on air after meeting all the famous people of Nashville. Instead, she wanted to dig a hole and climb into it to escape this familiar feeling of being unwanted.

Had she really thought she could blend in with people like those she'd met tonight? Jared had made it plain that she was only there because of the practice. She'd just been the hired help, at least that was what he thought. It had been stupid of her to think it was anything more than that.

Just like it had been stupid for her to think that sharing her secrets with Jared might have made a difference in how he saw her.

"Look, I just think it would be better if we remember that we are here to do a job. This isn't about us and all this..." he said, turning toward her and waving a hand between the two of them.

"This?" she asked, copying his waving hand gesture. "You mean the two of us acting human?"

Jared's eyes met hers and she saw a vulnerability there that surprised her. "What are you afraid of? Is it disappointing your father? Or is it me?"

She didn't want to think that there was something about her that scared him off from becoming involved with her. She had been over-the-top flirty with him, and sometimes she did push too hard when there was something that she wanted, but she'd only wanted him to notice her. "I'm sorry if I've been too pushy. I just thought…"

What had she thought? That he would jump at the chance of spending time with her on the dance floor? That he'd welcome her into his arms? That he'd secretly been harboring a crush on her just like she'd been harboring one on him?

"I just thought we could have a good time while we were here," she murmured, turning her head away from him so he wouldn't see the tears that she couldn't explain.

"It's not you, Sky. I just don't think the two of us getting involved would be a good thing. I'm sure you'll agree that the two of us are just too different. Things would get complicated."

He looked over at her as he started his truck, then sat there as if waiting for her to agree with him. Not that she did. All she knew was that when she'd been in Jared's arms, it had felt right. Finally, when she didn't speak, he put the truck in gear and started down the drive.

CHAPTER SIX

JARED WAS HAVING a bad day. From the time his alarm had gone off, nothing had gone right. He'd even growled at Tanya this morning when she'd reminded him that he had a lunch meeting with his dad and Sky at noon, though the office manager had only been doing her job He tried to tell himself it was just because it was a Monday and even he didn't like the first day of the workweek. But he knew it was more than that. He'd been in a foul mood ever since Friday night when he'd dropped Sky off at her home.

He knew he owed her an apology. He'd overstepped his place and in the process he'd ruined the night for her. He'd known she was excited about meeting all the famous people that had been sure to attend the Carters' party. He'd even overheard Lori talking to Tanya about helping Sky pick out a dress for the event. She'd wanted something to make her blend in with all those famous people.

Not that it had worked. She would never blend in with any crowd. She was too beautiful, too spirited for that. It was what drew Jared to her while at the same time making him want to be as far away as possible. He knew danger when he saw it and Sky was the most dangerous woman he'd ever met. She was like an atomic bomb that could blow the life he'd worked so hard to make right out of the Tennessee mountains. That was why he'd felt the need to remind Sky that nothing could happen between the two of them. But if he really believed that, why had he spent the rest of his weekend thinking about the dance the two of them had shared?

"Hey, Dr. Warner, can I speak to you for a moment?"

Jared looked up from his desk to see Lori's mom standing outside his door. "Sure, Maggie, and call me Jared, please."

"I don't want to disturb you, but they just took Jasmine back to the examination room and I wanted to talk to you before you see her," Maggie said as she stepped into the office. "You asked me to let you know if there were any changes with her blood pressure or her behavior."

Jared pushed the laptop he had been using out of the way. "How is she doing?"

"Her blood pressure is about the same with the medications you've given her and she is taking them without any trouble. It's her behavior that has me worried. She just seems so detached from the rest of the women in the household. She spends most of her time sleeping or at least in her bed."

"She told me the medication for her blood pressure was making her tired, but I don't think that's all there is to this. She's made too much of a change since she first came to see me with her mother. I'm wondering if she's homesick. Have her parents visited her?" He didn't know a lot about Jasmine and her parents' relationship. They'd seemed to be close on that first visit. Jasmine's mother had asked all the appropriate questions as a caring parent of a pregnant teenager. But something had happened between them, something big, and whatever it was, it had affected Jasmine badly. Sky had followed through on her offer to talk to Jasmine, but she'd told Jared that the girl had seemed very low energy and had no luck in getting her to open up.

"Her mother calls her I know, but the conversations I've heard were very short. From what I can tell, there was some type of disagreement between the two of them before Jasmine came to Legacy House. And as far as the medication is concerned, I don't think we can blame it for all of the changes. She's showing too many signs of a new onset of depression. I can't say she's not looking out for the baby. She's doing everything we ask as far as that is concerned. She's just not taking care of herself. There were times last week when she'd go days without bathing or dressing properly."

Jared sighed, then rose. They couldn't have found anyone to manage the home as well as Maggie did. With her medical background and her caring nature, she was the perfect stand-in mom for the women there. "Thanks for letting me know. I'll talk to her and try to get her to agree to see a counselor. Whatever is going on with her psychologically, it's not a good combination with her hypertension."

Maggie thanked him before returning to the waiting room, and Jared headed into the exam room to see Jasmine. Knocking and then opening the door, he saw immediately why Maggie had been concerned. The young girl lay on the examination table, not even opening her eyes when he entered. The last couple months with Jasmine had been like watching a thriving flower slowly wilt in front of him. There had to be something he could do to help this girl.

Pulling out his phone, he sent a message to Sky asking her to meet him in the examination room. He needed a second opinion along with any help he could give her. He hadn't seen Sky come into the office but he knew she normally had patient exams scheduled on Mondays.

"Good morning, Jasmine," he said, taking a seat and opening the room's computer where the patient's weight and vital signs had been recorded. Her blood pressure hadn't increased but neither had it decreased. He hated to add a second blood pressure medication but it looked like he was going to have to do it.

There was a knock on the door before Sky entered. She'd pulled her hair back into a pony-tail today and he found himself missing those curls of hers that spiraled all around her face. When her eyes met his, they were all business. Yeah, she was still mad at him. It was something they'd have to deal with but it would have to wait till later. Right now his priority was his patient.

"Jasmine, Sky is one of the midwives here. You met her the other day."

Jasmine opened her eyes for the first time, then sat up at the end of the exam table. He noted the dark circles around the girl's eyes, but it was the increased puffiness in her face that truly bothered him. What had started out as a concern for hypertension was now looking more and more like preeclampsia.

"Hi, Jasmine. We talked the other day when I was helping Ms. Maggie."

"I'm not stupid just because I got myself pregnant," Jasmine said, the first sign of life showing in her defiant eyes. "I thought you were my doctor. Why do I need a midwife?"

"Sky and I work together on some cases. And neither one of us thinks you're stupid. If I remember correctly, your mother said you had earned a scholarship for college next year. What are you planning on studying?" He had her talking to him now and he didn't want her to stop.

"I was going to do pre-law, but that's messed up now. Everything is messed up now." Jasmine's shoulders lowered along with her head, that small spark of defiance gone.

"My sister is a lawyer. She practices family law in our hometown. What type of practice are you planning on going into?" Sky asked, taking a seat in the chair beside Jasmine as the girl looked up at her.

There was pain and disappointment in the girl's eyes now. Was that what was bothering her? Did she think that because she was having a baby she couldn't go to college? Couldn't have a future? She definitely wasn't like most of the teenagers she dealt with that were more concerned about the here and now. Jasmine had planned a future that hadn't included raising a child.

"I told you. It's all messed up now. My parents… It's just messed up and I don't want to talk about it. Ms. Maggie said you wanted me to come in so that you could check my blood pressure and adjust my medication. That's why I'm here." And there was that spark of anger again. He didn't like the fact that making her angry could increase her already too high blood pressure. Still, at least he had an idea what the problem was now.

"I'm going to change your blood pressure medicine and I want to do some more tests," Jared said. "And I'd still like you to consider going to see a counselor."

"I don't need a counselor. I don't need anything except to have this baby," Jasmine said before falling back against the table.

"You still have a few weeks until it will be safe for the baby to be born. I'm going to step out and get someone to come in and draw some blood. If you're okay with it, Sky can do a fast exam of your heart and lungs for me and check you for swelling while I'm gone."

Jasmine sat back up and looked Sky over from head to toe. "You still haven't told me why she's here."

"Like I said, we work together sometimes. It's good to get a second opinion, don't you think? We're working together right now with a famous country star." Jared saw the interest in Jasmine's eyes before it disappeared. "I'll send someone right in to draw that lab work."

He left the room, hoping that with some privacy Jasmine might open up further to Sky. A few minutes later Sky appeared at his office doorway. "They're drawing Jasmine's labs now. I was going to let her go after that, but I wanted to check with you first."

"Did she say anything else to you?" Jared asked.

"I mainly talked to her about where my sister went to school and some of the courses she took. She seemed interested at first. Then she went back to the same line she used before. Everything is messed up because of the pregnancy. I don't know what happened between her and her parents, but I'm pretty sure that's at least part of the source of the depression she's having now. I'm supposed to help Maggie again Wednesday. I'll talk to her again then."

"At this point her blood pressure has got to be my main concern. And now that she's starting to have more swelling, I'm beginning to suspect she's becoming preeclamptic." Like the poor girl didn't have enough going wrong for her. "She could really use her parents' support right now, but I can't contact them without her okay. Maybe you can mention that?"

"I'll try to bring it up to her. She's seventeen. Whatever it is going on in that head of hers seems insurmountable right now. Hopefully, she'll let one of us help her." She started to turn away.

"We're supposed to have lunch with my father today," Jared said. He had to find a way to apologize for his actions Friday night but now didn't seem like the right time.

"Tanya reminded me. I'll meet you there." With that, Sky turned and hurried down the hall toward her own set of examination rooms. He probably owed her another apology for taking her away from her own patients. Not that she would be interested in one. She was just as worried as he was about Jasmine.

It seemed like the two of them would be working together even more now. And Jared found, even though he was well aware of the dangers after their dance, that he didn't mind that at all.

Jared and his father were waiting for Sky when she arrived at the Barbecue Shack down from the office. Unlike its name, the place was more modern barn chic than a shack. A large brisket turned in the rotisserie pit at the front entrance and the sweet smell of roasting meat pulled a nice crowd inside throughout the day.

She spotted both of the Warner men at a corner table, their heads together as they studied the menu. She still didn't understand why they couldn't have met in Jack's office, but when Tanya told you to be somewhere you just followed instructions.

"Sorry I'm running late," she said as she took a chair across from them. "I had a heavy load of patients this morning."

"I meant to thank you for helping me with Jasmine. I know you had your own patients to see," Jared said, his distant politeness setting her teeth on edge, though she shouldn't have been surprised by it. He'd made it clear that he didn't want anything to do with her except professionally.

"I didn't mind. I just don't know if I did any good. I'm going to talk to my sister tonight and see if she has any advice for someone with a child wanting to go to law school. I'm sure there are resources out there to help single moms like Jasmine." Sky kept her voice just as polite as his.

Dr. Warner followed their conversation, his head ping-ponging back and forth between them, without commenting. As always though, his eyes showed a merriment that Sky herself wasn't feeling.

"Again, thank you," Jared said. His words were sincere. They shouldn't have hurt.

"It's nice to see the two of you working together so well. I knew the two of you would find a way to make this work," Jack said as the waitress appeared to take their order.

After she left, Jack pulled out his phone and held it out to them. "I received this from our accountant this morning. It seems that you two and the Carters have been talking up Legacy House to a lot of people in their circle. We received four significant donations over the weekend. I don't know the last time we've received donations like this, so keep up the good work. You're making a difference in a lot of women's lives."

Sky skimmed down the email till she got to the names listed and the amounts that had been donated. She recognized two of the names, one being Nick and the other the producer of the Carters' reality show.

"Joe promised another twenty-five thousand for allowing him an interview for the show. Also, he is going to let us put a plug in for Legacy House in the interview."

"Why would they want to interview us? There's nothing exciting about the two of us." It would be good to get Legacy House on the show though. Maggie had been talking about needing to update some of the kitchen with large appliances. And she'd said that the electrician had recommended an electrical upgrade too.

"I think it's just to get more interest in the show. The audience seems to be obsessed with Mindy's pregnancy," Jared said, acting like it didn't bother him that people could be asking them personal questions when she knew it would be the last thing he wanted.

"And how are things going with Mindy and

Trey? It sounds like they are satisfied with their care so far," Jack said.

"Mindy's coming in Friday for her first visit. I'm going to let her in through the employee entrance so she won't have to come through the waiting room. I'm not expecting any problems as far as the pregnancy. She's done well so far. I do want to get an ultrasound to measure the baby's growth while she's there. What about you, Jared? Anything I'm forgetting?"

"It sounds fine. Except for her miscarriage she doesn't have any risk factors. Trey did specify that they didn't want to know the sex of the baby. It is really important to them to find out at the delivery."

"Well, that all sounds good," Jack said as their food arrived.

The rest of the meal they spent discussing what Jack wanted them to stress in the interview as far as the practice was concerned and Legacy House. It was like prepping for an examination and Sky wanted to make sure she was ready for any questions that might be directed at her.

She launched herself into her afternoon patients' exams feeling better than she had that morning when she'd come in. She and Jared had managed to share a lunch without either of them referring to the party they'd attended together. And if he wanted to pretend that the dance they had shared had never happened she could do that too. It had only been one dance, she told herself.

So why did it feel like it had changed everything?

CHAPTER SEVEN

WITH THE OFFICE closed and most of the staff gone for the day, Sky sat back in her chair and perched her bare feet on the desk. She'd gotten a blister on her foot while dancing Friday night and being on her feet all day had just aggravated it.

When the knock came on the door, she assumed that it was one of the techs saying goodnight. As Jared stuck his head into her office door, she started to put her legs down, then stopped. It was her office after all. If she wanted to put her feet up after hours, she could do it.

"Sorry, I don't mean to disturb you. I just wanted a minute of your time," he said. He was still being overly polite and she still didn't like it. He'd made it clear that he wasn't interested in her except professionally, But he didn't have to act so cold to her.

"Is there something we didn't cover at lunch concerning the Carters?"

"That's not what I wanted to talk about. I just wanted to tell you that I'm sorry for what happened. I know you were excited about the party and I'm sorry I ruined that for you."

Sky didn't know what to say. She *had* been excited about the party. And it had been amazing. She'd had a great time dancing with some of country music's biggest stars. She had enjoyed getting to know Mindy better too. But the thing she had enjoyed the most was the one thing Jared was apologizing for.

And why did they have to go over this again? Oh, he said he was sorry for ruining the party, but she knew what he meant. He was embarrassed that he had responded to her on the dance floor. The point being, *he had responded to her.* They both knew that. She just didn't understand why he was determined to ignore it. The two of them were single adults. And it wasn't like workplace relationships didn't take place there. As long as they were discreet, no one would care. There was something else keeping him tangled up that he couldn't seem to break free of. Something stronger than his desire to explore what the two of them had felt that night. If only she could understand what it was.

But that wasn't something she was going to

solve tonight. "I enjoyed the party. You didn't ruin it for me."

Her phone rang and she almost groaned when she saw it was the women's unit of the hospital. "This is Sky."

She listened as the nurse on the labor floor gave her report on one of her patients who was thirty-six weeks and expecting twins. Sky had been her midwife for her other two deliveries and they had hoped that she would be able to deliver both of them vaginally. Now it didn't look like that would happen.

"I'll be over to talk to her," she said before ending the call. "Are you on call tonight for surgery?" she asked him.

"I am. Why? What's wrong?"

"Nothing's wrong. I have a patient that is expecting twins. They were both head down on her ultrasound last week, but it looks like baby B decided he didn't want to follow his sister's direction. He's complete breech now." Sky put her feet down and toed her shoes back on. "Sarah's water is broken but she's only two centimeters and not having regular contractions yet. I delivered her other two babies without any difficulty, but she has a small outlet. We planned to try for a vaginal delivery with the twins if they were both cephalic, but I don't feel good about trying to turn baby B."

"I'll call over and tell them to get her ready for a C-section," Jared said. "Have you discussed with her the possibility of surgery with twins?"

"Of course I have. It was one of the first things we discussed. I know how to do my job, Jared." Why did he always make her feel like he thought she was incompetent? "When are you going to accept that midwives are as competent as doctors? What is it you have against us?"

"I know you are competent. I didn't mean anything by my question," Jared said. "I don't know this patient. I'm just asking for information."

"It isn't just this time. You said you don't have a problem with midwives, but you do it all the time. Is it something I've done?" She knew this wasn't the time to get into this, but she needed to know. She was tired of feeling like she wasn't good enough for him. Like she was lacking something. She knew that no matter how much she denied it, some of her insecurity came from the way her ex had treated her. Still, she wanted to know that Jared trusted her to take care of her patients. "What do I have to do to convince you that I'm a good midwife?"

The sincerity in Sky's blue eyes cut through his need to keep his most painful history private. "It's not you. It's just…"

He took the seat at the desk across from her. How was it that this woman had the power to make him bare his soul to her? "My mother died after childbirth."

"I'm so sorry, Jared," Sky said. "Do you want to tell me what happened?"

This was something that he didn't speak of to anyone, but he found himself now wanting to explain it all to her. Maybe then she'd understand that it wasn't that he doubted her capability. He just wanted to make sure what had happened to his mother didn't happen again.

"After I was born, my grandmother told the midwife taking care of my mother that something was wrong. My mother had begun complaining of feeling bad, feeling 'funny.' My grandmother had no medical training, but she told me she felt it in her soul that something was wrong. But before she could insist that the midwife do something my mother had a seizure. She aspirated and coded while the midwife was repairing her episiotomy. She had an anoxic brain injury and a week later she was declared brain dead and removed from life support. My grandmother discovered later that my mother's blood pressure had been rising during her pregnancy but the midwife hadn't followed up and ordered any of the diagnostic lab work she should have." He didn't tell her that his grandmother had blamed that midwife for the loss of her only child from that day until her death, while he'd grown up blaming himself. It had only been when he'd been older and had learned more about childbirth that he had understood the things his grandmother had told him.

"I'm so sorry that happened to your family," Sky said. "You didn't become a doctor because of Jack, did you? You became an obstetrician because of what happened to your mother."

"Jack was a part of it." He'd come to believe that having Jack, one of the most sought out obstetricians in Nashville, as his father had been more than fate. "But yes, most of it was because of my mother. I don't want another woman to die unnecessarily."

"That's what I want too. What we all want. But even with all the medical gains in our field, maternal deaths still happen," Sky said.

"That's why we have to work harder to find

ways to stop it from happening." Jared leaned forward, his hand reaching out to her in his need for her understanding. "Don't you see, Sky. That's why I double-check everything. I know I can be a bit intense, but I only want what's best for the patient."

"That's what we all want. Maybe working together, respecting the role each of us play in our patients' care is the best thing for our patients," Sky said, taking his hand and giving it a comforting squeeze. "Thank you for telling me about your mother."

Jared looked down to where their hands were joined. He felt as if a burden had been lifted from his shoulders. As if telling Sky had opened up something inside him. Maybe she was right? Maybe instead of working at cross-purposes, they could work together to ensure their patients' safety.

"Speaking of patients," Jared said as he let go of Sky's hand, "we need to go take care of those twins of yours."

"I'd like to assist you in surgery, if that's okay with you?" Sky asked as she stood and stretched. Jared knew that her day had been just as long as his.

"I think that would be a great idea," Jared said, rising and following her to the door.

"Okay, then. Let's go deliver these twins. I can't wait to meet the little troublemaker who decided he wanted to take his own path instead of following his sister." Sky took her jacket from the stand where she'd hung it.

"I think that sounds like a plan we can both agree on," Jared said, excited about the delivery. He told himself he was just looking forward to the birth of the twins, but he knew that having Sky right there beside him would make it even better.

"Hey, let me help with that," Sky said to Lori, grabbing one of the bags of groceries that her best friend was juggling as she tried to open the kitchen door to Legacy House.

"Thanks." Lori moved back so Sky could open the door. "Mom told me you would be here today. She appreciates all the help you've been with the spring cleaning. Though I don't know how you have the time with everything going on right now."

"I love helping out. I can't donate a lot of money so I give the time I have available instead."

"So how did the party go? I heard you and Jared got some significant donations," Lori said as they began putting away the groceries.

With everything going on in the office, Sky hadn't had a chance to tell her about that night. "It was amazing. It was like attending one of those parties you see pictures of after the CMA show. And Mindy was the perfect hostess."

"What about Jared? Did he have any fun?" Lori asked.

Sky grabbed a couple sodas from the fridge and sat them on the table. "I'm not sure. It's complicated."

"What do you mean?" Lori joined her at the table. "He didn't talk to you?"

It wasn't the talking that Sky was thinking about. She still couldn't get over how Jared had gone from hot to cold so fast. She hadn't planned to discuss any of what had happened between them with anyone, but maybe she needed to. Maybe talking with Lori would help her understand how he could change from one moment to the next. Or maybe it was her. Maybe she had just imagined the red-hot need that had flowed between the two of them.

"We talked. It wasn't the talking that was the problem. Well, at least it wasn't a problem until after the dance we shared."

"Really? What happened? Is he a bad dancer? Did he step on your feet?" Lori smiled, her eyes filled with amusement.

Was he a good dancer? She really couldn't remember much about the dancing or the music that was playing. She only remembered how perfect it felt to be in Jared's arms and how much she had wanted to stay there. And his eyes. She remembered the heat that had filled them. He'd wanted to kiss her, she was sure of that. "I think it was more like he stepped on my heart."

The amusement in Lori's eyes died. "Tell me what happened. Then give me a good reason I shouldn't kick his butt."

"You can't kick his butt. He's our boss's son. Besides, he didn't do anything wrong. At least, not intentionally."

"Tell me everything," Lori said.

So Sky told her. She told her about the people she met. How she had felt out of place amongst all the famous and talented people, though they'd all been kind and welcoming. She told her how Mindy had been especially sweet. Then she told her about dancing with Nick Thomas.

"What is he like? Is he going to call you?"

"I don't think he'll be calling me. Jared was pretty rude to him." She wondered if Jared would be calling Nick to apologize. She didn't think so.

"Jared? Our Jared? I've never heard him raise his voice before. It's like human emotions are something too menial for him."

"He's not like that, not really," she said, not liking the way Lori made him sound.

"Has anyone seen Ms. Maggie?" a voice asked from the doorway.

Sky turned to find Jasmine, still dressed in her pajamas. The circles under her eyes were even puffier than the last time she had seen her.

"I'll go get her," Lori murmured, giving the young girl a worried look.

"Come, sit down," Sky said. At first she thought the girl was going to refuse. But after glancing behind her, Jasmine took a seat across from her. "How are you feeling today?"

"I'm okay. Just still tired. Dr. Warner changed the medication but I'm still tired all the time. I'm getting behind in my classes."

That was the most Sky had heard the girl volunteer in any conversation. "I'm sorry. I'd be glad to help. Or Ms. Maggie knows several tutors that help with the students here. You're doing online courses, right?"

"I had to change when I got here. I was ahead of the class at my school." The words lacked the teenage sarcasm she'd been filled with earlier in the week. "And now I'm falling behind because of this stupid medicine."

"You're right. The medicine can make you feel bad. But I don't think that your being behind in your classes is all that is bothering you. Talk to me, Jasmine. Tell me what is wrong so I can help you."

"You can't help me. No one can now." Then the girl broke.

Sobs wracked Jasmine's body and Sky moved to put her arm around her. Over the girl's shoulders, she saw Maggie and Lori come into the room. Sky shook her head at them and they stepped back out.

"I can't promise to have the answer but I'm here to help if I can. You can't keep all of this bottled up inside of you. It's not good for you or the baby."

"It's the baby that's the problem," Jasmine said, looking up at her with eyes filled with tears she'd clearly been holding in for months. "I don't want to keep the baby. I know I'm being selfish. But I had my life planned. I've wanted to go to college for as long as I can remember."

"You can still go to college. You know that, right?" Sky didn't think that was the real problem but she wanted to make sure that Jasmine knew she had options.

"I know, but it won't be the same. I love this baby. I do." The girl's eyes begged Sky to believe her. "But I'm not ready to raise him. He needs someone that can do a better job than me. He deserves that."

Sky agreed with her that every baby deserved to be loved and cared for. If Jasmine didn't think it was something she could do, they needed to respect that.

"And there are a lot of people that would love him if that is what you want. Allowing someone to adopt your baby isn't something to be ashamed of. It's not selfish. It's one of the bravest things someone can do." Sky had been through that struggle before. "You know my sister, the one who's a lawyer?"

"You said she practices family law," Jasmine said as she wiped her eyes with the sleeve of her pajama top.

"She had a baby when she was just a little younger than you. She decided she wasn't ready to raise a child too. Her doctor put her in touch with an adoption agency and she found the perfect couple for her baby. They're very open about the adoption and my sister gets pictures and cards from them."

"My parents would never agree to that. They want me to keep the baby. They keep promising they'll help, but that isn't the problem. I'm just not ready to be someone's mom. I know that makes me a bad person."

"You're not a bad person. It takes a lot of courage to admit that you can't do something. And you're thinking about what is best for your baby." Sky hugged the young girl to her. Jasmine was being forced to make an adult decision about her baby when she was not much more than a child herself. She wanted to offer to speak to Jasmine's parents herself, but she knew it wouldn't help. Whether it was fair or not, Jasmine had to make that move herself.

"How about I get my sister to call you? She won't try to push you either way. It's a personal decision, not hers or your parents. She'll be honest with you about the process and how it has affected her life."

"That would be good. Did your parents try to talk her out of the adoption?"

"No. They weren't in our lives then. They left us with our grandmother when we were young. But my grandmother was ready to support her no matter what decision she made. Your parents might not agree with you, but I have the feeling that they will support your decision once you explain how you feel. They love you and want you to be happy. Just talk to them. Be honest with them."

Jasmine sighed and had just begun to stand when Maggie and Lori came back into the room. Sky had figured they were outside the door listening.

Maggie started fixing lunch. Jasmine volunteered to help, then Sky and Lori got up to join them. The girl still looked worn to the bone. It would take more than a talk with Sky to help her get back on track, however moving around and working instead of staying in bed and worrying was a first step.

CHAPTER EIGHT

SKY OPENED THE back office door and let Mindy inside. Dressed in a plain black hoodie that covered her hair, the country music star had none of the glamour that she was known for. In a worn pair of jeans and a pair of sneakers, she could have been any other patient in the practice. As Sky led her down the hall to her exam room, members of the staff walked by them without anyone looking twice.

She shut the door as Mindy pulled off the hoodie. "That's a pretty good disguise."

"Trey agreed to let me come by myself if I wore one of his old sweatshirts," Mindy said. "It actually was kind of fun sneaking in the back. Not that I want my life to always be like this."

Sky had a feeling Mindy hadn't accepted all the changes stardom was going to make for the rest of her life.

"Speaking of sneaking around, I didn't see you leave the party," Mindy said.

"I'm so sorry I didn't tell you we were leaving. It was kind of sudden."

"That wasn't a complaint. After watching you and Jared on the dance floor, I understand why you'd want to leave so fast. Though I'm confused about why you told me there wasn't anything happening between the two of you. That dance made it pretty plain that there's something between you."

"There wasn't. I mean, there *isn't* anything. We're just colleagues." Sky felt the flush of embarrassment flood her face. Now she definitely would look like she was lying. "Seriously, Mindy, we aren't dating."

"Honey, I know what I saw. The two of you were into each other. Even Trey said something about it after you left." Mindy's smile turned mischievous. "Though apparently Nick Thomas had his head in a barrel—either that or he needs glasses. He asked me for your phone number after you left."

Sky didn't know what to say to that bit of news. "We talked about Legacy House. He probably just wants some more information."

Nick seemed like a nice enough guy. There just hadn't been that connection she felt with

Jared. That attraction that drew her to him whenever he entered the room. Of course, that same attraction made him push her away every time they got close.

"I'm going to let Jared know you're here, then I want to get your vital signs and measurements," Sky said as she pulled out her phone to text Jared. "Have you had any new issues this week? Any cramping? Swelling?"

She was hoping to change the subject from her and Jared quickly. The last thing she wanted was for Mindy to say something in front of him.

"No. I feel perfectly healthy. I just wish Trey wasn't such a worrier. By the time I have this baby he'll have me swaddled in bubble wrap," Mindy complained as Sky helped her up onto the examination table.

Glad that Mindy was willing to let the subject go, Sky went through the exam quickly. When Jared knocked on the door, she already had Mindy draped and the ultrasound machine positioned.

"Okay, let's see how this little one is growing," Jared said as he moved the ultrasound wand over Mindy's abdomen. Within minutes he had all the measurements. And when the baby decided to give them that perfect view that would let them know its sex, Sky quickly changed the screen's direction.

"Everything looks perfect. The baby measures right at thirty weeks, which almost perfectly matches your due date," Jared said. "Would you like me to get a picture to send home for Trey?"

"I'd love that. He had planned to come, but there was some problem with the production of this week's show that he wanted to clear up. He and Joe get along well, don't get me wrong, but Trey knows Joe's job is to hype up the show with as much drama as possible. Sometimes he has to reel him in."

Jared handed Mindy a towel so she could wipe off all the ultrasound goo. "Joe's coming in Monday to interview the two of us here in the office after hours."

Sky looked over at him. She'd known that the interview was coming up. But Monday? She just hoped that Joe wouldn't ask any personal questions. The show was named *Carters' Way*, so she assumed they'd just be asked a couple questions in general about the care they gave their patients and maybe a question concerning the way the two of them were working together.

She was still thinking about the interview as she walked Mindy to the office's back entrance.

"I feel I should give you a heads-up about the interview," Mindy said as she adjusted the hood over her head. "Trey and I weren't the only ones who saw what was happening between you and Jared at the party. Trey was with Marjorie when you were dancing together."

"It was just a dance," Sky said as she opened the back door for her.

"You better keep practicing that line. Maybe Marjorie will believe it." Mindy grinned, then sprinted out the door toward her car.

As Sky stood and watched the country star get in her car, she repeated the words over and over, practicing putting emphasis on different words. "It *was* just a dance. It was *just* a dance. It was just a *dance*."

By the time she'd gotten back to her office, she had even almost convinced herself.

When Jared had agreed to a one-on-one interview, this wasn't what he was expecting. He'd assumed that the producer had meant to interview them himself. Instead it was Marjorie, wearing another red suit, sitting across from them. Her first couple of questions concerning their education and qualifications he had been prepared for. They each talked about the colleges they'd attended and where they had done residency. Sky managed to get in a few comments about Legacy House and the work they did there, but then something about Marjorie changed. There was a gleam in her eyes that put him on guard. This must be what a poor mouse felt like right before a snake went in for the killing strike.

"I can't tell you how happy Mindy and Trey are to have you and Sky taking care of Mindy and the baby. They've made several comments about how well the two of you get along." Marjorie's eyes took on a predatory look as her hands with their metallic red finger nails clasped together and she leaned in toward him. "And after seeing the way you were together at the party, I can see why. The two of you on a dance floor can really heat up a room."

He was stunned. This wasn't the type of question he had been expecting.

"Jared does look good on a dance floor, doesn't he? And we did enjoy the party." Sky's smile was perfect and there was sincerity in every word she said. "I can't thank Mindy and Trey enough for inviting us."

For a moment he thought Sky had shut down Marjorie on the subject of the party. Then the woman turned back to him and he suddenly felt like the weakest link.

"Jared, what about you? Sky seems to think you look good on the dance floor. How about her? What was it like to dance with this beautiful woman? It was plain to see that she was the hit of the party. Nick Thomas sure seemed to think so."

Why did the mention of that man's name bother him so much? It was time to get this interview back on track. "Sky is a beautiful woman inside and out. Her patients love her."

"I'm sure they do." Marjorie's eyes bounced between the two of them.

She was looking for another angle to go at him. He had to cut her off. "I just want to assure the audience that Mindy is in the best of hands with Sky. Working together, I know that we will be able to give the Carter family the best care in the country."

"I'm sure you will," Marjorie said, her eyes narrowing in warning that she'd come after them if they didn't take care of Mindy and her baby. Then she smiled. "You know, right now the two of you are almost the only people who know the sex of Mindy and Trey's baby. It seems that all of Nashville is wondering whether it will be a girl or a boy. Someone has even started an online betting pool. How does it feel to have such exclusive information?"

The woman seemed determined to find some kind of drama for this interview. "Actually, it's something we are very familiar with handling. Some of our patients want to wait till their baby is born to discover the sex."

"But I have to tell you, Marjorie, it *is* exciting having a secret that big," Sky said. Then leaning in to Marjorie, she whispered just loud enough for the camera to hear her, "But I'm still not telling."

The cameraman stopped filming. Marjorie clapped her hands together. "That was perfect, Sky. The sponsors will love it."

Jared had no idea why Marjorie was so excited, but if it kept her away from trying to hype up some type of romantic connection between him and Sky he was glad to go along with it.

As soon as he'd shown Marjorie and her cameraman out the door, he hunted down Sky in her office.

"Please explain to me what just happened," Jared muttered.

Sky gave him a smile then slung a bag over her shoulder as she headed for the door. "Marjorie wasn't going to let us go without getting something more exciting than the name of what colleges we attended. I watched this season's opener this weekend. It's a nice enough show, but there isn't a lot of drama because they are basically a happy couple. Happy couples don't draw ratings. I could tell that Marjorie and Joe wanted us to hype up the pregnancy. I just added a dramatic flair to the truth. We might know the sex of Mindy and Trey's baby, but we aren't going to tell anyone."

"So the questions about the party weren't just because Marjorie was being nosy? She was looking for some dirt to spread around?" Sky nodded, but it still didn't make sense to him. No one cared about two unimportant health care providers. It wasn't a glamorous job like being a country music star.

Which reminded him of Nick. "And I guess she was just trying to tie you and Nick together for ratings too?"

"Maybe," she said as he followed her down the hallway.

"I'll have to tell him about it the next time I talk to him." Sky opened the back door and when she turned to face him, he recognized that impish smile of hers.

Then after a wink that made his heart skip

a beat, she walked away, leaving him wanting to follow her. And not for the first time that week, he regretted that he couldn't do just that.

CHAPTER NINE

SKY HAD PLANNED a nice quiet Saturday. Instead she found herself sitting next to Jared on the Carters' band bus on the way to a concert in Knoxville.

"You didn't have to come," Sky said, before she spun herself around in the swivel chair set up at one of the tables in the bus.

"You're going to make yourself sick if you keep doing that," Jared pointed out. "And I did have to come. We're in this together. Remember?"

When Sky had received the phone call from Mindy asking if she could tag along for the tour stop, she'd been too excited to go to ask many questions. But after seeing Jared there and finding out that Trey's worry had caused Mindy to call Sky because she hadn't been feeling good, the trip had changed from fun to one of professional concern. Still, if you had to work on a Saturday night, you might as well enjoy yourself. And with a bus designed for comfort, this wasn't a bad trip.

"Of course, I remember," Sky answered. "But Mindy is fine now. I checked her blood pressure and she denied having any contractions. You could have stayed at home."

Not that she really minded him being there. He'd dressed the part tonight in jeans and a chambray buttoned-up shirt. His black boots had been shined to perfection. If she gave him a cowboy hat, he would have looked like another member of the band. With her own short, denim skirt and her brown, knee high boots, they both looked like part of the band, which worked out well since Mindy was adamant that no one suspect there were any worries about her health.

A couple of the band members came out of a back area, carrying their instruments. In minutes they were playing one of their new hits that had just come out. Sky smiled and tapped her bootheel to the rhythm. This was so much better than sitting around her house and doing her laundry.

She looked over at Jared and was surprised to see that he was enjoying the music just as much as she had. When she smiled at him and he smiled back at her, she thought her chest

would burst open. Was this the real Jared? The
one she'd caught a glimpse of while dancing
with him, the one who'd opened up to her about
his birth mom? She'd always known that he
was holding back something. Hiding some part
of him away from everyone. Was he so afraid
of letting someone in that he hid that smile,
those emotions of happiness and the joy of living, from everyone?

Then to her surprise, he picked up a guitar
that had been lying on the table and began to
play along with the band members.

Sky didn't move, afraid she'd break the spell
that the music had wrapped around Jared. She
listened with awe as the band changed the song,
flowing into another one, an older song about
loss and pain. It was a drinking song that had
been redone by many music stars and it only
took a few seconds for Jared to catch up with
the rest of the group. They played for half an
hour before the musicians set down their instruments and, after shaking Jared's hand and
inviting him to play with them again, they disappeared into the back of the bus to change for
the concert.

"That was amazing," she said when they
were once more alone. "Why didn't I know
that you could play?"

"I have my secrets," He said. His face was flushed with color. Embarrassment? He'd always had a confidence that Sky had admired, but she'd really only spent time with him at work until the last two weeks.

"Tell me one?" She loved seeing this side of him. Maybe if she kept him talking he wouldn't notice how much of himself he was allowing her to see.

"Like what?" he asked, his hands still strumming over the strings of the guitar.

"I don't know, just something you don't share. Like the fact that you can hold your own with a professional country band. It doesn't have to be something big. I'll even tell you some of my own secrets."

Jared looked up from the guitar he'd been studying. "Okay, but you go first. Tell me some more of those deep, dark secrets you are hiding behind that smile you always wear."

"First, I didn't say it would be that kind of secret. You already know most of my story anyhow. I mean more like something we don't know about each other. Like…" She searched for something insignificant to share. "I know. I hide chocolate bars around my house so that I have to look for them."

"Okay, that's just weird," Jared said. "Why

don't you put them in the kitchen like everyone else?"

"Because then I'd eat them. If I hide them I have to make a point of looking for them. It gives me a few moments to decide if it's really worth the trouble."

"So it keeps you from eating chocolate?" The corners of his lips rose in a small, knowing smirk.

"That's a secret for another time," she said, returning his smirk. "Now it's your turn."

He leaned in, copying the way she'd leaned in to Marjorie when they'd taped their interview for the reality show. "Every week, even though I know I shouldn't..."

Sky leaned in closer, his lips so close she could feel his breath against her own. For a moment she forgot what he was saying, and then his eyes met hers and something flashed between the two of them. Her breath caught and her lips parted. She wanted him to move closer. She wanted him to kiss her. It wouldn't take much. Their lips were only a few inches apart.

Jared pushed back from the table, leaving her straining toward him. "I make a really big homemade pizza and I eat the whole thing by myself."

Sky leaned back and glared at him. Was he

playing her? Didn't he know he'd just made her stomach flip inside out with the anticipation of feeling his lips on hers? "Why do you do that?"

"What? I like pizza," he said, beginning to strum the guitar again. She saw his body relax, just like it had when he'd been playing it earlier. She wanted to push him and discover why he kept pulling back from her, but at the same time she didn't want to have him shut her out again.

"Where did you learn to play?" she asked. Surely this was a safe subject. "Self-taught or lessons?"

"Mom made me take lessons when I was ten. I hated them at first. But she played herself and believed if you live in Music City you should at least give it a try. At least that's what she told me. I think she thought it would help me make friends."

"And did it?" She'd heard that Jared had been close to his mom. She could picture him as a young boy playing the guitar with her. Sharing something creative like music had to build a strong bond between them. It had to have been a hard blow on him to lose a second mother. Everything she'd heard about Katie Warner had been good, even the way she'd dealt with the cancer that had taken her away from her family too early.

"I made a few. Once I started playing though, I kind of forgot the people around me."

Sky could believe that. She could see how the music had affected him. He was more relaxed. More open. "I'm glad she made you take the lessons. You clearly enjoy it."

He looked at her, that deep groove between his eyebrows telling her that he had something more on his mind than music lessons. "So, you asked me a question and now I have one for you."

"Okay," Sky said, something about the intensity of his gaze making her stomach twist into knots with apprehension. "What do you want to know?"

She'd left her whole life open with that question. What had started as a way for her to find out more about Jared had taken an unexpected turn somewhere. She just hoped that it was a detour she was prepared to take.

"You told me about your life with your grandmother and your parents, but I still don't understand how or why you would fake feeling happy if you don't. It seems a lot like lying."

"I think we all lie about how we feel at some time. Don't you? I can't say I know all of your story, but you told me about losing your mother. I know you were hurt by that, anyone would be. And I know the Warners adopted you, so I take it you lost your grandmother or she couldn't take care of you."

"She died of cancer when I was six," Jared said, his voice a solemn whisper as if he didn't want to hear the words.

Sky could see that the memory of losing her still caused him pain after all these years. "I'm lucky that I still have mine. She's a tough woman. Strong and stubborn. I'll never forget the way she just accepted us when our parents left us. She might have been faking it, but if she was, I'm sure glad that she did. I guess that's where I learned you don't have a choice about what other people in your life do. But you do have a choice about how you deal with it. I dealt with my anger at my parents by accepting my grandmother's love even though my parents had convinced me that I didn't deserve it. I guess that means I owe my attitude toward life to her."

A door slammed in the back of the bus and Sky remembered where she was.

As members of the band started appearing, Jared leaned toward her and whispered, "I'm glad she was there for you. You deserve to be happy."

There was a sadness to that statement that she didn't understand. Did he think he didn't deserve to be happy? But why? Unfortunately, it was a question that would have to wait.

As the band started to assemble around them and they pulled into the parking lot of their venue, Sky reached out for the hand that was still strumming the strings of the guitar and covered it with her own. "We all deserve to be happy, Jared. Some of us just have to work harder than others to see that."

If the concert had been amazing, the after-party thrown by the Carters' reality show at the hotel where they were all staying was even better. They'd been treated to front row seats by Mindy and Trey for the concert, but as Sky wandered through the crowd of performers and invited guests in the hotel's ballroom, she found herself blown away once more by how far her country bumpkin self had come in the world.

Both she and Jared had checked on Mindy after the concert when some of the private se-curity had ushered them into her and Trey's dressing room. Mindy had looked tired physically but invigorated with an emotional energy at the same time. It was plain to see how much she enjoyed performing.

"Sky, come over here," someone from the band called out to her. She recognized the woman as a backup singer she'd met earlier in the evening. "I want to introduce you to my husband."

"Sky," another voice shouted over the noise of the room as she was pulled into a hug by the band member whose recommendation had gotten her there.

"Hey, Jenny, it was a great concert," Sky said, hugging her back. The woman was becoming one of the most sought out fiddle players in Nashville and after the performance tonight, Sky understood why. "I haven't gotten a chance to thank you for recommending me to Mindy."

"You are an amazing midwife. I knew she would get the best of care with you," she said.

"Jenny does say you are the best," the young woman who'd called her over earlier said. "I'm Carly and this is my husband, Zack. We just found out we're pregnant."

The whole group let out a scream of excitement mixed with congratulations. "We were hoping you would be our midwife."

Sky agreed and once again congratulated the couple. A few of the performers had picked up guitars and started to play and she turned and smiled when she saw that they'd invited Jared to join them.

As the crowd gathered around them, Sky moved to the front. She eased her phone out of her pocket and snapped a quick picture of Jared. His head was bent over the borrowed guitar as his hands changed chords and strummed the strings. Jenny joined them with her fiddle and the music changed to an upbeat song that had the crowd clapping along with the melody. An older man, white haired with spindle-thin legs, offered her his hand and the next thing Sky knew she was being swung around in a dance that took her breath away.

When the music stopped, the man bowed to her and moved back into the crowd. Laughing, she looked around the stage to see Jared walking her way. She laughed and did a twirl. This must have been what Cinderella would have felt when she'd made it to the prince's ball.

Before she could stop herself, her arms flew around his neck and she pulled him into her dance, twirling him around with her. They stopped spinning and she looked up at him, laughing as she tried to catch her breath, surprised to see him smiling. That smile. Every time she saw it her heart seemed to explode with happiness.

Pushing up on her toes, she went to press a kiss on his cheek, surprising him as he turned toward her. His lips brushed against hers and the world around them disappeared. She kissed him with an abandonment that came from too much excitement, not enough sleep and a whole lot of happiness.

Then she lost control of the kiss, giving it all up to him when his lips parted hers and the kiss went deeper. Her hands dug into his shoulders, needing to hold on to something as her legs went weak when his tongue swept across hers and her lips opened up to him.

Gone was the music that had woven itself through her just moments before. Her whole world was Jared and the feel of his lips on hers. It wasn't a sweet kiss. No, this kiss was primitive, hard and hot. When he let her go, she stumbled back, her lips feeling bruised and tender.

"What was that?" she asked as he stared at her. Looking around the room, she saw that, while they might have caught some of the crowd's attention, most everyone was gathered around where a new group of guitar players formed at the other end of the room.

"You kissed me," Jared said, his voice rough with an irritation she wasn't going to stand for.

"I let myself get a little too excited, I guess." Yes, she had instigated the kiss, but she'd planned on a quick smack on the cheek. Something fun. He'd been the one to deepen it.

"Well, I wasn't expecting it. I don't do things like this. You know that. I'm not like you," Jared said as he started to turn back to the impromptu stage set up by the group.

He was brushing her off again, just like he had the night they'd shared that dance. He was making her feel like she was unimportant, like she was the only one feeling this connection, like it was easy to walk away from her. It was the same thing her parents had done. The same thing her ex had done to her.

But she wasn't that little girl or that insecure woman anymore. She would never put up with someone ignoring her or not taking her seriously again.

"Go ahead, walk away. If you can ignore what we just shared, so can I. I'm sorry I kissed you. I won't bother you again."

She turned and walked toward the door leading out of the hotel's ballroom, glad that everyone was busy enjoying the music instead of watching her humiliate herself. If anyone had noticed the two of them kissing, they didn't seem to think there was anything unusual about it. It wasn't like the two of them were well-known among the people here.

Only she knew better. That kiss could have been the start of something special. Instead it had opened her eyes to the fact that Jared didn't want her. Oh, his body might respond to hers. That kiss, that dance they'd shared, had been proof of that. But if he couldn't admit that he wanted her, if he couldn't let go of that stubborn need for control that locked others out, she would have to be the one to let him go. And she wouldn't cry. Not now. Not ever. She'd wasted too many tears on people who didn't want her in their life when she was younger. That wasn't who she was now.

So, with her head held high, she walked out of the room and headed for the elevator that would take her to her room.

CHAPTER TEN

JARED STOOD OUTSIDE of Sky's door and knew this wasn't a good idea. She was mad at him. And though he'd like to deny it, he understood why. She had been right. There had been more to that kiss than he was willing to admit, just like there had been more to their dance.

Leave it to Sky to call him on his bull right in the middle of a ballroom. He was in awe of the way she was willing to just put herself out there. She was so open about her feelings, while he instinctively wanted to deny that he might want something more with her.

It wasn't something new. He'd struggled with admitting he needed anyone, or anything for that matter, since he was a child. It had taken him years to believe that Katie and Jack Warner really wanted him to be their son. Looking back, he knew that had hurt them, especially his mom. But after his grandmother's death when he was only six, then being sent from one foster home to another for the next two years, he'd learned that the only person he could rely on was himself and the best way to stay safe was not to draw attention to himself.

But Sky Benton had put a dent in the armor he'd always wrapped himself in, with every flirty smile and every sassy wink she'd given him over the last few months. Now the kiss they'd just shared had blown a hole straight through that armor, right over his heart. A hole that he had no idea how to patch.

Instead of going to his own room, which would have been the safe thing to do, all he wanted to do was find Sky. Maybe if he saw her, he'd find that he'd just imagined the attraction that somehow had grown from an irritating buzz of electricity when she was around him into the scorching heat of a lightning strike during that kiss.

"What are you doing out here?" Sky's voice came from the crack in her doorway.

He'd been so busy trying to make up his mind about what to do that he hadn't noticed when her door had opened.

"I'm sorry. I didn't mean to disturb you," he said as she opened the door a little more.

"I'm a woman on her own in a hotel. The sound of someone pacing outside my door is going to disturb me." She leaned against the doorframe with her arms crossed over her chest. There was no way the cartoon character pajamas she wore should be nearly as sexy as Jared was finding them.

"I wanted to…" he started.

"Whatever it is that you are about to say had better not be another criticism. I've had it with those." Her chin went up, her eyes challenging him like a defiant child.

The truth was he didn't know what he wanted to say. Sky was everything that scared him. She threw herself into life with an abandonment he didn't feel comfortable with. He'd seen her do it the night of the party at the Carters'. While he had been happy to stay on the sidelines, she'd quickly thrown herself into the center of all those famous people and fit right in. Then she'd pulled him in with her, with that dance they'd shared. She lived without any restraints—something he didn't understand. She'd been through as much as he had in her life, yet she saw no danger in opening herself up to people.

Tonight when she'd kissed him, he felt like someone had kicked him in the chest. Part of him wanted to believe her when she said they had something special. But another part of him worried that she was throwing herself into one more thing without thinking it through. She lived for the moment while he was a planner. He liked to know what the next step would be. He needed to have control of everything around him and with Sky he had no control. That need for her took it all away and it scared him.

"I'm not going to apologize," he said, though he did owe her one. He'd been brutal in his denial of how that kiss had affected him. "I know I handled everything wrong. It's just that we are such opposites."

"What does that have to do with anything? Because we have different personalities, we can't enjoy a kiss? I've never asked you for anything more than a dance or a kiss. We're two adults who are attracted to each other. It's that simple. What is wrong with the two of us enjoying ourselves for one night?"

"What we're doing here, working with the Carters, it's important for the practice and for Legacy House. We have to be professional." And this was why Sky scared him. Any other woman could have said those words and he would have agreed with her. He'd had relationships with women through college and med school that had been short and uncomplicated.

He'd always made it plain that his priority was his education. Even the women in his life since he'd gone into practice with his dad, he'd made sure they had careers of their own that left no more room for anything more serious than an occasional date. It had been a good arrangement. And if a woman started to act like they might want more from him, he backed off. What Sky was offering him was no different from what he had offered those women.

He wasn't even surprised by that. Sky lived her life to the fullest. She made it plain by her actions that she was there for a good time. He just didn't know if being another one of her good times would be enough for him.

Yeah, Sky's way of living scared him, but what choice did he have when all he could think of with her standing there in front of him was that he'd be a fool to walk away from her.

"Nothing," he said, his mind reeling from the realization that this had been inevitable all along. Somewhere in the back of his mind, when he'd made his way to Sky's room, he'd known that kiss had changed things between the two of them forever. There was no going back to ignoring how Sky affected him. He could no longer deny that his body went on alert every time she was near him. He could continue telling her that it had been just a kiss they'd shared, but he would be lying to them both. "Maybe we should try that kiss one more time and see what happens?"

Without thinking it through or trying to figure out how this would fit into his plans, he stepped toward her. One of his hands cupped that defiant chin she'd challenged him with just moments before, while his other hand reached behind her head and pulled her toward him. Their lips met and this time, there was no mistaking the magnetic energy that drew the two of them together until he didn't know which affected him the most: his desire or hers.

Her lips parted, welcoming him inside, and the sweet taste of her filled him. His hand slid lower and he pulled her closer to him.

"Well?" she asked him when he let her go. Her smile was back and as always, it made his heart beat a little faster. Knowing that somehow he put that smile on her face made it race even more.

"Why don't you invite me inside so we can try it again?" he said.

Sky wasn't sure what had changed in Jared in the last few minutes, but she wasn't going to complain. She had no doubt that he had shownd up at her door with just another of his apologies on his mind. She'd wanted to break through Jared's hard outer shell for months, her interest going from curiosity to caring when he'd started opening up to her, to full-blown desire once she'd seen that he had the same response to her as she had to him.

They'd played a game of cat and mouse, her being the cat for the most part. Some women wouldn't be comfortable with that, but with Jared it had been fun. But after the way he'd reacted to their first kiss, she'd been ready to walk away. With him now asking for an invitation inside her room, things had suddenly taken an unexpected turn.

"Come inside," she said. She turned away from him, not reaching for his hand. This had to be a decision he made by himself. She needed to know that he wanted to take this step on his own. She didn't want to wonder later if she had led him in there. Jared valued control of his own life more than anything else. And if he took that step inside her room, if he laid her on that bed, she would give him all the control he needed.

She felt his hand on her back as he joined her before closing the door behind them. The room wasn't large and the king-size bed took up most of it. Turning, she waited for him to make the first move. When his arms came around her waist, she wrapped her own around his neck, settling into his embrace. His lips touched hers, hesitant at first. Was he having second thoughts?

But when he deepened the kiss, she let all her doubts go. They stood there kissing for several minutes, his hands exploring her body with a thoroughness that was just a part of who Jared was. They moved up her body, skimming the sides of her breasts before running down her sides to cup her bottom, pulling her against the hard length of him. She arched her body until her most intimate parts slid against him.

Her nipples puckered from the cold air in the room and she realized she had somehow lost her top. When he lifted her against him, she wrapped her legs around his waist. She started to protest when he laid her on the bed and untangled her legs from him, then stopped herself.

"I want to see all of you," he said, rising back from the bed and pulling her pajama pants from her body.

Her panties came next and she felt exposed to him as he stood there in front of her, still wearing the clothes he'd worn to the concert.

Then she looked at his eyes and saw the heat there. She had never had a man look at her that way, with so much desire and need. She let herself relax into the bed as he began to remove his shirt. When his pants followed, she found it harder to keep from squirming. He was a beautiful man and the anticipation of touching all of him made it hard not to reach up and pull him down to her.

But she'd promised herself that she'd let him have control tonight. So she waited for him, all the while her body becoming more aroused by the sight of him. When he finally moved toward her, her breaths were coming quicker. She wanted to touch him. To kiss him. She wanted to take him inside of her and find the release her body craved.

"You are so beautiful," he said as he placed one knee between her legs and began to climb onto the bed. When he stopped and kissed her calf, then skimmed his tongue up to the top of that thigh, she couldn't help but squirm against him. When he parted her legs and moved between them her hips bucked up to greet him. She needed him inside her now. How could he still have so much control? Couldn't he see that he was driving her wild?

"Jared, I need..." Her voice broke off as his lips grazed one of her nipples.

"Tell me what you need," Jared murmured before his lips moved up her collarbone and behind her ear. "Tell me and I'll give it to you."

He knew what she wanted. He knew yet he held himself back from her. She started to protest but then she saw his hand tremble as it came up and pushed her hair from her face. No matter how strong his control, he was close to breaking. She could wait him out, knowing that he was reaching his limit, but why? She didn't want to play games anymore.

"I need you inside me," Sky said, the words barely out of her mouth before he was parting her legs and guiding himself inside her. Her body welcomed him as he filled her with his first thrust, but he still held himself back.

"Let go for me, Jared. Give me everything you have." As if her words had broken through all his restraints, his lips took hers in a kiss that left no doubt all his control had been abandoned. His hips thrust against her, filling her with every stroke. She wrapped her arms around his shoulders and held on as she rode out a storm of desire like she had never known.

He placed one of her legs around his waist

and she arched her body as the pleasure of this new position started to build.

Her release came over her with no notice, her body shuddering as she felt Jared's body stiffen against her before he thrust inside of her one more time.

She lay there, her body spent and empty while at the same time her heart was filled with something she couldn't recognize. Satisfaction? Oh, yes, she was definitely satisfied. She'd never felt so satisfied in her life. But that wasn't it. It was something more, something that she wasn't ready to admit. Not now. Not yet. Right then, all she wanted to do was enjoy the moment. Tomorrow would take care of itself. Didn't it always?

CHAPTER ELEVEN

SKY'S PHONE RANG and she blindly reached over to the nightstand. Pushing up in the bed, she realized two things. One, it had to be very early as the sky was just beginning to lighten. And two, Jared was gone.

"Hello," Sky said, disappointed that instead of Jared it was Mindy on the phone. She'd made plans to meet her for breakfast, but not this early.

"Hey, Sky, it's Trey. Mindy's not feeling good. I've already called Jared and he's on his way up to our room. He wanted me to call you too."

"What exactly is she feeling?" Sky asked as she hurried to slip on the clothes she'd laid out the night before.

"She was up several times last night with her stomach. She says it's only a stomach bug, but I'm not sure." The concern in the man's voice was enough to have Mindy walk out of her room while still trying to get her shoes on.

"What's the room number?" she asked as she hopped on one foot into the elevator, pulling the last shoe on.

She pushed the button to take her up. The elevator stopped on the next floor and Jared joined her.

She didn't say anything about the fact that he had left her room during the night. Had he regretted their night together? She refused to believe that. Jared had wanted her last night. Unlike the kiss she had initiated, he had been the one to come to her room. But now wasn't the time to discuss what had happened between the two of them.

"Thanks for having Trey call me," Sky said, feeling an awkwardness she wasn't familiar with. "He said she'd been sick during the night, but not much else."

"It could only be a stomach bug like she thinks or it could be something more serious. She might have to cut back on performing until after the baby is born." The elevator stopped at the penthouse floor and Jared waited for Sky to exit before following.

Trey met them at the door and took them to the bedroom, where Mindy sat in bed. Her face was pale and there were dark circles under her normally bright eyes.

"I'm feeling better," Mindy said. "I'm sure it's just a bug."

"Let Jared and Sky check you out," Trey said as he kneeled beside her.

"Okay, but I don't need both of y'all. Why don't you and Jared go get a cup of coffee?"

Sky waited for Jared to protest, but instead he handed her a satchel she hadn't seen him carrying. Opening it, she saw that there were several pairs of sterile gloves inside along with scissors, a clamp and a suction bulb. Leave it to Jared to have a bag readied in case he had to deliver an unexpected baby.

"So why don't you tell me exactly what you're feeling?" Sky asked Mindy once the men had left the room.

"It's just some cramping. My stomach is a little upset I guess. I don't think it's the baby."

"When is the last time you did a kick count?" Sky asked, as she casually placed her hand on Mindy's stomach. Sky didn't have anything to monitor contractions so she would have to do it the old-fashioned way.

"I just did one. The baby is very active. Do you think there's something wrong with them?" Mindy placed her own hand on her abdomen, whether to soothe herself or the baby inside her, Sky wasn't sure.

"I don't think so," she said, her hand remaining on Mindy's abdomen as it tightened, then after a few seconds relaxed. She hadn't grabbed her watch on her way out of her hotel room so she began to count manually in her head.

"Tell me about the pain you're feeling. Does it come and go?" Sky asked. The contraction she'd felt had only lasted a few seconds, but Mindy was only around thirty-one weeks now. She didn't need to be having any contractions.

"Just some stomach cramping, like period cramps. It's not too bad. It started last night after we went to bed."

"Any bleeding?" Sky moved her hand off Mindy's stomach.

"No. I would have called you if I'd had any bleeding," Mindy said. "Should I be worried about this?"

"Sometimes that period cramping can be short, weak contractions. It's not unusual to have them during the last trimester of your pregnancy. They're usually Braxton-Hicks. Some people call them false labor, but they actually tone your uterus and help it get ready for when you do go into labor."

"So is that what I'm having?" Mindy asked. "Is that the cramping feeling?"

"Probably. I did feel a couple contractions, but they weren't strong. But with your history of having an earlier miscarriage I'd like to have you monitored. Unfortunately, I don't have one here so we'll need to go to a local hospital."

"Can we do that? Will they let you use their equipment?" Mindy's apprehension seemed to grow with each word.

"Not like you're meaning, but you can be seen at any hospital when you are pregnant. No hospital can turn you down. But let's talk to Jared. Knoxville is a big city. He can probably contact a local obstetrician who will be willing to cover you in one of the local labor and delivery wards." Sky knew that neither Mindy nor Trey would like that idea.

"Trey's going to be upset. He'll probably cancel the rest of the tour. We only have two more concerts and they are both local."

"Let's see what's going on before y'all decide anything. If it's Braxton-Hicks and your cervix hasn't made any changes, you might manage two more concerts, though that is between you and Trey. I do think it would probably be best to rest more. Maybe cancel the after-parties?"

Mindy nodded her head in agreement. "The

party last night was fun, but I shouldn't have done all that dancing."

As if in afterthought, Mindy added, "I didn't see you or Jared on the dance floor."

"I headed to bed early while the party was still going. I'm not used to all that partying like you." It was a true statement if maybe not the whole story. Why she left and what happened afterward wasn't something she was prepared to tell anyone. She'd have to talk about it with Jared at some point. It wasn't like the two of them could ignore what happened, though, by the way he was acting, it wouldn't surprise her if Jared planned to do just that. And the fact that he had left during the night without saying anything to her still bothered her even though she knew it was probably just her insecurity that had her feeling as if he regretted the night. She'd been left one too many times for it not to bother her, even though she knew she was being oversensitive due to her history.

A knock came on the door before Trey entered the room, followed by Jared. When Sky explained that she was concerned that Mindy was having some mild contractions and wanted to have her transported to a hospital for further monitoring, Jared pulled out his phone and started calling the nearby hospitals.

It was only a few minutes before he returned. "Okay. I talked to Dr. Ward at Knoxville Medical. She knows my father and she agreed to let the hospital staff know you are coming in. She's aware of the circumstances of wanting privacy and she notified the labor and delivery staff. She speaks highly of them and assures me that they'll guard your privacy."

"Do we need to call 911? Or an ambulance?" Trey asked. He'd been pacing the whole time Jared had been on the phone.

Sky removed her hand from Mindy's abdomen. "I think if you can get us a car, it would be fine. The contractions she is having are weak and irregular right now."

Jared gave her a questioning look and she answered him with a smile. "I think Jared will agree with me that we are just doing this as a precaution."

"A car should be fine," he said. "I'll call downstairs and see if they can take care of that. I saw that they had shuttle vans available if needed."

Jared headed out the door to make the call and minutes later there was a knock on the door. Mindy scowled when she saw the wheelchair, but Jared assured her it was just another precaution.

* * *

Four hours later, the four of them were on their way back to Nashville with the assurance of Dr. Ward, as well as that of Jared and Sky, that Mindy and the baby were fine. Mindy had received a liter of IV fluid as it appeared that dehydration had been the reason for the early contractions. An exam showed she hadn't begun to dilate, and the baby's fetal heart tracing had been perfect. Once the contractions had stopped and after promising everyone that she would increase her fluid intake, Mindy had been discharged and cleared to travel.

When Trey had cornered him questioning if he should cancel the two concerts that were planned over the next two weeks, Jared had done the smart thing and recommended that he discuss it with his wife, as he had assured the man again that neither his wife nor his baby were in any danger at that time.

Jared had been in this situation before, with overprotective husbands worrying that something out of their control could happen to their wife or child. After the way Jared had lost his first mother, he understood their concerns. He knew that if it was him in that position, he would have wanted reassurances too. But he knew there were never any guarantees in life.

His mother had been in perfect health before the pregnancy and even then her pregnancy had been without complications. It wasn't until after she had delivered that things had gone bad.

"Thank you again for being here," Trey said after coming out of the large bedroom in the back of the bus, where Mindy had lain down to rest.

"I'm glad I was here, though you would have been fine with just Sky." His father had been right about it being a good thing for the two of them to work together. Sky was a good midwife and had handled everything with Mindy the same as he would have himself.

It was the change in their personal relationship that he wasn't sure about now. Last night had changed everything. Becoming involved with a coworker wasn't something that he had ever considered before. He knew it was always safer to keep your personal life separate from your professional life. He'd crossed that line last night.

Yet still, he didn't regret it. What he'd experienced with Sky was different than anything he'd ever experienced before. And if he was honest, at least to himself, he had to admit that it had been much more than just a night of sex.

Holding Sky while she slept in his arms had given him a feeling of possessiveness so strong that it scared him.

"So Mindy keeps reminding me. I know my overprotectiveness drives her up the wall, but I can't help it. I keep telling her that it's my responsibility to keep them safe." Trey scratched his head before looking back up at Jared. "You would be the same way, right? If you were married and expecting a baby?"

Thoughts of Sky pregnant with his child sprang into his mind with no warning. His imagination flared with visions of a pregnant Sky, her abdomen round with his baby. Another wave of possessiveness washed over him. Sky pregnant with his baby?

Somehow, having a wife and a baby had never seemed to fit inside his plans. He worked too much. He didn't have time for a family. He wouldn't be a good husband. There were a thousand reasons for why he didn't think he was husband or father material.

But the biggest obstacle was that he had never met anyone he wanted to share his life with. There had never been anyone that he could feel safe enough to trust his heart to. No one who he trusted enough to give up the control that ensured his life was orderly and secure. And if he had met that person, that one person who he was willing to risk his heart for, would he even have enough courage to love them knowing they could be taken away from him at any time?

"I'm sure I'd be just as protective." And that protectiveness would annoy Sky no end.

He had to stop this. He couldn't think of Sky that way. This was exactly what he'd been worried about happening just moments before. He was letting what they'd shared the night before trick his mind into thinking that they had some type of future. It had only been the two of them sharing a night together. They'd both agreed to that. Hadn't they?

And even if they hadn't, the two of them couldn't be more incompatible. Sky with her live-life-in-the-moment lifestyle and his obsessive need to make decisions in a practical manner would never work together.

He thought about the night before, how she'd given up all her control to him. He would have thought that would be hard for her, but she'd seemed to enjoy it. It made him wonder how it would feel to switch roles and let Sky take control. Thinking about her being in control of him in the bedroom sparked an interest he didn't need to explore. It had taken all his strength to leave her bed the night before, he couldn't allow himself to think of picking up where they had left off. Like she had said, they were adults and it had been only for the one night.

"She's asleep," Sky said, joining the two of them at the gathering room on the bus.

The rest of their group had been sent home earlier along with the reality show's production crew. Only a couple of the Carters' trusted bandmates had been informed of why Jared and Sky were staying behind and traveling back to Nashville with Mindy and Trey. And the people who had been informed knew that Trey did not want any of this shared with any of the production crew.

"She's worried that Joe and Marjorie are going to be mad when they hear she went to the hospital without informing them," Sky said as she took a chair beside him.

"She's right, but if we'd told them they probably would have wanted to have a crew there in the hospital recording it all for the show. I wish I'd never let Marjorie talk me into doing the show," Trey said as he pulled his phone out and headed to the front of the bus to place his call.

"I think Mindy is regretting it too, but what are they supposed to do? They signed the contract. According to Mindy they're stuck in it for another two years." Sky yawned and closed her eyes. "Hopefully something more interesting will happen to take all the show's concentration off of the pregnancy. I don't understand why Marjorie is pushing the focus on the pregnancy so much. She obviously cares about them."

"We still have an hour and a half till we get home. Go take a nap in one of the bunks. Maybe if we all get lucky, Marjorie will find something else to concentrate all her attention on."

"I hope so too," she said as she headed to the back of the bus to one of the curtained bunks, "just as long as it isn't us."

CHAPTER TWELVE

SKY HAD TO drag herself into the office Monday morning. She didn't know how Mindy did it with the late-night parties and all the traveling. After getting home Sunday afternoon, she'd barely finished the laundry she'd left for the weekend, before she was crawling into bed. She guessed the glamorous life of musicians came with a cost. Just like being a midwife came with her being on call the next twenty-four hours.

"Good morning," she called to the receptionist, stopping to see if there were any messages from any of her patients.

"Good morning. I see you had a good weekend," Leo said, handing her a couple notes. "Lori said for me to have you call her as soon as you came in."

Lori had been on for the weekend midwifery coverage at the hospital and would want to give a report on any of Sky's patients she had seen.

"I'll give her a call. Anything else I need to know?"

"Nope. What about you? Anything you'd like to share?" Leo moved in closer over his desk. "You know I can keep a secret."

Leo could keep a secret about as well as she could give up chocolate. "Nope. No secrets today."

Besides, the only secret that anyone at the office would be interested in concerned her and Jared, and that wasn't anything she planned on sharing with anyone...well, except maybe Lori.

She put her bag away and put on the white lab coat she wore around the office before glancing down at the messages Leo had taken for her. One was the message to call Lori. The other was a message from Jasmine asking her to call.

The call had been left with their answering service before the office had opened, which meant that the girl had been up early, probably getting ready for her classes. Sky put in the call but didn't get an answer. Jasmine had probably already started her classes for the day and couldn't answer.

Next she returned Lori's call. "Hey, what's up?"

"Where are you?" Lori asked, her words fast and breathless.

"I just got to the office. Why didn't you call my cell?" Sky asked, taking a seat at her desk. By the sound of Lori's voice, she knew something was wrong.

"I did call your cell. It goes straight to voicemail." Now Lori's words were clipped and sharp. Her best friend wasn't happy with her.

Sky pulled the phone out of her pocket and realized it was turned off. "Sorry. Just tell me what's up."

"Me? Why don't you tell me what's up? I wasn't off in Knoxville partying and I definitely wasn't making out with Jared."

Sky's stomach did a bounce, a twist, and then dove down to her toes as her heart rate did its own dangerous dip. "How do you know about that?"

Sky was sure Jared hadn't told anyone and she would have sworn no one had been paying attention to them at the party. But unless Lori had developed some new psychic abilities, someone had talked. She held her phone up and waited as it powered up then signaled that she had three missed calls and six text messages, most of them from Lori.

"Because ever since the office found out that Mindy has become one of our patients, the staff has been following the Carters' reality show on social media. Check your phone. I sent you the picture someone sent me."

Sky scrolled past a message from Mindy to the first message she had received from Lori this morning. A picture appeared on her screen and she recognized the room. It was the ballroom at the hotel. Trey Carter stood over to the side facing the camera with his arm around Mindy's waist. In front of him with their backs turned to the camera, some of the band members were playing. Sky could recognize Jenny from this view, but not the other players. But it wasn't the famous music stars who had been circled in red marker on the picture. From the angle of the camera, you could see two people in the background. It was unmistakably her and Jared tangled together in a kiss. That was what had been circled. That was what most of the staff had seen?

"Can we talk about it later? Maybe lunch?" Sky needed to make a call to Jared to warn him before his father saw the picture. And then she needed to have a talk with a certain receptionist who she was sure had sent the picture out to the staff.

Her phone beeped with a call from Jared. Someone must have already shown him the picture. While normally she'd be able to look at it as a reminder of a magical night she'd always treasure, she knew that this would upset him. He'd kept his life so private until they'd started working for the Carters.

And his father? He'd trusted them to represent the practice.

"I have to take another call. I'll call you back to get a report on the weekend."

She clicked over to Jared's call. "Hey. I'm sorry. I'll explain to your father that it's all my fault."

"Sky, I'm glad I got you. I'm over at the hospital. One of your patients, Khiana Johnson, just came in and it looks like she is having a placental abruption. They're taking her back to the operating room now, but I thought you might want to come over. I've got to go. I need to scrub up now." He hung up the phone and for a moment she just stared at it before she realized what he had been saying.

Khiana Johnson was a single mom and a nurse who worked at the hospital on the surgical floor. Jared hadn't said how the baby was doing but if they had been in distress she was sure he wouldn't have stopped to make a phone call.

The hospital was just across from the office, no more than a five-minute walk. If she hurried she'd be able to slip into the OR by the time the baby was delivered. She pulled off her lab jacket, threw it on the desk and headed for the back door.

Because she was starting her call rotation she was already dressed in scrubs, which meant she didn't have to change her clothes once she'd made it up to the L & D unit. She covered her shoes and hair, then after washing her hands donned her mask. Opening the door to the OB operating room, she heard the weak cry of a baby. Jared looked over at her as he handed the baby to the nursery nurse waiting with a blanket to receive the little one. The baby looked to be around five pounds, a good weight for being at only thirty-five weeks gestation, but the little boy was pale and cyanotic. Not good.

The anesthesiologist recognized her and offered her his stool beside Khiana, but she shook her head. The young mother appeared to be sleeping after receiving a dose of general anesthesia. She was in good hands. It was the baby that Khiana would want her to watch over.

"How are we doing?" she asked the pediatrician as she watched monitors being applied to the baby.

"Not bad. Usually we see this in preemies. I'm thinking his Dubowitz score will put him around thirty-five weeks gestation so he has that going for him. He's requiring some oxygen and we're getting stat labs. Just looking at his color, I suspect he's going to need a transfusion. Do you know if there was anyone here with his mom? I'll need to get consent."

"I don't. She's a floor nurse on one of the adult floors. She might have been at work. I've met her sister at one of Khiana's visits though, and I'm sure her number is in our paperwork. I'll call the office and get the number." Sky left the room feeling better now that she could at least do something to help Khiana. She wracked her brain for some missed sign that this could happen but there wasn't anything— Khiana had been in perfect health the last time she'd seen her. They'd both been happy with her weight gain and there had been no concerns for hypertension.

After calling the office, she called Khiana's sister and found out that she was already on her way to the hospital after receiving a call from Khiana's nursing manager. As soon as she hung up, her phone chimed with another call and she saw that it was Jasmine.

"Hey, Jasmine, I'm glad you called me back. What's up?"

"I'm going to tell my parents that I'm giving

the baby up for adoption today. I can't do it, Sky. I want to, for my parents, but every time I think of trying to raise the baby on my own it doesn't feel right. Maybe there's something wrong with me." The girl was becoming upset again, just like she had the day they'd talked at Legacy House.

"Take a deep breath, Jasmine. It's going to be okay. Jared told me that he could tell your mother cares about you when she came into your visits. You might disagree on what is best for you and the baby, but if you tell them what you've told me I'm sure they will support you. Give them a chance to see that you've thought this through. In the end, this is your decision, not theirs. Even if they don't understand it now, I'm sure they will come around. And until then you have a place to stay at Legacy House as long as you need it."

"Okay," Jasmine said, her voice calmer now. "Thanks for everything. I talked with your sister. She gave me the name of a local adoption agency where I can meet the people who would want to adopt the baby."

Sky gave Jasmine some more reassurance and asked her to call back after she talked to her parents. A few minutes later Jared joined her in the physician's consultation room.

"There wasn't anything I missed. Her blood pressure has been in the normal range her whole pregnancy. She doesn't smoke or do drugs. This shouldn't have happened." She'd had Leo pull up the vital signs from Khiana's last three visits and had been reassured that just like she'd remembered, there had been no issues.

"I thought I told you when I called. We know the cause of the abruption. She fell on the floor after someone spilt something and didn't clean it up. Her manager was livid."

Sky's body relaxed and she realized she'd been dreading this from the moment she'd gotten the call. She'd assumed that Jared would think it was something that she had missed. She'd hoped they were past that—working together so closely the last few weeks, he had to see that she took her patients' care as seriously as every other provider—but clearly she hadn't quite shaken off the fear that he would always view her, and possibly all midwives, as in some way less qualified, because of the circumstances of his birth mother's death.

There was nothing she could do to change that. A part of her would have even understood—an error had been made and his life had been changed forever. And still, she was surprised at the depth of her relief at hearing that he hadn't assumed she'd done something wrong with Khiana's care. His professional trust meant a lot to her.

"I'm glad you were here to take care of her. I'll go check on her before I go back to the office." She looked over to see Jared busy working on his operating report. She hated to interrupt him when he was busy. Waiting to talk to him at the office would probably be the best. Except there was no guarantee that someone wouldn't mention seeing the picture of them together before she could warn him... This might be the only chance she had.

"So, about this weekend..." Her voice trailed off. Why did this have to feel so awkward? The man had seen her naked. She should be able to talk about this without feeling so self-conscious.

"It's okay, Sky. It was one night. Like you said, we're both adults. And now that we're back to the real world, there's no reason to let it affect our professional association."

Professional association? Was he serious in thinking that nothing had changed between them?

"Look, I just need to know if anyone has

asked you about the two of us being in Knoxville with Mindy and Trey?"

"Who would know we went to Knoxville? I haven't even told my father yet," Jared said, his head still bent over the computer.

"Oh, I'd say most everyone at the office and even some of the nurses here in L & D know we were in Knoxville." There was no telling how many people had seen the picture posted on the *Carters' Way* socials. Fortunately, most would be concentrated on the stars of the show, not two lowly health care workers.

"What are you talking about?" His fingers went still on the computer and he turned in his chair so that he could see her.

"Apparently ever since it was announced that we would be taking care of Mindy during her pregnancy, most of the office has been following the reality show."

"You said you watched some of the shows. It's not surprising that some of the staff might be curious about it too. What does that have to do with us?" His shoulders shrugged and he turned back to the computer. "If they posted something about us going with them to Knoxville, it's not a big deal, though I doubt they said anything about their preterm contractions scare."

She could only beat around the bush about this for so long. It might have been easier on her if someone else had made a comment about that picture so she didn't have to be the one with news that she knew he wasn't going to like. "I don't think that was mentioned. Well, at least no one said anything about it. It's one of the pictures they posted of the two of us that's circulating through the office that has everyone's attention."

"Why? Everyone knew we would be working closely with Mindy. My father made it clear that good public relations with their reality show would be necessary. I don't see why a photo of us would be cause for much interest."

"Maybe you should see the photo. Then you'll understand." She waited for him to stop typing before she handed him her phone, where she'd pulled up the picture Lori had sent her.

He stared at the photo, not saying a word, for several moments before he handed her back the phone and turned once again to the computer without saying a word. For a second she thought about stealing the keyboard from him so he would be forced to talk to her. Then she thought of hitting him over the head with it to see if maybe that would be enough to get a human reaction out of him.

"How can you sit there and ignore this so calmly? If your father doesn't know about this already, he will soon."

"My father is not into reality shows, nor is anyone likely to have the nerve to send him the picture."

"I think we should tell him. I'll explain that it was all my fault. He knows how spontaneous I get sometimes. It might not be the kind of attention the practice needs, but except for our staff no one is going to recognize us in the background of that picture." She realized that she wasn't really worried about what other people's reaction would be to seeing her and Jared kissing. Why would she be? It wasn't like it was something she was ashamed of. It was only Jared's reaction that had worried her.

Everything between them was new and fragile. She'd convinced Jared, and almost herself, that she just wanted to have a casual relationship with him. Nothing serious. Just two adults enjoying a night together.

But after what they'd shared in Knoxville, she didn't know how that would really be enough for her now. Now she wanted time with Jared to discover if this thing between them was real. Because no matter how much she wanted to deny it, she'd fallen in love with him, something that he most definitely wasn't ready to hear. Jared was a planner and he always liked to play it safe and keep a low profile. The last thing she needed was for the two of them to come to everyone's attention, something that would be sure to have Jared running for cover. But it looked like it was too late to stop that now. All she could do was damage control.

"Telling my father isn't necessary. Like I said, it's not likely that he'll hear about this. The best thing we can do is ignore all this and not give them anything else to talk about. In a week everyone will have forgotten all about it," Jared said, his words calmly destroying all her hopes as he made it plain that was exactly what he planned to do.

So he was just going to ignore what they'd shared? Was it really possible that what had seemed so special to her had only been what she had claimed to want? Just one night for them to enjoy each other? She knew this was all her fault. She'd asked for just that one night without thinking it through. And now that she knew she wanted a chance for more, it was too late.

Without saying another word, she walked out of the room. Maybe he'd only meant they would let everyone *think* there was nothing going on between them, but she didn't think that was the case. He'd never felt comfortable getting involved with her. He saw her as someone who liked to rush into things without thinking them through.

And in this case he'd been right. She believed life was too short to measure out all the moves you made in advance. But that wasn't what this was between the two of them, she was sure of that now, because it had been building for a long time. She just hoped that Jared would see that.

She took her time getting back to the office from the hospital. The walk was mostly sidewalks and parking lots, but the spring air was soft and sweet. Spring had always been her favorite time of year. It held the promise that the cold, dark winter was over and the future held only sunshine and warmth. She used to love helping her grandmother with the planting of their garden. Then there was the waiting for those seeds to grow into the plants they would harvest. But sometimes, a late cold snap would come and freeze all the fragile ones. It always made her feel like everything she had worked for had been for nothing. Why put so much of yourself into something when you weren't going to get anything back?

That was how she felt about her relationship with Jared now. She'd tried everything to show him who she was, and to get him to let her see who he really was and what they could have together. She'd put herself out there and bared herself to him in a way she'd never done before. And for what?

She opened the back door of the office and glanced down the empty hallway, glad that everyone was busy with their patients. The last thing she wanted right now was to be questioned about her and Jared.

She'd almost made it when one of the exam rooms opened and Lori walked out followed by a very pregnant young woman with a baby on each hip.

"Megan, I promise you it won't be much longer," Lori said as she opened a door leading out to the waiting room. "I'll have the receptionist make you an appointment for next week just in case, but I suspect you'll be delivered before the weekend."

Sky had started back down the hallway when Lori caught up with her and, taking her arm, pulled her into the supply room.

"Don't think you're going to get away that

easily. Spill it, bestie. I want to know what happened in Knoxville. Don't leave out any of the details and maybe I'll forgive you for not telling me before everyone else in the office found out."

"I was going to tell you," she said, studying her hands before looking up to see one of Lori's eyebrows lift and her smile turn into a smirk that said she knew Sky wasn't telling the truth. "Okay, I don't know if I was going to tell you. I don't even know if there is anything to tell."

"I saw the picture. Why don't we start there?" Lori moved farther into the room until she came to an old exam table that had been stored in the room. Sky followed her and took a seat beside her.

"That was all my fault. The concert had been great and we were having so much fun at the party. Jared was playing with some of the band members and I was dancing with this cute old man."

"Wait. Jared was playing?" Lori asked. "Our Jared?"

"He's really good. His mom made him take lessons. He said it was so he would make friends, but I think she knew he had talent." Or maybe she was trying to give him a way to escape all the trauma he'd experienced as a child. "Anyway, it was just a spontaneous thing. He was having fun. I was having fun. I wrapped my arms around him and somehow we ended up kissing."

"And that's all it was? Just a once-and-done kiss?" Lori asked.

"Well, that was all it was supposed to be." And it would have been, except Jared had surprised her when he'd kissed her back and now there was no forgetting that kiss and the lovemaking that had followed that night. "We might have gotten a little carried away. You know how adrenaline works."

"I do. So did you tell Jared that your first kiss has now been captured for the world to see?" Lori had a wicked grin on her face. Her friend knew, just as she had, that it would be the last thing Jared would want to happen.

"I did. He seems to think as long as we ignore it, it will go away." She tried to keep the hurt from her voice.

"The attention from the kiss, or whatever it is that's happening between the two of you?" Lori asked.

Leave it to her friend to get right to the point. "I think he meant both."

They sat in silence for a moment. Sky knew she had to get to work. Her patients had been waiting too long already and she knew Lori had patients of her own to see.

She stood and stretched before heading for the door. "I wish you could see him play the guitar. It's like the music brings him out of his shell."

"I think he needs someone like you to do that. He might not know it, or at least he might not be ready to admit it, but you're good for him. He needs some fun in his life," Lori said as the two of them walked out of the supply room.

Sky went over Lori's words as she grabbed her jacket and made her way to see her first patient. She'd started out just wanting to put some fun in Jared's life with her teasing, but now she knew he deserved more. He deserved someone who would love and accept him, just the way he was. For a moment she'd thought that person might be her, but now she knew better. Because no matter what her brain tried to tell her, her heart knew she deserved to have someone accept her just the way she was just as much as Jared.

CHAPTER THIRTEEN

THERE WAS NOTHING Jared wanted more than to head home. With his day starting out with an unexpected surgery, his schedule had been thrown off from then on. The advantage of his running late was that he hadn't had time to think about Sky or the picture she'd showed him. If any of the staff were curious about it, they hadn't said anything to him. Like he'd told her, it was best just to ignore the whole thing and not give anyone else a reason to speculate about the two of them. She hadn't been happy about it, but she had to accept that he was right. He'd learned early in life that it was better to keep your head down and let people forget about you. It was safer that way when you were a foster kid who was easy prey for the bullies in the world. Without a mother or father to take up for you or protect you, becoming invisible was the only way to stay out of their way.

He'd almost made it out of the office when he heard his father's voice calling his name. He stopped and retraced his steps to his father's office.

"I thought you had gone home," he said, taking a seat in front of Jack's desk. "What are you doing here?"

"I was waiting for you to finish. I heard you started your day with an emergent C-section this morning. An abruption, Sky said." Jared's dad took off his glasses and laid them on his desk. He looked more tired than Jared felt, and that was saying a lot as Jared had barely slept since he'd come home from Knoxville.

"One of the nurses at the hospital had a fall. I just checked on the baby. He's received a transfusion and is doing well now. They expect him to get out of the NICU tomorrow if he continues without any setbacks."

"That's good," Jack said, his eyes studying his son a little too hard. "Sky told me the two of you traveled to Knoxville Saturday with the Carters and that Mindy had to be seen at the hospital there."

And what else had Sky told his father? He was afraid he knew the answer to that question. "She was a little dehydrated. She received some fluids. Nothing major."

His father's eyes still bore into him and it reminded him of the time when he was about eight and his father had questioned him about the dent in his mother's car. Jared had known that he was about to be sent back to the foster home when he'd admitted that he'd been riding his bicycle too fast on the driveway and had turned into the car to stop himself. After his dad had been assured that Jared wasn't injured, he'd sat him down and told him that he didn't need to hide things from them. If Jared messed up, his father wanted to know so he could help him make it right. It had been a turning point in their relationship. For the first time he'd felt safe in the knowledge that his parents had no intentions of sending him back into the foster system. He was their son. Forever.

"I guess Sky told you about that picture of us," Jared said. "I can explain."

"You mean the picture that I saw this morning on the *Carters' Way* show's socials?" his father asked. "No, Sky didn't say anything about it, though I gave her plenty of opportunities."

So she hadn't gone behind his back and told his father. Not that he'd had any right to ask her not to. She was involved in this as much as he was. "I asked her not to mention it. I didn't think you'd see it."

"I might not have if I hadn't overheard one of the techs chatting this morning. Do you want to talk about it?" his father asked.

Did he? It wasn't like the picture didn't explain itself. He and Sky had shared a kiss. Except it hadn't been just a kiss they'd shared. Not that he would be telling his father anything else about the night.

"I don't think so," Jared said. "I know it was very unprofessional and I'm sorry if we embarrassed you and the practice."

He started to promise his dad that it wouldn't happen again, but something held him back. No matter what he'd told Sky about the two of them, he knew there was still something between them and he didn't want to lie to his father.

"Who's embarrassed? In my day, you could kiss a girl without worrying about all the cameras people have these days. If anything, I owe you an apology for putting you in the situation. I know you value your privacy and I'm afraid you've lost some of that because of me."

"It's okay. I think you were right about me and Sky needing to work together with the Carters. You know I've had a problem with working with the midwives since they started here."

"Because of what happened with your mother. I know. It was a terrible thing to have had happen, Jared. But doctors make mistakes too. You can't hold what happened to your mother against every midwife you ever work with." They'd had this conversation a hundred times, yet it was like Jared was only now ready to hear it.

"I know. I was biased and wrong. Sky is as credible as any doctor I've worked with. We work differently, but I'm beginning to see that it doesn't have to be one or the other. Like I said, it's been good for me. I hope it's helped me grow as a doctor."

"And what about as a man?" Jack asked. "Sky's not only a competent practitioner. She's also a beautiful, strong woman."

She was all those things and more, yet still he held some part of himself back from her and he didn't even understand why. Would he ever get over being that little boy who was always too afraid to trust anyone?

"It's complicated," he said, hoping his father would let it go.

"Love's always complicated. And don't try to deny that you're in love with her. I saw the picture. That wasn't just any kiss. I'm not so old that I don't recognize the signs."

Jared started to argue with his father, then

just shook his head. Once Jack decided that he was right about something, you couldn't change his mind. Besides, Jared wasn't even sure that his father wasn't right.

For the past six months he'd told himself that he was doing his best to ignore Sky, when really he couldn't wait each day to see what outrageous thing she'd do next. He'd enjoyed every wink and every ridiculous flirty smile that she'd sent his way. Now he got up each morning looking forward not only to her smiles, but also to the time they spent working together.

"I think I'll leave now, before you get any more ideas about my love life," he said, noticing how tired his dad looked tonight. "You going to be long?"

"No, I'll be right behind you. I just want to finish this last chart of the day. Go on home."

As his dad waved him away, Jared resolved to talk to him the next day. His father had to start cutting back his time at the office. He'd worked hard building the practice and Jared knew it meant a lot to him, but it was starting to take a toll. Jared had lost too many people in his life sooner than he should have. He didn't want to lose his father too.

* * *

Sky jumped as a knock came against the door of the providers' sleep room. She couldn't complain about the interruption to her sleep. She'd only been called for one patient so far. She reached for her phone, then realized she had left it in her jacket that hung on the back of the door.

"I'm coming," she called as she rolled out of bed. The clock on the side of the bed said it was just past midnight. She couldn't have been asleep for more than an hour.

She grabbed her phone from her jacket before she opened the door. The night-shift charge nurse stood waiting for her. "What's up?"

"The emergency room just called. There's a patient on their way in by ambulance," Kelly said. "They want you down there."

"Why can't they just send the patient up here?" Sky asked as she badged herself into the unit. All obstetric patients were immediately taken up to the L & D floor unless they had a life-endangering injury.

"They didn't say, just that the emergency room doctor wanted you there when she rolled in. The report they got was the patient is pregnant and had a seizure," Kelly said as they both headed to the elevators that would take them down. "They said they weren't expecting a delivery, but I thought I'd come check out the situation."

"Thanks," Sky said as they stepped onto the elevator. The charge nurse had years more experience than Sky and more than once she'd asked the older woman for her advice with a patient.

The elevator doors opened up right in the middle of the busy emergency room. "Did they say which room they wanted me in?"

Before Kelly could answer, she recognized one of the pediatricians headed toward her as the one that had taken care of Khiana's baby.

"They called you too?" she asked, not sure why he would have been called unless they had expected a delivery.

"I was down here seeing another patient and they told me they had a pregnant seventeen-year-old coming in after having a seizure so I decided I'd stick around in case I was needed," the man said. They followed him when he turned toward the resuscitation rooms that were near the ambulance entrance.

Sky wished she had more information. She was going into this blind. If this was a real emergency then they should have called the doctor on call instead of the midwife on duty.

Her phone dinged with an incoming message and she pulled it out of her pocket. Her screen showed she'd missed three calls from the same number. And she recognized the number. Legacy House. The incoming message was from Maggie, asking her to call.

Then it hit her. Seventeen years old. Missed calls from Legacy House. And finally, a seizure that in pregnancy was usually brought on when a patient had high blood pressure and proteinuria.

She started to make a call as they reached the room only to be pushed back into the hall as a couple of EMTs came through the door with a stretcher, where Jasmine lay unresponsive and intubated.

Instead of following the stretcher into the room, Sky moved farther back from the crowd of people waiting for the patient to arrive. The phone rang twice before she heard Jared's voice. "Sky, what's up?"

She realized then that she should have waited until she had the ambulance crew's report before calling him. She needed more information to make a true diagnosis. "They just brought Jasmine into the hospital. She's had a seizure."

"I'll be right there," Jared said, before hanging up.

She knew he would be upset that he hadn't been called instead of her. Jasmine's condition was much too critical for a midwife's care, but until Jared made it there she could at least help as best she could by giving the emergency room staff the girl's background.

As the ambulance crew rolled out their empty stretcher, Sky made it inside the room. It was busy in that orderly chaotic way of emergency rooms everywhere. One nurse was applying the monitors that would give them the necessary vital signs and heart tracings while another nurse was starting an IV.

"Where's that midwife?" a young doctor called from the head of the stretcher. Sky waited as he applied his stethoscope to Jasmine's chest to check her lung sounds to make sure the ET tube was properly placed before calling out to him.

"The patient is one of my colleague Dr. Warner's patients. Jared Warner. I've called and he's on his way. I do know the patient and I can tell you that she's seventeen years old and a Gravida One, around thirty-five weeks. She's been treated for high blood pressure for the last few weeks and I know Jared was concerned about preeclampsia."

A nurse called out a blood pressure and heart rate. Both were too high.

"You need to give her a four-gram magnesium sulfate bolus, then a continual infusion of two grams per hour. Otherwise she's going to seize again." Sky turned to Kelly, who had come to stand beside her. "Find a Doppler and get fetal heart tones, then call upstairs and tell them to set up the OR for a C-section."

Kelly looked at her for a moment, then headed out of the room. Sky knew that it wasn't usual for a midwife to be the one initiating a cesarean section, but she also knew Jared wouldn't want to wait any longer than necessary to deliver the baby. Sky just prayed that the baby was okay.

She spotted a small ultrasound machine across the room. Instead of waiting for Kelly, she rolled the ultrasound over to Jasmine's side and after coating the wand with jelly, placed it on her abdomen. Taking a deep breath to prepare herself for the worst possible outcome, Sky maneuvered it till she could see Jasmine's little boy's heart. She let out her breath and her body relaxed for the first time since she'd arrived in the emergency room. She took a few screenshots for Jared, then turned to the ER doctor, who had been watching her.

"The baby's fine. Fetal heart tones look good on the ultrasound, but I want to get her on a continuous monitor." One of the baby's feet kicked out at the ultrasound wand and she laughed with relief. "I think he's ready to get out of there though."

Kelly appeared back in the doorway, the Doppler in her hand. "Sky, the patient's parents just showed up in L & D. I didn't know what you would want me to tell them."

"I wasn't sure where to send them when we picked up the patient. I guess they assumed she'd be taken up there since she's pregnant," said one of the EMTs that Sky recognized from Jasmine's arrival.

"Were her parents at Legacy House?" Sky asked. She remembered the conversation she'd had with Jasmine earlier that day. Had her parents come to the house to talk her out of going through with the adoption?

"No. She was brought in from home," the EMT said before leaving the room.

Sky needed to talk to Jasmine's parents to see what had happened and to let them know her condition, but she didn't want to leave her till Jared arrived.

"Okay, start the mag sulfate and then get her over to CT. We need to make sure her head is cleared. I want to rule out anything else going on," the ER doctor said, then nodded to Sky before leaving the room.

Though she'd seen a nurse check Jasmine for responsiveness, Sky went through the motions herself, checking Jasmine's pupils and response to pain. The minimum amount of sedation the EMTs had reported giving her to intubate could be part of the reason the girl was less responsive, or it could be that she was still postictal from the seizure.

"What happened?" Jared asked as he rushed into the room, an ER nurse behind him with the bag of magnesium sulfate Sky had requested.

"I don't know all the details, but it looks like she had a seizure. Her blood pressure when she arrived was two-twenty over one-seventeen. They're treating that, and with her history I asked them to bolus her with four grams of magnesium sulfate and then start her on two grams an hour."

Sky and Jared moved back as the nurse, having started the medication, began to roll Jasmine out of the room with the respiratory tech at her bedside assisting with the ventilator and other equipment. "They're taking her to CT now and I asked Kelly to have L & D set up for a cesarean section."

When Jared didn't say anything, Sky looked over at him to find his eyes glued to his patient. "I shouldn't have listened to her. I knew I should have admitted her last week but she got upset about being in the hospital because of her classes. She agreed to being on strict bed rest and her blood pressure reports from Maggie had been improving."

"I didn't know you'd put her on bed rest," Sky said. If Jasmine had been put on bed rest how had she been at her parents' house? Was that why the girl had called her earlier? Was she so determined to see her parents that she'd ignored Jared's orders?

"I don't understand what happened. I called Maggie on the way here and she said that when she went to give Jasmine her medications, she was gone."

None of this made sense. The last time Sky had talked to Jasmine she'd been determined to get her parents to agree with her about putting her baby up for adoption. Even though she hadn't known about the bed rest, Sky had assumed that Jasmine would call her parents on the phone or that she'd have them come see her at Legacy House.

Jared was quiet as they followed Jasmine's stretcher over to the CT department. She didn't have to ask to know that he was thinking about his mom. "This isn't your fault, Jared. I don't know everything that happened, but I do know that Jasmine left Legacy House to go see her parents."

"Why would she do that? I know she's been upset about whatever happened between her and them, but they could have come to see her."

"I don't know why she went there, but I do know…"

"Dr. Warner, the radiologist wants to see you," the charge nurse said, rushing over to them.

Sky waited while Jared and the radiologist reviewed the CT screens. Sky needed to tell him about the conversation she'd had with Jasmine and her suspicion that the young girl had gone to see her parents, hoping to get their support for her plan to find a couple to adopt her baby. But that would have to wait.

"The CT is clear. Call the ER and let them know that we are going straight up to the OB floor. I want to get her on a fetal monitor and talk to her parents," Jared said, before walking out of the room.

Unsure of what she could do to help him, Sky stayed back with Jasmine and called Kelly to see what room the charge nurse planned for them to use. Once Jasmine was taken to the pre-op area, where they were met by an anesthesiologist, Sky went to find Jared.

Jared had no problem picking Jasmine's mom out from the rest of the visitors in the waiting room, though he'd only met her a couple times. Even if he hadn't met her before he would have known Jasmine's parents anyway, because they were the only two huddled in a corner of the waiting room looking anything but excited as they waited for news of their daughter.

"Mr. and Mrs. Jameson?" he asked as he approached the couple. He'd been aware that Jasmine's parents were older than most parents of a seventeen-year-old, but the woman whose eyes met his seemed to have aged a decade since the last time he'd seen her. "Can we step out for a minute to talk?"

"Is she...is our Jasmine gone?" the woman asked him, her voice breaking with the last word.

"No. She's very sick but she's stable right now," Jared said. "What has Jasmine told you about her pregnancy?"

"Nothing, until today. She's barely talked to us since she left home. I call her every day, but she barely talks to me. She used to tell me everything…well, maybe not everything. The pregnancy was a surprise and maybe we didn't handle it as well as we should have." Jasmine's mom stopped and took a breath.

"It wasn't that we didn't support her. You know that, Lily. We told her from the first that we would help with the baby any way we could," Jasmine's father huffed, placing his arm around his wife's shoulders. "It doesn't make sense to me."

"Can you tell me what happened tonight?" Jared asked. Right now the only thing that mattered to him was the welfare of Jasmine and her baby. Everything else could be sorted out between this family later.

"Jasmine called and asked if she could come talk to us," Jasmine's mother said. "Of course I said yes. I thought she wanted to talk about coming back home. I was so excited. I offered to come pick her up but she insisted that she would take the bus."

"I thought that was why she looked so tired when she got there," the father said. "Remember, Lily? I told you that our girl didn't look good. That bus stop is three blocks from the house. She didn't have any business walking all that way."

"Actually, you are right, Mr. Jameson. I had

put Jasmine on strict bed rest due to her blood pressure being too high. She didn't tell you?"

"No, she didn't say anything about that. All she wanted to talk about was this idea that she didn't want to keep her baby. She said that she's been talking to someone in your office and she was going to help her with an adoption. We tried to make her see that she didn't need to do that. We're her parents, that baby's grandparents. She should be talking to us, not some stranger."

Why was Jared not surprised that Sky had gotten tangled up in this family's affairs?

"She said that was why she came to see us. That this woman, this midwife, told her that Jasmine had to tell us what she planned to do." Mrs. Jameson's grief had turned to anger now, something that Jared was all too familiar with.

"Like I was saying, I had put Jasmine on strict bed rest because of her blood pressure and because she was beginning to show signs of preeclampsia. From what I've been told, she had a seizure while she was at your house."

"That's right. One moment she was arguing with us and then she said she felt funny and sat down on the floor. That's when she started shaking. I didn't know what to do. Her eyes

were open but it was like she wasn't there,"
Lily said.

"I called 911 the moment I realized what
was happening. By the time they got there she
wasn't shaking, but she couldn't talk to us. The
EMTs said something about her airway being
bad so they put a tube down her and brought
her here," Jasmine's father said. "But none of
this matters. What we want to know is how is
she now?"

"And the baby. How is the baby?"

"Like I said, Jasmine is stable for now and
the baby looks good. We've got Jasmine on
some medicine to keep her from having more
seizures for now and she does have a tube
down her throat—more to protect her airway
if she has another seizure than because she
needs help breathing. Unfortunately, the only
way Jasmine is going to get better is for us to
take her to the operating room and deliver the
baby."

He had just finished explaining to the Jamesons about the procedure and the risks to both
Jasmine and the baby when he saw Sky coming toward them.

"Excuse me. I'll be back in just a moment,"
he said, then stepped in front of them to in-
tercept her before she could say anything that

would upset the couple. The last thing he needed was for Jasmine's parents to discover that it had been Sky who had been speaking to their daughter about giving up the baby.

"Can I talk to you?" he asked her, taking her arm and leading her farther down the hall.

"Anesthesia is here and the OR is ready," she said. "Are those Jasmine's parents?"

"Yes, and you are not to go anywhere near them," he said, keeping his voice low so he wouldn't be overheard. "They said someone told their daughter that she had to tell them that she didn't want to keep the baby, and they know it was someone from our office. They're going to blame this on you. They said that she went to see them because of what you told her to do."

For a moment Sky didn't say anything. When she finally spoke, her own voice was low and her face was expressionless. "Do *you* blame me for this?"

"I know you didn't make Jasmine have a seizure," he answered, brushing his hand across his face as if he could scrub away the night. Unfortunately, it didn't work. "I just think you should have talked to me before you began advising my patient about her baby."

"You asked me to talk to her," Sky said, her voice louder now.

"If you had talked to me maybe we could have found a way to help her without her having a fight with her parents. You knew I was concerned about her blood pressure. If you'd talked to me first you would have known that Jasmine had been put on bed rest and didn't need anyone upsetting her. Didn't you know that her facing off with her parents could make her blood pressure spike?" Jared found himself getting upset and he didn't know why. "I can't even disagree with her parents—it might be that argument that caused the seizure."

"Let me talk to them. I'll explain that I was just trying to help their daughter."

"No. The last thing they need right now is for you to get them more upset. You've done enough for now." Jared wanted to take the words back as soon as he saw the hurt in Sky's eyes. He wanted to tell her that he didn't blame her for any of this, but deep inside, a part of him—the part that still hadn't found a way to forgive the midwife he blamed for his mother's death—wasn't sure. He knew that she never would have intentionally done anything to hurt Jasmine. Of course she wouldn't.

But Sky did have a tendency to do things

without thinking them through. That was part of the reason he hadn't trusted this thing between the two of them. He didn't want to be yet another thing she got involved with without thinking it through.

Sky looked past him to Jasmine's parents before turning her gaze back to him. "I'm sorry."

With those two words, she turned and walked away, leaving him wondering what she was apologizing for. For getting too involved with Jasmine and her parents? Or for getting involved with him?

CHAPTER FOURTEEN

SKY WANDERED IN and out of the room as the nurses prepared Jasmine to be taken to the OR. She felt helpless in doing anything for Jasmine, and just as helpless in dealing with Jared. Could he really be blaming her for what had happened to Jasmine?

Was he right?

She wasn't sure why she hadn't talked to him about Jasmine and her problem with her parents. And while she hadn't thought to tell him about her advising Jasmine to contact her parents and being honest with them about the reasons she didn't want to keep the baby, he hadn't shared with her that Jasmine had been put on bed rest either. Had they both been so tied up in their personal drama that they'd forgotten what was really important?

"We're taking her back now," Kelly said to Sky just as she was about to step into the room. The team started to push past her as they rolled

Jasmine out toward the OR. "Are you coming with us?"

Sky started to say yes, then remembered the look Jared had given her and his warning for her to stay out of things. He'd made it clear that he didn't want her in his OR. She was pretty sure he didn't want her anywhere near him.

"No," she said, turning and walking away from Jasmine before she could give in to the need to stay with her.

That wasn't her place. Jared had also made that clear. Sky needed to take care of her own patients and stay away from his. She made one more pass through the unit to make sure a patient from their practice hadn't come in while she'd been dealing with Jasmine, then decided that instead of going back to the doctors' sleep room, she'd go back to the office and get some work done. She had to do something to keep her mind busy while she waited to see if Jasmine was going to be okay.

She found herself becoming angry now, and she didn't like the feeling at all. She didn't do angry. She believed in the power of positivity, but there was nothing about any of this that was positive. How could Jared expect her to just walk away from a young girl that she had come to care for? Just because he could walk away from people didn't mean that she could do the same thing.

Because that was exactly what he had done. Hadn't he made that clear when he'd left her bed after making love to her? She'd wanted to talk to him about their relationship, but he'd seemed happy to pretend the whole night had never happened.

No matter how it hurt, it was time for her to face the fact that no matter how much Jared might have wanted her that night, he regretted becoming involved with her. Once more, she hadn't measured up to be the person that someone she cared about wanted.

And once more, she would get up, dust herself off and start living her life again. Next time she'd be more careful. Next time she'd protect her heart better.

Jared stood over Jasmine with the scalpel in his hand and forced his mind to forget how hurt Sky had looked when he'd refused to let her talk to Jasmine's parents. He had no doubt that she only meant to help the girl. It wasn't her fault that Jasmine's parents weren't listening to their daughter.

He had to put his thoughts of Sky away now. She'd been all he had thought of since the night they'd spent together. No, it went farther back than that night. He'd fought against thinking about Sky for months now, ever since that first time she'd looked at him across that crowded conference room and given him a smile that was as sexy as it was sweet. When she'd followed it up with that flirty wink of hers, part of him had known his life would never be the same. He'd been defeated even before he'd begun the fight. Only he'd never told Sky that. He'd been too afraid to let her know just how defenseless he was where she was concerned. And now he'd hurt her when she'd only tried to help him. He had to make that up to her, though he didn't know how.

But for now, he'd have to put all of that aside. Right now, all that mattered was his patient.

Jared took a breath and looked around the room, taking in the NICU team that had gathered to take Jasmine's baby as soon as it was born. Then he turned to look at the anesthesiologist, who nodded his head that he was ready. With his hand steady and his mind cleared, Jared made his first incision.

Thirty minutes later, there was a screaming baby boy being taken care of by the NICU team and the anesthesiologist was discussing whether to extubate Jasmine then, as she was showing signs of becoming more responsive, or wait until her blood pressure was more controlled and she was out of danger of having another seizure. Agreeing to err on the side of caution, the two of them decided that for now Jasmine would be left intubated and transferred to the critical care department, where she could be watched more closely.

By the time Jared had met with the Jamesons and shown them to the unit where Jasmine would stay for the next few days, it was past two in the morning. He knew he needed to head home and get what sleep he could before he had to start his day, but he wanted to let Sky know that Jasmine was improving and that her baby was perfect.

He expected to find her waiting for him on the unit, but when he couldn't find her one of the nurses informed him that she'd said she was going to the office to work on some charting. He knew immediately that she had left because of him. He'd hurt her and she'd chosen to leave instead of facing him. He had to fix this. Besides, he didn't like the thought of her over in the office alone in the middle of the night.

Checking on Jasmine once more, he made the walk across the parking lot to the clinic.

When he opened the back door, the motion light above him came on, illuminating the entryway. Passing the exam rooms, he called out to Sky, not wanting to startle her. He started to take the hallway that led to her office when he heard a sound farther down the entry hallway.

His heart sped up and he looked around to see if there was something close he could use for a weapon.

"Jared? What are you doing here?" Sky asked as she came down the hall, stopping when he put his finger against his lips and listened.

He heard the sound again, this time recognizing it as a groan. Realizing that the only room left down that hallway was his father's office, he motioned Sky behind him and made his way there.

The pair of motionless legs sticking out from behind his father's desk was the first thing he saw when the lights came on in the room. "Dad?" he called as he and Sky rushed around the desk to find his father lying on the floor, his eyes closed but his chest rising irregularly.

"Dad?" he whispered, his voice sounding more like the little scared boy he'd once been than the grown man he was now. He barely registered Sky's urgent voice speaking behind him. When his father's eyes blinked open, his own eyes filled with tears.

"I had to wait. I had to tell you," his father began, his voice weak as he grimaced with pain.

"I've called 911," Sky said, before dropping down beside him. Jared watched as she applied a stethoscope to his father's chest. "Jack, just rest. There's help on the way."

"Just want to tell you, I love you, son. From that first day…" His father's voice gave out and his eyes closed.

"His pulse is irregular and weak. There are no signs of trauma. I don't think it was a fall," Sky said as she ran her hands down Jack's legs and then up his arms before turning her attention to his head, then standing and running out of the room.

"Can you hear me, Dad?" Jared asked as he took his father's hand and squeezed. He knew he should be doing something, anything, to help him, but he was frozen by the fear of losing him.

Sky rushed back into the room with the office AED. After turning on the monitor, she didn't take the time to unbutton his father's shirt, instead she just ripped it open and began applying pads. As the cardiac rhythm began to scroll across the machine and the AED machine told them that a shock wasn't advised.

Sky squatted down in front of it and studied the rhythm. "It looks like a STEMI. See how the ST segment is higher here." Jared looked at where she pointed but found he couldn't take in the information. "Stay here with him. I'm going to open the door for the EMTs. If anything changes call out for me." With that she jumped back up and was gone down the hall.

"She's something, isn't she?" his father whispered, then cleared his throat. "She reminds me of my Katie. So full of life. You'll be a lucky man if you don't mess things up with her."

His father's face became pale and his lips tightened.

Jared was a doctor. Surely there should be something that he could do for his father besides sitting there and holding his hand, but nothing came to mind.

Minutes later, Jared heard Sky's voice directing the EMT crew to the office. Jared started to move back but his father's hand tightened on his with a strength that surprised him. "You're going to be okay, son."

His father's hand let go of his as the ambulance crew moved him over to their stretcher. Moments later they were gone, leaving packaging from the IV they'd started and debris strewn across the floor.

"I just talked to the ER doctor. He's calling in the interventional team now. We can probably meet the ambulance in the ER if we cut across the parking lot."

Jared stared at her. The last few minutes had been a nightmare for him, but Sky had remained calm and had taken care of his father while Jared had been unable to form a complete thought. All he could do was think about the other losses he'd suffered, and how he wasn't ready to lose his father too.

"Thank you," Jared said as he closed his arms around her. From the moment he'd seen his father lying helplessly on the ground, Jared had felt cold and alone. The warmth of Sky's body against his took all those feelings away. He hadn't been alone. Sky had been there for him the whole time. "I don't know what I would have done without you."

Sky sat next to Jared as they waited for the interventional cardiologist. Jack had been taken straight from the ER to the cath lab as soon as the emergency room doctor had confirmed that he was indeed having an ST-elevation myocardial infarction. The fact that Jack had lain in his office, unable to call for help for all those hours, had her worried about what damage had been done to his heart.

"How's Jasmine?" she asked Jared. He'd said very little since they'd found his father.

"I forgot to tell you. That's why I came over to the office. I wanted to let you know she's stable. They'll probably extubate her today, once they decrease her sedation medication."

"Thanks. I appreciate you letting me know." At least he was still keeping her updated on the young girl.

They stood as the doctor came into the room. The man looked almost as tired as she did, and she knew that she and Jared weren't the only ones who had been up most of the night.

"How is he?" Jared asked. He surprised her when he reached out and took her hand in his. "Can I see him?"

"He's going to be sleeping for a while. We had to keep him sedated for longer than usual, but we were able to place two stents. I'm going to have him watched in the ICU overnight, but I think he'll move out to the floor tomorrow. I know he has a busy practice, but he's going to have to slow down. I don't want him working at all for the next few weeks."

Jared assured him that he'd make sure his father abided by his orders. Once the doctor left, Sky quickly removed her hand from Jared's. Now that she knew Jack would be okay, there wasn't really a reason for her to stay with him. Still, she waited until one of the cardiac intensive care nurses came to take him back to see his father.

"We need to talk," Jared said, looking over to where the nurse waited for him. "About everything."

There had been so many things that she wanted to tell him, but in reality none of them would make a difference. Jared's actions had made it clear that it was better the two of them forget their night together. He hadn't even wanted to tell his father about the picture that had captured their kiss. He believed that if they ignored it, it would all go away. At first she had thought he'd meant the attention from the picture, but now she knew he meant whatever it was that had been happening between the two of them. And the truth was he was probably right. If he ignored it, eventually she would have to give up on him. Looking back she could see that it had always been her that wanted more from him. Even though he'd come to her room the night they were in Knoxville, it had been her kiss that had compelled him.

Not once had he ever been the one to make

the first move. In fact, if she hadn't started flirting with him all those months ago, they'd still be nothing more than colleagues who passed in the hallway. That wasn't saying that she regretted anything they'd shared recently. She was just realistic enough to know that no matter what she thought the two of them could have together, it wasn't going to happen.

So instead of responding, she gave him the best smile she could muster. The moment he disappeared down the hallway, she headed for the closest elevator. She wanted to get out of the hospital and away from the man that she had almost let break her heart. But there was one more stop she needed to make, no matter how mad it would make Jared.

She took the elevator to the surgical ICU waiting room on the next floor, where she spotted Jasmine's parents.

"Mr. and Mrs. Jameson, my name is Sky. I'm a midwife at Legacy Clinic," Sky said. "I just wanted to check and see how you are doing."

"You're the woman Jasmine was talking about. You're the one that told her she could give her baby up," Mrs. Jameson said.

Sky noticed that the poor woman was probably too tired to be angry at this point. "Jasmine told me that she didn't want to be a mother right now. She didn't feel that she was ready for the responsibility of a baby and she didn't think she could give her son everything that he deserves. I think your daughter was very brave and selfless in making that decision, but I assure you that it was *her* decision. I only encouraged her to speak openly with you about it. She just wants to do the right thing for her child. She might change her mind about what she wants tomorrow when she sees her son, but I hope if she still wants to go ahead with the adoption you will listen to her and respect her wishes. As a child who had parents that never wanted her, I wish my parents would have considered what was best for me instead of themselves. I'm sure you have always done what was best for Jasmine even over your own desires. That's all she's asking for you to do now."

Sky waited for Jasmine's parents to yell at her, or at the very least to tell her that she needed to mind her own business, but they just stood there staring at Sky like she had been speaking a foreign language.

Without saying another word, Sky left the waiting room. She didn't know if the Jamesons would even consider what she had to say, but for their daughter's and grandson's sakes, she hoped they would.

* * *

Jared paused at the door of the waiting room to look back at Sky before he let the nurse lead him to his father's room, where he found his father asleep, his respirations deep and even. He sat down beside him and waited for him to wake.

He found himself questioning the look Sky had given him before he'd left her. There was something about the way she'd looked at him before he left that made his chest hurt. The smile she'd given him had been nothing like the smile that always took his breath away. Instead this smile had been a little sad and her eyes had been empty, with none of the happiness they usually shone with. It reminded him of the smiles from his time in the foster system when he had to leave a new friend, because he knew they'd never be together again. A goodbye smile. A smile that said, *So long, it's been great while it lasted.*

Jared shook his head to clear it. His mind was just playing tricks on him. Sky wasn't leaving. As soon as his father woke up he'd go get her. And tomorrow when he came into the office she would be there waiting to torture him with one of her usual sassy smiles. Right now, he had to take care of his dad. Then he'd make time to talk to Sky. She had been right, they needed to talk about what was happening between the two of them.

"Why the face? Am I dying?"

Jared had been so tangled up in his thoughts that he hadn't noticed when his father had awakened. "No. You're going to be fine, though we are definitely going to have a talk about your work schedule."

"So if I'm not dying, what's wrong?" his father asked, clearly hoping to avoid the necessary conversation about the amount of hours he'd been working. "Is it Sky?"

"Do you just want me to say you were right again? Our working together has been good. Seeing her in action when we found you has given me even more of a reason to appreciate her work."

"I didn't put the two of you together so that you could learn to work together, son. I wanted to force you to open your eyes and see that there was a woman who's perfect for you." His father's voice held a hint of irritation and Jared saw that his heart rate had jumped up into the one-twenties.

"Calm down before the nurse comes in here and throws me out," he told his dad. "And what do you mean you didn't put us together because of work? You said that the Carters asked for the two of us."

"Mindy did ask for Sky, and her husband requested that there be a doctor following his wife closely, but they had asked for it to be me. But I knew that you would never make a move past that flirting game the two of you have been playing for the last few months if I didn't step in and force you to acknowledge your feelings for her." His father sighed, then closed his eyes. "I hoped you'd have the good sense to make a move, especially after I saw that picture of you two kissing. What is it going to take to make you see what's right there in front of you? You're a smart man. You can't believe that a woman like Sky is going to wait around forever."

Jared thought of that smile she'd given him earlier. He might have tried to deny it, but he'd known that something was off with Sky. His father was right. He'd pushed her away every time she got close. She'd come into his life and shattered that old, dirt-streaked window he'd always used to look out into the world and she'd pulled him into a world of laughter and joy where she chose to spend her own life. And now, no matter how hard he tried to board up that old window, he knew what it felt like to live outside it now. Oh, there was still a part of him that wanted to play it safe, that wanted to hide back behind that window. Looking out at the world instead of living in it was where he was comfortable. But that part had been getting smaller every minute he spent with Sky. His father had seen a future for him that he'd always denied wanting. But with Sky, that future looked possible. Or at least it could be if he hadn't messed it up beyond repair.

"Sir," the nurse began as she walked into his father's room, "I'm sorry, but I'm going to have to ask you to go. Your father needs his rest."

Jared reached over and grasped his father's hand in his. He remembered the first time his dad had shaken his hand. Jared had been so scared when his foster mother had told him that a couple was coming over to meet him. That they were looking for a little boy just like him to be their own little boy. His father's grip wasn't nearly as strong as it had been that day when he'd dropped down on his knee in front of Jared and offered the scared little boy he'd been a handshake. He had thought his father was the strongest man he'd ever met then. Now, after all those years, he still believed that.

"I'll be back later to see you," Jared said, repeating the words his father had said that day, all those years ago. And even though young Jared had not believed the man's words as he watched the strong man and the beautiful woman walk away from him, he'd hoped with everything inside of him that he was wrong. Just like he hoped now that he'd been wrong about that sad smile Sky had given him.

But when he returned to the waiting room and found it empty, he knew he'd been right. He'd hesitated too long, making excuses for why he and Sky shouldn't be together. He'd let her be the one that made every move, unable to admit that he'd wanted her from the first time she'd given him that priceless smile and that outrageous wink. He felt the same as the little boy he'd been as he'd watched his future father and mother walk away. There hadn't been anything he could have done that day. He'd had to wait there, helpless to control his own future.

But he wasn't helpless anymore. He wasn't going to wait and hope that Sky would seek him out to give him another chance. He was going to take control. He would get her back. And he would show her just how much she meant to him. He was tired of fighting against the love he felt for her. Instead, he was ready to fight *for* that love. Fight for Sky. Now he just had to figure out how.

CHAPTER FIFTEEN

As SKY DROVE up to Mindy and Trey's house, she felt none of the excitement that she had felt the first time she'd seen it. Maybe she was already becoming jaded by all the glitz and glamour of the country music stars' life. Maybe she was just tired. Or maybe it was the fact that Jared wasn't beside her today.

Well, at least this time Marjorie wasn't running toward her waving a mile-high stack of papers for her to sign. To be honest, the place almost looked deserted. When Mindy had called and asked her if she could do her a really big favor and come to the taping of her reality show today, Sky had wanted to say no. But who could refuse Mindy? The woman was as sweet as Sky's grandmother's cane syrup. Still, she wasn't up to smiling for any cameras today. Right now she wasn't sure if she would ever smile again.

As soon as she'd left Jared at the hospital,

she'd gone home and slept the day away. She'd hoped that after finally making the decision to walk away from him she'd wake up ready to move on. She'd even thought of maybe leaving Nashville. There were so many places she'd never seen. Now might be the perfect time to go exploring the rest of the world.

She didn't know how long she'd sat there in the driveway before a man she hadn't met before knocked on her car window. "Ma'am, are you Skylar Benton?"

The man backed up as Sky opened the door and climbed out of the car. "That's me." She didn't know what she was expected to wear today so she'd settled on a blue flowered maxi dress and a pair of strappy sandals. Sky wasn't sure whether Mindy wanted her to actually be on the show or be there only for moral support as she explained to the show's viewers the reason for her hospital visit.

"They're waiting for you down at the barn," the man said before tipping his cowboy hat at her, turning and walking down a path along the side of the house.

"Mindy's in the barn?" Sky asked, confused. Where was everybody? Something about this didn't feel right. She felt like the heroine in one of those horror flicks being led to her demise.

"She's around there somewhere," the man said without turning around.

Sky had never been in Mindy's backyard and upon following him along the side of the house she was surprised to see that what the man was calling "a barn" wasn't the horse barn she had been expecting. Instead, it was a pretty cedar building half the size of the house, with old-fashioned Dutch doors. She could smell fresh cut hay before she made it to the opened half door, but there were none of the usual smells of horses. A huge chandelier suspended off a thick cedar beam that ran the length of the building. Other, smaller chandeliers had been hung throughout the space, bathing it in a golden light.

Then she saw him in the middle of the large open room sitting on a stack of hay. He'd traded his spotless white lab coat for a pair of faded jeans and a chambray buttoned-up shirt. He looked like a ranch hand who'd come in from work and decided to sit awhile. Sky's heart stuttered and her breath caught in her chest when he looked up at her and began to play the guitar in his hands.

She didn't see the man who'd led her there pull open the barn door. She'd made it halfway across the room before she'd even realized it.

What was she doing? She'd made the decision to walk away from this man. He'd made it plain that he didn't want her. Not like she wanted him. He hadn't been willing to give the two of them a real chance, though time after time she'd all but thrown herself at him.

She started to turn around, to leave before he could see the tears in her eyes. She didn't cry. Not anymore. She shed enough tears when her parents had left her and when the man she'd thought had loved her deserted her. The only tears she ever allowed herself nowadays were happy tears. So why was she crying now?

Then she recognized the song he played. It was an old Alabama song. A love song about falling in love. Then Jared began to sing, "How do you fall in love? When do you say 'I do'?"

His voice wasn't trained and he'd never be a country music star, but to her it was the most beautiful song she had ever heard. By the time he got to the end, she'd given up holding back the tears. Still, when he laid the guitar down and walked toward her, his arms held out, she couldn't move. She'd gone to him over and over. She'd flirted. She'd teased. She'd opened up to him and worked so hard to get his attention and still he'd fought against what she knew they could have together. If he wanted her, he had to say the words.

As if he'd heard her prayer to heaven, he stopped in front of her and took her hands in his. "I love you, Sky. I know I've been saying that the two of us are too different, but I think those differences are what make us perfect for each other. I need the sunshine and happiness that you've brought to my life and sometimes you need me to bring you down to earth. And no matter our differences, I can promise you that for the rest of my life, I'll always love you. Will you marry me?"

"Yes," she whispered, afraid to break the spell from Jared's song.

Then he brushed her tears from her face and with his hands on her cheeks, he kissed her. It was a sweet kiss, full of a love she had feared she'd never have. But when Jared's hands slid down to her waist, pulling her closer and deepening the kiss, the barn suddenly echoed with applause.

Pulling away, Sky turned to see the whole camera crew from Mindy and Trey's reality show. Beside them stood Mindy, looking as guilty as sin, and Marjorie looking as happy as if she'd won a CMA Award.

For a moment she was afraid this had all

been just a performance for the show, but when Jared's arms slid around her, she relaxed. He would never do something as callous as that. "I think you have some explaining to do, Dr. Warner."

"Well, we had cameras for our first dance and first kiss. It just seemed right that there should be cameras for the first time I tell you I love you," Jared said. He moved his lips down to her ear and whispered, "I had to sign a form saying that even if you walked away from me, I'd let them air the footage on the show."

"And what if I had refused to agree to this being on the show?" Sky asked, still stunned by all the trouble Jared had gone through to do this for her.

"Actually, one of those forms Marjorie had us signed covered it. They just wanted me to sign for backup since this was all my idea," Jared said before taking one of her hands in his and leading her over to the camera crew.

As he began to thank Joe and the crew, Mindy walked over to stand beside her. "Are you mad?"

"I can't believe any of this. Was this really Jared's idea?" Sky had a hard time believing that he would have ever wanted to take part in something like this, let alone that he had planned this.

"Oh, yeah, I even tried to talk him out of it. He'd have been the talk of the town if you'd walked away from him. Marjorie was hoping you'd do something dramatic like slap him across the face. Not that I thought you would do anything like that. Still, there was that chance… But he said he had to do something big to make you see he was serious."

"I guess you don't get much more serious than declaring your love on national TV," Sky said.

Once the camera crew was packed up, Jared asked Mindy and Trey if they could take a walk down to the pasture to see the horses. Holding hands as they made their way to the back of the property, Sky enjoyed the quiet of the farm after all the noise of the crowd in the barn. But there was still something they needed to clear up.

"I spoke to Jasmine's parents. They know I was the one who helped her get the information on giving her baby up for adoption."

"I know. I spoke with them too and explained that you were working with me. I also told them that you did the right think providing their daughter with information on all the options available to her."

"Thank you," she said. Having Jared's support meant everything to her.

"They assured me that they love their daughter and they only want what is best for her. And, most importantly, they're willing now to support her, no matter what choice she makes about her baby."

"I'm glad. Both Jasmine and her child deserve a chance at a good life," she said.

She knew she'd never been as happy as she was in that moment.

"I'm not sure you understand what you've done," Sky said. "Even though we're nobodies next to Mindy and Trey, we're bound to get some media attention."

"I know."

"We're really getting married," she said, stopping on the path as it all suddenly hit her now that they were alone. She could hear the note of panic in her voice. "I don't care what Marjorie offers us, they are *not* going to film any part of our wedding."

"Of course not," he said, his voice a little too calm. "I've already talked to her. She has no interest in filming the wedding."

"Oh, good," Sky said, starting back down the path.

"All she wants is to film the bachelor party. I declined that one also."

She looked over at Jared, who was smiling. "What that woman needs is a man of her own."

"Don't look at me, I'm taken," he said, squeezing her hand before raising it to his lips. He stopped as they came to the fence where they could see three horses galloping across a field. Still holding her hand, he held up a beautiful gold ring with a trio of diamonds, the one in the middle larger than the other two. He'd planned everything out so perfectly for her.

"Yes, you are," Sky said, as he slid the ring on her finger. "For now and forever. You're mine."

EPILOGUE

"JUST ONE MORE big push, Mindy. The baby's crowning. Just one more and you'll finally get to hold your baby," Sky said as Jared reached over her and wiped the sweat that had formed on her forehead.

"You can do it," Trey said, helping his wife get into position for that last push.

As Mindy took in a breath and began to push, Jared handed Sky a surgical towel to use to wrap around the baby. Carefully, she helped guide the baby out, first its head and then one shoulder after the other, until she held the new little baby who would soon be the talk of Music City.

"It's a boy!" Trey yelled as he hugged his wife, who had begun to cry the moment the baby began to cry.

"With a voice like that, I bet he'll be following in his parents' footsteps," Jared said as he handed Sky the instruments to clamp the baby's cord, then handed Trey the scissors to cut the cord.

"Here's your baby boy," Sky said, reaching across Mindy and handing her the baby.

While the nursery nurse began to help the new mother, Sky stood and turned to Jared. "I'm really going to miss us working together like this."

"Who knows? Maybe Mindy and Trey will have another one," he said, smiling down at her. "What I think you're going to miss is all the media attention."

"Speaking of which," Trey said as he moved to stand beside them. "I'm supposed to tell you that Marjorie has a camera ready to record all of us together so that we can announce the birth."

A few hours later, Sky found herself straightening the collar of Jared's lab coat. As always it was spotless and pressed to perfection. While he might have become a little more relaxed in his life since she had moved in with him, there were some things that would never change.

She'd been surprised about how well he'd taken the attention his proposal had gotten. As soon as it had aired, there'd been comments on the show's media accounts ranging from kind and sweet to some suggesting that her fiancé shouldn't quit his day job. He'd taken them all with good humor, along with the ribbing by the staff at the hospital.

But today would finally be their last time in front of the cameras. Something, no matter what Jared thought, Sky was glad of. Living a life of privacy with him was much more fun than being the center of attention. Not that the two of them would be the center of attention today. Today all the attention would be on Mindy and Trey.

"You ready?" Jared asked her as they made their way to Mindy's hospital room. "You know, if you find yourself missing the limelight, Marjorie might let you come back as a special guest on the show."

"The only person that's going to be recording me after today is the wedding photographer," Sky said as they made their way through the crowd in the hallway that had gathered to see the taping of the season finale of *Carters' Way*.

Sky and Jared followed Joe's direction as he placed the two of them behind the chair where Mindy sat holding her new baby boy. Trey sat beside her, his smile just as big as it had been the moment Sky had first shown him his son.

When Jared reached for her hand, Sky smiled

and looked over at him. His eyes caught hers and to her amazement, and right in front of the cameras for all the viewers to see, he winked.

* * * * *

MEDICAL

Life and love in the world of modern medicine.

NEW RELEASE

BESTSELLING AUTHOR

DELORES FOSSEN

Even a real-life hero needs a little healing sometimes…

After being injured during a routine test, Air Force pilot
Blue Donnelly must come to terms with what his future
holds if he can no longer fly, and whether that future
includes a beautiful horse whisperer who turns his life
upside down.

In stores and online June 2024.